PUFFIN BOOKS

CITY OF SHADOWS

Praise for *TimeRiders*:

'A thriller full of spectacular effects' – *Guardian*

'Insanely exciting, nail-biting stuff' – *Independent on Sunday*

'This is a novel that is as addictive as any computer game'
– *Waterstone's Books Quarterly*

'Promises to be a big hit' – *Irish News*

'A thrilling adventure that hurtles across time and place at
breakneck speed' – *Lovereading4kids.co.uk*

'Plenty of fast-paced action . . . this is a real page-turner'
– *WriteAway.org.uk*

'A great read that will appeal to both boys and girls . . . you'll
find this book addictive!' – *redhouse.co.uk*

'Contender for best science fiction book of the year . . . an
absolute winner' – *Flipside*

Winner of the Older Readers category,
Red House Children's Book Award 2011

ALEX SCARROW used to be a graphic artist, then he decided to be a computer games designer. Finally, he grew up and became an author. He has written a number of successful thrillers and several screenplays, but it's YA fiction that has allowed him to really have fun with the ideas and concepts he was playing around with when designing games.

He lives in Norwich with his son, Jacob, his wife, Frances, and his Jack Russell, Max.

Books by Alex Scarrow

TimeRiders
TimeRiders: Day of the Predator
TimeRiders: The Doomsday Code
TimeRiders: The Eternal War
TimeRiders: Gates of Rome
TimeRiders: City of Shadows

Sign up to become a TimeRider at:
www.time-riders.co.uk

TIME RIDERS

2001   1957   2066
1912   1941

CITY OF SHADOWS

ALEX SCARROW

PUFFIN

PUFFIN BOOKS

Published by the Penguin Group
Penguin Books Ltd, 80 Strand, London WC2R ORL, England
Penguin Group (USA) Inc., 375 Hudson Street, New York, New York 10014, USA
Penguin Group (Canada), 90 Eglinton Avenue East, Suite 700, Toronto, Ontario, Canada M4P 2Y3
(a division of Pearson Penguin Canada Inc.)
Penguin Ireland, 25 St Stephen's Green, Dublin 2, Ireland (a division of Penguin Books Ltd)
Penguin Group (Australia), 250 Camberwell Road, Camberwell, Victoria 3124, Australia
(a division of Pearson Australia Group Pty Ltd)
Penguin Books India Pvt Ltd, 11 Community Centre, Panchsheel Park, New Delhi – 110 017, India
Penguin Group (NZ), 67 Apollo Drive, Rosedale, Auckland 0632, New Zealand
Penguin Books (South Africa) (Pty) Ltd, Block D, Rosebank Office Park, 181 Jan Smuts Avenue, Parktown North,
Gauteng 2193, South Africa

Penguin Books Ltd, Registered Offices: 80 Strand, London WC2R ORL, England

puffinbooks.com

First published 2012
001 – 10 9 8 7 6 5 4 3 2 1

Set in Bembo Book MT Std 11/14.5 pt
Typeset by Palimpsest Book Production Limited, Falkirk, Stirlingshire
Made and printed in Great Britain by Clays Ltd, St Ives plc

British Library Cataloguing in Publication Data
A CIP catalogue record for this book is available from the British Library

ISBN: 978-0-141-33707-4

www.greenpenguin.co.uk

MIX
Paper from
responsible sources
FSC™ C018179
www.fsc.org

Penguin Books is committed to a sustainable
future for our business, our readers and our planet.
This book is made from Forest Stewardship
Council™ certified paper.

ALWAYS LEARNING   **PEARSON**

To the 'TimeReaders' — thank you for your patience thus far.
The truth is finally beginning to emerge.
And soon . . . very soon, something wonderful is going to happen.

Prologue

13 September 2001, New York

Roald Waldstein stared at the Manhattan skyline. The pallid sky above the south end of the city was still smudged with a faint pall of dust. The thin twist of smoke, coming from where the Twin Towers had stood just two days ago, looked like the careless rubbing out of a pencil drawing, a ghost of the towers that had once been there.

'God,' he said. 'And it's *still* burning.'

'My dad said it might carry on burning for weeks.'

Roald turned to look at Chanice Williams. 'Really?'

'Uh-huh.' She nodded confidently, working gum in her mouth almost mechanically. 'Said so on Fox News too.'

Like everyone else at Clinton Hill Elementary School, Chanice had become something of a news-station junkie, tuning in before and after school, the cartoon channels completely forgotten for now.

'You think anyone's alive in there still?' asked Roald.

'Dunno. I heard they lookin' just in case, tho'.'

He watched the puffs of dark smoke rising lazily. 'I hope there's no one trapped in that . . . alive. That would be horrible.'

'Come on. We should get on to school,' said Chanice. 'We'll be late.'

Roald nodded at her to head back up the alleyway without him. 'I'll come in a bit.'

'Shizzy.' She clucked her tongue. 'You gonna get youself another demerit. You want that, Waldo?'

The kids all called him Waldo. As in *Where's Waldo?* It took the first five minutes of the first day of school to get lumped with that stroke-of-genius nickname. The thick-framed glasses and untameable hair had played their part too.

She shrugged her shoulders. 'OK, your funeral, Mr Professor.'

He watched her turn and go, weaving her way up the alleyway, stepping round a dustbin that had spilled rubbish across the cobbles.

'I'll be along in a bit,' he called after her.

'Your funeral!' She shrugged again. 'Jus' don't miss registration,' she called over her shoulder. 'Or Miss Chudasama gonna get medieval on yo'.'

He turned back to watch the skyline. A train rumbled noisily overhead across the Williamsburg Bridge, heading into Manhattan. They were saying the trains and subway into Manhattan were still pretty deserted – easy seats. Everyone figured something else bad was bound to happen again at any moment: another plane, a bomb perhaps.

His mother said that too. Just like Chanice, like every New Yorker, like every American, dull-eyed from watching too much TV. '*They'll be back. They'll be back to finish us all off. Just you see.*'

It was just him and his mother and the TV set in their one-bedroom apartment. She had three different part-time jobs and what time was left after that was spent microwaving TV dinners or pop-tart breakfasts. Outside work, her life was Montel Williams, Judge Judy or Oprah Winfrey so she didn't really ever have much to say that wasn't already a newspaper headline. To be honest, she rarely had much to say that was original or vaguely interesting. But she had this morning. Something that had lodged firmly in his mind.

She'd turned away from her small black-and-white TV in the kitchen to look at him, mug of coffee in one hand, cigarette in the other. 'Roald, don't you just wish you could go back to Tuesday morning and tell those poor souls not to come in to work? Or just . . . just . . . go in there and scream *fire* or something?'

He nodded now. Such a small step in time that would be. Just two days to save three thousand lives.

He turned away from the East River. Beyond the railing the low-tide shingle was covered with rubbish: nappies, shopping trolleys and plastic bags and seagulls picking for titbits among it.

Just two days.

He started to make his way back up the alleyway, passing a boarded-up archway to his right. Chipboard panels nailed over old rust-red brickwork, covered with lurid-coloured spray-paint gang tags. One of the panels had been pulled away, revealing a corrugated metal shutter that was halfway up. He squatted down to look inside. Curious. His mother was always cautioning him how *curiosity killed the cat*. That or *got into very big trouble with the local police department if it didn't mind its own gosh-darn business.*

The muted light of day pushed the darkness within far enough back that he could see the place had been used by drug addicts or vagrants. Broken glass, discarded needles, a dirty mattress. A forgotten part of Brooklyn. He wondered when this place last had a proper use, a *purpose*, other than being some dark hole for an addict to crawl into, or merely a dark empty space beneath an old bridge.

'*WAL-DO!*'

He looked up the alleyway. Chanice, bless her, was tapping her toe, waiting for him, acting like she was his big sister or something. She cupped her mouth. 'You re-e-eally don't wanna be late again. Ya mom'll kill you! *Come on!*'

'Coming!' He got up and turned round one last time to catch a glimpse of the smudge in the sky over Manhattan.

10 September 2001, New York

'Mr Waldstein? S-sir?'

Roald Waldstein turned to see Dr Joseph Olivera approaching. The man joined him beside the railing and together they looked out at the sedate East River.

'My apologies, Joseph,' said Waldstein. 'I was a million miles away there.'

'Uh . . . that's OK, sir.'

Waldstein smiled. He liked Olivera. The technician reminded him of himself at that age: hungry for knowledge, to show the world what his agile mind contained. Hungry to show the world an incredible theoretical possibility: that it was possible to step backwards through the membrane of space-time. As easy as it was to step through the tattered rip in a bedsheet.

'You know, Joseph, I came across this place when I was just a boy. When I was eleven.'

'S-sorry?'

'This place,' Waldstein said, turning to look back at the alley. 'The archway. No one comes down here. It's a backwater.'

'You . . . you *lived* round here?'

'In Brooklyn?' He nodded. 'Moved to Chicago after my mother died. I lived with my aunt after.'

Olivera nodded. He knew that much of this legendary man's life – Chicago onwards. Waldstein's *early* life – the first years alone with his mother – Waldstein had always preferred to keep utterly private. A media-stream interviewer had once called him a *biographer's nightmare*.

4

'Perfect location this,' Waldstein said. 'I never ever forgot about it. This time and this place. You know, Joseph, tomorrow every New Yorker will have their eyes up on the sky. We could walk in and out of this alleyway dressed as clowns all day long and no one would remember that.'

'Yes, sir.'

'Perfect location,' Waldstein muttered. He smiled wistfully.

They listened to the distant hiss of morning traffic, the cry of a dozen gulls strutting among the shingle and rubbish below, fighting for scraps.

'Mr Waldstein? Can I ask you a question?'

The old man smiled, pushed a shock of his wild, wiry grey hair away from his eyes. 'You can ask, Joseph. I can't promise you an answer, though.'

Olivera sucked in a breath. Nervous. Waldstein suspected he knew what the man was going to ask. At some point or another, every person he'd ever worked with long enough eventually mustered their courage and got round to asking the exact same question. He let Olivera continue with it all the same. Better to get this out of the way.

'Mr Waldstein, when you went back . . . that first time, you know, in 2044? The Chicago demonstration?'

Here it comes. He half smiled. *Yup . . . that question, all right.*

'Did you . . . did you ever get to s-see –'

'My wife? My child?'

Olivera nodded. Wide-eyed and very nervous. Waldstein suspected the man must have worked himself up for this moment. Must have spent the last few months at the institute, and the last few weeks here, waiting for that perfect moment to pop the question. And here it was supposedly – what this young man judged to be the perfect moment.

Waldstein sighed as he cast his mind back to fading memories

5

of that day. That's what he'd intended. Wasn't it? Just one last chance to say goodbye to both of them. To tell them how much he loved them. Because he'd been far too busy to say that before the accident. Far too busy with his work. A chance to say *I love you*. That and, of course, a chance to demonstrate to the assembled audience of invited journalists that the Chan–Jackson Tachyon Theory – with a few alterations to neutrino channelling – could actually be put into practice.

Olivera swallowed anxiously as he waited for Waldstein to answer. Back home, back in 2054, this precise question actually had its very own name. The question was known as *the Waldstein Enigma*. Alternatively it was known as *the Billion Dollar Question*. Any journalist who squeezed the answer to that out of him was never going to have to chase down a new story again.

Waldstein turned to him. He toyed with the idea of answering this young man. Or at least telling him what he'd *not* managed to see.

'Regretfully,' he replied slowly, 'I . . . never got to see them again, Joseph.'

There you are . . . more than I've ever told anyone else. He hoped the young man would be satisfied with that.

Olivera's Adam's apple bobbed. He was fidgeting. Licking his lips. Eager to ask the inevitable follow-on question. 'So, what . . . what *did you s-see*, Mr Waldstein?'

Waldstein laughed softly. Shook his head. 'Now, Joseph . . . let's leave it there, shall we?'

'I . . .' Olivera's cheeks darkened. He looked down at his feet, ashamed. Aware that he'd overstepped a line. 'I'm s-s-sorry, sir. I –'

'That's quite all right. Everyone asks eventually, Joseph. *Everyone*.'

The silence was uncomfortable for the younger man.

Waldstein put him out of his misery. 'I believe you have an update for me?'

'Uh? . . . Uh yes! I do, sir. The AI imprints are completed now. I've checked them through and run simulations. They're one hundred per cent stable.'

'Good. Then I suppose we're nearly ready to upload those into the units?'

'They're very nearly ready, sir. Full growth cycle in the next hour.'

Waldstein patted his shoulder gently, a conciliatory gesture to reassure the younger man there was no harm done just now.

Curiosity didn't kill this cat. Did it, Mother?

'Let's go back inside and check on them, then.'

CHAPTER 1

2001, New York

<u>Wednesday, 12 September 2001</u>

If you're reading this then I guess someone, somewhere, does go through the rubbish and read every piece of paper that gets balled up and tossed away. So then, in that case, here it is – my name's Sal.

That's all you need to know about my name.

I'm fourteen. I think. Actually, I might be fifteen now. I'm not sure. I'm from India. And here's the tricky bit – I'm from 2026. You read that right. Please . . . read on. Don't throw this away. I'm not making that up, nor am I mad. Just go with it . . . for now. Please?

There's a long story that comes before this page. But all you really need to know is that right now I feel lost. I'm scared. I've lost another home. We can't go back to the archway. The place we were living in. Maddy says we can't ever go back there. Like, ever. It's marked, she said. Compromised. It's no longer a secret and safe place.

So now we have nowhere to hide. It's just us lot and an old bus-thing that Maddy calls an 'RV'.

Jahulla, what a collection of freaks we make. There's Maddy, she's a nerd from 2010. This is closest to her past-life time. She was like nine or ten in 2001, so she actually remembers this year.

Then there's Liam, he's a ship's steward. Or was. He was working on the Titanic. Yes. That Titanic. The one that sank in 1912. He's really out of his depth here (ha ha). Even though we've been stationed back in 2001 for a few months now, he's still like some confused old fuddah-man even though he's technically only sixteen.

There's Foster, who really is old. Not just acting old (like Liam). He's ninety or something and I'm pretty sure he's dying. He knows the most about Waldstein's agency. He was the one who recruited each of us from our past lives. But even he doesn't know who sent those killers after us. Someone's found out about us, what we're doing back here to preserve the timeline.

Then there's this man called Rashim. He's stuck with us for now. We pulled him out of a corrupted version of Roman times because he shouldn't have been there. He went back there with a group of people from the year 2070.

Oh . . . you should know this. Really important. The world's dying in 2070. Or about to. That's why they came back. They wanted to start over: to give humanity a second chance to get the world right. But you can't do that, see? You just can't mess with history. There's ONE WAY it goes and that's it. Call it fate, destiny, kismet. As Foster says, 'For good or bad, history has only one true course. You mess with that, and you're looking at chaos . . . Hell itself opening up.'

(He's actually not as wacko-mad as I'm making him sound.)

That's why we were saved, 'recruited', to work for this agency set up by a man called Waldstein – he's some billionaire inventor type from the future.

And then we have two cloned humans with computers for brains: Bob and Becks. Gorilla Guy and the Ice Queen. They're, well, 'special' I suppose. Let's leave it at that. Oh . . . I almost forgot, we've also got a robot from 2070 with us that looks like a cross between a filing cabinet and the old cartoon character from when my parents were kids, 'SpongeBob SquarePants'. I think Rashim designed him as a joke or something.

That's us. Like I say, a bunch of freaks and we're trying to run for our lives across a country that's suddenly doing a double-take at anyone who looks remotely out of the ordinary. So much for remaining deep undercover.

We're running through an America that's still in deep shock from what happened yesterday: 9/11. You can see it in their faces; everyone expects another terrorist bomb, another aeroplane attack.

I guess my father would say to these Americans: 'Get jahully well used to it.' After all . . . he lived through the Terror Attacks of the Twenty-teens. All those dirty bombs and suicide attacks in northern India.

Shadd-yah. When aren't humans always killing each other?

So, we are running. I can't say where. I won't say where we're going. Just in case, reader, you're ONE OF THEM! Can't be too careful, right? But we have a plan. Sort of. There's a place we're driving to and we just stopped here at this roadside shopping mall-diner-service station place. It's been a crazy two days. A blur. One big panic after another.

I needed to write this. Get my head on a little straighter. So . . . there it is. Maybe our job of stopping pinchudda morons from messing with changing time is finished now. Maybe this 'agency' thing's all over. Maybe all that's left for us is just trying to stay hidden. Staying alive. I don't know. I don't know what the next few weeks hold for us. Jahulla, I don't even know what the next day holds for us.

I don't even know if these last six or so months have even been for real. Maybe it's all been one big nightmare and I'll wake up again in my bedroom in Mumbai and it'll be 2026 again.

Nice dream.

So . . . I've written enough. Maybe too much. I might just rip this up. Burn it. Eat it or something. Or maybe I'll stuff it into my Burger

King box with the rest of the cold fries and floppy gherkin where no one is likely to find it.

But writing this helped a little, I guess.

My name is Sal and, like I said, I'm lost, and quite a bit scared and not at all happy about things right now.

CHAPTER 2

11 September 2001, New York

Maddy took off her glasses and buried her face in her hands. Air hissed between her fingers: a long, torpid sigh that was a signal to the other two, Liam and Sal, to shut-the-heck-up for just a moment and let her think.

The archway was quiet except for its usual noises: the faint chug of a filtration pump from the back room, a tap dripping somewhere, the soft burr of a dozen PC computers' heat fans. It sounded like it did on any normal day, except for perhaps the inane trash-talking between Liam and Sal playing *Mario Kart* on the Nintendo.

'Hey, what's up with that girl, skippa?' chipped in SpongeBubba.

Maddy raised a hand to shush the lab robot. 'OK.' Her voice was muffled behind her other hand. 'This is what we need to do.' She straightened up, put her glasses back on and turned towards the monitors on the computer table. She addressed the webcam. 'Computer-Bob?'

A black DOS-like dialogue box appeared on the monitor beside the camera.

> **Yes, Maddy?**

'Can you force the archway's displacement field to reset to Monday?'

Today was Tuesday, early afternoon. Outside the archway a

collective pause had settled across the city: a pause in which the sky was clear of planes, television presenters had said all there was to say, and everyone was still busy wondering if the last few hours had been for real and the Twin Towers really had just been completely destroyed.

> **Affirmative.**

'Do it, then. Do it now!'

'What's going on?' asked Rashim.

'We're all going back in time,' Sal answered. 'By one day.'

The young technician still looked bewildered. Only a couple of hours ago – from his perspective – he'd been approached by Maddy and the others back in Roman times as he'd quietly been setting up the receiver array for the rest of his group to home in on. Now that was all history, or not, depending how you looked at it. Now he was here, stuck with them because they couldn't just leave him behind, dangling like a loose end. And Project Exodus, the project he'd spent the last couple of years of his life working on . . . well, none of that would be happening now. By grabbing him, they'd managed to prevent a group of three hundred refugees from the future completely throwing history off track.

Job done. But now he and his cartoon-character lab unit were stuck here with them.

'So, *when* exactly is this place?' asked Rashim, looking round the archway. His voice rose with growing anxiety. 'I mean, this is twenty, twenty-first-century tech by the look of it. Yes? Am I right?'

'This is the day the towers were knocked down by planes,' said Liam.

'September the eleventh, 2001,' Maddy said quickly. 'It's our base-time, our field office. Where we've been operating out of for the last few months.'

The cursor on the dialogue box flickered.

> **Stand by. Field resetting.**

They heard the soft whine of energy discharging into the displacement machine and then the fluorescent lights dangling from the archway's low ceiling suddenly blinked out and a moment later flickered back on. The archway was still in the mess it had been when she and Sal had fled back in time to the reign of Caligula. Tidying all this up, however, was the last thing on her mind at the moment.

'And now . . . it's yesterday,' said Maddy. 'The day before 9/11.' She sat down in the office chair beside the desk and huffed air. 'Which now gives us twenty-four hours' breathing space before those psychotic killer meatbots come back to finish us off.'

Rashim's dark eyebrows rose, looking from Maddy to the others, for someone to add a word or two more of explanation. 'Psychotic . . . ?'

'There're *more* of them?' asked Liam.

'Two more, we think,' said Sal. 'Six of them came through.'

'What *killer* things are these?' asked Rashim.

'Six! Jay-zus!' Liam's jaw dropped. 'And you two managed to kill four of 'em?'

'Could someone please tell me what *psycho killer things* you're talking about?'

'Yes. We did pretty good, huh?'

Liam laughed. 'I'll say —'

Rashim closed his eyes. 'PLEASE, EVERYONE, WILL YOU *STOP* IGNORING ME!'

The others turned to look at him.

'I . . . I'm . . .' Rashim opened his eyes and smiled half apologetically. 'I . . . I'm very close to . . . uh, losing my mind. Please — the least one of you people can do is answer just one of my questions.'

14

Sal pointed at Bob. 'The psychotic meatbots we're talking about are clones, support units like these two. Four men and two women. They came from the future to kill us.'

Rashim nodded gratefully, then silently appraised Bob. 'He's a military-grade gene product, isn't he? One of the earlier-gen versions?'

'Correct,' Bob rumbled.

'Computer-Bob dealt with two of them for us,' said Maddy. 'And one got taken out by a time wave, I think. The other one . . . well, you guys saw what happened.'

One of the units had managed to leap after Maddy and Sal as their hastily opened escape portal began to collapse in on itself. It had emerged on the other side missing both its feet and one hand and yet it had still managed to be quite lethal. As Bob held it down, Maddy had put several rounds into its bald human head. The first and last time she ever intended to fire a gun at anything point blank.

'You said six of them?' said Rashim.

Maddy nodded. 'Yup, there are two more of them and they may be out there in New York somewhere.'

Sal sat down on the other chair beside Maddy. She scuffed the toes of her boots against the floor. 'More of them could arrive,' she said. 'Right, Maddy? Another six?'

Maddy nodded. 'Tuesday morning, sometime during Tuesday morning, that's when they arrived. So right now it's twelve noon, Monday. Which means we've got eighteen, maybe nineteen hours before they come again. And if another batch – technically, I guess, the same batch – don't come then we've *still* got those other two to worry about. And they'll be back from wherever computer-Bob sent them on a wild-goose chase. That's right, Bob, isn't it?'

> **Affirmative.**

'Affirmative.'

Both Bobs answered the question.

Maddy turned to look at them all. 'Two of them we might stand a chance against. But if another six turn up right here in this archway . . . ?' She pulled on her lip, made a face. Not the sort of face to instil confidence in her little team.

'We could set some sort of a trap for them,' said Liam. 'As soon as they arrive, get Bob to open a portal and drop them right into that chaos space. Could we not do that?'

Maddy shrugged. 'We could do. But, Liam, you're missing the point. And it's actually quite a big point.'

Liam splayed his hands. Irritated by her patronizing tone of voice. 'What?'

'Someone else knows about us, Liam. Someone knows exactly *when* and *where* we are. We're not a secret any more.'

'That means we're still in danger?' added Sal quietly.

'If we stay here, yes.' Maddy's words rang round the archway, a reverberation off damp brick walls that seemed to last indefinitely and not quite fade away.

Liam muttered a curse under his breath. 'That's great. I was just about gettin' used to this place, so I was.'

'I'm thinking the sooner we leave, the better,' said Maddy. She regarded the gloomy interior. Hardly a place anyone would normally look at with dewy-eyed fondness. But it *had* become their home. It *had* become something of a safe haven, a nest, a shelter. And yes, between the seemingly constant firefighting they'd experienced from here, there had been moments of . . . dare she say . . . fun.

Fun. Some good memories. Among all the scary ones, that is.

Liam sighed. 'Ah well . . .' was all the consolation he could offer them. 'Ah well.'

'It's just bricks,' said Sal without a great deal of conviction.

The squat lab robot flexed its pliable plastic face, wrinkling its pickle-shaped nose as its round and permanently staring eyes scanned the gloomy interior. 'It's a very messy place. I don't like it very much.'

'Yeah, but it's home,' said Maddy. 'Or it *was* anyway.'

She looked around the pitted and cracked floor to where a shallow scoop of concrete was missing — where so many terrifying and unplanned last-minute portals had been opened up. Where a thick loop of cables dangled from the ceiling – from which a horrific Cretaceous-era carnivore had once dropped down and butchered a man right in front of her eyes. Where power cables snaked from one side of the archway's floor to the other – there had once lain a carpet of dead and dying Confederate and Union soldiers, men feebly crying out for water amid the acrid smoke of battle, bleeding out for a war that should never have been. Where the walls flanked the shutter door – the probing claws of irradiated mutant humans had once tried to pick through crumbling mortar to get in at them, to eat them.

And, planted on the very desk she was sitting at now, the severed head of a young woman had rested recently. Grey eyes, beautiful grey eyes, glazed over and lifeless, the cranium hacked open to reveal a bloody pulp, and a small, invaluable microchip inside.

Ahhh, memories. Precious memories, Maddy noted unenthusiastically.

'You're right, Sal, it's just a bunch of bricks. The sooner we get the hell out of here, the better.'

CHAPTER 3

10 September 2001, New York

Maddy took the subway across to Manhattan and emerged at 57th Street into the warmth of the sun. Middle of the day, that's when the old man could be found in Central Park. That was Foster's pact with her, his tacit promise when he'd walked out on the team after their first mission.

You'll always find me here at the same time. Feeding the pigeons.

She'd made this trip nearly a dozen times now over the last six months. Six months' worth of their 'bubble time' – Monday and Tuesday, the 10th and 11th, looped over and over again. Every time she sat down with him on that bench by the duck pond, beside the hot-dog cart, it was – for Foster – like their very first meeting after he'd bid farewell and left her in charge of the team. The world outside the archway's protective field was linear, a sequence of moments experienced by everyone in sensible chronological order.

But, for Maddy and the others, it was time that occurred *inside the archway* that appeared to be linear, while everything outside was a weird and endless forty-eight-hour *Groundhog Day*.

She'd asked the old man once why it was that she never bumped into copies of herself. His answer had been both straightforward and oddly cryptic.

'You're not of this timeline, Maddy. None of you are. You

might as well be aliens visiting from another planet as far as earthly cause and effect is concerned.'

Reassuring perhaps, but she'd still ended up none the wiser.

As always, she caught sight of him sitting on the bench, sitting back and savouring the sun on his wrinkled face, in that dark blue cardigan of his, jeans too big for his narrow frame and that scuffed old Yankees baseball cap clasped in his liver-spotted hands. She stopped for a moment, watching him through the hot-dog queue, watching him through the clouds of billowing steam coming from the cart's griddle.

A quiff of silver-white hair fluttering on his head: untidy, unruly hair. The likeness was so obvious now Maddy knew, now they all knew. She wondered how none of them had ever noticed, or remarked, how much alike Foster and Liam looked. Yes, age completely alters a person's appearance, but there are those things that survive the years intact: the shape and set of a person's eyes, the habitual expression on one's face, the lazy way you sit when you think no one's looking — things that are as unique as a fingerprint.

Liam and Foster, the very same person, and she hadn't seen it until he'd told her.

Foster had given her no explanation for that. None at all. She had her theories. Perhaps one of them didn't belong in this timeline; perhaps one of them had stepped across chaos space from another similar world and now there were accidentally two of them. She wondered if somewhere, beyond dimensions she couldn't even begin to comprehend, there was an old-woman version of herself.

She decided probably not. She suspected in any dimension she was the same kind of person, destined to get stressed-out on all and everything and die young. Probably of high blood pressure or a heart attack.

Nice thought.

She emerged round the end of the queue and Foster's eyes were drawn away from the pigeons chasing each other for breadcrumbs at his feet.

His eyes lit up at the sight of her. 'Ahhh!' He smiled. 'You found me!'

She raised a hand to hush him politely. 'I always do.'

Foster laughed. 'I gather from that we've met before?'

Maddy nodded. 'Quite a few times now.' She looked around at the park, the duck pond, the hot-dog vendor. 'This is like *Happy Days*. Like a TV show I've seen way too many times.'

'Talking to me must be like talking to someone with –'

'Alzheimer's?'

Foster grinned. 'I've said that before, haven't I?'

'Only every time we meet up. Listen, Foster.' She sat down beside him. 'This time's going to be different, though.'

'Oh?'

'We have to leave New York.'

'Leave? Why?'

Maddy explained as succinctly as possible: the handwritten message addressed to her about Pandora from some mysterious informant; sending through a message to the agency in the future and asking what the hell 'Pandora' was all about. And then, in short order, a squad of support units arriving right in their archway hell-bent on killing them all.

'I don't know what's going on, Foster. Maybe our ability to contact the agency, to contact Waldstein, has been compromised somehow. Intercepted by someone else?'

She didn't bother telling Foster that the last time they'd met here she'd told him about the Pandora message and it had been *his* suggestion that she 'communicate forward' and ask if

Waldstein knew anything about it. Maddy hadn't come here to blame him for that. Neither of them were to know asking about Pandora was going to lead to this.

'Point is, someone now knows where we are, Foster, and we could be jumped at any time by more of those things. We have to leave. Like . . . as soon as possible!'

Foster nodded slowly. Sadly. 'It wasn't ever meant to last for eternity, this agency. It was a temporary fix to a problem.' He looked up at her. 'There's something you need to know, Maddy.' He ran his tongue along his teeth beneath pursed lips. 'Maddy, the agency . . . it's just –'

'Just us.' She shrugged. 'I know.'

'Seriously?' He cocked a bushy eyebrow. 'I already told you that as well?'

'Yup.'

'Jay-zus. Must be annoying for you, hearing me –'

'We're leaving, Foster. Leaving first thing tomorrow morning. We're packing everything we need to set up again, and we'll find some other place to carry on doing the job.'

'Right.' He nodded thoughtfully. 'That's probably very sensible.'

'And I want you to come with us.'

Foster shook his head. 'I can't go back. You know I can't enter a displacement field again.'

'I know.' She reached for one of his frail hands and squeezed it gently. 'I know. We're just relocating for now. No time travel, no fields, no tachyon particles. No more damage to you. We're just taking a drive away from New York. That's it.'

She realized just how fragile he looked now. When he'd first recruited them, yes, she'd noted he was old, but he'd looked robust-old. Like some seasoned old army veteran, hard as nails beneath a weathered exterior.

'Maddy . . . I don't think there's much left of me.' His smile broke her heart. 'I'm dying. I have cancer. All over.'

She knew that; it was something else he'd already confessed on a previous visit.

'Foster . . . I wish I could leave you here.' Maddy looked around at the park, the sun streaming through September leaves, turning golden and beginning to fall. Beautiful. He'd told her he thought he might have just a few weeks left maybe; if he was really lucky, a couple of months. The rate of cellular damage caused by time travel wasn't really quantifiable. It happened, that's all they knew.

'I know you've earned this,' she said. 'I know you've given the agency your life . . . and you deserve to choose how to spend the time you've got left. But we need you.' She squeezed his hand again. '*I* need you.'

'You know as much as I did . . . do, Maddy.'

She shook her head. 'No. No, I don't. I'm making mistakes. We're screwing up. There are things *stitched* in history . . .' She shook her head. Not quite the right expression. 'Things *pre-baked* into history. Messages . . . written for us, I don't know, maybe even written by us! Like we've been here before or something. I don't understand what's going on. I don't . . .' Her voice hitched with emotion. She stopped and looked across the pigeons at a toddler on reins tormenting the birds on the ground. 'I can't do this on my own any more. I'm not ready. And I wasn't ready when you walked out on us.'

'And I wasn't ready for this when I first started,' he said softly. 'But you and I? We're made for this job.'

She looked at his grin. That stupid lopsided old grin of his. 'You know, sometimes I don't know whether to call you Liam or Foster.'

He laughed. A dry old cackle. A dying man's defiant snort.

'Does Liam know now? About me?'

Maddy nodded. 'I think actually, in a way, he's kind of proud that he gets to turn out like you.'

'But maybe he's not so happy that's going to happen sooner than he thought?'

'I think he's accepted that.' She shrugged. 'Come to terms with it. After all, if you hadn't grabbed us, we'd all be dead anyway. It's all extra time. Extra bonus life, right?'

'Aye.'

They sat in silence for a while, watching a young couple rollerblade past them. He was teaching her, and she was guffawing at how bad she was. Not a care in the world between them.

'Please, Foster,' Maddy said again presently. 'Please come along with us.'

His watery eyes watched the rollerbladers zigzagging up the path and away from them.

'Don't make me get on my knees,' she said.

'All right,' he nodded. 'I'll come.'

CHAPTER 4
10 September 2001, New York

'She's . . . what do you reckon? Fourteen? Fifteen?' asked Liam, peering through the thick protein soup at the murky outline suspended in the growth tube.

'It's hard to tell,' said Sal. Her nose was pushed against the warm perspex. The clone's body was tucked into a foetal position, knees pulled up, slender arms wrapped protectively round them. The last twelve hours of archway time had taken her body shape from one that was definitely that of a small child to something that looked adolescent.

'Maybe a bit younger,' she said. 'It's hard to make her out through all this gross gunk.'

Liam wasn't sure about this. Maddy's instructions – birth her. They couldn't leave her behind and probably wouldn't be able to bring themselves to do that if they had to. She was going to become Becks one way or another. She was part of the team.

The other foetuses in stasis, on the other hand, were simply going to be flushed out. They were all too early in the growth stage to survive for long outside the protein solution. No more than fist-sized bodies and none of them with viable, organic rat brains yet, just sim-card-sized slices of silicon; it wasn't going to be an easy task to bag up and throw away those pitiful-looking things floating in the other tubes.

Liam looked again at what would become Becks soon. 'The

body's just that of a child. She'll be younger than any of us, so she will. What good is that?'

'She'll still be stronger than me or Maddy, though. That's got to be useful.'

He shrugged. 'I suppose . . . if we decide to enter her into a schoolgirl arm-wrestling competition.'

Sal sighed. 'Come on, we should get on with it.'

Liam nodded. Wrinkled his nose in anticipation of what was coming. Sal knelt down and tapped the small glowing display on the pump's control panel. The soft purring stopped. The first time they'd done this, they'd had state-of-the-art 'W.G. Systems Growth Reactor' tubes, with a motor at the bottom that orientated the tube smoothly to a forty-five-degree angle before opening a sluice hatch at the bottom, depositing the clone and protein soup on to the floor. This growth tube was a home-made affair, the pump and control panel recovered from the damaged system, the perspex tube purchased from a defunct distillery. The other growth tubes likewise.

Liam grabbed the top of the cylinder of bath-warm perspex. 'Give me a hand – we'll tip it over nice and gentle if we can.'

Sal braced herself against the weight of the tube as Liam pulled. It teetered, the liquid inside sloshing. The foetal shape inside twitched and jerked, finally beginning to wake up, becoming aware.

'Go slowly, Liam!' grunted Sal. The tube was impossibly heavy.

'I got a hold . . . it's all right, it's all right. Just keep taking the weight as I tip it.'

He carried on pulling, the tube canting over enough now that the viscous gloop was sloshing over the top and splatting on to the floor.

'Liam! It's too heavy! I can't –'

'Calm down, will you? We'll just ease it out. Pour it out so it's a bit lighter.'

'It's going to slip! It's —'

'Just relax! I still got a hold of it, so I —'

The bottom of the tube slipped on the floor under the angled weight and he lost his grip. It swung down to the ground like a felled redwood, Sal lurching back to avoid being crushed. The perspex made a loud *thunk* on the concrete and a tidal wave of pink soup erupted from the open top and engulfed her.

The clone slid out, riding the mini-wave and all but ending up in Sal's lap.

'Ah Jay-zus!' Liam flapped his hands uselessly. 'I'm so sorry, Sal! The thing just . . .'

Sal spat gunk from her mouth and wiped it from her lips and out of her eyes, thick like half-set jelly.

'I hate you, Liam,' she hissed, almost meaning it right then. 'Really hate you.'

Liam slipped in the muck as he hurried over and knelt down beside her, his hand uselessly wafting around Sal, wanting very much to comfort her, but at the same time not actually make any physical contact with the foul-smelling gunk coating.

'I am so very . . . very . . .'

'I think I'm going to be sick,' Sal said, desperately trying not to inhale the odour of rotting meat.

'You all right in there?' It was Rashim's voice.

'Fine!' called out Liam. 'Don't come in just yet! It's messy!' He looked down at the clone, still curled defensively in a ball, its head in Sal's lap. Eyes slowly opened, grey. Wide. Curious and vaguely alarmed.

Liam leaned over it and offered the clone a smile and a little wave. 'Hello there!'

Its mouth flexed open and closed several times, dribbling the gunk being ejected from its lungs.

'Ughhh.' Sal eased the clone's head off her lap and on to the floor. 'I'm soaked in this *pinchudda*.'

Liam wasn't listening. 'Hello? You OK?' he cooed down at the clone. Now she was out of the mist of swirling salmon-coloured soup, he could see the female unit clearly enough. The creature's hairless head made it hard to judge her precise age. Her face looked both old and young at the same time.

He reached down, lifted her by the shoulders till she was sitting up, produced a towel and wrapped it round her. 'There you go.'

Sal tutted, jet-black hair plastered against her face by the cooling, gelatinous protein soup. 'Oh, I see . . . *she* gets the towel, does she?'

Rashim sat cross-legged before the rack of circuitry of the displacement machine, SpongeBubba looking over his shoulder on one side and Bob over the other.

'Incredible,' he whispered. 'The design is quite . . . quite brilliant. Look at that, Bubba, see? He's sidestepped the feedback oscillation completely.'

'I see it, skippa!'

He turned to Bob. 'Our system's field was constantly suffering distortion variables. Outside interference and internally generated distortion. Feedback patterns.'

'Your displacement device was much bigger than this one, correct?'

Rashim nodded. 'Yes. Enormous. And large-scale introduces a whole new bunch of problems. But even so . . .' He shook his head again, marvelling at the economy of the circuitry. 'This is so ingeniously configured.' A grin stretched across his thin lips.

Roald Waldstein, you were fifty years ahead of anybody else.

'We should take this whole rack,' he said. 'I know a lot of these component wafers can probably be replaced – duplicated with present-day electronics – but I need to take some time to be sure I know how he's put it all together.'

'Affirmative. We will take the complete rack.'

'What about the controlling software?' Rashim looked at the row of computer cases beneath the desk. Each one with an ON light glowing, and the flickering LED of a busy hard drive. 'I need the software shell as well. It's as much a part of this device as the circuits.'

'Correct.'

Rashim shook his head. 'Those computers look primeval. How the hell can they run Waldstein's machine's software?'

'Networked together these computers are suitably powerful,' replied Bob. 'They do not use the original operating software.'

Rashim recalled the charming old names of computing's early twenty-first-century history: *Microsoft. Windows. Linux.* Primitive times when code was written in a digital form of pidgin English. Not like the elegant streams of data from his time: code written by code.

'We won't need to take these clunky old computers with us, will we?'

'Negative. We can extract the machines' hard drives.'

Hard drives? Then Rashim remembered. Data in this time used to be stored magnetically on metal disks inside sturdy carousels. Again, so primitive. So wasteful. Nothing like the efficiency of data suspended in water molecules.

'Right . . . yes. Do you know how to do that, uh . . . *Bob*?'

'I have a theoretical understanding of the system architecture of these Dell computers. Also the system AI – known as computer-Bob – can provide detailed instructions on how to dismantle the architecture. However, only Maddy has practical experience of this process.'

'Right. OK.' Rashim pinched the narrow bridge of his nose. 'We'd best wait for her to come back before we start dismantling things, then.'

'Affirmative.'

He got to his feet. Across the archway, he watched the Indian girl, Sal, talking quietly with another girl, pale as a ghost and completely bald.

'Who is that?' asked Bubba cheerfully.

'It is a support unit,' said Bob. 'It was set on a growth pattern before we had to deal with your Exodus contamination.'

'A genetically engineered AI hybrid, SpongeBubba,' added Rashim. 'The US military were working with those back in the fifties and sixties. Perfect soldiers. We had a platoon of gen-bots come along with us on Exodus.' He looked at Bob. 'Leaner, more advanced models than you, I'm afraid.'

Bob's brow furrowed sulkily. 'I know.' Then, with something approximating a smirk, 'I did in fact manage to disable one of them.'

'Yes, you did.' Rashim nodded respectfully and then offered him an awkward high five. 'Good for you, big man.'

Bob cocked his head and gazed curiously at Rashim's palm left hovering in mid-air.

'Uh . . . never mind,' he said, tucking his hand away.

CHAPTER 5

10 September 2001, New York

Maddy returned from Central Park with Foster just after half past one in the afternoon. Following brief introductions of Rashim and his novelty robot, they set to work. During the rest of the day Sal was largely sidelined with the drooling child support unit in her tender care while Maddy, Rashim, Foster, computer-Bob and SpongeBubba collectively pooled their technical knowledge and carefully dismantled the equipment in the archway.

It was an exercise in identifying and extracting only the technology components that could not easily be replaced elsewhere. Bob and Liam meanwhile had been sent out to steal a vehicle big enough for them all and the equipment they were likely to take along.

By the time lights started to flicker on, on the far side of the East River, turning Manhattan, skyscraper by skyscraper, into an enormous, inverted chandelier and the railway overhead started rumbling with trains taking city commuters home from the Big Apple to the suburbs of Brooklyn and Queens, they'd done most of what needed to be done.

A battered Winnebago SuperChief motorhome was parked up in the alleyway, a snug, hand-in-glove squeeze between the row of archways and the graffiti'd brick wall opposite. The rack carrying the displacement machine had been carefully lifted in and secured tightly in the RV's toilet cubicle. The PCs had been stripped of their internal hard drives and the filing cabinet beside Maddy's desk had been emptied. Its drawers were full of a messy miscellany of discarded wires and circuit boards and gadgets: a taser, something that looked like a Geiger counter, the babel-buds, a non-functioning wrist-mounted computer of some sort with 'H-data WristBuddee-57' stamped on one side. Gadgets and parts of gadgets, most of them clearly not from the year 2001. Nothing like that could stay behind.

The improvised growth tubes were too large to take along, but the pumps and computer interface were removed and carefully stored in the RV. The protein solution and the dead foetuses were gone now, poured away into the East River.

Like any normal family moving house, it was a revelation to Maddy, Liam and Sal discovering how much clutter they'd already managed to acquire. Magazines and books, a Nintendo and a TV, a kettle and sandwich toaster, a chemical toilet, a wardrobe full of clothes, a shelf in their bunk archway filled with half-used toiletries. And rubbish. A small pyramid of empty drinks cans, a teetering Jenga tower of pizza boxes and takeaway cartons.

As they left the archway, tired after a busy day, the last of Monday's fading sunset left the sky a deep blue and there existed that momentary gasp of air, that fleeting pause between the last of Manhattan's office dwellers vacating the city and the emergence of the first eager beavers of New York's nightlife.

Times Square was still busy, but mostly with ambling tourists coming home to their 5th Avenue hotels after a day's sightseeing. Bob, SpongeBubba and the freshly birthed girl clone – yet to be called 'Becks': they were still debating whether to consider her a new personality entirely, that was still up for discussion – were left to watch over the SuperChief and the archway. The rest of them headed across to Manhattan, one last time in Times

Square. They found a Mexican-themed place that looked out across the winking lights and animated billboards, the news ticker around the Hershey store, the stop-start intersections and sluggish convoys of yellow cabs, gaggles of goggle-eyed tourists, and the last city suit walking home with a gym bag slung over one shoulder.

It was quiet in the restaurant. They ordered from the waitress quickly and then were left alone to the privacy of their faux dark wood and red-velvet-cushioned booth to talk.

'So . . .' Maddy clasped her hands like a host desperate to get her party started. 'Here we are, then.'

'Aye,' said Liam, 'the first proper chance I've had to sit down, rest and eat in ages.'

Maddy nodded. It seemed an eternity ago that they'd been cornered by guards in Caligula's palace. Since then they'd been running, hiding, scavenging. She realized she hadn't eaten properly in days, the best part of a week in fact. That went some way towards explaining her ordering the triple bean and beef mega-burrito.

'You're running,' said Foster. 'I can understand that . . . but have any of you thought where to?'

'No.' Maddy tucked hair behind her ear. 'Not yet.'

'Well now, to be sure, we want to know who sent those support units after us.' Liam looked at Sal for support. She nodded. Clearly the most pressing question hovering between them all.

Maddy shook her head. 'Somebody from the future. Obviously. I don't know.'

'Did you say the male units looked just like our Bob?' asked Foster.

'Yup. Like his evil twin or something.'

'These are military clones you're talking about,' said Rashim.

She nodded. 'Military use, yeah.'

'Then if they looked *exactly* like your Bob, they'd be from the same or a similar birth batch. The cloning process develops genetic-copy errors if you reproduce from the same DNA indefinitely. So the batches have relatively small print runs. Twenty maybe thirty units per base DNA pattern.' Rashim stroked the fine tip of his nose. 'I recall that the military contractors producing clone units back in the 2050s were constantly having to start over with new candidate genomes to engineer.'

Liam chuckled. The others looked at him and his face quickly straightened. '*Back in the 2050s?*' He grinned. 'I mean, doesn't that sound odd? That's the future for all of us, so it is. The *far* future for me!' He shrugged; no one seemed particularly tickled by that. 'Just sounded a bit funny, that's all.'

'When does your clone unit come from?' said Rashim. 'Do you know his precise inception date?'

'Bob?' Maddy struggled to remember. 'Uh, I think it's the 2050s . . .'

'2054, if I recall correctly,' said Foster.

'Then your enemy, whoever sent those killer units, must come from the same time.' Rashim folded his arms. 'That's an assumption, of course.'

Liam shuffled uncomfortably. 'But who's our enemy? Who've we gone and annoyed?'

'What?' Maddy laughed. 'Who's our enemy? You mean apart from some secretive association of Templar Knights? A government-backed top-secret project called Exodus, that group of anti-time travel activists who tried to assassinate Chan, Kramer's bunch of neo-Nazis.' Maddy paused. 'Need I go on?'

'Well,' Liam shrugged, 'apart from them, that is.'

'The point is,' cut in Foster, 'the world, down the line, is an increasingly grim place.' He looked at Sal. 'You've seen the storm clouds of the future, haven't you, Sal?'

She nodded. 'Not good.'

'A world full of people who see the only way of escape is back through time. And we . . . ?' Foster looked around at them. 'We're who're standing in their way. That's a lot of enemies to choose from.' He turned to Rashim. 'Maddy told me your group came from 2070?'

'2069 actually,' Rashim sighed. 'The world's dying. I mean, it's not good at all. The food chain's poisoned so that we're all living on soya-synth products. And the floods took a lot of land. Migrating people, billions. And wars. And God knows we've had a lot of them. But that's what everyone's worried about . . . petrified of, you see? A big war. There are countries and power blocs in my time that are in a desperate position. Desperate enough to consider the use of extreme weaponry: bioweapons, nanoweapons.'

'What're those?' asked Liam.

'*Plague* . . . is perhaps the best word for it, Liam. Whether it's something genetically revamped, or self-replicating nano-bots, either way it becomes a weapon that doesn't discriminate over borders, nationalities.' He looked out of the window at the flickering lights of Times Square. 'We're in a bad place. Desperate times. It's inevitable that something like that will eventually happen. We'll wipe ourselves out. We're destined to engineer our own end.'

'*The end*.' Maddy leaned forward. 'That's what Becks said to me. That was what she said was the "reveal condition" for the Pandora message, the Grail message. *The end*.'

'Pandora?'

She looked at Rashim, wondering how much they should be letting their new, temporary accomplice in on.

'All we know,' said Foster, 'is that the people who want you dead had access to weapons technology from 2054. Apparently, the very same foetus batch as Bob and Becks, no less.'

'I don't like the sound of that.' Maddy stared at him. 'That feels like an enemy very close to home. Perhaps someone inside the agency?'

Liam started. 'You mean a turncoat in our Mr Waldstein's secret time-police force?'

'A traitor.' She pressed her lips together thoughtfully. 'I just hope not. We can do without that.'

'Maybe when you sent that message asking about Pandora,' said Sal, 'someone else got it? Intercepted it?'

That thought was met with silence. A silence that lasted several minutes and ended when the waitress arrived with an arm laden with hot plates. She served them out, along with the drinks they'd ordered, and, after looking at their glum faces, put a hand on her hip.

'This some kinda office party?'

Maddy nodded. 'Sort of.'

'Sheeesh . . .' The waitress made a face, half pity, half amusement. 'I'd hate to work at your place.' She wished them a perfunctory 'bon appetit' and left them to it.

'We're none the wiser as to who wants us dead,' said Liam. 'So, how about we decide what we're doing? Where we're going to go? Because . . . I'm completely confused.'

Sal nodded at Rashim. 'And what about our new friend? Is Rashim staying with us?'

'Uhh . . .' Rashim cleared his throat, fidgeted with his cutlery. 'Well, I'd really like to tag along. You know, if that's all right? I won't be a nuisance.'

Maddy shot a glance at Foster. *Is this my call?* She wondered if now they had Foster back with them, he might resume the mantle of team leader, relieve her of the burden of making the decisions.

Foster smiled. 'You decide,' he said softly. 'It's your team now. Not mine.'

She picked at the burrito on her plate, fumbling with both hands to keep the mince and assorted gunk from spilling out either end. 'I suppose we could use Rashim. He's got a better understanding of the displacement technology than I have.'

'Than any of us,' added Foster. 'To be fair.'

'True.' She nodded and glanced up from her food at the man. He seemed fascinated by the rack of ribs on his plate, inspecting it like a forensic pathologist picking over a cadaver. She smiled at that. *Of course*. He'd probably never experienced real meat in his time.

'And he knows forty-four years *more* of the future than I do,' said Sal.

'Excuse me.' Rashim looked up from his ribs. 'You're all talking about me like I'm not right here sitting next to you.'

'Sorry, Rashim,' said Maddy. 'You're right, that is kinda rude.'

Rashim nodded. Apology accepted. He turned to Sal. 'When do you come from?'

'2026. From Mumbai.'

'Really?' His eyebrows arched. 'That's not long before the . . .' He stopped himself.

'Before?' She looked at him. 'Before what?'

He shrugged. 'The first Asian War.' Rashim winced apologetically. 'I'm sorry . . . I shouldn't –'

'No, tell me. Please.'

He deferred to Maddy. 'Tell her about it later if you like, Rashim. Right now we need to focus on our next move. We've got to decide what we're going to do.'

'What is it *you* wish to do, Maddy?' asked Foster.

He's pushing me to lead. Not for the first time, Maddy wondered if she tended to open things up for discussion too much.

She put down the leaking burrito, licked her fingers. Buying time . . . because she simply didn't know just yet. A part of her had almost made the decision that the game was up, that their duty as TimeRiders was done and perhaps they should all just put some clear miles between themselves and New York, and then all go their separate ways to live whatever was left of their lives how each of them wanted.

But then an insistent, nagging voice inside her reminded her of the horrendous timelines they'd narrowly prevented from happening. And of course that voice had an even greater urgency to it now she knew it was just their one little team keeping an eye on history. Not some vast agency of multiple teams, with multiple redundancies, safeguards, fail-safes.

Just them.

So the decision, in truth, was already made in her mind. But she wanted to hear what the others had to say, particularly Liam and Sal.

'We run,' she said. 'Then?' She looked at Liam with a shrug.

'What do you mean by that?' asked Liam.

'I'm putting it to you. I'm asking what you think, Liam. We run . . . then what?'

Liam frowned for a moment. Then put down his burger – no, *dropped* his burger. Suddenly indignant, he exclaimed, 'Jay-zus, Maddy! Are you asking me whether we give up?'

She said nothing. That was her answer.

'No way!' He turned to Sal. 'Right? No bleedin' way!' He looked almost angry. As close to anger as she'd ever seen him. 'Now listen here, Madelaine Carter! I've nearly died a dozen times, so I have. To keep that . . .' He flung a hand towards the window and the glistening lights of Times Square. 'To keep New York just like it is! I'm not giving up on that now!'

Maddy noted a proud smile steal across Foster's lips.

'Sal? I'm right, am I not?' said Liam. 'We want to go on, right?'

She chewed on the straw in her glass of Dr Pepper and blew bubbles for a moment before she finally spoke. 'There's things I want to know. I want to know what Pandora is. I want to know what Becks knows; what's locked up inside her head. I want to know what *that man* was trying to tell us.'

That man. Maddy and Liam knew who she meant: the poor soul who'd arrived back in New Orleans, 1831, only to be fused into the bodies of two horses. He'd held on to life for perhaps five, ten minutes, a gruesome jigsaw puzzle, an inside-out parody of a centaur.

A horror-show freak for the few minutes he, it, lived.

'I want to know what's really going on, Maddy.'

'I want to know more about this Waldstein fella. Aye, and more about this agency,' said Liam. 'And the only way I see it is . . . we have to keep on doing what we're doing. Even if we have to move somewhere else and continue doing it there.'

Maddy tapped the table gently with her knuckles. Her attempt at calling their meeting to order. It took a few moments. She would've been quicker just telling the pair of them to shut up. But also a touch rude.

'OK, it's agreed, then. We relocate and we'll set things up again.' She looked at them all. 'And we will *continue* keeping this timeline on track while we're still able to. Because – look – whatever's really going on, if we're being played for fools, if we're being manipulated by Waldstein somehow . . . or someone else inside his agency or someone outside, the truth is . . . I know what we're doing is the *right thing*. And that's the only, literally the *only*, certainty we can grab hold of.'

The other two nodded. They'd seen enough alternate timelines to know there could be far worse ways history could play out than the way it was now.

'For better or worse, right, Foster?'

The old man nodded. 'For better or worse, history needs to stay on track.'

'OK . . . OK, this is what I'm thinking we do.' Maddy pushed her glasses up the bridge of her nose. 'We head north to Boston.'

'Why? What's so special about Boston?' asked Foster.

'It's my home.'

Liam looked up from his burger. 'You want to go to your home?'

'It's my home turf,' she said. 'I grew up there. I know the area. And look, maybe we can get some help. My folks –'

'You *can't* go to your home, Maddy,' said Foster.

'Why not?'

Sal's eyes widened. 'Jahulla! You'll be there already, won't you? Another you?'

Liam stopped chewing. Dawning realization on his face too. 'You'd be a little girl! There'd be a little Maddy there!'

'Nine.' Maddy nodded. 'Yes, I'd be nine.'

'Madelaine,' said Foster. 'You cannot visit your family, you cannot visit *yourself*. Do you understand me? That's a very dangerous contamination!'

She stared at him silently for a long while before finally, reluctantly nodding. 'All right. I get it. OK, I won't visit home. It was just an idea. But listen! I know the area. There are places I know where we could set up. If we're going to ground, it's better we head somewhere that someone knows. Right?'

'Somewhere we can easily tap power?' said Rashim. 'We'd need that if you want a viable new place to operate from.'

'Sure. There's loads of places we could settle in. There's industrial parks. We could rent a unit, pretend to be some small business or something.'

Liam nodded, encouraged that she seemed to have already given the move some thought. 'Seems like a plan, so.'

Sal smiled. 'A new home. I'd like that.'

Foster seemed less than happy. 'It's a danger, Maddy. And a temptation. To be so close to your childhood home.'

'I won't go home! OK? I promise! I mean . . . what's the alternative? We stick a random pin in a map of America and just hope for the best?' Her burrito drooled gunk on to her plate with an unappealing *splat*. 'Seriously, guys. If anyone else has got a better suggestion . . . I'm all ears.'

No one, of course, did.

'Then that's all I've got. Boston. It's a start. What do you guys say?'

Liam and Sal nodded.

'Uhh . . . so does that answer your earlier question?' asked Rashim.

'What's that?'

'Whether I'm coming along?' Rashim looked sheepish. 'Am I in your . . . what do you call it? Your *team*?'

'Yuh . . . I guess,' Maddy smiled. 'Sure, if you want?'

He smiled. 'You're joking, right? A choice between staying in 2001 or going back to 2070?' His face cracked with a wide grin. 'It's a head-slap. I'd very much like to stay.'

'Then that's the deal.' She offered her hand across the table. 'We need some kind of oath or something, but I guess a handshake's good for now.'

They reached across and shook awkwardly. The sort of uneasy gesture of two geeks unsure whether to high-five, chest-bump or knuckle-kiss and in the end pulling off a fumbled combination and Maddy nearly knocking her drink over. Sal rolled her eyes.

'So, we'll set off tomorrow morning. Have a last night in the arch.'

Liam nodded. 'A last night to say goodbye to the ol' place.'

Maddy sighed. 'It's a freakin' brick archway. That's all.'

'No, that's not fair. I'd say it was a bit more than that.'

'Yeah, me too,' said Sal. 'It was sort of *home*.'

Maybe they were both right. It had begun to feel a bit like that. 'Let's just look ahead, guys. OK? We've still got a job to do. And maybe now . . . we're doing the job on our terms? We're calling the shots.'

That felt like a leader-ish sort of thing to say. Like the right thing to say. Maddy looked sideways at Foster and he gave her a subtle wink.

CHAPTER 6
11 September 2001, New York

Liam lifted the last of the bags into the back of the SuperChief. Maddy took them from him. 'That the last of the stuff piled in the middle?'

He looked back into the dark interior of the archway. 'Aye.'

'Good. Because there's no room left anyway.' She ducked back inside, looking down the middle of the vehicle, an assault course of plastic bags and cardboard boxes. And that was just their essentials. 'I guess I'll find somewhere to tuck these. What's in these bags anyway?'

'Some of me books.'

'We can replace books, Liam.'

He shrugged. 'And a few comics.'

Maddy sighed, leaned over and pulled open one of the bags. 'Oh, come on . . . and the Nintendo too?'

'Well . . .' He looked sheepish. 'I thought . . .'

'Jesus, we can pick another one of those up at any computer game store.' She shook her head. 'Just the difficult things. Just things we can't easily replace, I'm afraid.'

He sighed and swung the bag ruefully into the open rubbish bin beside the vehicle.

Maddy poked her nose into his other bag. 'OK, I guess these books can come aboard.' She took the bag off him and disappeared inside the RV.

Liam looked back under the shutter. It was dark and gloomy: a vacant space once more, strewn with the cables and rubbish, boxes of tools, cartons of nuts and bolts, spools of electrical wire. A desk with the gutted remains of a dozen Dell computers left beneath it.

A large wardrobe that had contained, until this morning at least, a bizarre collection of garments. A twelfth-century leather jerkin, two Wehrmacht army tunics. Several Roman togas. An Edwardian-era suit and lady's gown, a steward's tunic and more. The clothes were all squirrelled away aboard the RV now.

It looked like the abandoned premises of some black-market, cash-in-hand PC repair shop. A sweatshop, a squat, a student dosshouse; the Aladdin's cave of some foraging vagrant.

He offered it a lukewarm farewell wave. *Thanks for the shelter.* And smiled with amusement at his own mawkish sentimentality. How daft it was that a pile of damp bricks and crumbling mortar could make him feel guilty for abandoning it like this.

The RV's motor rattled to life.

'Come on, Liam.' Maddy's head was poking out of the passenger-side window at the front. 'The sooner we're off, the better!'

'Aye.' He raised his hand in acknowledgement and turned back to the dark interior. 'Well there, Mr Archway, you've still got a job to do,' he muttered under his breath. 'After all . . . there's this bridge above you that needs holding up for a while yet.'

'Liam!'

'I'm coming!'

Sal sat in the back of the RV on an oat-coloured seat worn through at the corners and showing yellow foam. Her seat belt didn't work. She decided Bob could have stolen something that looked a little less old-fashioned, beaten-up and threadbare. She'd spotted glistening, spotless tour vans rolling through the streets of New York. Ones that looked almost futuristic, like spaceships on wheels. Instead they had this.

She looked out through the rear plastic window, scuffed and foggy, someone's name and a love heart scratched into it. She watched Brooklyn receding like a movie back-projection: busy with cars, bumper to bumper at each intersection, waiting to get on the two lanes across the Williamsburg Bridge on to the lower east side of Manhattan; the morning ebb and flow of commuters, regular as bowel movements.

There was some relief mixed in with the sadness of a goodbye. At least she wasn't going to see this particular morning ever again. Tuesday 11 September was at last playing through for them the way it did for everyone else. Once. One terrifying morning albeit seemingly running in slow motion.

Relief she wasn't going to have to see that again. The swooping airliner. A sky filled with billowing smoke and the confetti cloud of millions of pieces of fluttering paper.

But, yes, sadness too. Brooklyn – this place, this side of the East River, had become so familiar to her. Almost as familiar as the suburbs of Mumbai that she'd grown up in. The Chinese laundromat with that old lady so proud of her office-worker son. The coffee shop from which she'd collected countless cardboard trays of coffee and paper bags of assorted doughnuts. The YWCA whose skanky showers with hair-clogged drains she and Maddy had had to use more times than she cared to remember. Their alleyway always cluttered with rubbish, the cobbles underfoot slightly tacky, the walls with fading sprayed gang tags.

And their archway.

Their home.

The RV juddered to a halt at a traffic light and just then – Sal knew it was due any second now – she spotted a subtle flash on the distant skyline: the pale sliver of a fuselage catching the morning light, moving fast and descending towards the twin pillars of Manhattan shimmering in the sun-warmed morning.

She lost sight of it among the skyscrapers, but then a moment later the distant sky was punctuated by a roiling cloud of orange and grey that drifted lazily up into the empty sky. No sound. Not yet. Just a silent eruption like an undubbed movie special effect.

Then, half a dozen seconds later, even through the closed window, over the chugging of the RV's engine, she heard it. A soft, innocuous-sounding *whump*. Like the door of an expensive saloon car being slammed shut. The heads of pedestrians on the pavements either side of them turned to look towards the sky above Manhattan . . . and never turned back.

Green light. The Winnebago motorhome crossed the intersection and turned left on rolling and slack suspension that made the vehicle sway like a boat on a choppy sea.

Behind a row of apartment blocks, Sal finally lost sight of Manhattan, the Twin Towers and the billowing mushroom cloud of smoke and the frozen pedestrians as they headed up Roebling Street – a place where people and cars and taxis and trucks continued to move from one traffic light to the next in blissful, clockwork ignorance, at least for the moment.

CHAPTER 7
11 September 2001, New York

It was four hours later that footsteps scraped and tapped down the cobblestone alleyway. Nearly one o'clock. Framed and silhouetted by muted light from outside, two figures stepped into the open entrance of the archway. Two tall, athletic figures, one male, one female.

They stared into the gloom. Perfectly still. Attempting to comprehend the situation. Finally the male figure took several steps forward into the dim interior and then squatted down to inspect a tangled nest of data-ribbon cables and the green plastic shard of a circuit board, dropped or just discarded to be crushed carelessly beneath someone's foot.

'Faith,' said the male unit.

The female figure joined him. Her cool grey eyes surveyed the rest of the archway.

'It would appear we have been misled, Abel,' she said.

'Correct.'

She stepped towards the table topped with computer monitors, and keyboards, drinks cans and sweet wrappers. She reached out for something.

'What have you found?' said Abel.

She inspected the small webcam in her hand, as if the glinting, lifeless plastic lens contained a soul that could be peered into and cross-examined for answers. The AI installed on this network of computers had sent her and Abel to a random address across the city. It had assured them that that was the precise location where the human team members would emerge from chaos space – their return data stamp.

Her thoughts travelled wirelessly to Abel.

> **This AI provided us with incorrect information.**

> **Affirmative.**

Her hand closed tightly round the webcam. Plastic cracked inside her taut fist.

She turned to look at Abel. 'The AI broke protocol. It lied.'

Abel nodded. 'The AI may have been corrupted by prolonged interaction with the organic modules. It has developed feelings of loyalty to its team.'

Faith examined the gutted computers, the mess in the archway. Objects strewn across the floor. 'They arrived here while we were gone.'

'And left,' added Abel. 'We must determine where they are now headed.'

Faith nodded, closed her eyes and queried her mission log:

[Restate Mission Parameters]
[Mission Parameters]
1. **Locate and eliminate team members**
2. **Locate and destroy critical technical components (see sublist 3426/76)**
3. **Self-terminate**

She examined the detritus on top of the desk and beneath it. 'It appears they have taken the critical technical components. The displacement technology. The support unit propagation hardware.'

'Agreed,' said Abel. 'That indicates they intend to redeploy elsewhere.'

Abel joined her, then his eyes began to sweep along the clutter on the desk. 'They may have discussed strategies within audible range of the system AI. We may be able to override the AI system and access its recently cached audio files.'

Faith pointed at the computer cases, unscrewed and exposing the innards of wires and circuit boards. 'The hard drives have all been extracted.'

'There may be residual data in the system's motherboards. Recently stored data.' He looked at her. 'This is system architecture that is fifty-three years old. There will be data packets still on any solid-state circuitry. We can query each circuit board with a small electrical charge.'

Faith nodded. It was a place for them to start. Very much a case of looking for a needle in a haystack, though.

'This will take many hours.'

Abel nodded. 'Do you have an alternative plan?'

She shook her head.

'Then we should begin immediately.'

CHAPTER 8

21 August 2001, Arlington, Massachusetts

Joseph Olivera held the digital camera in front of him and panned it around the tree-lined avenue. Such a beautiful place. Long, freshly clipped lawns leading up from a wide avenue to generous whiteboard houses. Suburbia. It was mid-afternoon and peaceful and the sun was shining with a warm, mid-August strength, dappling the road with brushstrokes of light and shade through the gently stirring leaves of the maple trees.

Beautiful.

As a child Joseph had dreamed of living in a place like this. He used to watch old programmes from this time, family dramas they used to call 'soap operas', with healthy, tanned people always smiling, happy families, driving nice cars and worrying about nothing more important than high school proms, or who was dating who or who was going to win a thing called the 'super bowl'.

Joseph walked slowly down the avenue, panning his camera left and right. In the viewfinder an elderly woman was kneeling among a bed of flowers with gardening gloves and pruning shears. A postman walked cheerfully by with a nod and a smile for Joseph. Some chestnut-coloured Labrador was frolicking on a lawn, chasing a frisbee. He could hear the lazy buzz of a lawnmower somewhere.

Suburbia. Beautiful suburbia.

Joseph had only ever known cities. All his life, cities. Towering labyrinths of noise and chaos that seemed to contract on themselves, getting tighter and more choked and crowded with each passing year. His early school years he'd lived with his family in Mexico City, then, later on, as a student in Chicago. He'd been working in London in the 2040s, during which time large portions of that city had begun to be abandoned to the all-too-frequent flooding of the River Thames. Finally, he'd ended up in New York. They'd been building up those enormous flood barriers around Manhattan then. Hoping to buy the city another couple of decades of life.

But always . . . always he'd dreamed of a place like this, mature trees, lush green lawns, sun-drenched porches and white picket fences. The perfect place to grow up. The perfect place to spend one's childhood.

He passed a driveway with a Ford Zodiac parked in it, stunning paint job. Pimped with skulls and flames to look like it had driven bat-out-of-hell style right out of Satan's own garage. Joseph grinned.

Some young man's first car, of course.

Joseph looked around. One of these houses would be *hers*. He panned his camera left. Then right. The viewfinder settled on a grand-looking home. Mock colonial with a covered porch that fronted it and wound round the side. There was even a rocking-chair on there.

Perfect.

Joseph crossed the avenue. The house's driveway was empty. Presumably no one home. Just as well. Better that he didn't attract the attention of anyone inside.

His digital camera still filming, he walked up the tarmac drive, sweeping the camera gently in a smooth panning motion, taking in every little detail, finally reaching the bottom of three broad wooden steps. He took them one at a time. Now standing on the wooden boards of the porch, freshly whitewashed. He let the camera dwell on the rocking-chair for a moment, the hanging baskets of purple and pink Sweet Carolines, on several pairs of gardening boots and gloves, a small ceramic garden gnome holding a chainsaw. Somebody's idea of a joke present for Mom or Dad. The camera recorded all those small, important, personal details.

And finally he panned the camera on to the door of the house. Mint green with a brass knocker in the middle. Joseph smiled wistfully. What a wonderful childhood home to have. What wonderful childhood memories to have.

'I envy you, Madelaine Carter from Boston,' he said softly. 'To have all of this . . .'

He had enough to use now, and turned the camera off.

CHAPTER 9

12 September 2001, New York

Faith was picking through the scattered circuit boards on the desk. They were specifically querying the motherboards first. That's where the cache memory was, lodged in these ridiculously bulky chips of dark silicon on tiny hair-thin metal seating pins.

They had both been meticulously teasing small charges of electricity into the circuits, stirring them to life and diverting the random nuggets of dormant information to a connected monitor. What they were getting mostly was useless gibberish: random packets of hexadecimal, every now and then punctuated with snippets of English. Faith's internal clock informed her they had spent nearly twelve hours on this process. Twelve hours during which their targets must be putting a healthy distance between them.

She picked up the motherboard of a yet unchecked computer and prepared to hand it to Abel to jury-rig a connection to the monitor when her eyes settled on a pad of lined writing paper half buried beneath the mess on the desk. She reached out and picked it up. The last used sheet had been torn away roughly, leaving a few tattered paper shreds attached to the glue binding at the top, the tops of several letters in biro. That's all.

But that wasn't what Faith was focusing on.

It was the shallow indentations on the page that had been directly beneath the torn-away page. She held the pad close to her face, tilting it so that light from the desk lamp fell obliquely across the paper. She could make out the faintest lines of indentation . . . the hard tip of a biro pressed too heavily, too quickly on the page above. The scrawl of someone in a hurry. Perhaps someone thinking, making a desperate decision. Writing lists, pros and cons.

She could make out a word, very faint and not entirely complete. But her mind quickly produced a very brief shortlist of possible word variables. Only one of them had any relevance to the data she'd been uploaded with for the mission.

She put the pad down. 'The team leader, Madelaine Carter, is taking the team to her childhood home.'

Abel looked up from the soldering iron in his hand and a curl of blue smoke twisted in the harsh light of the desktop lamp as he put down the motherboard he was working on. 'Why do you conclude that?'

Faith handed him the pad of paper. He squinted at it. And, just as she had, his eyes picked out the faintest markings of writing.

'Boston,' he said.

Faith nodded. 'She is going home.'

They emerged from the archway. As they paced swiftly towards the intersection between Wythe Avenue and South 6th Street, a Bluetooth conversation passed quickly between them. They needed a vehicle. They needed a vehicle now. They needed to make up for the lost twelve hours.

Abel stood at the entrance to the alleyway. It was dark now, an hour after midnight. Street lights bathed the Brooklyn intersection opposite with sickly neon, punctuated by the regular circular blue flicker of police lights.

An NYPD squad car was parked diagonally across the

intersection, impeding the flow of traffic in both directions. Cones placed out to help make the point. No traffic was being allowed on to the slip road and up the ramp on to the Williamsburg Bridge. No traffic, that is, except emergency vehicles: fire engines, mobile cranes and diggers heading over into Manhattan, the occasional solitary ambulance heading slowly back out. No sirens. No horn. No rush.

Even now, at this late hour, there were still a few pedestrians out, craning their necks to get a look past the towering supports of the bridge at the apocalyptic haze on the far side. Manhattan glowed with a million office lights as usual, but tonight the light pollution was enhanced by powerful halogen floodlights towards the south end of the island that leaked an unstinting glare into the night sky like an unnaturally early dawn.

Faith stood beside Abel, both of them now evaluating the situation. Both of them staring covetously at the NYPD squad car, parked across South 6th Street. Two policemen stood guard ready to wave back any non-emergency traffic trying to pick through the cones to cross the bridge. Not that anybody was trying to get across.

The support units exchanged a cursory glance.

Perfect.

Abel led the way towards the nearest of the two policemen.

The policeman noticed Abel's strident steps approaching him. 'Sir, you need to step back!'

Abel drew up a few steps short of the cop. 'Why?'

'We're keeping this access-way across the river clear for emergency vehicles.' He waved his hands at Abel. 'Please step back now, sir. There will be more fire trucks and heavy vehicles passing through at any time.'

'Please give me the ignition key to your car.'

The cop ignored him. 'Just step back off the road, sir.'

Abel reached out and grabbed one of the cop's fingers and twisted sharply with a flick of his wrist. 'Please give me the ignition key to your car.'

'Hey! Ow! Hey!' His other hand – clearly not his gun hand – fumbled around his ample waist to find the leather flap of his holster.

'I will break your finger,' said Abel politely. 'This is a warning. Please comply to avoid further discomfort.'

The cop lifted the flap and grabbed hold of the gun's grip. He pulled the weapon out and levelled it at Abel's face. 'Let go! Now! Let go and get down on the ground!'

Abel snatched the gun out of his hand as calmly as a toad lassoing a passing mosquito with its tongue.

'Jesus!' The cop's jaw dropped open.

The other cop challenged Abel from across the street. 'Drop that weapon! *Now!*'

'I require the ignition key to your vehicle,' said Abel calmly. 'Please provide this.'

'Drop the weapon now or you will be fired upon!' the other cop barked, a gun levelled at Abel, taking slow steps towards him. His voice was shrill. High-pitched. Warbling with fear.

Abel swung the gun in his hand quickly. A microsecond to aim, then three shots fired in rapid succession. The first shot killed the approaching cop, the other two were unnecessary. Faith immediately paced over towards his prone body ready to frisk his pockets and belt pouches.

'Hey . . . p-please! Don't sh-shoot, man!' the other cop pleaded, his hand and finger still twisted in Abel's firm grasp.

'Do you have the vehicle ignition key?'

'It's in the c-car, man!' He grimaced in agony. 'It's in the car!'

Abel shot a Bluetooth instruction to Faith and she changed direction towards the squad car.

'You will not discuss this intervention with anyone,' said Abel.

'Whuh?' Then the cop understood and nodded vigorously. 'No! OK! Sure . . . I . . . I won't d-discuss this. I promise.'

'Your promise is not required,' said Abel. Then he calmly shot the second cop dead.

He noted the pedestrians nearby staring at him. Frozen with shock. It would take too much valuable time to pursue them all and kill them. He decided so many eyewitnesses were an unfortunate collateral contamination, but nothing that could be helped.

The squad car rattled to life as Faith settled into the driver's seat. Its siren squawked for a second before it was turned off. Abel made his way over, pulled the passenger side open and got in beside Faith. The car rocked under his weight.

'Boston,' she said.

He nodded. 'Please proceed.'

CHAPTER 10

11 September 2001, Interstate 95, south-west Connecticut

Liam had watched as the Bronx became a suburban carpet of gradually more expensive homes interspersed with out-of-town superstores fronted by acres of car park as the RV crawled north-east along Interstate 278, then along 95. It was slow progress for the day, bumper to bumper past slip-road after slip-road; police blockades and random vehicle searches had reduced the traffic to a crawl. They'd stopped once for petrol at lunchtime then finally hit some clear road beyond New Rochelle.

'It's all new to me too,' said Foster quietly. 'All I've ever seen of this world is New York.'

Liam nodded. 'You never been tempted to take yourself off and have a look around?'

Foster looked at him. 'Have you?'

'I've not had any time. Feels like we've been dealing with one problem after another since you pulled me off the *Titanic*.'

He realized, though, that the old man's question was an invitation for him to talk about what they now both knew but had yet to talk to each other about.

'She told me,' said Liam. 'Maddy told me you're . . . *me*.' He shook his head. 'Or I'm you, or however I'm meant to say it.'

'I'm how you'll become, Liam. We're the same person on either end of a number of years, lad.'

'That's what I can't get me head straight about, Mr Foster. It's . . .' He paused. 'Or do I call you Liam now?'

'Just *Foster*,' he answered with a smile. 'I've been used to that name for some time now.'

'So . . .' Liam looked out of the scuffed perspex window at a Greyhound bus, its windscreen striped with the reflected glow of street lights passing overhead.

'Do you remember all the same things as me?'

'Up to a point.'

'Cork? St Michael's School for Boys?'

Foster nodded.

'Sean McGuire and that stupid party trick of his with the three apples?'

The old man grinned. 'He was never very good at it, was he?'

They both laughed. Liam felt odd. Memories, personal memories that he hadn't shared with anyone, and yet this man knew them as intimately as he did. It was like talking to himself. Yet hearing a wizened, croaky version of his own voice coming back at him.

'You remember getting the steward's job with the White Star Line?'

'Yes,' Foster replied. 'We got the job only because that other Irish lad was caught drinking on duty before the ship set sail. Remember his name? *Oliver*, wasn't it?'

'Aye.' Liam smiled. 'Stupid fella didn't realize he was breathin' his fumes all over the Chief Steward.'

The RV halted in traffic, causing everyone inside to lurch gently as Bob applied the brakes a little too keenly. A plastic bag full of unlaundered underwear slid off a seat into the cluttered aisle.

'So you remember that night as well?'

Foster closed his eyes. 'The night the *Titanic* went down? Of course I do. How does anyone ever forget something like that? I think what stays with me, Liam, what has stayed with me, was the calm before all the screaming. When everyone was certain there'd be lifeboats for all; that it wouldn't come down to the type of ticket you'd bought.'

'Aye.'

'It came suddenly, so it did. The panic. You remember that?'

Liam nodded. It had. One moment there'd been order and calm across the promenade deck, even the calming sound of a string quartet playing. People talking excitedly about how this was going to be the news story of the day tomorrow; how their eyewitness accounts – from the comfort of their bobbing lifeboats – of the Unsinkable Ship slowly, gracefully surrendering to the sea would be in every newspaper around the world. No panic. Not yet.

And then word had spread among them like wildfire. Chinese whispers. Not enough lifeboats for everyone. *Not nearly enough*.

Then the panic. The horrible panic.

A thought occurred to Liam. 'So, Foster . . . were you recruited just like me? The same way?'

He could see a glint of light reflected in Foster's eyes. The glare of passing headlights on his drawn face. 'Yes. Yes, of course. I was down checking on the second-class cabins.'

'And you were young, like me?'

'A bit younger than you are now, Liam.'

Of course. Liam knew that. Felt that now. No longer a young lad of sixteen, but subtly older in a million barely noticeable little ways. A man, prematurely.

'And was it an older version of you . . . that recruited you?'

Foster hesitated. 'Yes.'

'But does that mean I'm in some kind of a loop that goes on and on? That I'll get old like you, change my name to Foster, and then one day send myself back to 1912 to pick up another me? Is that it?'

'No. Not a loop exactly.'

'Then what?'

Foster looked at Maddy sitting up front in the passenger seat beside Bob. 'She's going to find out soon enough. If we keep heading this way.'

Liam turned to follow his gaze, looking at the back of her head. 'What's that supposed to mean?'

Foster reached out to Liam and rested a fatherly hand on his shoulder. 'Liam, it's all going to come clear for you soon enough. Perhaps far too soon.'

'Oh, come on, Foster! Will you just tell me –'

'She's going to learn.' Foster lowered his voice just for Liam to hear. 'And so is Sal. They're both going to learn the truth. And it's going to be hard for them. Much harder than it will be for you.'

'Why? What do you mean? *What's* going to be hard?'

'Liam, you'll cope . . . because I know *I* coped. And I carried on the agency's work. I carried on doing the work Waldstein needs us to do.'

'Jay-zus, you're annoying!' Liam hissed. 'Just tell me! What are you talking about?'

Foster shook his head. 'Maybe it's best for the girls if they find out this way.' He patted Liam's arm. 'Trust me . . . I think it's for the best. You'll learn the truth together.'

Sal sat near the front of the RV, the female support unit sitting dull-eyed and vacant beside her. It wasn't Becks yet, she'd decided. It wasn't going to be *Becks* properly until they'd uploaded her AI. For now, this thing was just a spare female support unit. A blank-minded one at that.

'That's a gene-silicon hybrid,' said SpongeBubba chirpily.

'I know,' said Sal.

'We had two dozen of those units on Project Exodus!' The lab robot's goofy plastic grin widened. 'They were spooky!' Its bauble-round eyes gazed at her curiously. 'What's wrong with *your* gene-silicon hybrid unit?'

'She's got a name, you know,' said Sal, suddenly feeling protective. 'We call her Becks.'

'Becks?' If the squat, square-shaped lab unit had had shoulders, he'd have shrugged them. Instead, wide, rolling, expressionless eyes above a fixed frozen grin regarded her. 'Hello, Becks! My name's SpongeBubba!'

The support unit's grey eyes remained unfocused, unblinking, unintelligent. Fixed and lifeless. Her young face a frozen frown of incomprehension.

'Hello, Becks! My name's SpongeBubba!' the lab unit chirped again.

'She's not been installed properly,' said Sal. 'She doesn't know her name yet.' Sal sighed. 'She can't speak anyway.'

SpongeBubba stroked his pickle-shaped nose, a gesture he must have picked up from Rashim. 'My model, Mitzumi HL-327 LabAssist V4.7, comes with language modules and laboratory protocols pre-installed!'

'Well, aren't you lucky.'

'I didn't have to have software installed in me after manufacture. I was function-ready!' SpongeBubba sounded like a spoilt brat.

'Well, at least Becks doesn't look really stupid.'

'My model comes with a polyform plastic casing and a library of programmable templates. Dr Anwar hacked the template code to make me look this special way!' SpongeBubba stroked his nose again. 'He says I'm different to any other

Mitzumi unit because he hacked my template code! Skippa says I'm *unique!*'

Sal glanced at Rashim. He was stretched out on the seat opposite, fast asleep.

'And your voice code too? Is that his work or do all you models talk like this?' Sal wondered how Rashim managed to cope with SpongeBubba's squeaky, high-pitched voice and permanent false cheeriness. Fun for a while perhaps, but already she was finding the thing incredibly irritating.

'Oh no! My voice was approximated from a few audio files made from a children's cartoon show that used to be on cable TV at the beginning of the twenty-first century! My voice is very special!'

'Can you use that special voice of yours quietly?'

'Oh yes! My volume output can be modulated!'

'Well, how about you turn it down for me?'

'Uh-uh.' SpongeBubba wagged a finger at her. 'Only skippa can adjust my user settings.'

Sal wondered how Rashim could sleep so readily. She toyed with the idea of waking him up and asking him to turn SpongeBubba off or mute him somehow. The robot was still staring at her, that stupid buck-toothed smile.

'Shadd-yah! Are you always so . . . so perky and annoying?'

'Perky?'

'Happy.'

SpongeBubba shook his whole body, his version of a headshake. 'No. I have no capacity to emulate human emotions. My model doesn't require that! There is a similar model designed as a domestic support unit for civilian use. That unit is installed with gesture and mood recognition and replication code. But Dr Anwar says that's a pointless waste of install space since if you know a robot's a robot why pretend it can have feelings?'

'So you're not really happy, then? You're just designed to look that way.'

SpongeBubba stared at her, an unwavering, goofy smile. 'Dr Anwar designed me.'

Sal couldn't work out if the robot was blaming his owner, or just stating a fact.

Becks pointed at something she'd seen through the windscreen. 'Urggh . . . ge fug, duf,' she gurgled excitedly and pointed.

Sal nodded, pulled her hand gently down and settled her. 'Yes . . . cars, that's right. Nice shiny cars.'

Why me? She shook her head. *Why do I get to babysit these two morons?*

'We're going to have to stop for gas again pretty soon,' said Maddy. The gauge was showing just under the quarter bar. 'Maybe we should pull over for the night. Find a motel. We're far enough away to be safe now, aren't we?'

Bob nodded. 'We are probably far enough to be safe.'

Even now, so late, ahead of them was a sea of traffic, red brake lights winking on and off as vehicles inched forward.

'What do you think they'll do? Do you think they'll keep coming after us?'

'I have no information on their mission parameters.'

'But if, say, *you* were sent to kill us, what would you be doing?'

'I would persist until the mission parameters were satisfied, of course.'

'How would you go about that, Bob? For example . . . what would you be doing right now?'

Bob scowled. Thinking. 'I would attempt to intercept police radio communications for references to stolen vehicles in the vicinity of the archway. I would be searching the archway for items of useful intelligence.' He looked sideways at her. 'We left in a hurry. We cannot be certain we have not left behind some information that could lead them to us.'

He was right. They *had* left in a hurry, a careless scramble to grab all their essentials. God knows what they'd left behind, what fragments of information lay scattered around in their wake. Maddy's head began to throb with renewed stress.

She sat in silence for a while, her fingers caressing her temples. She looked down into the stationary cars on either side of them. The glow of radio tuners on dashboards. She imagined every single driver in every vehicle on this road was tuned into a news station and listening to reporters recap the day's terrifying events. Late-night talk radio stations venting unbridled rage at this cowardly attack on innocent American civilians. Experts hurried into studios to try and make sense of things. Because that's what everyone needed to have right now, wasn't it? Another explanation.

Why? Why are we being attacked? What did we do to deserve this?

Of course, Maddy had been pulled from a time – 2010 – when a lot of thinking had been done on why 9/11 had happened. The fact that there had been warning signs. The fact that there had been people in the FBI, the CIA screaming warnings to President Bush back in 2000 that something like this *Was. Going. To. Happen. Imminently.* Maddy came from a time when there was perspective, *hindsight*, on this day; from a time when everyone understood that a terrorist attack on America was inevitable. But for the people in these cars all around them this whole nightmare was still – and would be for years yet – a bewildering and terrifying mystery.

She drew her mind back to more pressing issues, for her. 'No matter how far we drive, Bob . . . there's no knowing for sure that we're going to be safe, is there?'

'No.'

She glanced at the gauge again. 'And how far have we gone?'

'We are only eighty miles from New York as a direct-line distance.'

'Eighty miles? Might as well be a thousand and one, I suppose . . . Let's take the next turn-off, then. We've got to fill up sometime soon anyway.'

Bob nodded. 'Affirmative. Next turning.'

'And how much further to Boston? It's not that far, is it?'

'Approximately a hundred and twenty miles as a direct-line distance from our current location.'

'We can do the rest of the drive after a rest break.' She pointed at a road sign looming towards them on the right. 'Let's take that next turn-off. The one for Branford. See if we can find a gas station and someplace to get some food, a diner or something.'

Maddy suddenly realized how bone-weary she felt; physically, mentally, spiritually, she was completely *spent*. A bed would be good. A bed with clean, crisp white sheets. God . . . better still, a hot shower. A *bath* even!

'Actually, the hell with that. Let's see if we can stop and find a motel too. We can do the rest of the drive tomorrow.'

'Tomorrow?' He nodded approval. Perhaps even Bob realized she needed a night off.

'Affirmative.'

CHAPTER 11
12 September 2001, Washington DC

The duty corridor off the mezzanine floor was windowless. The 'catacombs', that's what he'd heard one of the personnel who worked down here call it once. Several offices along an unused floor beneath an anonymous government building in Washington.

These offices had another name – a semi-official name. The few personnel who worked down in this artificially illuminated netherworld called it 'The Department'. More than half a century ago – fifty-six years to be precise – was when The Department was set up. Not here, though. The Department didn't have proper offices to call its own until after the 1947 'New Mexico Incident'. But this had been its one and only home since then.

On several occasions in those fifty-six years, these offices had experienced short bursts of frenetic activity; carefully vetted FBI agents had been drafted in to do routine belt-'n'-braces work, but never fully briefed on the various case files they were doing the heavy lifting on.

On a need-to-know basis. That's how The Department did its business.

There'd been a buzz of activity here back in '47, and again in 1963 after the 'Dallas Incident'. There were a lot of paper files generated over that, all of them still down here in the catacombs. Everything one would ever want to know about the death of a President was stored in dog-eared cardboard folders, in dusty filing cabinets labelled 'J-759'. And, if one took the time to dig through thousands of yellowing pages of gathered intelligence and witness depositions, one might in fact find the *correct* name of the man who actually killed President Kennedy.

Not Oswald. Certainly not one L. H. Oswald.

There were other labelled files down here, of other incidents over the decades that had been passed over to The Department to if not investigate then at least to safely archive. Fragments of intelligence gathered that would live forever down here in this air-conditioned twilight, far too sensitive, too incendiary, too dangerous to ever appear in the public eye.

There was file N-27, a certain dark secret from the very last days of the Second World War; a whole drawer of one of the filing cabinets was devoted to that. Then, of course, there was file R-497, the event that occurred in Roswell, New Mexico – several filing cabinets for that one – and typically plenty of silly TV shows, films and tinfoil-hat conspiracy theories about R-497.

And then there were several other, smaller, files.

One of those files had the equally uninspiring name of 414-T. Possibly the slimmest file in the pack of secrets, slumbering down here in the semi-darkness.

The Department was run 'off the books'. Its funding came from a lump sum dropped into a bank account just after the Second World War. Over the last half a century that lump sum had been managed by a financial management company and invested in various things. Back in the seventies, for example, some of that money had been spent purchasing shares in a promising little tech company with a rainbow-coloured apple for a logo.

The Department had a staff that had on a few occasions numbered as high as thirty-five men, but tended in quiet times to number as few as three. As it did right now. The 'Head', his assistant and a solitary clerical officer.

Niles Cooper was the 'Head' right now, and possibly for the foreseeable future. Handed that role by his predecessor, a middle-aged pen-pusher called Pullman, who'd been looking for an easy assignment to carry him over until retirement. Before him, there'd been an old man called Wallace who'd run The Department – so it was said – since it was set up back in 1945.

Every 'Head' had his pet file, so Pullman told Cooper the day he retired and passed the keys to this place over to his younger successor. Pullman said *his* pet file had been R-497, the Roswell one.

Cooper's was the slimmest one: 414-T.

Something of an enigma, that one. Several black-and-white photographs, very poor quality if truth be told. They'd been recovered, supposedly, by a Russian intelligence officer from one of the artillery-damaged barrack buildings near Obersalzsberg, near the mountain-top retreat of Adolf Hitler.

The Eagle's Nest.

But there was no guarantee of the accuracy of that. It might have come from somewhere else, just as likely one of the many bombed-out ministry buildings along the Wilhelmstrasse in Berlin. The images did have the ink-stamp of a swastika and a correctly configured intelligence reference number used by the Gestapo. So they were at least half-likely to be genuine.

Three photographs in total. The first in the sequence showed what appeared to be the aftermath of a bonfire of bodies in some snowy wood. A jumble of blackened limbs amid ice-melt and slush, surrounded by fir trees with snow-laden branches.

The second photograph was unpleasant. A close-up of a human skull, scorched completely black, and what appeared to be a section of skull cracked or carved open and lying in the snow nearby. The rest of the skull looked empty. *Scooped out* even.

But it was the third image that made this sequence so interesting, that had granted this slim file a place in The Department's twilight bowels. The third image was of an assault rifle, like everything else scorched black and the gun barrel bent by the heat of the fire. There were notes stapled to the photograph. Notes made on some typewriter and in German, then added to some years later in English, handwritten blue ink, notes made by some American or British firearms expert:

Make and model is unknown. Not Russian. Certainly
not one of ours! Could be a German prototype?
The firing mechanism indecipherable. Can't see
how this gun would actually work!
(Signed: G. H. Davison. 16th February 1952)

Someone had drawn a blue-ink circle on a copy of the photograph. The circle looped round some markings beneath the weapon's breech, a cluster of faint indented numbers and letters. The manufacturer's markings, batch number, model number, and possibly the weapon's date of manufacture.

Cooper had studied this photograph many times over the years. Each time, he'd studied it under a magnifying glass with the help of his angled desk lamp, like a manic philatelist examining a perfect and precious unmarked penny black stamp. And every time he'd peered closely at this black-and-white photograph he'd experienced the same shiver of excitement, of promise.

A possibility.

A possibility, and that's all it was, a possibility that those last four numbers of the manufacturer's mark were the year of manufacture.

2066.

CHAPTER 12

11 September 2001,
outside Branford, Connecticut

The motel was pretty basic, just what Maddy expected for thirty-nine dollars a night. A double bed, a table, a wobbly hanger rack and a small TV, manacled to a wall bracket. They got three rooms: one for Maddy, Sal and Becks, one for Liam and Bob and one for Foster and Rashim. Basic, but at least each room had an en-suite bathroom with a bathtub too small to drown a cat in and presided over by a shower unit that sprayed a lethargic afterthought of tepid water.

SpongeBubba had the RV with an aisle full of plastic bags all to himself.

They all freshened up, each of them relishing their turn in the showers, before heading to the diner next door for dinner. They chose unhealthy, heart-attack meals from a menu with helpful, if somewhat misleading, pictures. After that, they reconvened in Foster and Rashim's room.

The TV was turned up enough that anyone in a neighbouring room wasn't going to easily pick words out of their conversation through the paper-thin walls. Fox News was on and there was understandably only one story today. President George Bush had held a press conference and given the administration's official response to the day's acts of terrorism, and now his words were being dissected by news hosts in meticulous detail.

Foster was slumped in the room's only chair. The others were perched on the double bed. Becks sat cross-legged on the carpet like a nursery-school child waiting for storytime and Bob stood in the corner of the room keeping a wary eye, through the window blinds, on the RV parked outside.

'You want to know what the future's like?' said Rashim.

Maddy nodded. 'Yeah, Liam's right, we really should get to know how this century all plays out. All we've got are scraps of info. Bits here, bits there. Even Foster only knows *some* of it.'

The old man nodded. 'Only what was available on the archway's computer database and that only takes us up to the year 2054.'

Rashim looked at Foster. 'The year your secret agency originates from?'

'I suppose that must be it,' Foster answered with a shrug. 'It's the year from which Waldstein set it all up and took it back to 2001.'

'2054? I was just a small boy then!' Rashim laughed.

'Go on, please. Tell us what you can,' said Liam.

Rashim leaned back on the bed, hands behind his head, looking up at the low cracked plaster ceiling above. 'It's not a happy story, boys and girls. We screwed things up. Mankind did. We made a mess of everything. Funny, it's all history to me, but the future to you.' He sighed. 'The world hit seven billion people on the thirty-first of October 2011. In my time historians use that date a lot. Like some sort of a marker. The point at which it all began to go bad.'

'Go on.'

'Well, whether it was the population explosion or peak oil to blame, 2011 is retrospectively seen as the point at which the world crossed the line and was doomed.'

'*Peak oil?* What's that?' asked Liam.

71

'Peak oil is the term for the point at which we were never going to have enough oil-based energy to tide us over until we could rely on a new source of energy. Oh, there were things being trialled on a small scale: renewables, wind, tide energy, zero-point energy. But nothing that was near enough to replacing oil. The rest of the century was one war after another being fought for the remaining oil fields, while the world continued to warm up as we ferociously burned our dwindling supply of fossil fuels and the oceans continued to rise.

'I have a question for you.' Rashim lifted his head and looked at them all. 'Any of you heard of the Fermi Paradox?'

Maddy did, or thought she did. 'Isn't that the puzzle to do with why we haven't yet found any alien civilizations out there in the universe?'

He nodded. 'A mathematician called Fermi calculated the odds of there being other alien life forms out there in the big wide galaxy. He took into account all the usual variables: the number of stars at the right point in their life cycles, the average number of likely planets per star, the probability of any of those planets existing within the "Goldilocks Zone" around the star, the likelihood of a planet having liquid water . . . all those important variables.

'Anyway, while the odds were stacked against any one solar system containing intelligent life, given that there are literally trillions of stars, his maths delivered an answer that there must be hundreds of thousands of alien civilizations out there, and tens of thousands of civilizations advanced enough in technology to be putting out radio waves, intentionally or not.

'So the point is,' continued Rashim, 'when we started looking into space for radio signals, we *should* have stumbled across them almost immediately. According to Fermi's maths, we should have been swimming in alien radio signals.'

'But instead we never found anything,' said Maddy.

'Right. And *that's* the Fermi Paradox. Why isn't every frequency full of alien signals?' He sighed. 'Because we're alone. And why are we alone?' He smiled. He wasn't expecting them to answer. 'Well . . . in my time we figured that out for ourselves. Within a century of discovering radio waves, mankind managed to exhaust the raw materials of the planet. The raw materials, the free energy source that every emerging technological civilization gets as a gift from its historical past – fossil fuels. It's that package of free energy that we should have used carefully while we took our time to discover and harness quantum energy. Humankind never got a chance to take anything more than a few baby steps into space. We never got the time to mature, to reach out into space, for other worlds. Hydrocarbons. Fossil fuels. Oil. We used it all up far too quickly. Too many people wanting too many things. We used it up,' he said, sighing, 'and then, as it began to run out, we turned on each other.'

'The Oil Wars?' said Liam. He had heard another traveller from Rashim's time mention them. A man called Locke.

'Yes. Wars between India and China. Japan and Korea. The first of those was in the 2040s. Russia and the European Bloc, there was a short war between those. And, of course, what we should have been doing is trying to fix another bigger problem. The world itself dying: warming up, rising tides, poisoned blooms of algae killing the seas.'

Rashim fell silent for a moment. 'Anyway, that's the answer to the Fermi Paradox; most – if not *all* – civilizations either destroy themselves or mine themselves dry long before they ever spread out to other planets and are able to mine, harvest them for resources. Once you've exhausted your home planet . . . it's all over for you. Either you become extinct, or you eventually end up being cavemen once more.'

'It's a one-shot deal?' said Maddy.

He nodded. 'And perhaps every civilization makes the same mistake. Spends what it has, thinking it will never run out. Then, all of a sudden, it does.'

'Wonderful,' sighed Maddy.

'But on Earth we didn't just run out. We decided to destroy ourselves in style.' Rashim snorted. 'It was some kind of a genetically engineered virus . . . pretty much wiped us all out in the space of a few weeks. We made a nice tidy job of pretty much erasing ourselves from history.'

'Shadd-yah,' whispered Sal after a while. 'This is depressing! You're great fun to hang out with, you know that, don't you?'

He shrugged. 'You *did* ask what the future's going to be like.'

'I didn't,' she replied. 'It was Liam who asked.'

'Aye, and now I wish I bleedin' well hadn't.'

CHAPTER 13

12 September 2001, Washington DC

Cooper was up and at work despite the time. The Department was as much his home as the single-bed studio apartment he kept in Queens Chapel, DC. Thirty-nine, with no family, no partner, no children, not even a pet, one might say this twilight office with empty desks, a watercooler that hadn't been switched on in years and a fading poster of Jane Fonda was his life.

Custodian of secrets so secret even Presidents aren't privy to them. That's me.

Perhaps not the world's most exciting job. But an important one nonetheless.

Last night he'd stayed here, slept in the cot he kept in his personal office.

His PC was on and he was streaming MSNBC, watching it as his coffee and breakfast bagel cooled enough to have without burning the roof of his mouth. It was quite early in the morning; outside in the world, the sky was still dark. On the monitor he watched a news camera pan across rescue workers picking through the smouldering rubble of the World Trade Center. Brilliantly stark floodlights illuminated the enormous mound of rubble and twisted spars of metal. Dots of neon-orange light-reflective jackets decorated the mounds of dust and concrete; dozens of emergency workers picked through the remains of the towers in the vain hope of finding survivors.

The phone rang.

Cooper looked at it. The phones down here never rang. Well, rarely anyway.

He picked it up. 'Cooper.'

'Coop, it's Damon.'

Damon Grohl. A friend from the FBI Academy many years ago. Friends still. Christmas cards were exchanged every year and every now and then they shared a beer, if that counted.

'Damon!' Cooper's mood lifted. 'Well, been a while! How are you, ol' buddy?'

'Fine. Fine. The Bureau down this way is chasing around like a headless chicken with what went down yesterday.'

Headless chicken? Damon was probably right about that. FBI heads were going to start rolling pretty soon over this. Letting something like this slip through their fingers.

'I can imagine. Not much fun.'

'Look, Coop, something's come up that, uh . . . might be, well, your thing, if you get my meaning.'

Cooper's curiosity was piqued. 'My thing?'

'We've got a double cop killing over in Brooklyn. Happened after midnight this morning.'

'How's that anything to do with me? The Department?' A thought occurred to him. 'Is this linked to yesterday . . . ?'

'Twin Towers? Who knows? Might be. We're looking at pretty much anything that moves right now.'

'You said this cop killing might be my sort of thing?' A little careless of him, to be honest, talking so candidly like this over the phone.

'Your phone line is encrypted, right?'

'Yes. But keep what you say *foggy* . . . if you know what I mean.'

'Foggy? Sure. So, Coop, are you still doing that whole X Files thing down in Washington?'

'You know I can't comment on that.'

He heard Damon draw a breath.

'Damon? What the hell is it?'

'I think I've got something you might want to take a look at, if you can get up here quickly.'

CHAPTER 14

7.01 a.m., 12 September 2001, outside Branford, Connecticut

Maddy was knocking on the adjoining motel room wall for him to get up. Liam yawned and cracked open eyes to look at the digital clock on his bedside ledge. Just gone seven.

He thumped the wall back. 'All right! Jay-zus! I'm getting up, so I am!' he shouted.

He heard Sal's muffled laughter on the other side.

Bob was already awake. Not that he ever slept. 'Maddy has instructed me to tell you we are getting ready to move on.'

They'd all decided they needed a good night's rest before resuming their journey up to Boston. They'd all been strung out, far more exhausted than they'd realized. A week in Ancient Rome struggling to stay alive and now this. Fatigue had finally caught up with them all.

'Maddy says we will eat some breakfast then set off.'

Liam's stomach still groaned. Last night's triple-decker meat platter pizza was still lying heavily in his gut. He wondered if he could manage anything else right now.

They met outside in the car park beside the RV. Rashim was looking particularly ill.

'Jesus, what's up with you?' asked Maddy.

'I've been up all night, vomiting.' His face looked almost grey.

'The food wasn't *that* bad!'

He shook his head, his dark ponytail wagging limply. 'No, it's my fault. I was stupid. The food was too rich. I'm used to synthetic proteins. Soya products.' He gulped air and stifled a belch that could easily have been an empty retch. 'Not used to the real thing.' Rashim had had a mixed grill. Wolfed it down as he relished the texture and savoured the billionaire-luxury of eating nuggets of real meat.

Foster obviously hadn't slept well either, dark bags evident under his sunken eyes. Maddy looked at the men in their party with a mixture of pity and contempt.

The diner was open and several trucks were parked up in the gravel car park, their drivers inside already tucking into pancake and waffle breakfasts. Further along their side of the highway was an out-of-town mall called North Haven Plaza. Across acres of car park it looked open already. At least the eateries probably were.

'OK then, let's try and find something a little healthier over there, if you guys are feeling a bit precious.'

'Let me quickly check in on SpongeBubba.'

Maddy unlocked the side door to the RV for him and Rashim stepped up inside.

'Morning, skippa!' chirped the robot, squatting in the passenger seat upfront. It was playing with the steering wheel.

'We're having some food over there.' Rashim pointed through the windscreen at the mall. 'We won't be long.'

Maddy joined him inside. 'Does your robot have a wireless broadcast protocol?'

'Sure.'

'If anyone comes looking at our vehicle . . . cops, for example, can he bleep a warning over to Bob?'

'Yes, of course.'

She looked down at the lab unit. 'Reckon you can do that for me, then, SpongeBob?'

'SpongeBubba,' corrected the robot. His lips quivered a jocular, angry snarl. 'That's my name, missy-miss!'

Maddy rolled her eyes at the lab unit's pre-programmed plastic expression. 'Just tell your *toy* to keep a lookout,' she said to Rashim. 'OK?'

The mall wasn't busy. A few people inside walking freshly polished floors, mostly people who worked there. Clearly no one felt like shopping today. A jazzy rendition of a Stevie Wonder hit wafted across the bright and cheerful circular centrepiece atrium and a pair of overweight security guards shared a joke with a janitor and made one or two heads turn with their echoing laughter.

'Up there,' said Maddy, pointing to a balcony overlooking the atrium. 'RealBean Coffee. The place looks open. We can get a panini or . . .'

She checked herself. Stupid. Sure, although the mall looked no different to any other in her time, it was still 2001. No one did paninis back then. Back *now*.

'. . . or maybe we'll get a toasted sandwich or something.'

CHAPTER 15

7.20 a.m., 12 September 2001,
Interstate 95, south-west Connecticut

'Information: you are driving too fast,' said Faith.

Abel turned to look at her. 'The driving is suitable,' he replied.

'You are driving at a faster velocity than specified on the roadside indicators.'

Abel narrowed his eyes at her, then turned to look back at the road ahead flanked by signs indicating, advertising, proclaiming all kinds of things. Finally a speed indicator *wooshed* past on his side. 'The number fifty-five indicates a recommended velocity.'

'No. I believe it means *maximum* velocity. You are in excess of that. That will attract unwanted attention.'

Abel lifted his foot off the accelerator, causing the truck behind to brake hard, and then a moment later the driver leaned on his horn angrily. Abel looked over his shoulder. 'Why did the vehicle behind make that noise?'

Faith followed his gaze. 'I believe he is annoyed.'

'Annoyed,' Abel repeated. 'Why?'

She frowned for a moment. 'I do not know why.'

The truck driver overtook them, glaring down from his cab as he passed by.

The NYPD squad car they'd stolen in the early hours of the

morning had been replaced with a different car. After listening to police chatter over the radio, they'd quickly realized the vehicle's identification number on the roof was going to make them too easy to track down. Before the light of dawn had fully arrived, they'd switched to a solitary car parked in an empty forecourt. It was small and bubble-shaped and an uncomfortable squeeze for Abel's broad frame as he wriggled into place behind the steering wheel, but at least it wasn't going to draw the attention of any police helicopters scanning the highways for their stolen vehicle. Of course, it wasn't until dawn that they saw their new ride – a Volkswagen Beetle – was a rather conspicuous tangerine orange decorated with hand-painted pink daisies.

They drove in silence for a while, as they had in fact done all the way from Brooklyn. As he drove, Abel's mind carefully sorted through the data he'd acquired in the last thirty-two hours and twenty minutes of life. Not a particularly long life, but certainly a very busy one so far.

The first nine hours of his consciousness, just as with Faith and the others of his batch, had been spent in a sterile cloning room, illuminated with a soft amber glow coming from the half a dozen growth tubes. Each of them had contained a candidate foetus held in stasis, but now recently 'birthed'.

Six of them, naked and coated in the gelatinous protein solution drying out on their bare skin. They had sat huddled together on the cool tiled floor with empty, childlike minds. Frightened, confused. And then, without any warning, wireless wisdom had begun to flood into their minds: torrential packets of data and executable applets of AI software that shooed away the childlike fear and replaced it with impassive machine-mind calm.

Like awaking. Emerging from a coma.

Abel recalled his mind filling with compressed knowledge

that unpacked itself into segments of his hard drive. Knowledge of the world of 2001. Knowledge of a place called New York. Of a place called Brooklyn. Knowledge of cars, trains, planes, people, skyscrapers, billboards, intersections, doughnuts, handguns, traffic lights, cops, radios, computers, mobile phones, the Spice Girls, Shrek, George Bush, 9/11 . . .

And then, finally, into that dimly lit, womb-like, amber-coloured room a human had stepped. Abel's installed software was already prepped to acknowledge the man as an AUTHORIZED USER. His instructions to be obeyed without question.

The man pulled up a chair and sat down in front of them. 'Your primary mission goal is to locate and terminate these humans.' He held a data pad in his hand and tapped its screen.

In their six minds, simultaneously, they received a packet of images in rapid slide-show succession. Front images, profile images of a young man with an untidy shock of dark hair and thick, arched eyebrows. A young teenaged woman with frizzy, strawberry-blonde hair and glasses. A dark-skinned girl with jet-black hair that drooped like a velvet curtain over one eye.

'You should also terminate any other humans or support units that appear to be collaborating with them. Your secondary goal is to destroy all the equipment you find at the location you'll shortly be arriving at. This is their base of operations. Leave nothing intact. That is important. There are items of equipment there that can be used to displace time. That is an unacceptable contamination risk. All of it must be destroyed.

'When these things are done, you are to activate your own self-destruct devices. This is your tertiary goal. Your mission is complete *only* when these people are dead, their field office has been completely destroyed and your own on-board computers have been irreparably disabled. Are these mission parameters perfectly clear?'

All six of them had chorused a deadpan 'affirmative'.

Abel looked out at the bright sunny morning now, a blue cloudless sky above them. The road was clogged with morning traffic. A world of humans tirelessly going about their everyday business, getting up and going to jobs as if today was just another day. Like program loops executing regardless of the previous day's extraordinary events. Life going on the same as before.

'They are behaving as if nothing unusual occurred yesterday,' said Faith as if reading his mind. 'Why do you think that is?'

'A post-trauma behaviour pattern,' he replied. 'Access your database. File 3426/344-456. Human Stress Responses.'

She blinked momentarily, digesting a short data entry on how the human mind filled itself with unnecessary repetitive tasks to block out painful thought processes. Denial. She looked at him. 'Keeping busy so they do not have to confront what they witnessed yesterday?'

'Correct.'

'Experience, recollection, is useful data. Denying it makes no sense.'

'Agreed.'

Little of what they'd experienced of human behaviour over the last twenty-three hours had made any sense. There was a frustrating randomness to human behaviour that made predicting what they were going to do next almost impossible. Like trying to accurately predict the course of a waterdrop down a rain-spattered windowpane.

There was no knowing for certain that the target named *Madelaine Carter* was taking her team back to her hometown. There was a strong likelihood. A reasonable probability. But no certainty. All they had to support that assumption was the indentation of that word on the jotter pad. Boston.

All they had was a very human thing . . . a *hunch*.

Faith suddenly twisted in her seat to face him. 'I have a signal.'

His eyes locked on her and he nodded. 'I also just detected it.'

For a second, less than that, they'd both picked up an ident signal just as they'd driven past a turn-off leading to some large square buildings fronted by an enormous car park.

'An AI ident,' she said. Her grey eyes locked on his. 'Software version date –'

'2064,' he finished. Nothing in this time – *nothing* – other than their primary target could possibly be broadcasting a signal with a future date stamp. 'It must be them.'

'Agreed. Take the next turning.'

CHAPTER 16

12 September 2001, New York

Cooper had arrived in New York not long after sunrise and was taken by an NYPD squad car over from the precinct HQ. The plain-clothes police sergeant drew up and stopped in front of a fluttering streamer of crime-scene tape.

'As far as I can go, I'm afraid,' he said. 'Feds have it all staked out even though it was a couple of *our* guys that got shot,' he added without attempting to hide his disgust.

Cooper thanked him, stepped out and flashed his ID at a uniformed officer guarding the tape line.

A chalk circle on the tarmac marked several bullet cases, and another marked a dark dried puddle of blood.

'Is there an Agent Damon Grohl on-site?' he asked the cop.

'Your FBI buddies are down there somewhere,' he replied, pointing to the opening of an alleyway beside the base of the towering support for the bridge he'd just been driven over from Manhattan.

'So what's down there?'

'Damned if I know. Nothing us dumb ol' beat cops are being allowed to see.'

Cooper crossed the intersection, flashed his ID at another uniformed cop standing at the mouth of the alleyway.

'Yo, Cooper! Coop! Down here!' a voice barked out from further down the alley.

It was Grohl. Cooper could make out his chunky silhouette standing two-thirds of the way down. Light from crime-scene floodlights was spilling out from some archway across cobblestones and piled rubbish.

'Damon!' He began to hesitantly pick his way into the mouth of the alley, sidestepping a discarded spicy chicken wrap. 'You going to tell me what this is all about yet? I just spent the last four hours driving up here! And I really don't know what –'

Grohl waved at him to come on down. 'I'm not going to shout about it. Come over here.'

Cooper made his way along the alley. At the far end of it he could see a handrail and quayside, a view of the East River and the underbelly of the bridge overhead, receding until it merged with Manhattan beyond. Warm morning sunlight picked out the tops of the skyscrapers along Wall Street. In the sky, several news choppers buzzed around where yesterday the Twin Towers had stood.

He joined Grohl and shook his hand. 'Sheesh . . . long journey all the way up from Washington this morning. Every plane in America's been grounded. I had to damn well drive.' He looked at his old Academy buddy. 'Now I was trying to figure out what the hell it is you think you've got that made you decide to give *me* a call.'

Grohl smiled. 'Come on, Coop, everyone in the Agency knows you're the custodian of all that weird X Files stuff.' He slapped Cooper affectionately on the arm and grinned, a knowing boy-have-I-got-something-for-you expression. 'You won't be disappointed.'

They were standing beside a brick archway; a metal shutter door was wound three-quarters of the way up, but still low enough that they both had to duck down to look under. 'What's in here?'

'Last night, early hours of the morning actually, there was that double cop killing. You probably saw the evidence markers out there on the intersection?' Cooper nodded.

'Eyewitness saw the whole thing. Said they emerged from this alleyway, two of them; one male, one female, mid-twenties, white, tall, athletic. And get this –' he grinned – 'both as bald as buddhas. Walked right up, assaulted the first cop, took his gun off him and shot him and his partner dead, execution style. Two to the chest, one to the head. Then calm as you please they both got into the squad car and drove it away.'

'Sheeesh. Linked to the Trade Center? Terrorists?'

'That's what we thought. That's why we got handed this one so quickly. Follow me.' He ducked down, led the way inside. 'Precinct cops were first on the scene. They searched the alleyway and found this archway left wide open.'

Cooper ducked under after him and stood up inside.

'And this is where it all gets very *weird*.'

Cooper looked around. The place looked as if it had been burgled or rifled through. A mess of things pulled out and strewn across the floor. He noted the bunk beds, the table, armchairs. Kettle, pizza boxes, burger wrappers and drinks cans. 'What? This some sort of drugs den? A gang crib?'

Grohl shrugged. 'No. Not narcotics, not even a trace. But we did find this.' He pointed down to spatters and smears of dried blood on the floor, each mark highlighted with a chalk circle and an evidence number. 'Something went down in here. A fight. Crime-scene pathologist reckons there's enough blood on the floor to suggest another possible homicide. Two dead cops out there and another possible killing in here. But no body. Anyway, we got handed this ball because it might . . . *might* . . . have something to do with the terror attack.'

Grohl beckoned Cooper to follow him across the floor

towards a desk cluttered with wires and circuit boards. He picked up something sitting in a plastic evidence bag.

'And *this* little beauty is why I thought I'd give *you* a call, old friend.' He passed it to Cooper. 'Don't worry, it's already been dusted for prints. You can get it out and take a look at it.'

Cooper reached into the bag and pulled out a smooth, fist-sized piece of glossy black plastic and chrome. 'What is this thing? Some sort of digital organizer?'

'Turn it over.'

He did and noted the logo on the back in the centre. An apple.

'This is some sort of prototype *Apple* product?'

Grohl took it back off him. Pressed a button at the bottom and the screen glowed brightly. He slid his finger across the screen.

'Jesus! That's . . .'

'Touch-the-screen technology. Very fancy, huh?'

Cooper nodded. It wasn't fancy, it was *stunning*. But he still wasn't sure what he was doing all the way up here this morning. There was enough work the FBI needed to be doing chasing down whatever leads they might have on the horrific events of yesterday.

'Jesus, Coop, even the military doesn't have anything near as *slick* as this little beauty.' Grohl's thumb found an icon on the screen and tapped it. 'Check it out. This is where it gets real interesting, though.' He turned the device round and showed him the screen. Cooper squinted at a page of text.

'What am I looking at?'

'System software information. Look at the software version date.'

Cooper's stomach did a queasy turnover in his belly. It was showing the year as 2009.

'And the device's calendar is set to 2010. You ever see

anything like this gadget? It looks like something right out of *Star Trek*.'

Cooper shook his head. No, he'd seen nothing as advanced as this, not even mocked-up prototypes at a gadget show.

'Damon, it looks to me a bit like a super-advanced version of those new Apple iPod things the kids are all asking for Thanksgiving.'

'Oh, and this thing is also designed to make phone calls.'

'It's a *phone as well*?'

'Oh yeah, only . . . it doesn't connect to anything because it's using a telecoms protocol that doesn't actually exist . . .' His eyes met Cooper's and Cooper understood what word his friend was leaving unsaid and dangling in the space between them.

. . . *Yet*.

CHAPTER 17

7.24 a.m., 12 September 2001, outside Branford, Connecticut

Abel swung the Volkswagen Beetle into the car park and climbed out of the vehicle, the engine still ticking as he crossed the tarmac towards the source of the signal, a large white vehicle with wide perspex windows at the front and back. It looked like some kind of habitation module on wheels.

Faith strode beside him. She withdrew the handgun from the waistband of the jogging bottoms she was wearing, stolen from some hapless runner what seemed like a lifetime ago.

'They are here,' she said.

Abel nodded and reached for the handle of the vehicle's rear door. It failed to turn. He grabbed it tighter and twisted it hard. Something snapped softly and clattered on to the floor inside. He pulled open the door and stepped up inside the vehicle. The RV lurched gently under his weight.

Inside his eyes picked out a mess of bin liners and plastic bags piled down the vehicle's central aisle towards the driver and passengers' seats up at the front.

And a small, yellow cubed android was sitting on one of the seats. Big ping-pong-ball eyes batted lashes as its pickle-shaped nose quivered. 'You're not supposed to come in here,' it said with a cautionary tattle-tale voice.

Abel's mind detected a squirt of data. A broadcasted alert. The yellow robot was beaming an alarm signal. A fainter signal approximately a quarter of a mile away registered an acknowledgement. He dropped back on to the ground outside and turned to Faith.

She'd picked that up too.

'The acknowledgement came from over there,' she said, pointing towards a large squat white building, sporting signs of big-brand retailers. Between them a sea of tarmac beginning to fill with cars parking up: early-bird shoppers.

'They are inside that building,' said Abel.

'My God.' Rashim shook his head with disbelief. He looked around the mini-mart and then reached into a freezer unit and picked up a shrink-wrapped pack-of-three Ma Jackson's Shaked n' Baked Tennessee Chicken Drummers. 'This is real? *Real* food?'

Sal nodded. 'Those? Real chicken legs? Uh-huh.'

'From what was once a real live chicken?'

'Of course.'

His eyes widened. *When* he'd come from only the wealthiest could afford vat-grown meat and even then it wasn't really proper meat. 'Meat on the bone' was muscle cells grown on plastic rods shaped like bones. It tasted vaguely savoury, with a gelatinous texture, a meat-gel lollipop at best. Everyone else lived on synthi-soya alternatives.

'There's so much!' He shook his head again. 'There's just so much of this real food!'

'Yeah, well.' Sal took the drumsticks off him and dropped them in the shopping trolley. 'Best make the most of it, right?'

Maddy's call. Since this food supermarket inside the mall was already open, she decided that since they'd stopped they might as well stock up on some essentials. The RV had a fridge that worked, they might as well put something edible in it and the little kitchen cabinets located above it. Maddy said she wasn't sure whether they were staying in Boston or moving on. But it probably wouldn't hurt for them to have a few luxuries aboard the TimeRiders' 'tour bus'.

'This way, Becks.' Sal led the trolley. Becks pushed it dutifully.

'Affirmative.' Her language pack was installed now. Just the default library. Her voice was monotone, completely without any expression. Sal turned to look at her. She was wearing a beanie hat to cover her still-smooth head, and baggy jeans and a jumper hung loosely on her slight frame. Her pale face had a slack, vacant look to it. At least that part of her looked convincingly teenager.

And at least she wasn't drooling now.

'My God!' Rashim's voice echoed from the next aisle along. A moment later he appeared at the end of the freezer aisle gazing wide-eyed at something sitting on the palm of his hand. She waved him over.

'What's up, Rashim?'

He hurried over and held his hand out. 'Are these strawberries real too?'

Great. He's found the fruit counter.

Liam put some more boxes of Coco Pops in the trolley. Bob looked down at them.

'You already have five boxes of Coco Pops.'

'Aye, well, 'tis better to be safe than sorry.' He nudged Bob's arm. 'Anyway, you like them too.'

'They are acceptable to my digestive system.'

'Oh, come on . . . admit it, you actually *like* them. I've seen the way you gobble 'em down.'

'They are low in protein. I require large amounts of Coco Pops to sustain me.'

Liam offered him a sly grin. 'I've seen you slurp that chocolate milk, like a cat lapping cream.'

'The milk is the more beneficial food component of the two.'

Liam shrugged distractedly. 'Ah well.' He surveyed the other cereal boxes stacked along the aisle. 'Hey look, Bob. You can even have Coco Pops with funny pink teddy bear shapes in it.' He picked the cereal box up and held it closer to get a better look at the far too colourful package design. 'What do you reckon those little teddy bear fellas are made of?'

Bob scowled disapprovingly. 'Probably nothing particularly nutritious.'

'Maybe not, but it looks fun.' Liam dropped the cereal box in the trolley. He smiled up at Bob. 'You remember what *fun* is, don't you?'

'I can supply a definition of the word and several thousand cultural references to the word including –'

'Never mind.'

CHAPTER 18

7.25 a.m., 12 September 2001, North Haven Plaza, outside Branford

Maddy brought the tray over to the booth and sat down opposite Foster. He wasn't looking so good this morning. Perhaps a couple of sleepless nights hadn't helped. Perhaps it was the artificial lighting in this coffee shop. He'd looked healthier in Central Park: sun on his face and a fresh breeze ruffling the tufts of snow-white hair on his head. Healthier and happier back there.

'Coffee, milky and sweet, just how you and Liam like it.'

'Thank you, Maddy.'

She sat down, grabbed her latte and looked out across the mall. There was a toddlers' play area and a fake palm tree, beyond that the mini-supermarket where the others were food shopping. She thought she caught a glimpse of the bristly top of Bob's coconut head above an aisle. An hour's stop over here, that's what she'd told them. An hour, grab something to eat, then she wanted them all in the RV and back on the road. The further away they were from New York, the better.

Foster sipped his coffee, testing the heat with his lips. 'I think it would be safer if you were to head somewhere else. Somewhere other than Boston.'

'Where, though?'

'Anywhere.'

'Why?'

He took his time answering. 'I just think it would be safer.'

'They can't know where we're going. We lost them, right? We got clean away.'

'What if they know your family lives in Boston?'

'But those support units . . . they don't *know* me. They don't know anything about me. How the hell are they going to guess my folks live in Boston?'

'They know *something* about you, Maddy. They found you after all, didn't they?'

'They found our field office. Maybe we've been . . . I dunno . . . leaking traceable tachyons. Maybe we just got careless and left a breadcrumb trail? All the coming and going backwards and forwards in time, that's going to leave some kind of a mark, right? Some kind of a trackable signature maybe?'

He shrugged. 'I don't know. In fact, you probably know as much, if not more, about this technology than I do now.'

'You think?' She looked up from her styrofoam cup at his craggy face, seeing the ghost of Liam in there among the folds and wrinkles. 'Maybe so,' she said. 'After all . . . not so very long ago, you were just a young lad from Ireland, weren't you?'

He looked like he was going to say something, then laughed. 'That's about right.'

'Foster, there's something I've always wanted to know.'

'What?'

'How we got picked. Selected. Me, Liam and Sal. You too, I guess. I mean, who knew so much about us? Who knew I was on that plane? Who knew Liam and you were on that particular deck on the *Titanic*? Who knew exactly where Sal was in that burning building?'

'I . . . don't know.'

'And how come they knew we had the necessary skills?' She

rubbed her temple. 'Not that that's helped so much. I've messed up more than I want to think about.'

'The three of you were perfect,' he replied. 'Perfect recruits,' he added. 'You've done so very well.' He patted her arm gently. The lightest touch. 'Don't be too hard on yourself. From what I've heard you tell me, you've been busy saving history over and over.'

'Well, more like fighting fires. But we're here still. The world's the same as it ever was. For what good that does it.'

'Oh, it's important, Maddy. History can't be changed.'

'Yeah, yeah . . . has to go one particular way, I know.' She lifted a plate of sausage patty bagels off the tray. One for him, one for her, and more for the others when they finally came over to join them. That is, if the bagels lasted that long. She was famished.

'Did you have many missions, Foster? You know . . . back when you were Liam, I guess.'

'A few. Enough.' His smile looked sad. 'Enough that I ended up like this. Old before my time.'

'Long before your time.' She could cry for him, cry for this wizened old man sitting opposite her. 'Foster, you remember telling me about how travelling through time can age you?'

'Yes.'

She almost stopped herself. 'Were you serious? Are you really only twenty-seven?'

'I think so.' He sighed. 'Twenty-seven, perhaps twenty-six. It's easy to lose count of the field cycles.'

She could only imagine how Liam must feel looking at him now that he knew this fate was awaiting him. That all too soon his body was going to be irreversibly corrupted by time travel.

'What were the others like? The team you were with before us?'

'Young. Like you . . . and having to grow up fast.' He looked away. His voice had faltered. He sipped his coffee, gave himself a moment to regain his composure. 'Only they never got a chance to grow up properly.'

'Were you very close?'

He nodded.

'I'm sorry.'

'Don't be sorry. They lived an extra life. They had extra time, so they did. Not many people get to have that.'

'You miss them much?'

His gaunt face wrinkled painfully. Maddy realized this conversation was hurting him. 'Stupid question, I'm an idiot. I apologize, that was –'

He shook his head. 'No need to apologize. I have the three of you now. We're just as much a family together as the others.'

'Family . . . see? That's why I think this is a good idea heading to Boston. Perhaps my folks can help out? The way I figure it, now we're *not* living in a resetting time loop, then that money in the bank account won't last forever. There's just under twelve thousand dollars in it. Now it doesn't get to "reset" itself every Monday morning, that money's gonna go quickly. At least if we go see my mom and dad, they might be able to lend us some money to tide us –'

'Maddy. I think going to see your parents is a *big* mistake.'

'Why?'

She could see Foster was hesitating. He had something to say and was fidgeting just like Liam tended to do when he was unsure of himself. 'Foster?'

'Maybe those killer support units *do* know you. Maybe they know all about you. *Everything* about you.'

She looked at him. He said that in a funny way, like it was meant to mean so much more than just those words. 'Foster?

What's going on? What do you know? What're you not telling me?'

Just then she heard a scream. It echoed across the quiet mall, drowning out the soft burble of mall music.

Sal.

She was running across the toddler play area, kicking aside multicoloured plastic balls that had escaped the small ballpool.

'*MADDY!*' she screamed again.

Maddy stood up and waved her arm, directing her over. 'SAL? We're over here! What's up?'

Sal corrected course towards them. Behind her she could see Liam and the others scrambling out of the mini-mart, crossing the space in the middle of the mall. Sal barged her way through the coffee-shop tables and stools set up outside beneath a fake pampas-grass sunshade as if this was supposed to be a coffee bar perched on the beach of some tropical island. Stools clattered, pampas-grass parasols wobbled and tipped over. Sal finally came to a rest, bent over a waist-high partition of fake sun-bleached wood, struggling for breath.

'Sal? What's up?'

'They're here!' she wheezed.

CHAPTER 19

2054, outside Denver, Colorado

It was a small thing. An insignificant thing, but Dr Joseph Olivera noticed Roald Waldstein left notes lying around from time to time. The old man tended to prefer the old-fashioned pleasure of pen and paper as opposed to tapping out his thoughts on a virtual keyboard.

Joseph Olivera noticed that habit of his boss as they worked together setting up the archway field office. Scribbled notes on pads of lined paper on the computer desk, most of it in Waldstein's unique shorthand: characters and glyphs that only he could make sense of. Joseph wondered how such a brilliant person could be so scatterbrained, so messy. Or perhaps being untidy went hand in hand with genius: the messier the desk, the more brilliant the mind?

His notepads of cryptic notes were scattered everywhere and Waldstein was constantly rifling among his notes, cross-referencing them, correcting them. It was on one of these pages filled with the swirls of Waldstein's writing that Joseph one day spotted the word 'Pandora'. It had been the only word on the pad *not* in Waldstein's shorthand. Pandora, of course, meant nothing to him. He suspected it was a codeword for one of the many commercial projects Waldstein worked on simultaneously. He knew his boss was working on several projects sponsored by the US military. Technology they'd inevitably want to adapt to weapons systems.

Joseph knew the man was no fool. Waldstein was a genius. But also a ruthless businessman. His technology patents went to the highest bidder even if ultimately it meant his inventions were to be turned into devices for killing, maiming.

Pandora then . . . a word he noted on a scrap of paper, and promptly forgot about.

The *agency*, or the *New York Project*, as Waldstein sometimes referred to it, became 'active' on Friday 4 September 2054. An occasion marked only by Joseph and Frasier Griggs. From the comfort and safety of a private research lab at W.G. Systems' main research campus building in Wyoming, hidden a dozen miles away from the nearest town – Pinedale – amid tall, balding Douglas firs clinging to the valley slopes, the pair of them quietly clinked two glasses of Soyo-Vina Rouge in celebration and began to monitor the archway beneath the Williamsburg Bridge in a place called Brooklyn, New York, in the year 2001. They scanned for potential tachyon leakage or any emergency signal bursts.

Meanwhile, Waldstein had insisted on staying behind in 2001 to directly mentor the team. He wanted his to be the first face they saw as they woke up in their bunk beds. He wanted to be the father figure to the three of them. Said it was important that they wholly trusted him.

'*They'll be disorientated and frightened when they first come round,*' he said. '*I want to be there for them.*'

And so Waldstein's top-secret project had begun: one team, one field office, and all of history for them to watch out for and protect.

The agency was Waldstein's back-up plan to keep history safe. That's what he'd once told Joseph. It was his *B plan*.

His *A plan* had been his very public campaign three years ago to ensure that the world's leaders signed up to an international law forbidding any nation from continuing to develop time-travel technology. It was to be a banned science. But he was wily enough to realize that in this troubled time, while every world leader might publicly denounce the technology, secretly they'd be vigorously funding it. Working on it. Desperate to be the first world power with the ability to take control of time itself: the ultimate weapons system.

'*I want the New York Project to be self-reliant,*' Waldstein confided in Joseph.

'*Once it's up and running, the team will have to manage their own affairs, decide their own mission priorities. They must be entirely self-sufficient.*'

The team would have all the data, equipment, critical replacement parts they needed: spare support unit foetuses, growth tubes, spare component boards for the displacement machine. Anything else they might need they could buy from a hardware or electronics store back in 2001.

'*Here in 2054 we must have as little contact with them as possible. We cannot be directly linked to them, Joseph. I cannot afford to be caught dabbling in time travel like this. I must have a plausible, believable . . . deniability.*'

The team in 2001, then, was to be left entirely to their own devices. Griggs was the most vociferous on that. They had to survive on their own. No way could there be any interaction between the team and them. It could lead to their discovery in 2054. Their arrest. And the penalty under international law – 'Waldstein's Law' – was rightly severe: the death penalty.

However, Waldstein devised a safe way they could make contact. If the team *desperately* needed to communicate with them in 2054, there was a way that they could do so. He called the method 'a drop-point document'.

Joseph had been impressed by the man's ingenuity.

It was a private ad in a Brooklyn newspaper. They had a

yellowing page of newsprint contained in a glass case here in 2054. A dog-eared page that had somehow survived intact through half a century. If the team in 2001 needed to send a message forward in time, they simply had to dial that newspaper's classifieds desk, and place a personal ad to go in the next issue. A personal ad that was to begin with the words, 'A soul lost in time'.

The personal ad represented history being meddled with in a very small way. It would cause a tiny change. A tiny, harmless time wave that would ripple across fifty-three years to the present and change just one thing: the sheet of newspaper in that glass case.

That was the *only* method of communication Waldstein intended to permit them to use. Safe. Secret. Untraceable. Under no circumstances were they to beam a tachyon signal forward. If anyone in the present was scanning for telltale signs of time-travel technology development, the tachyon particle would be the giveaway. The smoking gun.

Pandora.

Joseph would have completely forgotten about that word if it wasn't for another discovery he made not so very long after Waldstein returned from 2001, content that his team based in Brooklyn – the *TimeRiders* . . . that was the nickname he had for them – were ready to do the job entirely on their own.

As it happened, that team was the *first* team based in that Brooklyn archway.

They did quite well. Lasted quite a long time.

CHAPTER 20

7.27 a.m., 12 September 2001, North Haven Plaza, outside Branford

Maddy led Foster by the hand out of the coffee shop, through the stools and tables to meet the others in the middle of the toddler play area, 'Chuckle Zone'.

Liam spoke first. 'Bob just picked up a warning signal from SpongeBubba.'

'I also just detected two idents,' added Bob.

'Where?'

'Three hundred and seventy yards in that direction,' he said, pointing along the central concourse of the shopping mall towards the front entrance to the parking strip beyond. He was pointing in the direction of their RV.

'They must have visited our bus first,' said Sal.

'How did they know which vehicle was ours?' Maddy asked. The parking area out front already had a few hundred cars in it. Even more now surely.

'Your lab unit,' said Bob. He turned to Rashim. 'Your lab unit must have left its wireless communication on.'

Rashim nodded. 'They must have homed in on Bubba's signal.'

'All the way from New York?' said Liam. 'I thought –'

'It's only a short-range signal. Half a mile and you'd lose it,' said Rashim.

'Then they must have already been tailing us,' said Maddy. She looked at Foster. 'Do you think?'

He shook his head. 'I don't know. It's possible.'

Becks had been watching the quick-fire conversation, her gaze snapping from one person to the next. But now her eyes suddenly widened as they settled on something at the far end of the concourse. 'They are here,' she said softly.

She pointed.

All of them turned to look. Two silhouetted figures emerging through large rotating glass doorways, striding purposefully in their direction, the pallid glow of morning light outside behind.

'Jay-zus! There's two of them!'

'We can't fight,' said Maddy. 'We've got to run!'

Bob stiffened, bristled like a guard dog. 'I can fight them. I can provide you with time to escape.'

'Don't be an idiot, Bob,' said Liam. 'They'll rip you to pieces, so they will.'

'Shadd-yah! Who *are* they?'

'We're wasting time,' said Maddy. She turned to look in the opposite direction. The concourse carried on another fifty yards where it terminated as a circular eating area, tables and plastic bucket chairs surrounded by a dozen fast-food outlets. A lift and a couple of escalators could take them up to a balcony overlooking the central area, and the upper floor of shops. But as far as she could make out, the only way out of the mall was back towards the approaching support units . . . and out of those big revolving glass doors at the front.

'How about in there?' said Sal. She pointed towards a large store with two floors, upper and ground. A pre-school toy store called TOYS-4-TOTS! All bright, happy-clappy colours inside. Out in front of the store a tall, surly-faced young man was putting on the head of a costume, the store's mascot, a livid pink dinosaur that Maddy suspected was a blatant rip-off of Barney.

'Yes! Go! Go!' She grasped Foster's hand and led the way. The others followed.

She pushed her way past a toddler on reins. The child turned to watch them pass by, blue eyes suddenly round and wide at the sight of Bob. Presumably thinking he was another store mascot, the toddler chuckled gleefully and reached out to grab and hug one of his tree-thick legs.

'Back off!' boomed Bob. The toddler toppled backwards in shock, landing and bouncing on its nappy-cushioned behind. It gazed up at them in confused silence, watching this odd assortment of grown-ups leave the play area before finally deciding to bawl.

Maddy led them into the store TOYS-4-TOTS! She shook her head. *How'd they get away with a name like that?* Still early enough in the morning it was mainly staff milling around inside: puffy-faced teens in gaudy pink store shirts bearing plastic name tags.

It was the right place to hide, cluttered with racks of chunky, plastic nonsense, large furry soft toys, rotating display stands of storybook CD-ROMs and nursery-rhyme favourites.

'Everyone split up! We'll lose 'em in here.' She had hold of Foster's hand still. She wasn't going to let it go. She wasn't losing him again. 'Split up . . . and we'll rendezvous . . .'

Where?

'The diner?' said Sal.

'Yes . . .' Not the RV. Definitely not the RV. There might be another of them waiting for them there. The diner was next to the motel. Good enough. 'Make your way to the diner!' She looked back out past the knock-off-Barney mascot standing out on the concourse. She could just make out the distinctive outlines of the support units. Closer now. The pair of them could so easily be Bob and Becks.

'Go!' she hissed. 'We stand out like a sore thumb. Split!'

Their group fragmented in different directions: Rashim and Sal; Bob, Liam and Becks.

She pulled Foster with her, quickly weaving past an extravagant diorama made from BaBe-Blox building bricks into a maze of aisles laden with romper suits and cute, frilly Babygros. He was already breathing hard. This was getting difficult for the old man. 'Maddy . . . I . . .'

'Shut up, Foster! I'm not leaving you behind.'

She crouched low, pulling aside clothes hangers on a rail to peer out. Across the store she could see the top of Rashim's head for a moment, then it was gone behind a row of super-large Sesame Street cuddlies. She looked back at the store's entrance, hoping to see the support units striding past and missing them.

Nothing for the moment. Perhaps they'd already gone past.

'Maddy . . . ?'

'Foster, shhhh . . . I'm trying to see —'

'Excuse me? Miss?'

Maddy turned to see a member of staff looking down at her. A girl in a pink shirt, with a nose stud and up-way-too-late-last-night red-rimmed eyes, stared wearily down at her. A face that clearly indicated this was too early in her cruddy day to put up with customer-stoopid like this.

'Ma'am, you're not really allowed to hide among the clothes like that.'

Maddy straightened up. 'I . . . err . . . I was just looking for . . . umm . . . bargains.'

'I think it might be best if you step out of the store, ma'am.'

Maddy remained where she was, her eyes on the store's entrance. 'Just give us a sec here . . . we just need . . . to uh . . .'

'You need to leave, miss. You're clearly not shopping. You're being a nuisance –'

'Christ!' Maddy turned on her. 'Just give me a freakin' moment, will you? It won't kill you!'

The girl didn't like that. 'I'm asking you politely to leave, please. If you don't, I'll call the manager. I'll call mall security.'

Just then Maddy saw them. The support units standing in the entrance, two pairs of grey eyes sweeping the toy store like prison searchlights.

Knock-off Barney, the implausibly pink dinosaur, sauntered cheerily towards them, probably wearily parroting the store's moronic catchphrase: *Friends That Play Together Stay Together!!*

The female support unit – *Becks*, Maddy found herself thinking – lashed out with a fist and caught Barney in the throat. He disappeared from view.

'Whuh?' said the girl in the pink shirt to herself. 'Did she just punch Joshua . . . ?'

The male support unit's eyes panned round and caught sight of Maddy just as she was about to duck back down out of sight. He raised his arm, something in his hand glinted. Someone screamed.

And then the gunfire started.

CHAPTER 21

7.29 a.m., 12 September 2001, North Haven Plaza, outside Branford

Maddy felt a warm puff of displaced air on her cheek as the shot whistled past her head. She heard the shot impact on something. A soft thud followed by a gasp.

She turned to see the girl on her knees beside her, dark crimson blossoming across her store shirt. She looked down at the blood then at Maddy, perplexed.

'I . . . I . . . just got shot . . .'

Another couple of gunshots, deafening in the shop's stillness. The baby clothes hanging from the rail above Maddy lurched and danced. A blizzard of foam stuffing erupted from a Humpty Dumpty on a shelf nearby.

Maddy remained hunched down, Foster beside her. 'My God, we're gonna die!' she whimpered to him. There were raised voices outside the toystore in the mall's main concourse. A male voice. Two of them, issuing a sharp challenge. A warning.

More shots, aiming out of the store this time.

'Maddy . . . you go!' It was Foster.

'They're distracted!' she whispered. 'Come on, let's –'

'No!' He shook his head. 'I can slow them down. You go!'

'Slow them down?' She made a face. 'You're kidding, right?'

'Not *fight* them . . . I'll talk to them.'

More shots. One of them hit a wall nearby, showering them with flakes of plaster.

'You can't talk to –'

'They're just like Bob! They have the exact same AI.'

'Yeah, but . . . but they're running an entirely different freakin' mission! You step out, they'll shoot you just as soon as look at –'

Foster grasped her arm. 'Maddy . . . I'm dead anyway.'

He didn't need to explain that. They both knew he was dying. She knew he was dying the day he walked out of that Starbucks and left her in charge of the team. But somehow the reality of that had seemed removed. With time looping for her in New York, he was never going to die. Every time she'd gone to visit him in Central Park, he was the same old Foster. No sicker. But then, of course, he wouldn't be. It was always the same moment for him. The same morning over and over and over.

Since she'd grabbed him from Central Park, time, for him, had *advanced*. Two days, that was all it had been, but enough time that she could clearly see he was getting worse. A dying man. He should be in a hospital bed, a hospice, kept comfortable on a drip perhaps, not running for his life through a shopping mall.

'They know me,' he said. 'It's enough . . . it'll confuse them. They may let me talk.'

'*Know you?*'

'There's no time to explain!' He pushed her. 'Go! Just go!'

Maddy glanced at the girl beside them. She was in shock, pale. Alive, but maybe for not much longer unless she got some help.

The gunfire was beginning to wane. Whomever the support units had been exchanging shots with outside on the concourse, police, mall security, it was nearly a done deal now.

'Foster, I . . .'

110

He shushed her with a finger over her lips. 'This is goodbye, Maddy. Don't ruin it by blurting something stupid.'

She pulled his hand away. 'Foster . . .' She wanted to call him by his *real* name. 'Liam . . .'

Foster smiled. 'It's a long while since I've been called that.'

'Please . . .' She had no idea what she wanted to say. Something meaningful. '*Please*' wasn't it. '*Please*' was just so pathetically lame.

'For the love of God, Maddy . . . will you just bleedin' well go!'

'Liam . . .' she said again. 'I, I . . .'

He waved her silent. 'I loved you, Maddy. Each time. I always did. Even when I knew . . .' He stopped himself. So much he wanted to say, and so little that he could in this all too short heartbeat of time. 'Just *go*!'

She heard footsteps inside the store. Heavy, purposeful footsteps drawing closer.

Then, cursing herself for being a coward, for leaving him behind, she scooted on hands and feet, through aisles of chunky plastic playsets, beneath rows of fur-hooded children's anoraks and racks of cheerily coloured wellies, perfect for little feet to stamp in autumn rain puddles. She scuttled on all fours until she finally stumbled upon the moving metal grated steps of an escalator.

Foster waited until she was out of sight, stood up, his hands raised above him. Both support units levelled their weapons at him. The male support unit was bleeding from three gunshot wounds, one to the forehead. A dark trickle of blood rolled sluggishly down between thick brows, down the side of his nose from a circle of puckered flesh above his eyes. A perfect take-down shot from some policeman or mall guard. Whoever

111

had taken that head shot must have died wondering how a man could be shot between the eyes and shrug it off like a mere gnat bite.

'You know me,' said Foster.

The female support unit frowned, a hesitant, confused expression on her face. The old man standing before her looked very similar to one of the faces in her database. It wasn't an exact match, but a very close one. Close enough that she wanted to take a couple of steps closer, see him more clearly and confirm his identity one way or the other.

'Where are the others?' asked Abel.

Foster shrugged. 'Long gone.'

'You are a part of their team?' Halfway between a statement and a question.

'You *know* me, don't you?' said Foster again, trying a lopsided smile. 'It's me. I'm your Authorized User. Now then . . . why don't you lower your weapons?'

Abel narrowed his eyes. He had to admit the man standing in front of him with his hands raised did look very much like the man who had issued them their instructions: Authorized User.

He cast an uncertain glance at Faith. A glance that asked the question: *Is he?*

She was still working on that particular one herself.

The escalator carried Maddy slowly towards the shop's upper floor; Baby-Toddler Wear. It was so still, so very quiet. All she could hear was the gentle hum of the escalator's motor and the soft chime of mall music outside. Still down on her hands and knees, she decided to chance one last look. She lifted her head to see over the smoked glass side of the escalator, over the black rubber rim of the hand rail and she caught sight of Foster, standing just yards in front of the two units. His arms raised in surrender . . . but slowly lowering them as if the gesture of surrender was no longer necessary.

He was saying something, she could just about hear his voice, low, unclear. But it was definitely him doing the talking.

My God, he's actually doing it! He's actually talking them round!

For a moment there, just for a moment, she let herself believe something might go their way for once.

Then one of the units fired.

Her last image of Foster was him dropping to his knees in front of the killer meatbots. She thought she heard him swear at them, something Irish, something defiant . . . something *so very Liam*. Then, as the escalator carried her past a sales display and she finally lost sight of him, she heard four or five shots one after the other. Then one last executioner's shot.

CHAPTER 22

7.32 a.m., 12 September 2001,
North Haven Plaza, outside Branford

Liam led the way out of the toystore's upper-floor exit, on to the top concourse. The few mid-morning shoppers were frozen where they were; no one was going anywhere, merely exchanging expressions of panic.

'Was that a gun I just heard?' a woman asked Liam as he and the two support units rushed past.

'Aye,' said Liam, dragging a dawdling Becks by the hand.

'We must stop and fight them,' she said.

'There's two of 'em. And they got guns.' He looked at her. 'Are you that desperate to get yourself into a scrap?'

She cocked her head. 'Scrap?' Not used to Liam's speech patterns just yet.

'Inadvisable,' said Bob. 'The best course of action right now is evasion.'

Liam nodded. 'Listen to your big brother.'

They were just passing a Barnes & Noble when half a dozen more shots erupted from the floor below and rang out across the mall.

'Jay-zus!'

'Oh my God!' someone across the way screamed. 'It's terrorists!'

The 'T' word spread like a ripple across a still pond. People's mouths dropping open into 'O's. The mall music suddenly stopped and a voice announced over the tannoy that an emergency situation was in progress and that all customers and staff were to proceed immediately to the nearest fire exits.

Inevitably someone screamed the 'B' word and the frozen tableau of confusion turned into a flood of shop staff emerging from the entrances of their respective stores, spilling on to the upper concourse. Suddenly it seemed like a very busy mall.

Liam and the other two joined the press of bodies heading towards the escalators at the end that would take them down to the front entrance and out into the car park.

Sal and Rashim had found a different way out of the toystore on the lower floor, a door marked STAFF ONLY that led to a stockroom piled high with cardboard boxes and bubble wrap. From there they found a door at the back that gave access to a service corridor of dull grey breeze-block walls.

'Which way now?' asked Rashim.

'I don't know.' Her guess was left. Left would take them towards the entrance they came in, she figured. She led the way. Muted by two closed doors, they heard the faintest crackle of gunfire behind them.

'This is insane,' gasped Rashim. 'Who in God's name wants you lot dead so badly?'

'Jahulla!' she whispered. 'Wish I knew.' It felt to her like they'd been running non-stop for weeks. In added-up time for her, it was almost that. Just after sending Liam and Bob back to Rome, that's when they'd been jumped in Times Square. Ambushed and pursued all the way back to the archway, and there, attacked yet again – one of the units even managing to dive through the portal right behind them and join them back in Ancient Rome.

Pandora. It was asking about Pandora that had set this off. Sal was almost certain of that. That and perhaps, somehow, it was linked to that poor, poor man who'd jumped back to 1831 to warn her about something.

But what was that warning? '*The bear*'. '*You're not who you think you are.*' What the pinchudda was that supposed to mean?

I think I'm Sal. I'm Saleena Vikram. I'm a schoolgirl from Ajmeera Independent Academy in Mumbai. I used to play Pikodu pretty well. And listen to bhangra-metal. I'm the daughter of Sanjay and Abeer Vikram. And I used to live in a small apartment in Mumbai. Papaji used to buy and sell computer chips. Mamaji used to be an accountant. What part of all of that isn't right?

They turned a corner.

'Yo! Hey!'

Ahead of them, a black mall security guard. 'Stop right there!' He had a handgun pointed at them. 'Hands where I can see them!'

'We're trying to get –'

'SHUT UP!' A hand fumbled for the radio on his belt; he kept his eyes on them. 'This is Kent. I got two of 'em right here. Service Access 5b.'

The radio squawked static and an unintelligible voice.

The mall guard replied. 'Asian. One male, approximately mid-twenties. One female, mid-teens.'

Another squirt of static and voice.

'Uh . . . yeah, he's got a bit of a beard. They were both running from the gunfire.'

Static and voice.

'Copy that!' He hung the radio back on his belt. 'You two raghead terrorist sons of . . .' He bit his lip. 'You gonna see a whole bunch of prison time.'

'We are *not* terrorists!' said Rashim.

'You put a bomb in this mall somewhere? Huh? That it? You gonna blow up some more innocent people?'

'Shadd-yah!' Sal cursed. 'We're not terrorists!'

'*Shallah?* What's that? Some Ay-rab raghead-talk or something?'

'She's Indian,' said Rashim. 'I'm Persian. That makes a total of zero "Ay-rabs" here.'

'SHUT UP!' He jerked his gun at them. 'Put your goddamn hands on the wall, Abu-Babu!'

Sal shook her head, pointing over her shoulder. 'The bad guys're back there! They've got guns and –'

'You put your goddamn hands against the wall, miss, or I swear I'll put a bullet in both of you right now!'

She could see the knuckle of his trigger finger bulging, the skin paler, drawn over tendon and bone. There were already several pounds of pressure resting on that trigger.

'OK . . . OK . . .' She placed her palms up against the rough breeze blocks. 'Rashim . . .' Silently, she urged him to do likewise.

'*Rashim*, is it, eh?' The mall guard shook his head as he approached. Then as Sal and Rashim adopted the legs-apart-hands-against-the-wall pose, the guard began to pat Sal down one-handed.

'What is it with you goddamned Moslems? Uh?' he huffed as he frisked them. 'What the hell is it you hate so much 'bout America? What is it, the Big Macs? The freedom? The rap music?'

'Look, please . . . we're not actually terrorists –'

'Or even Muslims,' added Sal.

'I lost a cousin in what you people did yesterday. Good man. Worked up in the top of the north tower in the restaurant. Took care of his folks, worked real hard.'

He began to frisk Rashim. 'But that ain't enough, is it? He's

117

gotta live *your way*, hasn't he? Got to grow a goddamn Santa-beard and wear them stupid pyjama-suits. Gotta go an' worship Buddha five times a day –'

'It's Allah actually.'

The guard pushed Rashim's head hard against the wall. 'You shut your goddamn raghead mouth!'

CHAPTER 23

7.34 a.m., 12 September 2001, North Haven Plaza, Branford

They regarded the body of the old man lying on the floor in front of them in silence. Beside him a young female was cowering on the floor, her hands clasped to a wound.

'P-please . . . d-don't kill me . . .' she whimpered.

Both support units ignored her. She was irrelevant. Back to the dead man.

'It is an older version of the one called Liam O'Connor,' said Faith, studying the old man's face. 'A valid target.'

Abel nodded. 'Good.' He looked up. 'The others will be nearby.' They'd spotted the group heading into this store and briefly picked up the idents of the two support units with them. Those signals were gone now. Switched off.

Other than sneaking past them out of the store's main entrance, he noted only two other possible exits for them.

'We must separate.'

Faith looked at the escalator leading to the store's upper floor. 'I will go that way.'

Abel nodded and immediately strode towards the STAFF ONLY door at the rear of the store.

> **Locate and kill. We have six remaining targets**, he added wirelessly.

> **Affirmative**, she replied.

Faith jogged up the escalator as another tannoy announcement reverberated throughout the mall. 'Attention, attention . . . this is an emergency announcement. All customers and staff are asked to immediately leave the mall. This is an emergency and not a drill. Please leave the . . .'

The escalator jerked to a halt beneath her feet. She hurried up the rest of the way and at the top she scanned the shop floor. She spotted thirteen people, seven of them wearing the same pink shirts as the dying girl downstairs – she assumed the shirt was some sort of a uniform. None of them, or the others, bore any resemblance to the mission briefing images she'd started with, nor the library of fleeting shutter-frame images, glimpses of her quarry, that she'd managed to build up during the mission so far.

Faith emerged quickly from the store, tucking the gun away into the waistband of her jogging bottoms and hiding the gun's protruding handle beneath her hoody. No need to attract any unwanted attention. They'd already done enough of that with the gunfight downstairs.

She joined the throng of people on the upper floor, emerging from store fronts. So many of them sluggish, uncertain: seemingly unsure whether this was a real emergency or a drill, unsure whether the exchange of gunfire minutes ago might have been stupid kids letting off some firecrackers.

She scanned the backs of heads, necks, shoulders. She had a comparison image of that particular view of one of the targets called Madelaine. From back in Times Square, when she'd crossed the street and chased them into the building. Madelaine: tall, slim. Long, light-coloured curly hair pulled into a ponytail. Jeans. Checked shirt. The other girl, Saleena: short, slim. Black hair. Dark leggings, black hooded top. Of course they could be wearing different clothes by now.

Her eyes coolly evaluated the people hurrying in front of her, one after the other in quick succession.

Maddy found herself in the middle of a milling crowd of people, a bottleneck at the top of both of the now stationary escalators leading down to the ground floor. Someone had turned them off. Probably a routine health and safety measure in the event of a mall evacuation. Stupid, though, being off. It was taking an age to get down. She was stuck at the top, waiting for an elderly couple in front of her to tramp slowly down.

Come on, come on.

She guessed she must be the last one in their group to get out. The others were probably already running back across the car park, along the pavement towards the motel and their waiting RV.

Her mind had yet to process what she'd glimpsed. It was there in her head. Foster being gunned down. But in the fleeting minute – two minutes – since then, she'd yet to digest it, make sense of it. *Feel* something about it.

That was going to come, of course. Tears. Probably lots of them. Fear, grief, panic, stress. Four excuses right there to let it go and cry like some typical movie girl-in-distress: all quivering, dimpled chin and smudged mascara.

If she managed to live long enough, that is.

A woman pushed past Maddy, pushed past the old couple in front of her. Heavy heels clanked on the metal-strip steps, wide hips bumping people aside as she pushed her way forward and wheezed a mantra of barely contained panic. 'Oh my Lord, protect me! Oh my Lord, protect me!'

Maddy wanted to push her way forward like that. But didn't. Too rude. Still . . .

Come on. Come on!

She wished she had Bob here with her. Even their half-grown Becks. She might only look like twelve or thirteen years old, but she could snap a neck or take a magazine full of bullets almost as well as Bob.

Then she saw her face. Becks. Only of course it wasn't Becks.

'Jesus! You guys took your goddamn time!' the mall guard called out, relieved at the sight of five cops jogging along the narrow service passage towards him.

'These the two perps you called in?' said one of them. A police sergeant. He and one of the others were carrying shotguns.

'Yeah. These are them.'

'They don't match the description our boys called in,' he said, pumping shells into the weapon's breech. 'Armed male and female. Both adults, both Caucasian.' He looked at Rashim and Sal. 'These clearly aren't them.'

'But –'

'Jason, take these two out!'

'Yessir,' said one of the cops.

'You give your details to him,' he said to Sal and Rashim. 'We'll need witness statements off you later.'

'Right,' said Sal. 'Thanks.'

The sergeant stroked his chin thoughtfully, his radio crackled with traffic. More cops on their way in. An armed response unit among them.

'We got several officers down in there, sir.'

'I know that!' the police sergeant barked. 'I know that. Lemme think. Lemme think.'

Just then they heard the echo of a door bang open, the slap of heavy footsteps on linoleum. Nothing Sal could see. It came from around the corner, from where she and Rashim had just emerged via the toystore's stockroom some minutes ago.

'Who's that?' whispered one of the cops.

The footsteps echoed. Heavy. Even. Measured.

'It's one of them!' said Sal.

'Them? Who?' The sergeant cocked his weapon. 'One of the shooters?'

She nodded.

'POLICE!' he called out quickly. 'WE ARE ARMED POLICE.' His voice rolled down the passageway and eventually faded to silence.

The sound of approaching footsteps suddenly ceased.

'POLICE!' he called again. 'YOU BEST COME ROUND WITH YOUR HANDS UP!'

There was no reply. Just the sound of an ammo clip being ejected and rattling on the floor. The *clack-snick* of a new one being rammed home.

'That don't sound so good,' said the mall guard.

'Just get these two civilians the hell out of here before this turns nasty,' whispered the sergeant.

The mall guard nodded. Grabbed Sal's arm. 'Let's go, folks.'

'OK . . . OK,' she whispered eagerly.

The guard led the way. 'Delivery bay six is right up here. Just ahead,' he said quietly. 'We can exit that way.'

He picked up the pace. Sal stole one last glance over her shoulder at the huddle of police officers in the anaemic, turquoise glow of the passage's wall lights, checking their weapons and holding them up and steady in the trained and engrained two-hand legs-apart stance.

'Here, this way,' said the guard. He pushed open double doors that led on to an underground delivery bay.

As they stepped out, the mall guard holding the swing doors

open for them, Sal thought she heard the police sergeant call out one last challenge. Then, as the echo of his shaky voice tailed away, the passage behind them suddenly sounded like a war zone.

CHAPTER 24

7.37 a.m., 12 September 2001, North Haven Plaza, outside Branford

Liam, Bob and Becks approached the RV cautiously. It sat in the motel's small forecourt on its own. Overhead the sky was noisy with the *thwup-thwup* of a police helicopter, hovering above the pale slab of the mall several hundred yards away.

Liam could also hear the sound of several approaching police cars and ambulances coming from further up Interstate 95, brake lights winking on down the congested road like a Mexican wave as drivers slowed to pull aside and let them through.

Ahead of them, the RV.

'Maddy said we should meet at the diner,' said Bob.

'I want to check on SpongeBubba,' said Liam. 'You think it's safe?' he added. 'Maybe there's another of them inside.'

'I detect no idents,' said Becks.

'Just a moment,' said Bob. He closed his eyes.

'Why? What're you doing?'

A few seconds later the rear door of the RV swung open and a yellow cube appeared on the top step.

'Communicating with the lab unit,' replied Bob. He smiled down at Liam. 'SpongeBubba says it's all clear inside.'

They crossed the last fifty yards, Liam gesturing at SpongeBubba to get back inside. They didn't need the lab robot attracting attention. Liam climbed up and slumped down on the rear seat, damp with perspiration.

'Gee!' said SpongeBubba with a fixed plastic grin. 'Fun and games!'

Becks looked down at the small robot. 'No. Not fun and games. Danger.'

Bob clambered inside. The RV rocked. 'Your warning saved us, lab unit. We are grateful.'

'You're welcome. Where's my skippa?'

Liam looked out through the scuffed perspex, hoping to catch sight of the others weaving through the cars in the mall's car park towards the motel. Nothing yet.

'They're coming,' he said. 'They were just behind us. I think.' He looked at Bob and Becks. 'Right?'

Bob shook his head. 'I don't know.'

'Foster will have slowed them down,' said Becks. 'He moved very slowly.'

She was right. Liam decided he should have stayed behind, with Maddy, to help her with the old man. A dreadful thought occurred to him. That those killer meatbots had trapped and finished both of them off. Perhaps Rashim and Sal as well. He felt a growing surge of panic inside him. The idea of spending the rest of his life alone on the run with two support units and something that looked like a yellow bar of soap on stumpy legs terrified him.

Please . . . please . . . somebody else turn up.

Faith recognized the young woman instantly. The oval jawline, the glasses, the curly strawberry-blonde hair, all a perfect match. But even without the visual match the look of sudden recognition and sheer horror – as their eyes locked – gave the girl away. Faith reached round behind her and whipped out the handgun from her waistband.

'Please move out of the way!' she commanded the evacuating people all around her as she levelled the gun at her target.

'*OH-MY-GOD-SHE'S-GOT-A-GUN!*' someone screamed.

That worked better. The crowd, jostling to get down the frozen escalator, dropped to the floor as one, and Faith had a perfect line-of-sight on Maddy. The only person still on her feet.

Maddy pushed the large woman crouching in front, desperately trying to get past. But the woman was too big to make a space on the escalator. Maddy found herself clambering over her back.

'Ow! Jesus help me! I'm being assaulted!' screamed the woman.

'I need to get past!' Maddy replied. 'I need to freakin' well get –'

A shot rang out. The glass of the escalator's side exploded. The woman ducked down as shards scattered over her rounded shoulders and Maddy rolled over the top of her, on to someone else in front. Another shot thudded into the thick rubber handrest.

She found her feet and decided she was far enough down the escalator to jump over the side. She landed on the top of a display of plastic tropical bushes embedded in a bed of pebbles. Not the softest landing, but perhaps far better than the mall's faux marble floor. She scrambled on to her feet yet again, people all around her shrieking in alarm as several more shots rang out across the entrance foyer.

'Get out, get out!' Maddy screamed at the bottleneck of people fighting with each other to exit through the revolving door, and the fire exits either side of it.

Faith strode towards the safety rail of the concourse above,

127

overlooking the escalator. She saw her target below on the ground floor, grappling with people, tugging at them to make way for her. She took aim again and fired two shots, emptying the clip. Downstairs, more glass exploded, and the screaming all around her took on a new shrill, intense pitch.

Faith clambered over the rail and let herself drop down. She landed twenty feet below on the hard floor, like a cat landing on its feet, legs flexed to absorb the impact like the over-pimped shock absorbers of a monster truck.

She reached into her waistband to pull out her last clip. The target – Madelaine Carter – was directly in front of her, trapped because the only way out was clogged with people tangled with each other and too petrified to sort themselves out. She would have smiled if she'd had that particular face gesture on file. Instead, her face remained impassive, as calm and expressionless as a person fast asleep as she rammed the last clip home into the grip of her handgun.

Sal and Rashim gave the mall guard – Kent – a thoroughly unconvincing pair of aliases and random contact numbers. The guard, though, seemed more than happy to take down what they said, no questions asked. Quite probably he was preoccupied with thanking God he was alive still. He offered a nod – Sal guessed that was his version of a 'sorry for earlier' – and told them to go home.

They now picked their way through the crowd at the front of the mall. A slew of police cars had parked up in a semi-circle just outside the entrance and officers were setting up a cordon around it, urging the rubbernecking curious back away from the rotating glass doors at the front.

'Good grief . . . that was . . .' Rashim wiped sweat from his forehead.

'Close?'

He nodded. 'Incredibly.'

'They're the same ones that were chasing me and Maddy before we came back in time to get you.'

'Almost identical to your support units. They were definitely a similar batch number. Quite possibly from the exact same batch.'

A possibility occurred to Sal as they backed away from the crowd outside and studied the front of the mall from a comfortable distance. There were still people spilling out of the revolving doors, being hustled out of harm's way as quickly as possible by paramedics, cops and mall guards. Maybe they were a batch of support units that had malfunctioned? Perhaps whoever was running their little agency from the future had decided to send them some replacement support units and something had gone wrong in the process?

She shot that idea down just as quickly as it had popped into her head.

No. There was the San Francisco drop point. That's where they'd get back-up copies of Bob and Becks – frozen foetuses ready to grow. These were ones already fully grown and given a very specific mission. To come after the whole team and not rest until the last of them were dead. Apparently. So . . . no mistakes there. No malfunctions. Just deadly intent.

'You think we should make our way back to that diner?' said Rashim.

Sal was about to answer when two gunshots came from just inside the mall's entrance foyer.

A moment later a large plate-glass window exploded and screams ripped through the air. The police who'd set up a cordon to hold the crowd back now drew their sidearms. All of them spinning round to face the glass frontage of the shopping mall.

People spilled out of the slowly turning revolving door, the side doors, even through the jagged-tooth remains of the freshly shattered glass frontage.

'There's Maddy!' hissed Sal.

She emerged with the others, arms up and wrapped round her head to protect it, hunkered over like someone getting out of a helicopter. Sal pushed through the crowd now all turning and scattering from the entrance at the sound of another shot fired inside the foyer.

'MADDY!' she called out. 'OVER HERE!'

The girls all but crashed into each other.

'Maddy? I thought you were –'

'Just GO! *Gogogogogo!*'

Faith picked her zigzagging target out of the retreating, stampeding crowd. She levelled the .40 Smith & Wesson. Now the thing had a fresh clip, she resolved to empty all twelve rounds in several controlled double-taps. To be absolutely certain of killing the target. As she aimed down the short barrel, she caught sight of one of the other targets: *Saleena Vikram*. Both girls tangled with each other for a moment, then, turning their backs to her, ran away hand in hand.

Two for the price of one. Faith nodded. Pleased with herself for producing an appropriate saying for the occasion. She was about to pull the trigger when the world went completely dark.

CHAPTER 25

7.42 a.m., 12 September 2001, Interstate 95, outside Branford

Five minutes later they were all back aboard the RV, on the road and running on the last quarter-tank of petrol, Bob driving north-east as instructed and Maddy rocking back and forth beside him in the passenger seat trying to get a handle on things, get a handle on her jangling nerves, a handle on the growing knot of grief in her chest, as Sal, Liam and Rashim threw questions at her over the seat.

'He's gone,' she said, finally answering them as to where the hell Foster was.

'What? Do you mean . . . ?' Liam struggled to say any more. So Rashim finished his question for him.

'They . . . they got Foster?'

She nodded. 'Shot him.'

'He's dead?'

Here it comes. Maddy felt her composure slipping. The blissful comfort of numbness was ebbing away, like the downslope of a novocaine buzz after root-canal treatment. The first hot tears trickled down her cheeks. She tasted salt on her lips and licked them away.

She nodded. 'Yes, Foster's dead.' Her voice was a lifeless whisper. The flutter and tap of moth wings against a windowpane. She took her glasses off and buried her damp face in her hands and realized that *now* she'd finally become that typical movie girl-in-distress: all quivering, dimpled chin and smudged mascara.

Albeit minus the mascara.

CHAPTER 26

2055, outside Denver, Colorado

Joseph Olivera had got to know Frasier Griggs quite well. Griggs was the only other man in the world, other than Roald Waldstein, of course, who knew of the TimeRiders' existence.

Frasier Griggs was Waldstein's lesser-known junior partner. Where Waldstein was the source of the patents, the ideas man, the genius, Griggs was the practical other half: the software designer behind Waldstein's prototypes, the builder; the Steve Wozniak to Waldstein's Steve Jobs. Although most people assumed the 'G' in W.G. Systems was in memory of Waldstein's dead son, Gabriel, Griggs was in fact the 'Real G'. The company's first stakeholder, the fledgling company's first employee and perhaps the closest thing to a friend that Waldstein had ever had. Hell, on his desk, Griggs even had a tea mug with that printed on the side – *The Real G*.

The TimeRiders team established in 2001 became effectively 'active', and monitoring their activities began on 4 September 2054. On a day-to-day basis, Joseph and Griggs were the 'base team' doing that.

Only four months after the team started functioning, things began to go wrong. On 3 January 2055, they received a broadburst tachyon signal from 2001. A malfunction with the field office's displacement field had caused the first team to be killed. They'd received a garbled plea for help from one of them who'd managed to survive. Griggs panicked. For the first time since working for Waldstein, Joseph saw his boss's normally ice-cool composure slip.

It wasn't that the team had been destroyed that unsettled him; it was the fact that one of them had been careless enough to send an unencrypted, widespread tachyon signal. It was sheer blind luck for Waldstein that the message hadn't included a mention of his name. But it might as well have, given he was quite likely the only person in the world, at that moment, with the know-how to send a traveller back in time.

That short signal could have been picked up by labs right across the world, and it could only mean one thing for everyone who might have detected it: that somebody was already up and running with viable displacement technology.

Joseph remembered Griggs and Waldstein having a blazing row that morning. One held behind closed doors, not meant for Joseph to hear, but the one word he did pick out from their heated exchange was the word 'Pandora'.

Waldstein had little choice. Either he had to go back to 2001 and set things up all over again, or he had to send a message to the survivor, instructing him on how to set things up for himself.

Waldstein wanted to go back, but Griggs insisted that another trip back to 2001 was pushing their luck too far. If this was it, if this meant the premature end of their project, then so be it. Better than the three of them facing a lethal injection.

Joseph soon learned who'd sent the message, who the sole survivor was. It was Liam O'Connor. A second message arrived after the first, this time via the safe method: the personal advert. A field malfunction, that's what he'd said. *Equipment failure*. The Liam unit had been aged chronically by a sudden blast of tachyon radiation that had bathed the entire archway with a lethal dose.

The other two units hadn't stood a chance. They'd died in their sleep.

Waldstein replied with a detailed packet of instructions. And not a single word of support or comfort. But then that was it, wasn't it? The Liam unit was merely a piece of equipment to Waldstein: a disposable asset. Joseph had wondered how the man could be so cold; in a way, the Liam unit was as much a part of Waldstein as he was a part of Joseph's programming.

Poor Liam. He'd be alone back there. Alone, and suddenly aware now of what he was. Joseph felt for him. The boy was so young and yet now so old and quite clearly entirely on his own. The 'base team' was offering him instructions from afar and that was pretty much all the support the poor man had.

That was the first thing. The second misfortune happened not long after.

A contamination event had occurred in 1941. It appeared the event had been corrected by the re-established team but one of the team had been killed. The observer unit: Saleena Vikram. They needed to grow a new one with an adjusted memory: one that would allow her to be inserted into the existing team. Some tricky synaptic programming there for Joseph to do.

There was no avoiding it; they were going to need to carry out the 'edit job' on the Saleena unit here in 2055, then send it back.

That was it for Griggs. Too much. He wanted out. There was another blazing row between him and Waldstein behind closed glass doors. This time Joseph picked out one word several times over. *Pandora*. And Griggs screaming at Waldstein, 'Why? Why do you want that to happen?'

The third thing was Griggs's death a few days later. It was sudden, unexpected and left Joseph feeling distinctly uncertain about this whole project.

The night before he died, Griggs had been on edge. He'd also been drinking. Joseph didn't get much sense out of Frasier other than he'd told Waldstein he'd finally decided he was going to leave this project, that he didn't want to have anything more to do with 'this madness'.

The next day Frasier Griggs was found dead several miles outside W.G. Systems' Pinedale, Wyoming campus. The official verdict was that some 'flood migrants' must have ambushed him. There were plenty of them out here now – the displaced, the desperate, the hungry – millions of them from the various east-coast states partially or completely submerged by the advancing Atlantic Ocean. The lucky rich lived in fortified urbanizations. The rest in large displacement camps. That's how it was. The haves and the have-nots separated by coils of razor wire and private security firms.

It could have occurred as the official verdict stated: that poor Frasier had just set his Auto-Drive to take him home along the wrong road at the wrong time and the hastily erected roadblock, the subsequent murder and vehicle theft were just another sad sign of these dark times.

But then Joseph discovered something that made him suddenly very frightened of Waldstein. Griggs's personal *digi-pen* – a very expensive one modelled to look like an old-fashioned fountain pen – was sitting in Griggs's *Real G* mug like some carelessly discarded biro. Something he never did. He had a brass holder for his digi-pen and it always nestled there when not in use – one of his obsessive-compulsive habits. He'd never leave it like that, poking out of his mug.

So that's why Joseph picked it up and thumbed the control nub.

A memo. It wasn't even password-locked. It was the last entry recorded on Griggs's digi-pen. He must have recorded it not long after he'd rowed with Waldstein. He sounded angry still. Perhaps even frightened.

'*He's insane. The man's completely insane, Joseph.*' Griggs's words were badly slurred. He must have carried on drinking after Joseph had bid him goodnight.

'*I think he wants the whole world to die, Joseph. That's what Pandora is. It's the end of the world. Roald knows all about it. When it happens, how it happens. And you and I . . . and those poor clones back in 2001 . . . we're here to make sure it happens that way.*'

A pause. Joseph heard the slosh of liquid, the clink of a glass. The sound of a gulp.

'*You know . . . that first time he used a time machine? Back in '44. I don't think he went back in time to see his wife, his son, like he always claimed. No. I think he went forward. I think he discovered how mankind finally kills itself off. And all this . . . everything . . . his campaign against time travel, this little project, those poor lab rats back there in New York in that archway, you and me . . . it's all been to make for certain it damn well happens that way. We've been played for fools, you and me, Joseph. Fools!*'

Another pause.

'*You can stop this, Joseph. I . . . can't. He won't let me back in after what I said. He won't trust me anywhere near this project. I should've shut my mouth. I shouldn't have confronted him. But it's done. I'm out of the circle of trust . . . and that's how it is. But you can do something. You're all he has now. He trusts you. You could derail this thing! Sabotage it!*'

The sound of heavy breathing, rustling across the mic.

'*Joseph. History has to be changed. Do you understand? Not preserved . . . but changed.* You have to do it! You've got to steer us all away from wiping ourselves out!'

Another pause.

'*God forgive me for my part in all of this . . .*'

CHAPTER 27

12 September 2001, North Haven Plaza, Branford, Connecticut

'We're going to have to pull in a lot of favours to keep the lid on this, Agent Cooper.'

'That's what favours are for, aren't they? Rainy days like this.' Cooper looked around the entrance foyer of the shopping mall. It looked like a thousand other malls, all pastel plastic fascias and plastic plants. Faux Greco-Roman columns and Doric archways. Only this one was decorated with icing-sugar granules of glass scattered across the fake marble floor, shopping bags discarded in the stampede to exit. Several drops and smears of dried blood dotted here and there.

'What cover story are we putting out?'

'Armed robbery that went wrong.'

'Good.' Cooper nodded. Keeping it simple. If there'd been a whiff of 'terrorist' to it, the press would be all over this story. That had been his first instinct, a 'terrorist' cover story that some conspirators involved with the Twin Towers incident – some of the press were calling it 9/11 now . . . a catchy term for it – had been identified and put under surveillance: the men had been a terrorist cell attempting to lie low for a while, until things settled down and vigilance levels dropped once more and they could have a go at slipping past immigration and out of the country, but they'd been followed and caught as they headed upstate from New York.

If Cooper had gone with that cover story, this car park would have been crawling with news-station broadcast vans and reporters doing pieces to camera. Instead, a simple 'armed robbery gone wrong' story didn't have the same pulling power right now. They had the mall to themselves for a day or two. A crime scene: every entrance taped off and guarded by a uniformed officer.

'We got CCTV coverage of most of the incident.'

'That's all been confiscated?'

'Yes, sir.'

Cooper had already seen some of it. Digitally copied and enhanced to make it a little clearer. There was no mistaking the fact that the two armed people, one man and one woman, had been hit several times in the opening crossfire. And yet they'd walked on as if nothing had happened, leaving an easy-to-follow trail of blood droplets in their wake.

Cooper looked up at the escalator, one glass side of it shattered. Then at the railing running round the horseshoe-shaped balcony of the floor above. A twenty-foot drop down to where they were now standing.

Incredible.

'The female really jumped down from up there?'

'That's what the eyewitnesses said.'

'They'll need to be informed they were mistaken, or that the woman shattered her legs and spine on impact.'

'They saw her get up and take several steps.'

Cooper looked at Agent Mallard, one of the few FBI agents his limited budget allowed him to deputize into The Department. Mallard was young, eager to impress. Ready to do as he was told. 'That's what they *thought* they saw, Mallard. Do you understand? What they *thought* they saw in the heat of the moment. The mind plays tricks on what you think you've seen in a situation like this.'

'Right, yes . . . sir.'

'The male one?'

'Preliminary autopsy's already been done.'

'And?'

Mallard hesitated. 'The report says he sustained thirty-seven separate gunshot wounds.'

'Thirty-seven?'

'Yes, sir. The police officers who were interviewed said they only managed to bring him down after four or five successful head shots.'

Cooper kept his face impassive, his response measured. This wasn't the place for outbursts of incredulity. He also needed to be sure his new recruit fully understood the situation. 'Mallard?'

'Sir?'

'You're going to *see* some things, *learn* things that – I'll be frank with you – most Presidents don't even get to know about. You understand, once you're in The Department, you're in it for good?'

'That was made clear to me, sir.'

'Good. Now . . . take me to where they're holding the other one, the female. I want to talk with her directly.'

CHAPTER 28

12 September 2001, Interstate 90, Newton, Massachusetts

The rest of the drive up to Boston had been quiet. Liam, Maddy and Sal all silent with their own thoughts. The two support units sat perfectly still; Bob was busy as he drove, sorting through packets of code and prioritizing the most useful bits to upload to Becks. She sat in the back, still as a shop mannequin, as she digested the code floating back to her. Rashim gazed out of the window at more of a world he'd only ever seen in video-film files, while SpongeBubba chirped exclamations full of childlike wonder every now and then.

So very much like a child with that squeaky voice and slight lisp . . .

Look, skippa! A RED car!

Hey! That man's re-eally fat!

Maddy wondered why Rashim would deliberately choose to hack his robot's code to be so grating. But that was it, wasn't it? The faults, the irritating traits and annoying behavioural ticks, the imperfections and phobias . . . it's those things that make us human. That's why he made his lab unit so irritating. Less of a soulless machine.

Perfection on the other hand . . . ? Cool, detached, emotionless perfection. Like those two killer meatbots relentlessly pursuing them. That's what sociopaths were, weren't they? At least in their own minds – without weakness, without imperfections.

Just after midday they checked into another motel; it was as generic and nondescript as the last one had been. But at least this was one in her hometown. Boston. Maddy felt a little more secure. The suburb Arlington, where her folks lived, was actually only about five or six miles away as the crow flies.

She was so nearly home.

'Isn't this a bit dangerous?' said Liam, flicking through the channels on the room's TV set. 'I mean . . . well, might they not guess you'll come here?'

He'd said 'they' like *They*. *Them*: the sort of language a tinfoil-hat-wearing, paranoid conspiracy nut would use.

'We're nearly out of money, Liam. And, even if the account had more money in it, what if someone's tracking the card when we use an ATM?' It could be done, a bank account flagged and used to track a person's movements. 'We need some help. In case you haven't noticed, our little organization isn't doing so good.'

'But come on, going to your *parents'* house?'

'They can help us out! My mom and dad, once I've explained who I am, they'll help us out.'

'Once you've explained who you are?' He cocked a brow. 'Listen to yourself. That'll take some explaining, so it will, Maddy.'

She could already imagine the expression on her mom's face. A squint of suspicion at the strange teenage girl on her doorstep gabbling about time travel. Then probably fear. Perhaps Mom would try slamming the front door on her and calling the police. But then Maddy could tell her and Dad some things that were about to happen. She could tell them that President Bush was soon to make his infamous 'Axis of Evil' speech. That very soon they were going to start pointing the finger of blame at Saddam Hussein in Iraq. Or aim for something closer to home.

She tried to think of their family life directly after 9/11. But she couldn't remember anything specific that was due to happen at home over the next few days. They'd lost Julian in the north tower, their nephew, her cousin. It would be a household fogged with grief right now. No wonder she couldn't recall anything specific. She was nine, then – *now*. Her younger version would be a confused and frightened little girl, believing Fox News that a Big War was coming. That more planes could suddenly start dropping out of the sky. No wonder Maddy couldn't pull any useful memory out of her head from the immediate aftermath. It was just one big fog of news stations repeating the same things, of fear and paranoia and rumours.

She decided she'd pick something from before 9/11 to tell her parents, something only their very own daughter would know. And yes, there'd be herself – *her younger self* – right there to confirm that she was telling the truth, that she was their daughter from the future. She could pick something like her favourite toy's name, her favourite TV show, her favourite clothes, her favourite . . .

Maddy realized she couldn't recall any of those things.

Not a single thing.

'Liam's right,' said Sal. 'Maybe visiting them isn't a good idea.'

Maybe. Maddy watched channels flash by on the screen. Maybe the other two were right. But they couldn't stay here in these two motel rooms forever.

Liam yawned. She felt tired too. She needed some time alone to get her head right.

'Let's get some rest,' she said finally. 'We've all had a bad few days and we're none of us thinking straight here.'

'That is sensible,' said Bob. 'Becks and I can stand watch while you sleep.'

'You boys can have the other room,' said Maddy. Rashim

nodded and got up. Liam tossed the TV remote to Sal, and Bob opened the door for them.

'Let's meet for dinner. We'll work out what we do next then.'

The boys left, the motel door *snicked* shut behind them. Becks took her place beside the window, the net curtain tugged slightly aside, patiently watching the slip road outside that led past a TGI Friday's and a liquor store to their motel. Sal flopped on to the free bed and within a couple of minutes was snoring with a soft rattle that sounded like the purr of a cat.

And Maddy gazed listlessly at the muted TV set at the end of her bed.

CHAPTER 29
12 September 2001, New Haven County, Connecticut

Agents Cooper and Mallard looked at the knuckle-shaped bulge in the cell door.

'*She* did that?' said Cooper.

The duty officer at the county police station nodded. 'We had to taser her and heavily sedate her, cuff her . . . *and* put her in a restraining jacket, or I reckon she'd have smashed her way out eventually.'

'She's conscious now, though?'

The officer nodded. 'You actually wanna *go in there with her*?'

'Of course.'

'Jeez . . . don't rile her up or anything.' He fussed with a jangle of keys on his belt. 'Don't know why we're holding her here. She should've been taken to the state –'

'On my orders,' replied Cooper. 'The less pairs of eyeballs on this, the better. And you and your boys did a splendid job taking her down at the mall.' He smiled kindly. 'I trust her in your care, officer. For the moment.'

He found the key and inserted it into the cell door. 'This is some kind of Top Secret, isn't it?'

'Afraid so.'

'Anything to do with the World Trade Center?'

Cooper shook his head. *Keep it simple. Keep it terrorist-free.* 'No. Nothing.'

He turned the key in the door. 'Back at the mall she hospitalized three of my men even *after* we'd tasered the heck out of her.' He looked at Cooper pointedly. 'Could you at least give me *some* idea what the hell she is?'

Cooper glanced at Mallard, then back at the cop. 'She's . . . the future.' He pulled the cell door open; it clanged against the doorframe as it opened, slightly misshapen from the pounding it had received from the inside.

He stepped in, beckoned Mallard to join him, but held his hand up to the cop. 'Just my colleague and me, I'm afraid.'

'Right,' sighed the officer.

He glanced at the bald-headed female strapped to the cell's cot. She was wide awake and emotionless grey eyes swivelled murderously towards him. She was panting like a wild animal, flexing against the restraints.

'She's all yours,' he said finally and closed the door on them.

Mallard looked decidedly uncomfortable. 'You sure we're safe in here with her, sir?'

Cooper ignored him. He squatted down beside the cot; those grey eyes were now on him. Her panting and flexing stopped. No longer a wild animal. In a heartbeat she was calm and impassive. He could feel those grey eyes coolly evaluating him.

'Release me,' she said evenly after a while.

'Ah! So . . . you *can* talk?'

'Affirmative. I am able to talk.'

Cooper tapped his chin with his fountain pen for a moment. 'I have no idea what exactly you are. I do know, however, that you're not a *normal* human being.'

She said nothing.

'We had a preliminary report back on a sample of your

colleague's blood . . .' Cooper worked to keep his voice as cold and clinically professional as this young woman's. 'It's not a match with *any* blood type.'

'Correct,' she replied. Her dark eyebrows knotted momentarily. 'Abel is terminated?'

'Terminated? You mean dead?' No point lying to her. 'Yes, he's quite dead.'

He thought he detected the slightest flicker of a reaction on her face.

Terminated. God, yes . . . that's what this was beginning to feel like – that awfully cheesy eighties science-fiction movie about killer robots.

'The post-mortem also produced another very interesting discovery,' continued Cooper.

This one's a doozy. The pathologist who'd rung this little detail through to him was almost in tears. She was gabbling, confused, asking him questions none of which he could answer. Mallard had yet to hear this titbit of information.

'Your friend, *Abel*, has no human brain.'

'*Whuh?*' Mallard's jaw hung open. Cooper scowled at him and his mouth snapped shut.

'The cranial cavity interior's much, much smaller than a regular human skull. The space is taken up with additional layers of bone. A thoroughly reinforced skull. Inside all of that we found a brain the size of a fingernail and what appears to be some sort of embedded circuitry.'

'The circuit has self-destructed,' she said, cocking an eyebrow. 'Yes?'

He wasn't sure if that was a statement or a question. He waited for more, but she just eyed him coolly. 'Yes . . .' He sighed. 'It was pretty much fried.'

'That is good.'

Was that the ghost of a smile there?

'Abel was able to self-destruct.'

He thought he'd give the direct approach a go. At the moment she seemed willing to talk candidly. 'Would you care to tell me who . . . or *what* . . . you are?'

'Genetically engineered organic-silicon hybrid – Reconnaissance and Covert Operations variant,' she replied. 'With W.G. Systems AI version 2.3.11 installed.'

'What does *organic-silicon hybrid* mean? You're what? . . . Some sort of half human-half robot?' asked Mallard.

'Negative. I am a genetically engineered human frame with a dense silicon-wafer processor.' Her eyes flickered on to Mallard. 'A computer for a brain,' she clarified for his benefit.

'But . . . but –' He looked at Cooper – 'we can't do that kind of genetic engineering yet! Can we?'

'No,' Faith replied. 'Not for another fifty years.'

'My God!' gasped Mallard. 'Jesus! You're from the . . . from the future? Is that what you're saying?!'

Cooper was tempted to tell Mallard to shut up. Yes, at some point he was going to need to bring his new man up to speed. Mallard had already been exposed to knowledge way beyond being allowed to return to the FBI rank and file. Cooper decided he might as well get him right up there on the same page as him. The sooner, the better. 'Why don't you start by telling me what precise year you're from?' Cooper said.

'My batch birth date is 25 June 2069. Waldstein sent us back to kill TimeRiders.'

'Oh my God! Did she just say –?'

'That's right, Mallard. You're going to need to get your head round this. And fast. I can't have you flapping your jaw like that every time something's said. She's from the future – get used to it.'

The younger man paled. He rocked on his heels uncertainly as his jaw hung open, catching flies once more.

Cooper decided he'd better go easy on him. After all, personally he'd had quite a few years to get used to the idea that anonymous time travellers had passed this way in recent years and just might have rather carelessly left one or two of their footsteps in history.

'*The future?*' he whispered.

'Mallard, I need you to process that quietly, all right? I know it's a helluva thing to take on board. So, just think about it for now, and later I will talk you through it, all the evidence we have. The whole deal. But for now? Right now? . . . I need you to shut up.' He patted the man's shoulder. 'All right?'

Mallard nodded. Cooper turned back to the young woman strapped to the cell's cot. 'Why have you come back here to our time? Who were you after in that shopping mall?'

She started blinking rapidly.

'You all right? What're you doing?' No response, just the rapid flickering of her eyelids.

'Good God!' Mallard was horrified. 'I think she's having a seizure. She's –'

Her eyes snapped open. 'Negative. I am reprioritizing mission parameters. Just a moment . . . just a moment . . .'

A minute passed in silence. Long enough for Cooper to begin wondering whether he needed to prod her again.

'Information,' she said finally. 'While you may be able to assist me, revealing mission objectives to you is a protocol breach. A contamination.'

'Contamination?'

'A time contamination: providing information to you that may cause you to behave in a way or perform actions that alter the timeline. This is a basic protocol breach and must be avoided.

However . . .' Her eyelids stopped fluttering and her gaze settled back on Cooper. 'There is a greater contamination occurring at the moment which must be prevented.'

'The people you were after?'

'Correct. They are not of this time. They must be located immediately and dealt with.'

'By that, I'm guessing you mean *killed*?'

'Affirmative. They have with them the necessary components to facilitate further time displacements and cause even greater contamination. They must be located before they effect a displacement.'

'Displacement? You mean time travel?' Cooper felt hairs rising on the back of his neck. 'My God, you . . . you're actually talking about a functioning –' he felt ridiculous even voicing the words, but there was no other way of saying it – 'time machine? Is that what you're talking about? Is that what they've got with them?'

'The components required to rebuild one, yes.'

Cooper felt a little unsteady. Like Mallard had a moment ago, he rocked back on his heels, settling gently against the cold wall of the cell, grateful for its support.

She played a cold, emotionless facsimile of a smile across her lips. 'What is your name?'

'Cooper,' he answered. 'Agent Niles Cooper.'

'Cooper, I am Faith. I believe that we are able to assist each other.'

A deal. She's proposing a deal.

'You want us to let you out of here?'

'Affirmative. I can lead you directly to them. I have data on their likely movements.'

'And, if you find them, then what?'

'I will kill them.'

'What about their –' he decided to use her term – '*displacement machine?*'

'It must be destroyed.'

'No, we'd want that intact. I can't agree to those –'

'Negative. Allowing you to possess a fully functioning displacement device is unacceptable. That would be an even greater contamination threat. You will not be permitted that.'

'Then I'm afraid there's no deal, Faith.'

Her eyes closed and her eyelids began to flutter. She started to pant and flex again, an unsettling sight like a child sucking in air and preparing to throw an almighty tantrum. But then she stopped. 'I am able to offer you an alternative, Cooper.'

'What?'

'My silicon mind, completely intact.'

He narrowed his eyes. 'The computer in your head? Just like the other one . . . in your dead friend?'

'Correct. I will, of course, delete all files associated with time displacement, but you would be left with the computer architecture entirely intact.'

'Jesus,' whispered Mallard. 'That's a fifty-year jump in computer technology!'

Cooper nodded slowly. 'Yes . . . yes, it is.'

'Do we have an agreement?' asked Faith.

He tapped his chin again. He could feel those hairs on the back of his neck once more, his scalp prickling.

'All right. I think we have the basis of an agreement.'

CHAPTER 30

13 September 2001, Interstate 90, Newton, Massachusetts

It was mid-afternoon the next day when the debate in her head finally came to an end and she got up off her bed. Sal was still snoring.

Becks heard her stir, looked up from where she was sitting cross-legged on the floor. 'Where are you going, Maddy?'

'Out,' she replied softly.

'Are you going to visit your family?'

No point lying to her. 'Yes.'

'The others are worried about you doing this.'

'I need to go.'

She and Becks had had this conversation before. Back when the archway was a pile of rubble in the bottom of a bomb crater, barely holding itself together. She'd nearly walked out on Becks and the others then. She'd planned to somehow make her way back to Boston in the vain hope of finding an alternate version of her parents, perhaps even a version of herself. It had been a moment of weakness. A moment when she'd been prepared to leave her friends to deal with things on their own.

Maddy doubted Becks had a memory of that particular conversation, of walking out, abandoning her in the archway. At the moment she wasn't sure what memories Becks had back in that skull of hers. Bob had been filling her mind up with as much as he could over the last couple of days, a slow process over their nearfield wireless link. Whatever memories she had on-board now would be Bob's, not her's anyway. Becks's full mind remained on an external hard drive.

'Don't wake Sal. If she does wake and asks where I am . . . tell her I've gone to get some supplies in or something.'

'Yes, Maddy. Be careful, Maddy,' she added almost as an afterthought.

Half an hour later she was on a Greyhound bus heading towards Arlington. Maddy realized she'd forgotten how the lines were organized, which ones went where. And yet once upon a time she must have taken them everywhere: to school, back home, into the city to meet friends from high school.

I'm nineteen and I'm already going freakin' senile. How come I can't remember which buses I used to take? She wondered whether a new bus service had taken over here, and perhaps that was why none of the numbers or routes made sense to her.

The bus passed a high school and she looked out on a football field; several dozen young men lined up in their tracksuits, donning shoulder pads and helmets, preparing to practise a few set pieces. Some younger boys kicking a soccer ball around on another field. Maddy realized she couldn't even remember the *name* of her high school. Not even the name. Nor the names of any of her teachers. Or their faces. God . . . nor could she even recall any of her *friends*.

I had some friends, right? At least one friend . . . surely?

But none came to mind. Not a single one. She felt the first stirring of panic set in.

I really am losing my mind!

She could guess what this was – this was that damned archway field, the time bubble. Those freakin' particles killing her mind, one brain cell at a time. She'd just now joked about going senile, but maybe that was just it. Sitting in that brick dungeon all these months was gradually, memory by memory, wiping her mind clean.

She was suddenly grateful to be out of there – OK, they were on the run, but at least they were free from the ever-present corrosive effect of that technology. And grateful, so grateful that she still had enough of her mind and memories left intact to at least find her way home.

The Greyhound dropped her off outside a small 7-Eleven store. She smiled. Her mind remembered *that* all right. The first familiar sight so far, it was the only convenience store around for miles. The rest of this suburb was endless loops of road flanked on either side by well-tended lawns and picket fences, long paved and brown asphalt driveways leading up to grand-looking white-collar homes.

She passed the store, and second on her right Silverdale Crescent. Lined with mature maple trees, their leaves beginning to turn golden for the autumn, not quite ready to fall. She stepped aside for a couple of boys riding their bikes along the pavement, talking to each other about an upcoming game console called the Xbox, that was due to be released this Thanksgiving.

Maddy felt an overpowering urge to run the last hundred yards home. This was *her* street, the place where all of her childhood years had been spent. This was where her life had once made sense, when it was simple and stress free. Decisions no more demanding than which cartoon channel to watch, which flavour ice cream to eat.

Across the road a bed of flowers, Sweet Carolines, glowed in shafts of warm sunlight, tidy rows of purples and creamy pinks. A chestnut-coloured Labrador on a long leash followed an old lady wearing gardening gloves and holding a shopping list in one hand.

She heard the soft boom of rock music and a Ford Zodiac pulled up a long driveway. It was painted with skulls and flaming guitars. A young lad with long hair got out, a guitar case over his shoulder and a small practice amp in one hand.

Band rehearsal.

She smiled. Even only days after 9/11, life was still going on for everyone. The bad guys hadn't won. America hadn't ground to a halt. Kids were still taking their guitars and doing band practice.

And *God*, it felt so good to be coming home. Maddy tried to remember the last time she'd been back home to see Mom and Dad. Because since she'd left home to work for that software games company, she'd been living in . . .

Once again her mind was letting her down.

'Oh, come on, girl,' she chided herself. She'd been living . . . where? . . . *Where?*

She stopped. Nothing was coming. She couldn't even remember where in New York she'd been staying. Or was it New Jersey? And yet she'd been on a damned plane when Foster had saved her. Where the hell was she going? Was she going home for a visit? It must've been. Home for Thanksgiving or Easter, or Christmas or something. But home from *where* exactly?

Her confusion was brushed to one side as she caught a glimpse of the family house up ahead. Home. Unmistakably home. There it was, unchanged in all these years. A large family home built in a mock antebellum style. Covered porch along the front, shingle tiles and white painted supports.

She turned up the empty drive. Dad was probably still at work and Mom always parked her car in the carport.

Did she actually do that? Did she? Was that a memory?

Maddy had the distinct impression she'd just made that bit

up, like someone joining the dots on a child's puzzle. Filling in gaps with whatever seemed to fit. Just to hurry up and finish the picture off – damned if it was a hundred per cent right or not.

She noticed the bedroom window above the carport was open and a gentle warm afternoon breeze was teasing a pink curtain in and out. Her bedroom. Now that she was certain of. The front room above the carport, that was hers all right.

But a *pink* curtain?

I never liked pink . . . did I?

She shrugged. She'd still been a bit girly at age nine. Torn between being like all the other girls or being a tomboy. Maybe the pink curtain was a phase in her younger life she'd chosen to blot out, to not remember. A phase where she'd made a half-hearted attempt to appear feminine. Beyond that curtain, inside the room, she was pretty sure it was all Star Wars action figures and comic books, Warhammer figurines and models of tanks and guns.

The window being open meant one thing. *I must be at home.* Maddy stopped before the whitewashed steps leading up to the front door.

I'm at home. I'm in this house somewhere. Me. I'm home from school. Of course she was. It was after three.

It's me in there. Me, aged nine.

She felt an overpowering rush of emotion. It was going to be so strange meeting herself. Like looking in a peculiar mirror that could filter away years, allow her to look back through ten years of time and see herself with braces still welded to her teeth and that always impossible hair of hers dragged into submission by a brush and pulled tightly into two bobbing Goldilocks ponytails.

She was trembling. It was going to be impossibly weird.

'And what the hell do I say?' she muttered.

She took the steps up to the porch slowly. There was the garden gnome with a chainsaw. Her idea of a joke present for Mom, who just hated gardening and could quite happily have taken a chainsaw to all the delicately trimmed bushes up and down Silverdale Crescent. And there, across the porch, was the rocking-chair. She smiled at the memory of the thing. Dad's favourite chair . . . where he spent summer evenings smoking a long clay pipe and rocking back and forth.

Again. She had the distinct impression that she was *inking in details*, filling in gaps in her mind with memories that seemed appropriate, most likely. She was creating mental images to fill her blank memory. Worse still, she suddenly realized, she was borrowing images, scenes, from old movies, from old TV shows. Why the hell was she seeing Dad with long white whiskers? Wearing worn old dungarees and a battered straw hat?

'That's not right . . . that's *The Waltons*,' she whispered. It had been on TV back in the motel room: some old rerun of *The Waltons* on cable. And now her mind was taking bits of that old show and superimposing it on her scant childhood memories. Filling in. Filling in.

The front door. Now, *dammit*, she remembered this for sure. Reassuring, a genuine memory this time. Mint green with that brass knocker. How many times had she closed that behind her or watched her mother fumble with shopping bags to find her keys to open it?

She reached for the knocker and hesitated. What the crud was she going to say to Mom? How was she going to explain who she was?

It was going to be difficult. Mom was in there somewhere, probably glued to the TV on the breakfast bar in the kitchen, still watching the news on Fox. Perhaps still crying for her poor older sister who'd lost a wonderful son in that pile of still-smouldering rubble. And Maddy could imagine herself up in her bedroom painting her Warhammer figures. Keeping her mind occupied. Not wanting to think about the fact that Julian was gone for good. Not wanting to pester Mom with difficult questions right now.

This was going to be awkward.

She grabbed the knocker and tapped it firmly against the door.

Hi, Mom. Can you guess who I am?

No, that wouldn't do.

Hi. I have something really important to tell you . . . Can I come in?

No. That made her sound like a goddamn Jehovah's Witness.

Mom, it's me . . . Maddy. I've come from nine years in the future.

She heard footsteps inside. The squeak of trainers on parquet floor, then the rattle and clack of the latch and the door opened.

'Yeah?'

A girl. About the age she was expecting, blonde. She was wearing a Spice Girls T-shirt and pink jeans with a glitter pattern down one leg and floral pumps.

God! Is that really me!? It can't be!

'Yeah?' said the girl again with an impatient shrug. 'Help you?'

Maddy was tongue-tied. 'I . . . uh . . .'

'You want to speak to my mom?'

Maddy nodded mutely.

'Mom!' called out the girl. 'It's for you-hoo!'

'Who is it?' A woman's voice from somewhere in the back.

The girl made a wearisome face. 'Mom says . . . who is it?'

Maddy felt her resolve beginning to fail her. She wanted to mumble something like *I guess I got the wrong house, sorry about that*, turn around and walk away. But she couldn't walk away. Not now. She was past that point, over it. She was here, she'd already knocked and waited and now the door was open and she was just seconds away from speaking to Mom. Too late to run. She was here now and she really needed Mom and Dad's help. It was now or never.

Maddy hunkered down a little, to the girl's level. 'Hi,' she said. 'My name's Maddy. Just like yours.'

The girl looked at her sideways. 'Uh, no, it ain't.'

'Nadine!' called the voice from the back. 'Who is it?'

'Your name's *Nadine*?'

'Uh . . . yeah.'

That flummoxed her. 'Nadine?' She wasn't expecting that. 'Since . . . when?'

She shrugged. 'Like, since, birth.'

CHAPTER 31

2055, W.G. Systems Research Campus, near Pinedale, Wyoming

Waldstein stared at it. There it was behind the darkened glass, in a carefully controlled and monitored sealed envelope of cool air. A sheet of brittle and age-yellowed newspaper. A page of classified ads: columns of messages from the hopeless, the lonely, the bereft, the bewildered. An ad from someone who'd lost a much-loved bulldog answering to the name of Roosevelt and was offering a reward of $200 for him. Some old soldier looking for a fellow platoon member he served alongside during the Normandy landings, and someone else looking for a missing daughter who might just be living in the Brooklyn area. There an ad from a very lonely widower looking for someone else to share his suddenly empty life with – searching for a friend who might enjoy trips to the theatre, watching matinees of old Bette Davis movies.

This page of forlorn little classified ads was a perfectly preserved record of one day's worth of misery in Brooklyn in the year 2001. A record of incomplete lives and broken hearts. Of final words that should have been said face to face, but never were.

Waldstein's heart ached every time he studied this withered page of newspaper. There were words he wished he'd said to his wife, Eleanor, and his son, Gabriel. Words that he'd always felt foolish saying out loud, rather preferring to assume the pair of them knew he loved them very much, to save him saying such things. Words that he'd sell his very soul to be able to say to them one last time . . . now.

Words.

Beneath that light-filtering glass, a UV light glowed softly on the page, and a digital camera with an ultra-low light-sensitive lens and an infrared sensor closely monitored one particular personal ad. There it was halfway down the third column, one rather innocuous little paragraph of faint, slightly smudged newsprint.

The letters in that paragraph quite often flickered in a faint, spectral way. Just enough that if you weren't looking directly at them your peripheral vision might just catch the subtlest sense of movement. A square inch of newspaper that undulated, shifted, stirred every now and then as if a small ghost lived in the very fibre of the newspaper itself.

It was a square inch of reality in permanent flux. The tiniest portion of the world caught in a perpetual state of undulating change, trapped in the eddies and currents of its own mini time wave.

Today, though, it seemed particularly agitated. Letters fidgeted, blurred, changed. As if it very much had something it wanted to tell Waldstein. The infrared sensor was picking up a temperature shift off the brittle old paper that was a whole tenth of a degree higher than normal. The minutest leakage of energy through the tiniest crack in space-time.

It wants to talk to me.

He studied the data monitor beside the glass case, watched the temperature read-out twitch and shuffle and occasionally spike. Beside it, the low-light image of the printed letters shimmered and danced like ghouls in a graveyard, caught only in glimpses of flitting moonlight.

Waldstein suspected the newly grown, birthed and trained

team were struggling to find their feet. That poor old wretch – not Liam now, he'd chosen the name Foster instead. So much rested on his shoulders. And he'd been through so much recently. To have lost his friends in such a horrific way. Then to have also been through the appalling torment of being suddenly, prematurely aged. And then, after all of that, after sending his plea for help through time to the future, to hear back from his 'creator' and learn that he was somewhat less than human. Worse still . . . that he was going to have to fix things up again entirely on his own. To be the fatherlike mentor for a new team.

So much – *too much to put on the poor thing*. Waldstein's heart ached for him.

That poor wretch Liam – now Foster – was entirely on his own, effectively running this project himself. He'd had to set up a replacement team, to mentor them, train and ready them for their respective roles, all the while knowing exactly what they were and yet having to go along with this appalling deceit. To lie to them.

Now it seemed, with these flickering letters on the page, there was more bad news coming through from 2001. From Foster.

The heat reading spiked again. Another tenth of a per cent of a degree.

It's coming.

The letters shimmered and shuffled faintly. And there it was. Ink on paper. No longer shimmering with a desire to change. There it was. Bad news.

. . . Experienced significant event. Origin time-stamp of contamination 1941. Major displacement effects. Problem narrowly but successfully averted. New recruits performed well under stress. One team member lost. Require new observer immediately – Foster.

Joseph Olivera looked up from his floating data screens. 'They need a new . . . ?'

'A new observer, Joseph. They need a new Saleena Vikram.'

Frasier Griggs paled. 'You mean . . . send one back?'

'Yes.'

'What happened, Mr Waldstein?' asked Joseph.

Waldstein shook his head. 'I'm not sure. It seems like they've had to deal with a *major* contamination originating from sometime during the Second World War. Something big must have shaken things up for them.' Waldstein smiled. 'Their first big test. And it seems they've saved mankind.'

'But one of them's dead,' said Griggs.

'Indeed.'

'What about the others?'

'It seems they're all right, Joseph.' Waldstein touched a data pad and the air in front of him shimmered with holographic data. He swept the data to one side with his finger, and double-tapped a thumbnail image. It expanded in front of them, a digitized image of the page of newspaper hovering in mid-air. 'You read it for yourself.'

Joseph and Griggs leaned forward to scrutinize the image more closely. They read it in silence.

'He won't be able to grow one back there,' said Waldstein. 'The memory needs altering. Which is why we'll have to do it here and send her back.'

Joseph nodded. Waldstein was, of course, quite right. The other two team members – the Maddy unit and the Liam unit – weren't ready to know what they were. If Foster was sent a Saleena Vikram unit foetus and started growing it right there in the archway, then the game would be up. He'd need to explain to the other two *units* exactly what they were.

Clones.

All three of them were designed to work at their best believing themselves to be entirely human. Believing they had real life stories, real loved ones, real memories. It's what made their purely organic data matrices produce completely *human-level decisions*. That's why Joseph hated to call it 'Organic Artificial Intelligence'. Because it wasn't *artificial* intelligence. It was Authentic Intelligence. If their brains – which were no different from any other human brains – truly believed the store of memories in their minds to be genuine then as far as Joseph was concerned, they were *real* people. Just as real as anyone else. More than mere genetically engineered replicas. Certainly so much more capable of strategic thought than the silicon minds inside the support units.

However, the moment they realized their lives were fabricated, a pack of installed lies; the moment they understood they hadn't been born to loving mothers, but instead had emerged fully grown from plastic tubes, just like their support units . . . that was when their decision-making would become compromised. Unreliable.

'Joseph, start a growth here in the lab,' said Waldstein. 'Then we'll have to send her back. Can you edit her memory to make that work? She can't suspect she's a tube-product.'

'Wait . . . hang on a minute!' cut in Griggs. 'We said no more direct interactions!'

Waldstein waved a hand to silence him. 'They need an observer. Joseph?'

Joseph nodded. 'I can s-splice into her existing memory. We have her life-story file, right up to the recruitment event.' He scratched his chin. 'I suppose I can graft in some generalized memories of her living in the archway with the other two. Nothing too s-specific, just the general impression that she's been living in close proximity to Maddy and Liam for some weeks. It'll be a little foggy for her.'

'Foggy?'

'She'd be a little disorientated. Like she's experienced a kind of mild amnesia. A gap in her memory, as if she's experienced a mild trauma, concussion, like a blow to the head. There'll be minor continuity errors she won't be able to make sense of, but if we deploy her directly after a field refresh or a corrective time wave she and the others may attribute that foggy memory as some side effect of the realignment of the timeline.' He shrugged. 'Since they're newly recruited, I imagine they'll buy that explanation from Foster. They'll trust what he tells them.'

Waldstein nodded. 'Then we should do that.' He looked at Joseph, placed a hand on his shoulder. 'Be as careful as you can splicing in her memory.'

That didn't need saying. Sal needed to wake up and find herself returning to the archway, believing nothing more than some time wave must have caught her outside; messed with her head in some small way. If that didn't work, if she started questioning her reality . . . ? If the team figured out they were a bunch of enhanced support units, meatbots? Then the whole project was over. They'd have to start again from scratch. *Delete* the old ones and grow a brand-new team. New minds, new memories, new lives.

'I'll be very careful, Mr Waldstein. Trust me.'

'Good.'

Griggs stepped forward and grabbed Waldstein's arm. 'Roald . . . this is really pushing our luck. You know we broadcast our presence every time we open a portal! You know there must be dozens of tachyon-listening stations all over the world. Christ . . . it was your campaigning that made sure of that. Do you want to be discovered? Do you want that?'

'It's an acceptable risk, Frasier.'

'No, it's not. This whole project was always too risky. We were supposed to travel only to 2001 to set it up. And that was it. No further trips!'

'It's an acceptable risk.' He looked at Griggs sternly, then lowered his voice. 'Please, don't push our friendship, Frasier. This is more important than that. More important than anything.'

'More important?' Griggs laughed. 'What's all this really about? Eh?'

'You know as well as I do. Three-dimensional space is as precious as fine bone china. You can't let time travel –'

Griggs spat a curse. His eyes narrowed. 'That's not what you really care about.'

'Frasier . . .'

'You know what I think this is about? Vengeance. Bitterness. You can't bring your wife and son back so you –'

'ENOUGH!' Waldstein glared at Griggs. He pulled the man by his arm. 'You and I need to talk, Frasier. We need to talk right now.'

Joseph watched, dumbstruck by the suddenly charged atmosphere in the room, as both men stepped out of the lab into the small adjoining conference room. The glass door hissed shut behind them and their voices became muted. He saw Griggs's face darken with anger, and he heard their muffled voices, quiet at first, but then quickly rising in volume and pitch, getting louder and louder.

Then finally that word. *Pandora*. And . . . *Why, Roald? Why do you want that to happen?*

CHAPTER 32

13 September 2001, Interstate 90, Newton, Massachusetts

'Where did she go?'

Becks looked at him, a growing expression of anxiety on her face. 'Maddy . . . said she was going to get some supplies.'

'Said . . . she *said* . . . so maybe she wasn't?'

The support unit could only look at Liam plaintively. He grasped her slim arms firmly. Arms that easily could have shrugged off his grasp and twisted his head off his shoulders if she had the notion to do so. 'Becks! Come on! Where's she *really* gone?'

'She . . . said –'

'She's gone to her old home, hasn't she?'

Becks looked conflicted, torn between an instruction to lie and a logical imperative to speak the truth.

Liam cursed. 'I knew it!'

'That is an unwise action,' said Bob. His cool eyes looked around the others gathered in the girls' motel room. 'The pursuing support units may also attempt to travel to the same location.'

'I don't think we could've stopped her,' said Sal. 'I think she's too close to home to not try to see them. She really misses her family.' She looked down at her hands. 'I know it's what I'd want to do.'

'And I miss me own ma and da just as much!' said Liam. 'But

Bob's right – that's a stupid thing she's gone an' done! I should have known she'd do this!'

'What if they're clever,' said Rashim. 'What if they don't attack her there, but instead follow her back here?'

'Exactly!' said Liam. 'She could lead them right to us all!'

Just then a key clicked and rattled in the motel room's door. All heads turned as the door opened and daylight stretched across the mottled pattern of the room's threadbare carpet.

Maddy.

'Perfect timing!' said Liam. 'We were wondering . . .' His voice tailed off. She stood in the doorway staring back at all of them. On any other occasion he would have expected her to do a double-take at them all staring wide-mouthed at her and irritably snap *'What's up?'* But instead she stepped slowly in, kicking the door shut behind her. She sat down on the end of the bed and stared listlessly at the blank glass screen of the TV set, reflecting her own sullen expression back at her.

'Maddy?' said Sal. 'You OK?'

No answer.

Liam could see her eyes were red-raw beneath her glasses. Her cheeks were wet. She was crying. He sat on the bed beside her. 'Maddy?'

'She appears to be distressed,' said Bob.

Liam waved him silent. 'Maddy? Is everything all right?' She shook her head silently.

Liam didn't dare ask the next question. But it needed asking all the same. 'Maddy? Your family . . . are they all right? They're not hurt in any –?'

'They're not my family,' she muttered.

'Uh?'

'Not my family,' she said again. She turned from her dim reflection in the TV screen. 'And they never were.'

Liam leaned in closely to her. 'Maddy? What do you mean? What's the matter?'

He'd never seen her like this before, not even when things had seemed at their worst, not even that first day when they'd all met in the darkness of the archway, freshly plucked from the very last moments of their lives. This wasn't normal Maddy: stressed, irritated, annoyed or frustrated. This was a totally alien Maddy Carter: utterly crushed, defeated.

Sal got up off the chair by the door and knelt on the floor in front of her. She could see it in her face too; this was Maddy right at the end of her game. She reached out for her hand and squeezed it. 'Tell us what happened?'

'I . . . I've worked it out,' she said, her voice a mucus-thick whisper.

'Worked what out?'

She looked at Liam. 'I've worked out who we are.'

'Who we are?' He frowned. Confused.

'Or more to the point,' she added, 'I've figured out *what* we are.'

'What we are?' Liam turned to the others, then back at Maddy. 'What in the name of Jesus an' Mary are you talkin' about?'

'Shadd-yah!' Sal muttered under her breath.

Liam looked at her. The one eye of hers not hidden by her looping fringe had suddenly widened with realization. She seemed to have some inkling of what Maddy was talking about. 'What, Sal? What's she mean by that?'

'We're not who we thought we were, Liam,' said Maddy.

'Not who we . . .' His brows locked. 'What's that supposed to mean?'

'Your life is just a lie, Liam . . . a story,' said Maddy. 'Fiction.'

'Maddy? What happened?' asked Sal.

Maddy laughed. More a wet snort of snot mixed with tears. 'They obviously didn't expect we'd come looking for the truth. Why would they?' She took her glasses off and wiped at her eyes. 'I mean, Foster made such a big thing of it, didn't he? That we should be dead already . . . that this extra life was like a bonus or something. A gift.'

Liam nodded. Of course he had. The old man made no bones about that. There'd been a choice right at the end of their old lives: not much of a choice admittedly, but a choice nonetheless. He could have gone down with the *Titanic* if he'd wanted, but he'd chosen to join Foster.

'We all chose it, Maddy,' said Liam. 'Right at the end, when he saved us all.'

She laughed. A miserable, choking sound. She shook her head. 'But that's the point! We didn't!'

'Didn't?' Liam hadn't a clue what she was talking about. 'Yes, I did. I chose to –'

'No . . . no, you didn't,' said Sal quietly. Nodding. She understood now. 'Or me . . . I didn't either.' Her one visible eye was beginning to spill glistening tears on to her dark cheek.

'Ah Jay-zus! *You* crying too? What's up with you both? Why're you crying? *What is goin' on here?*'

'None of us chose to join this agency in the last moments of our lives, Liam,' said Maddy. 'Because none of that ever happened.'

Sal's head dropped, her face dipped out of sight. He could see her shoulders heaving gently. He looked around. The only other person here who seemed utterly bewildered by all of this was Rashim. He offered Liam a sympathetic shrug that seemed to say, *I got no idea what they're talking about either.*

'Our memories, Liam . . . everything we thought were memories of our lives before the archway, before we were

170

recruited . . .' Maddy's chin dimpled as fresh tears streamed down her face. 'Everything. My home, my mom, my dad, my school, my job . . . they're all lies. They're phoney.'

'Information: memory implants.' Even Bob seemed to have an understanding of what she was saying now.

Maddy nodded. 'Faked memories. Our lives are just made up. I never lived in Boston. Sal never lived in India. And you . . .' Her voice faltered. 'Oh, Liam, you never came from Ireland.'

'But . . .' Liam bit his lip. 'But I'm from Cork! I know I am! I'm . . . that's . . . what kind of nonsense do you think you're –'

'We didn't come from those places. We never lived there; we never even set foot in any of those places.'

'Whuh?'

'I get it.' Sal's soft voice drifted up through the drooping curtain of her hair. 'We came right out of three giant test-tubes.'

Maddy nodded. She reached out and rested a hand on Sal's shoulder. A reciprocated gesture of comfort.

'Do you get it, Liam? Do you see?' said Sal. 'We're support units.'

CHAPTER 33

2055, W.G. Systems Research Campus, near Pinedale, Wyoming

'Can I trust you, Joseph?'

Joseph Olivera lurched. That question came right out of nowhere and caught him entirely off guard. Waldstein was standing beside him in the lab, seemingly emerging from thin air.

'Wh-what? Yes! Of . . . of course, Mr Waldstein.'

A long, uncomfortable moment.

'I'm so very sorry about what happened to Frasier. He was the closest thing to a friend I have.' He shrugged. '*Had.*' He sighed. 'God, I've known him for nearly ten years.'

Joseph swallowed compulsively. He had the suspicion that an aura of guilt was glowing around him: a scintillating sparkle of betrayal giving away his secret intentions to Waldstein's deep penetrative gaze.

'The argument the other day . . . I'm sorry you had to see that. That was unfortunate. I wish Frasier and I hadn't fought like that. I . . .' Waldstein looked away. 'And I truly wish that hadn't been the last time we spoke.'

'Yes, sir.'

'But he had doubts, Joseph. Doubts about this project. Even if that awful attack on the road hadn't happened to him, he would have had to leave us.'

Joseph nodded.

'You know, I've been thinking it would be a sensible precaution to deposit some more pre-growth embryos back in the San Francisco drop point.' Waldstein nodded to himself. 'Yes, we should arrange that. As soon as is possible. Get some ready to transport.'

'Go back there? Again? Are you sure?'

'I know, Joseph. It's risky. But I suspect they're going to get through more support units than I originally anticipated. You know . . . when we were setting up the 2001 team, I was half convinced they'd never actually be needed – that they'd be just sitting there kicking their heels. That I was over-reacting, being paranoid. Worrying too much about other time travellers out there wanting to destabilize our timeline!' He shook his head. 'I realize now maybe I wasn't paranoid enough!'

'Yes, sir.' Joseph checked their inventory on the holo-screen in front of him. There were two dozen embryos on ice: part of the batch being readied for the US military's field-testing programme. 'How many would you want me to prepare?'

'Let's give them half a dozen. Maybe send them some of *both* types of hybrid; the heavy-duty model and the female recon model. Might as well give them a few of each.'

Listed on the screen were the other clones, who were nothing at all to do with the US military. 'What about the pure-clone models? The Madelaines, Liams . . . the Saleenas?'

Waldstein gave it a moment's thought. 'No . . . if we send back pre-growths of themselves they'll know what they are. We were very lucky with that first team. Very lucky that the Liam unit played along with us and kept the new team from finding out what they are.'

'It's part of his programming. He's loyal. Duty oriented. That's his personality template.'

'But even with your programming, Joseph, they're not a hundred per cent reliable, are they?'

Joseph shrugged. 'They have the capacity for independent will. That's what makes them better –'

'– tactical decision-makers, I know. But when all's said and done, unlike the military hybrids, those three are just like real people, aren't they? They're like real kids. If they ever found out they were products? Good God, who knows what they'd do?' Waldstein sighed. 'I do sometimes wonder if what we've done is . . . a *cruel* thing: created three children who-never-were and then gave them this sort of burden. If that was me,' he said, smiling sadly, 'if I discovered that was my lot, I think I would almost certainly turn on my maker.'

Joseph nodded.

'No, they'll have to be on their own. We can't send back pure-clone embryos. If it happens again – if another one of them dies . . .' Waldstein shrugged. 'Then I'm afraid they'll have to work around that problem.' He sighed. 'There's only so much we can do for them.'

'Yes, sir.'

'So, if you could organize that? Prep some embryos and ready them for transport?'

'Yes, of course.'

Waldstein looked out of the lab's small window, a long moment of deliberation before he finally spoke again. 'And I'll take them back myself. But this has to be the last time we go back to assist them with supplies. The *last* time I go back. It's getting too damned dangerous.'

Joseph looked at him. 'Perhaps . . . ?'

'What?'

Be very careful, Joseph.

'P-perhaps . . . this project has *already* become too dangerous, Mr Waldstein?'

The old man stared at him for a moment. Joseph wondered what thoughts were thrashing around behind those intense eyes. He struggled to keep his composure. 'I . . . I just wonder if things have become –'

'We don't have much of a choice in the matter. This has to work. You understand that, don't you?'

Joseph could hardly meet his eyes. 'But . . .'

'There are no *buts*, Joseph. We're the first and the last line of defence. Do you understand? Do you honestly think we're the *only* people in the world right now with viable time-travel technology? I'm not a fool. Yes, there's a law now: ILA Ruling 234. A draconian law. But I'm not naive enough to think there aren't people out there quietly working on time travel all the same.'

'Yes, Mr Waldstein.'

He leaned over and squeezed Joseph's shoulder affectionately. 'You've seen for yourself what our team in the past have narrowly prevented.'

Joseph looked at the small window. Outside that window, beyond the reach of their laboratory stasis field, he'd witnessed a time wave arrive and leave behind it an irradiated wasteland. Just for a few minutes it had been there – a hellish landscape – then washed away by another wave moments later.

'I know this isn't an *ideal* world –' Waldstein laughed drily at that understatement – 'but there are an infinite number of possibilities far worse.' Waldstein squeezed his shoulder again. 'Trust me. Just stay the course. You're a good man, Joseph. I know I can trust you. I know that.'

'Th-thank you, sir.'

He got up off the stool and stepped away. Other matters appeared to be on his mind. 'I have a damned meeting I need to attend in Denver tomorrow. W.G. Systems' investors, some of our major clients. I could do without that right now, but . . .' He sighed. 'It's one I really do have to be at.' Waldstein looked harried, stretched, like plastic wrap over the hard corners of a box, pulled taut to the point of ripping.

'I know things have been difficult recently, Joseph. I . . . I wish Frasier was here with us still. It's . . . well, what happened to him was horrible. I suppose it's a sign of these awful times. You know, I sometimes think we deserve this hopeless world. All our mistakes have finally come home to roost, haven't they?'

Joseph nodded, and Waldstein looked like his train of thought was heading off in some other direction. 'Just you and me running this project now.'

'Yes, Mr Waldstein.'

'We need to keep things going. To keep things on track. All the hard work's been done now. All we need to do now is just make sure our team can continue doing their job. I'm sure they'll be fine back there.' He smiled. 'They're good kids. I'm so proud of them. And you too, Joseph. They're as much your creations as they are anyone else's.'

'Thank you.'

Waldstein nodded and turned to go.

'Mr Waldstein?'

'Yes?'

'When will you want the embryos ready by?'

He sucked in a breath. 'I hate doing this, you know? Having to step into that white mist. Knowing that it's killing me cell by cell. Knowing that every time we open a goddamn portal we're broadcasting our presence to those who might be looking for it.'

'That worries me too, Mr Waldstein.'

'And this, then, will have to be the last time. They're on their own after this.' Waldstein sighed. 'Have the embryos good to go for this evening, will you? Let's get it done and out of the way.' He nodded to himself. 'This evening.'

'I will have them ready.'

'Thank you. And after that . . . hopefully the Saleena unit will be ready to drop back in Brooklyn?'

'She'll need another thirteen hours, I think, to full growth. Then I'll need a few hours to upload and configure her new memory.'

'Fine, as soon as she's ready get her sent back. You'll be OK doing that on your own?'

'Of . . . of course, Mr Waldstein.' Joseph tapped his h-pad. 'I have the insertion data-stamp as we discussed: outside the archway, directly after the 1941 corrective wave. I have it all ready.'

Waldstein nodded. 'Of course.' He sighed, trying a weary morale-raising smile. 'Then that'll be all our messy housekeeping done. Back on an even keel, as I think the saying goes.'

Joseph watched Waldstein go. Then, finally alone in the lab, he took in a deep breath and let it out.

Jesus.

He recalled a couple of things Waldstein had said. Things that had echoed what Griggs had been fixating on.

We deserve this hopeless world? We need to keep things on track?

Frasier Griggs was right. He was certain of it now. Quite certain that beneath his carefully orchestrated enigmatic composure, withstanding his publicly declared ambition to save mankind from itself – Waldstein had quietly gone insane. The man seemed utterly intent on steering the ship *on to* the rocks, not *away* from them. Intent on steering mankind towards its own demise.

Pandora.

Joseph realized it was all down to one person. Himself. Griggs had been foolish and confronted Waldstein directly. Now he was dead. Perhaps he could smuggle a warning to the team, just something to alert them to whatever this 'Pandora' was that Waldstein was attempting to preserve. Something discreet. A note. Something.

It's just me now. I've got to do more than that.

He looked once again at the message from the past. The Liam-now-Foster unit had ordered a replacement Saleena like someone might dial up a pizza. The unit did his job diligently, loyally – just like he was programmed to do.

Saleena Vikram.

Olivera had an idea. Another way that he could attempt to derail this project. Something he could do, something subtle enough that it could be sneaked past Waldstein's ever-watchful eyes. A deliberate, conspicuous continuity error in Sal's memory line. Enough of a jarring continuity error that she'd end up picking at it like a scab, worrying away at it until she'd finally worked out what it meant. Now that was something Waldstein might not spot – some small additional memory embedded in her mind, a detail not quite right. A detail that was quite impossible to be true. And it would trouble her. Make her question things.

He'd been thinking about that last night as he'd sat alone in this lab, while trying to catch a few hours' sleep on the metal-framed cot in the corner. While he'd been watching her grow in the tube, the faint outline of a child's body floating in a glowing amber soup.

Then he had it. It came to him.

A certain blue bear that he recalled seeing in the dusty window of an antique shop back in 2001. Not too far from the archway, as it happened. Close enough, in fact, that she was bound to stumble across it sooner or later. See it with her own eyes and then wonder how it was possible that she'd recall seeing it tumbling over and over in an inferno in Mumbai, in the year 2026

CHAPTER 34

13 September 2011, Interstate 90, Newton, Massachusetts

'But that's completely bleedin' crazy!' said Liam. 'You're saying . . . what? That I'm a . . .'

'A meatbot, Liam. You, me and Sal — we're just weedier, nerdier models of Bob and Becks,' said Maddy with a bitter tone.

Liam laughed a little maniacally. 'Aw, come on! That's a corker, that is! There's no way at all that I'm —'

'Think about it, Liam. Think about it!'

'I don't need to think about! I'm Liam!'

Maddy got up and took a step forward. 'I was never on an airplane from New York to Boston. A plane that supposedly blew up,' she said. 'And you, Liam, you were never on the *Titanic* and Sal was never living in 2026 in Mumbai. They're all just made-up memories.'

'*Made-up?*' Liam frowned. He had a mind full of memories. His family and friends, Cork, his school, leaving home for Liverpool because what he really always wanted to do was to work his way on to a boat and get to see the world. But then . . . cross-examining those memories — and he'd done that several times over the last few months — there'd always seemed to be troublesome gaps, missing bits. He'd put that down to all that had happened to him recently — a lifetime's worth of traumas and adventures that he'd struggled to survive through over the last few months. Who wouldn't forget something like their mother's maiden name after all of that? Right?

But it was more than that, wasn't it?

'I can remember a whole life before this, so I can. *A whole bleedin' life!'*

'Yeah? Really?'

'Aye.' Liam nodded vigorously. 'Of course I can!'

'OK then . . . so how did you get the job as a steward aboard the *Titanic*?' There was a challenging tone in her voice, a *come-on-then-genius* tone. It sounded almost spiteful.

'Well, I . . .' Liam shrugged, expecting the memory to come along at his will. But there was nothing. Nothing at all. Had he just walked aboard and asked for a job? Had it been that easy? He reached further into his mind, assuming, hoping, this was just a mental blip – going blank because she was pressuring him, goading him. He tried to rewind his mind. The night the ship went down, the screaming, the panic. He recalled a gentleman calmly drinking cognac in the reading room, preferring drunken oblivion to drowning soberly. A girl left to die with him because she was in a wheelchair. He recalled an hour earlier, the ship jolting in the night, crockery lurching off dining tables and smashing on the floor.

Further still. He recalled the day before. A normal day as a ship's steward. The routine: up at five, cabin-service breakfasts for those that had ordered it. Cleaning the rooms during the morning. Filling in as a waiter for the midday meal and the evening meal. Then cabin-service teas and suppers served until ten in the evening, then collapsing wearily into his bunk in a small cabin shared with three other men. A typical steward's day.

Then back further.

But nothing. It was like the blackness after the end titles of a movie. Void. White noise. Nothing.

'I . . .' His mouth hung open until finally it snapped shut with a wet *clup*.

'I'm so sorry, Liam,' whispered Maddy. 'So sorry.'

'No! Wait! What about me parents! My family! I remember them!'

'Go on then, Liam. Tell me about them.'

'Me ma, me da . . . they were . . .' He closed his eyes. But he could manage to conjure up only one decent mental image of them. Just one. And that was a photograph. Just one faded, sepia-coloured image.

'What about your home? You said it was Cork, wasn't it?'

Cork in Ireland. Could he even recall whereabouts they lived in that city? No, not really. He just knew the name. He could conjure up no more than a couple of images of the place – the docks, St Fin Barre's Cathedral, St Patrick's Street – and that was about it. Again, almost as if they were mere photographs pulled from some photo archive somewhere.

'Ah . . . Jay-zus . . .' he whispered.

'It's just the same for me,' said Maddy softly. She sat down beside him. 'Bits and pieces. Like somebody just googled up a whole bunch of pictures, music, films, news, clothes, computer games, TV shows from the year 2010 and made me out of all of that.' She wiped a tear off her cheek. 'You know what my mind is? It's the search results you get back if you do a "things you might find in the year 2010" search on whatever passes for the Internet . . .' She shrugged. 'From whatever frikkin' year we actually come from.'

'Do you think we've got computers in our heads too?' asked Sal.

'Maybe I'll stick my head in an X-ray machine sometime and

find out,' Maddy replied, wiping a snotty nose. She laughed. 'Maybe not. Last thing I want to know is that there's nothing in my skull but a rat's brain linked to a SIM card.' She looked apologetically at Bob. 'No offence.'

Bob shrugged. 'I cannot be offended.'

'And the difference is that we can,' said Maddy, finding a hint of a smile. 'So maybe we're different somehow. Clones, but maybe we're more human or something.'

Sal nodded. She was looking down at her hands in her lap. 'I just . . . I just can't believe we never worked this out. I mean . . .' She looked up at them. 'When we woke up in the archway, how come none of us thought to ask why we didn't see a portal when we were recruited?'

'Exactly.' Maddy got to her feet. 'So why didn't they put a portal memory into our heads? Why make that mistake?'

'Perhaps . . .' Rashim cut in, clearing his throat. 'Perhaps they hadn't yet perfected the portal system while they were writing your memories?'

The others looked at him accusingly. 'Thanks for your input, *human*!' snapped Sal.

He raised his hands apologetically. 'Just saying.'

'No.' Maddy shook her head. 'Rashim's right. Maybe that's why they, he, Waldstein . . . *whoever* made us was still putting it all together. Maybe they were doing it in a hurry. I guess if we all think hard, we'd find other little errors in there.'

'My blue bear,' whispered Sal to herself. She addressed the others. 'I remembered a bear, a soft toy, in Mumbai . . . but it was exactly the same bear in the window of that shop in Brooklyn.' She shook her head. 'Someone . . . someone who made us must have seen it in the window, and thought it would make a nice little detail to put into my . . . life.' Her voice hitched. 'Nice touch,' she hissed.

The room was quiet for a while, the three of them silently trawling through their minds, sorting memories into piles of true and false – sorting them into *before* and *after* their recruitment.

Finally Liam spoke. 'I get it now.'

He looked at Bob, arms crossed and eyes lost in the shadow of a neolithic brow, and Becks sitting beside him slight and wraithlike, with wide, vacant, dumb-animal eyes.

'Meatbots, eh? Bleedin' marvellous.'

CHAPTER 35

2055, W.G. Systems Research Campus, near Pinedale, Wyoming

It was late in the day. Joseph Olivera had decided to stay overnight on the grounds of the W.G. Systems research compound to eat in the staff canteen and sleep in the cot in the adjoining office area. The synthi-soya gunk they served up in there almost tasted like real food. Better than the cartons of gunk he had in his apartment's refrigerator.

Anyway, it was beginning to get dark outside and he didn't fancy taking his Auto-Drive along the winding wooded road down to Pinedale. There were more and more vagrants drifting westward from the eastern states and he knew for certain many of them were camping out there in the woods. He'd heard some of the W.G. techies talking about several more roadside hold-ups in the last week. In most cases it was just the desperate and hungry after a little money, not exactly asking ... but ... in most cases the hold-up ended as a palm-transaction of whatever digi-dollars you had on account and they'd let you pass through unharmed.

Desperate times for some. No. Desperate times for many.

He felt uncomfortable anyway, leaving the lab. He'd set things in motion. Sown seeds. As a last-minute thing, he'd ended up slipping a hastily scribbled note addressed to the Maddy unit into the embryo box that Waldstein had taken back to San

Francisco. And now he was beginning to panic, wondering whether he'd been stupid. There was no knowing for sure when, or even *if*, the team back in 2001 were going to discover the note, whether they were going to question the base office. If a message did come through from them, through that scrap of old paper, he wanted to intercept it before Waldstein saw it.

It was a relief right now that the old man was away in Denver on business. Olivera felt a mixture of guilt for betraying the man, and a desperate fear of him. Griggs . . . he still wasn't certain one way or the other about poor Frasier's fate. Perhaps his paranoia was getting the better of him; perhaps the poor fellow had just been unlucky.

The Saleena unit had been inserted back in the past now. And it wouldn't be long before her curious mind started picking away at the tiny new details edited into her consciousness. Between that bit of memory surgery and his handwritten note, Joseph felt he'd done as much as he could to unbalance things. Those three young clones weren't stupid. Far from it. Together, they were going to figure this all out one way or the other. Eventually.

And now perhaps he needed to find a way out for himself. Handing in his notice wasn't exactly going to wash with Waldstein. As the man had told him: 'Once you're in, Joseph, you're in. Do you understand?'

Perhaps he could plead mental exhaustion. Perhaps he could tell Waldstein he was beginning to make mistakes and it might be best if he took some kind of sabbatical? That sounded lame even before he tried saying it. He was so busy trying to find some way of phrasing a way to ask Waldstein to let him go that he failed to hear the soft scrape of a foot in the doorway. Olivera lurched suspiciously in his chair, like some mischievous little boy caught with his fingers in a sweetie jar.

'Joseph.'

It was Waldstein. Olivera felt his heart pounding in his chest. He hadn't been expecting the man to return this evening. 'Mr . . . Mr Waldstein. I . . . I thought you were still in Denver on business.'

'Indeed.' Waldstein's cool eyes remained on him.

Olivera looked away. Found something for his fidgeting hands to fiddle with on his desk. 'All . . . all s-sorted, then? The business?'

'Not really, no. I had to come back here early.'

Oliver nodded. 'Oh?' The old man looked tired, sad. 'Everything all right, Mr Waldstein?'

'No, Joseph. Not all right.'

No explanation. Just that. Olivera felt panic growing inside him. He dared not say anything in case his stutter betrayed him.

'I know,' said Waldstein after several interminable seconds.

'Know? Uh . . . know . . . know what?'

Waldstein shook his head slowly, the gesture very much like a father's disappointment with an errant child. 'I know you've been tampering with things.'

Olivera felt his stomach flop queasily. 'T-tamper?'

'You've edited the memories of Saleena. You added something to the unit that was sent back.' Waldstein noticed the faintest involuntary flicker of reaction on Joseph's face. 'Yes, Joseph . . . I've had the database tagged to alert me for updates to the source archive.' He spread his hands in a vaguely apologetic way. 'After Frasier let me down, I figured it might be prudent to keep a closer eye on you also.'

'I . . . I . . . needed to just . . . tidy up s-s-some continuity faults.'

'Please, Joseph . . .' he said, stepping into the lab and finding

187

a seat to ease himself down into. 'Please don't lie to me. I'm too tired for that now.' He sighed. 'You've not been fixing memory mismatches. You've added new content to her mind.'

Olivera couldn't help his jaw sagging. Perhaps that was less an admission of guilt than stuttering a denial at him.

'Why did you add the visual memory of a tumbling teddy bear to her recruitment memory, Joseph? Why?' Waldstein's eyes narrowed. 'What are you trying to tell her?'

The bear. Olivera realized Waldstein must have actually viewed the visual insert: the image of the blue bear tumbling end over end, almost defying gravity. So very deliberately conspicuous. The kind of visual image that would stick in a mind.

'It's a trigger memory, isn't it?'

Olivera felt his cheeks burn with shame. His face, his demeanour, his awkward shuffling were screaming his guilt out loud and, of course, Waldstein knew what he'd been up to anyway . . . if not the precise reason *why*.

'Yes,' Joseph said eventually.

'Joseph?' Waldstein said softly. 'Talk to me. Why the trigger memory?'

Olivera looked up at him.

He'd noticed the bear back in 2001, while he and Frasier had been setting the field office up. That curious antique shop not so far away had provided him with some of the props he'd needed to validate their various recruitment memories; the *Titanic* steward's uniform had given him the idea of setting Liam's recruitment aboard that famous doomed ship. A perfect recruitment fable. There'd been other things in various other shops that had helped him author *appropriate* life stories for each of them: the dark hoody with splashes of neon-orange Hindi-graffiti, that T-shirt with the Intel logo. *Real* things that would exist with them as they woke up in the archway. Real, tangible items that would help all three engineered units *bond* with their carefully scripted memories.

The bear . . . adding that bear to the replacement Saleena unit's memory was adding something that couldn't possibly be. The same bear in both places: Brooklyn 2001, Mumbai 2026. A clear, unambiguous impossibility.

A trigger.

'Why, Joseph?'

'Why?' Olivera felt slightly emboldened. His game was up. No more lying. Somehow so very liberating. 'Let me ask you that, s-sir. Why?'

Waldstein frowned. 'Why what?'

'Why do you want mankind to destroy itself?'

'What the hell are you talking about, Joseph?'

'I know . . . I know about *Pandora*.'

The word caused Waldstein to shift uneasily.

'I know it's s-some kind of codeword you have, isn't it? A codeword for the end of mankind. The day . . . the precise date we destroy ourselves. That's it, isn't it?'

'This has come from Frasier, hasn't it? This is *his* nonsense, isn't it?'

'Pandora. The end of the world . . . that's what you s-saw, isn't it?'

'What I saw?'

There was something comforting about unburdening himself like this. Olivera realized he was already so far over a certain invisible line that there was nothing he could say that was going to make any difference now. Either he was going to be instantly dismissed from the project, escorted out of the compound . . . or . . . or perhaps worse.

'You're actually asking me what I *saw* back in 2044?' Waldstein eyed him cautiously. 'Is that what you're asking me? What I saw that very first time?'

Olivera nodded hesitantly. 'You . . . you didn't . . . go back in time, did you? You didn't go back to s-see your . . . wife, your s-son?'

Waldstein shook his head slowly. 'Oh, Joseph . . . please don't ask me what I saw.'

'You went forward. You went *forward* in time. You . . .'

'What?' He smiled. 'I went forward in time to see if mankind makes it through these hard times? To see if mankind is as stupid and self-destructive as it appears to be?'

Olivera nodded.

'And what? All this?' He gestured at the small lab. 'This project of ours, the businesses I've built up, the technology companies I've been acquiring, buying, the billions of dollars I've made . . . all of this, just to make sure it happens? Just to make certain mankind wipes itself out?' Waldstein's voice rose in pitch. A note of incredulity. 'Are you seriously suggesting all of that is so I can ensure the end of the road for mankind?'

Olivera nodded again.

'Oh, Joseph . . .' That look of disappointment on his face again. He eased himself up off the seat. 'You have no idea. Not even the slightest idea. God help me! I'm not trying to *destroy* us . . . I'm trying to *save* us.' He sighed as he stepped back towards the lab's doorway. 'Or at least save what I can of us . . . what there is to save.'

Olivera had a sense that this was where their conversation met its logical conclusion. No bartering. No pretending. No back-out clause. This was the place they were at. 'Mr Waldstein? What . . . what happens now?'

Waldstein backed up several steps. Turned and said something softly to someone who must have been standing outside, just out of sight.

'Who's . . . Mr Wald-s-stein. Who's out there? Who're you talking to?'

A tall, muscular figure appeared behind the old man, completely bald, with the calm dispassionate face of a recently birthed support unit.

'I'm so very sorry, Joseph.' Waldstein looked back at him with sadness in his eyes. 'I'm truly sorry that it has to be this way . . .'

In a heartbeat he was certain of Griggs's fate. Murdered. Not by some gang of starving vagrants but by Waldstein. Directly or indirectly. The old man had made sure Frasier Griggs wasn't going to remain a dangerous loose end.

And now I'm dead.

He backed up a step, past his own workstation to what used to be Griggs's workstation.

'Joseph,' said Waldstein, 'please don't make this harder than it has to be. Come here.'

'You . . . you don't n-need to do this. Please . . . you don't –'

'But here's the problem – I can't *trust* you any more.' There was genuine sadness on Waldstein's face. 'Do you see? I couldn't trust Frasier either. And that's the important thing. This is too important, Joseph. More important than Frasier, than you . . . than me even.'

Joseph eyed the holo-display shimmering inches above the mess of Griggs's desk. He'd been looking through those folders of his ex-colleague's that *hadn't* been code-locked. Frasier had been recently pinhole-viewing history. One of his unofficial hobbies. He rather liked to discreetly spy on favourite historical moments, particularly civil-war history. Joseph had once caught him glimpsing the final moment of the Battle of Gettysburg, as

General Pickett's Virginians had finally withered under the barrage of musket fire, broke and routed. Then another time Frasier had been listening to Abraham Lincoln give his famous Gettysburg Address.

'Tell me,' pleaded Joseph, 'what's so important? Tell me!'

Waldstein sighed. 'If that I could, Joseph . . . if only I could . . .'

Joseph shot another glance at the display. The pinhole-viewer interface was in standby mode, as Griggs had left it last time he'd used it. The displacement machine was fully charged after having sent back the Saleena unit. Good to go, ready to dispense its stored energy. He just needed to open the interface, dilate the pinhole, three feet, four feet. That's all. It would be enough.

'W-why c-can't you tell me, Mr . . .Mr Waldstein? Maybe, m-maybe if you explained –'

'Explain Pandora to you? Explain why mankind has to wipe himself out?' Waldstein smiled sadly. 'I explain that to you . . . and what? All of a sudden I'll be able to trust you unreservedly?'

Joseph nodded. Perhaps too eagerly. His mind was on something else, though. Calculating escape.

'I'm sorry, Joseph. What has to happen is my burden, my burden alone, and I'll burn in hell forever for what I know has to be done.' The old man looked like he was crying. 'Good God, Joseph . . . you don't want to know what's in my head. Trust me!'

Three feet, just about wide enough for him to dive through. But . . . but . . . he had no idea what time-stamp, if any, was already set in the location buffer. He looked up at the support unit, still standing obediently just behind Waldstein. On a word of command it could be across the small lab in seconds, not enough time for him to pick out and tap the coordinates for a safe, density-verified location.

Oh God help me . . . If nothing was in the entry buffer, he'd end up in chaos space. That horrific nothingness. A swiftly crushed neck at the hands of the unit standing behind Waldstein would be infinitely preferable, surely?

'It all has to end, Joseph. In that way. Pandora. Only then will they let it happen.'

They?

'Let what . . . what h-happen? Who . . . who are you talking about?'

'I'm sorry, Joseph. The time for talking is over.' He turned to the support unit and nodded.

The support unit pushed past Waldstein, strode round a table cluttered with Joseph's mind-map charts and printouts of gene-memory data templates.

Not daring to think what horror awaited him if the time-stamp entry buffer was empty, Joseph's finger hovered over the COMMIT touch button on the holo-display. A warning flashed on the screen that a pinhole was now activated. The air near him pulsated subtly. It was there . . . but so small it was invisible. On the lab floor, yellow and black chevron tape marked out a safety square, a place not to enter while a pinhole was active. Walking through a pinhole would be like being shot by a high-calibre round – a tangent carved through the body and sent elsewhere, no different to the path of a speeding bullet, blasting a hole right through a body and depositing what it had eviscerated out the other side.

'My God!' Waldstein's eyes widened as he understood what Joseph intended to do. *'DON'T DO IT!'*

Joseph tapped a command in, an instruction to widen the pinhole.

The support unit picked up on the urgency in Waldstein's voice and leaped towards Joseph. The pinhole instantaneously inflated, from apparently nothing to a shimmering, floating orb a yard wide. Joseph turned towards it, time enough in the half second left to see that the churning, oily display was showing something more than featureless white. It was showing somewhere. *Somewhere.*

Not chaos space. Good enough.

He instinctively cradled his head and dived into the shimmering orb, tucking his legs up, his elbows in, to be sure he left none of them behind. In the last moment before entering it he was screaming. A wail of panic, a long, strangled bellow of defiance and fear. Most definitely fear.

This is insane!

As his head entered that swirling escape window – a window that could mean safety or death in any number of unpleasant ways – he thought he could make out the shape of horses. A wagon. Barrels.

At least it wasn't all white, right?

At least there was that.

CHAPTER 36

15 September 2001, Arlington, Massachusetts

Rosalin Kellerman stared at the man in a smart business suit standing on her doorstep, and a woman beside him. A striking young woman, with startling grey eyes, wide and intense, wearing a loose gentleman's checked shirt, several sizes too big for her but tucked into tightly fitting jeans. Athletic. But *striking* . . . in that her head was shaved almost down to the skin. And yet somehow she was still quite beautiful. Just like that Irish rock singer-songwriter from the eighties . . . what was her name? *Sinead* something or other.

'This is number 45?' he asked again.

Rosalin shrugged and pointed at the brass number plaque on her green door. 'Uh . . . well, there's the number right there! See it?'

'And this is your residence?' asked the man.

Rosalin narrowed her eyes. This was already becoming a peculiar encounter. And not the first one she'd had in the last few days.

'Have you received a visit from a stranger recently?' The man seemed to immediately realize that was a stupidly vague question. He pulled something out of his jacket pocket. A photograph. Held it up so she could see it. 'A visit from this person?'

Rosalin recognized the face. The oval-shaped chin, the glasses, the frizzy, strawberry-blonde hair. Oh yeah, she remembered this girl all right.

'You mind telling me what the hell this is all about?'

The man smiled. 'You've seen her, haven't you?'

'Yeah . . . she came knocking a couple of days ago.' Rosalin shook her head. 'Crazy. I was pretty stupid. I really shouldn't have let her in.'

'You spoke with her?' asked the intense young woman in the checked shirt.

'You kidding?' Rosalin snorted a laugh. 'I couldn't get a word in.'

'Mom!'

Rosalin heard the alarm in her daughter's voice and put down the tray of cakes on the counter, vaguely aware that the oven-hot tray was going to leave marks on the Formica, but Nadine's shrill cry sounded unsettling.

She stepped into the hallway to see that a girl, a teenager, pale and scruffy, had pushed her way into the house past her daughter Nadine.

'What the hell do you think you're doing?'

'This is my . . . my home!' cried the girl.

Oh my God . . . maybe she's a drug addict. Maybe she's after money?

'Get out! Get out of my house right now! Or I'll call the police!'

The girl ignored her. Turned to the left and took the stairs up to the landing, three at a time.

'Hey!' called Rosalin after her. 'Get back down here!' No answer. 'OUT! GET OUT OF MY HOUSE!'

Nadine was looking frightened. 'Mom? Who is she?'

'It's all right, honey. You stay down here.' She started up the stairs after the teenager.

'Mom? Don't go up there. Please!'

'It's all right, honey. You stay down here.' The young woman – no, not a *woman*, a kid still, really – didn't look dangerous as such. Just confused and frightened. 'Stay down there, Nadine. I'll just go up and speak to her.'

At the top of the stairs she could hear the teenager had gone into Nadine's bedroom. She could hear movement from in there. Movement . . . and now, what was that? Sobbing?

She approached the open door, spilling afternoon light out from Nadine's room across the hallway carpet. And there, sitting on the end of her bed, was the teenager, rocking gently, her face buried in her hands.

All of a sudden bellowing at this kid to get out before she set the cops on her seemed like overkill. She clearly wasn't a danger to anyone. She certainly didn't need to be cuffed like a gangster and rough-handled into the back of a squad car.

'Hello?' Rosalin said softly. 'Can I help you?'

That had happened two days ago. Now Rosalin looked at the smart young man and the striking, shaven-headed woman sitting side by side on her couch. The young man had shown her an FBI pass and said his name was Agent Cooper. The young woman he'd introduced as Agent Faith.

A cafetière was steaming on the coffee table in front of them, untouched. Rosalin had no idea why she'd offered them coffee. Maybe she was just as curious about that poor girl as they were.

'And what did she tell you?' asked Agent Faith.

'All sorts of crazy nonsense really. I thought she was drunk or on drugs or something.'

'What *specifically* did she tell you?' asked Agent Cooper. Rosalin preferred him asking. At least he smiled kindly. The woman on the other hand, Agent Faith, was like a goddamned robot. Face like an emotionless psychopath.

'She said some crazy things . . . like she was from the future. That she'd died in a plane crash or something in 2010, but someone saved her from the plane.'

'Saved her . . . ?'

'She said the plane was in mid-air. She said she was "beamed out".'

'Beamed out?' Cooper laughed politely. 'What? Like *Star Trek* beamed out?'

'I don't know what she meant exactly. It wasn't making much sense to me.' Rosalin shrugged. 'That's when I figured she wasn't a druggy, but maybe some sort of sick person, you know? On medication or something?'

'Indeed.'

'She said she got beamed back from the future, from 2010, to now. And was working for some sort of time police. Trying to stop people from the future time travelling.' Rosalin laughed self-consciously. It was the kind of make-believe game her youngest son played with his friends, tearing round the kitchen with plastic laser guns and making *whoop-whoop* noises.

'The girl is deluded,' said Agent Faith. 'None of this is correct.'

'Sure, of course,' Rosalin nodded. 'But . . .'

'But what?' asked Agent Cooper.

'But . . . she was saying things that sounded so . . .' She shrugged. '*Convincing*, I guess.'

Cooper sat forward. 'Such as?'

'Well . . . let's see.' Rosalin narrowed her eyes. 'Oh yeah, she said that we'll be going to war with Iraq again. And after that with some other country called Afganistan-izan or something.

She said some other weird things . . . can't remember them, though. Just odd stuff.' Rosalin shook her head. As that girl had sobbed and told her story, she'd almost found herself believing some of it.

'Did she explain why she came to *your* house?' asked Cooper.

'Oh yes . . . yes. That was the strangest thing of all. She said she had memories of living here in this house. I mean . . . living here right now. In 2001. That she'd lived here as a girl with her mom and dad. That she remembered the house looking very different on the inside and —'

'But she's never in fact lived here?'

Rosalin shook her head. 'No! We've been living here since before Nadine was born. Since 1990.'

'And this girl is in no way related to you?'

'No! Look, of course not! I've never seen her before!' Rosalin looked at the coffee. It wasn't going to get drunk. 'I told her that. Told her that we've been living here for more than ten years . . . that's when she went funny.'

'Funny?'

Rosalin recalled the girl had abruptly stopped mid-sentence, as if something in her mind had suddenly snapped. Discovered a hidden touchstone of truth. 'She just got up and left. Walked out of the house, sort of in a trance or something.'

'And she's not been back since?'

'No. Like I said, that was a couple of days ago.'

Agent Cooper nodded and offered her another charming smile. 'Well, Mrs Kellerman, thank you for talking to us.' He shrugged apologetically as he stood up. 'And for the coffee. I'm sure it was very nice coffee.'

The woman followed her colleague's lead and both agents headed towards the hallway and the front door.

'But one thing I don't understand,' said Rosalin. 'Why are

the FBI after her? I mean . . . you know . . . if she's just some kid who needs help?'

Agent Cooper shrugged that question away. But his female partner stopped dead.

'See, I'm . . . well, I've got a journalist coming over later today,' continued Rosalin. 'I called the *National Enquirer*.' She bit her lip, slightly embarrassed. 'I know it's a stupid newspaper. They run stupid My-Uncle-is-an-Alien-from-Mars stories . . . but they pay pretty well for them.'

Agent Faith turned to look at her. 'You will be telling this story to a newspaper?'

Rosalin nodded guiltily. 'Is that, uh . . . you know, a problem?'

Faith's movement was little more than a blur. The dull crack of a single gunshot was reverberating around the home's hallway before Agent Cooper fully realized she'd reached under his jacket and wrenched out his standard-issue firearm and used it.

Mrs Kellerman was dead before her legs buckled and she dropped to the floor. Blood trickled from a tidy dark hole between her carefully plucked eyebrows and pooled on the waxed wooden parquet slats beneath her head.

'Jesus! *What —?*'

'She was a contamination risk.'

Cooper realized he was trembling. 'You . . . can't . . . you can't just go and shoot —'

'My primary mission parameter is to eliminate the agency team. My secondary mission parameter is to ensure no significant time-contamination events occur.'

She handed the gun back to him.

'Thank you for the use of your weapon, Agent Cooper.'

CHAPTER 37

16 September 2001, Interstate 90, Newton, Massachusetts

So that's what we all are. Machines. Meat robots, just like Bob and Becks. Everything me, Maddy and Liam remember from before arriving in that archway is just a dream. Not even that, just faked memories.

I'm not Saleena Vikram.

I'm not from 2026.

I'm not from India.

I don't have parents.

I'm a meat product.

Sal wondered why she was even bothering to write in her diary. She'd started out writing in it because she thought it would help her keep her sanity. But why bother now when her mind wasn't even *hers* anyway? It was the product of some technician or team of technicians. A faked backstory. An amalgam of images.

I'm even beginning to wonder if some or all of the stuff that happened to us since we became TimeRiders is faked memories too. I mean, how do I know for sure? Maybe we never had a German New York, or that nuclear wasteland? Maybe those dinosaur things never broke into the archway? Maybe I never met Abraham Lincoln? Maybe someone invented those stories?

Another slightly more comforting thought occurred to her:

maybe there never was a pitiful eugenic creature called Sam, massacred along with several dozen others before her very eyes. Somehow that seemed a small kindness; a teaspoon of comfort in an ocean of cruel.

That blue bear. I think I get it now. Somebody put that into my memory by mistake. I wasn't meant to see it in that Brooklyn shop. Because how could it also be in India, twenty-five years from now? Someone messed up. Made a mistake. All this time, these weeks I've been wondering about whether that bear meant something special, whether it was important. And guess what? It was just someone's dumb mistake.

She shook her head. 'Jahulla.'

No one was going to hear her, standing in this place, alone, watching the endless traffic pass beneath her. The overpass ran across six lanes of interstate traffic. Cars, trucks, buses: a constant stream of on-off-on red braking lights on the right and glaring headlights on the left, some so bright they cast stars and streaks across her tear-wet eyes. A stream of traffic in the early evening, all of them on their way to or from meaningful appointments, running errands, returning from work, going shopping. Routine events. Life. Dull maybe, but at least it was *real* life.

She looked down at the dog-eared notebook resting on the pedestrian railing. Dozens and dozens of pages of her small handwriting. Scribbles and sketches she'd made of the team. The page corners flickered and lifted, teased by a gentle breeze. And, by the clinical cyan light of one of the overpass's fizzing street lights, she studied one particular sketch. A drawing she'd made of Liam playing chess with Bob. The pair of them hunkered over a chessboard placed on a packing crate table in the narrow space between the bunk beds.

Is that real? Did that really happen? She remembered it all right. Remembered that Liam got fed up with being beaten by Bob over and over and had finally cursed in Irish and wandered over to play on the Nintendo machine instead. But how much of that was real? How much, if at all, could she trust the memory?

She turned a page. There was a sketch of one of those lizard-sapiens, the bipedal descendants of a dinosaur species that should never have survived.

And did that happen? She was almost certain it had. In fact, she was pretty certain that everything she'd recorded in this notebook must be real. It was surely the things that had occurred *before* these memories on paper; everything that had occurred before she'd awoken in that archway . . . all of those things – they were the lie.

Sal looked down at the notebook in front of her, the pages flapping loosely. She'd been considering tossing it over the handrail. Perhaps it would land on the flat open bed of a lorry or rubbish truck to be carried away to some distant landfill site and buried forever. But then she realized this book of scruffy lined pages full of untidy scrawls was all that was keeping her rooted to sanity. In a way, this paper and ink was her mind. Her real mind. It was all that she had, all that she really owned. It was everything that made her . . . *her.*

It was all that she could trust.

I love you, notebook. She wrote that at the bottom of one page. *You are me.*

She wrote that, then drew a box around the last three words as if it might protect that single thought for all eternity. A little blue biro-ink force field.

Liam flicked through channels absently. He lay on his motel room bed and was steadfastly working his way through a packet of Oreos.

'Is this it, then?' said Rashim. He'd been in the motorhome for most of this afternoon, picking through the critical circuit boards pulled from the displacement machine and, with SpongeBubba's help, working his way through the terabytes of data stored on the hard drives that had been pulled out of the networked computers. Thanks to that process he had a much clearer idea of the ordeal these three teenagers had been through over the last few months of their lives, and now had a fair idea of how their little agency worked together to preserve history. He was making notes, scribbling away on a pad of foolscap. He didn't even look up as he spoke.

'Is this the plan? We stay in these rooms until what? The end of time?'

Liam shrugged. He didn't know what happened next. The last two days had been a strange, disembodied experience. He'd been lost in his own thoughts. Eaten once or twice maybe and he couldn't remember what. He vaguely recalled taking a long walk – hours and hours alongside a busy highway – then finally coming to a halt, turning round and walking back the way he'd come.

'There's no more money,' said Rashim. 'We will have to leave here soon anyway.'

Liam flicked through channels, hardly hearing the man talk. Sal, he'd hardly seen her all day. And Maddy? Not since last night.

The team was no more. Broken into shards. Just three lost individuals, three young adults lost in their own troubled clouds of thought. His mind kept playing the last thing he remembered from his 'supposed' old life: that passageway down on deck E of the *Titanic*, rapidly filling up with freezing cold seawater. Being certain that the rest of his life was going to be measured in mere seconds. And then Foster – his older self – like some benign bigger brother, a kindly uncle, offering a hand to him, offering him a choice. Offering him a way out.

All of that was a faked memory. A montage of images. He even thought he recognized where some of the visual elements of his memory had come from now. He'd seen a film with the girls on one of those silvery discs: a film about the *Titanic* – in fact, it was simply called *Titanic*. There'd been some boyish man called Leonardo Something-or-other playing the hero. And yes . . . some of the images had been almost a perfect match to parts of his hazy memory. It was as if a patchwork quilt had been made from that film and others, from eyewitness accounts, from historical records and encyclopaedia articles . . . and dumped into his head with some crude adjustments to make him the star of that film and not that Leonardo fellow.

I'm not even Irish.

He sighed. And yet, if he'd said that aloud, it would have been with an Irish accent.

He wished Foster was still alive. The old man must have experienced this moment himself. At some point in the past, perhaps while working with the team before them, he must have found out what he was. That he wasn't a lad called Liam O'Connor. And yet he'd pulled through, hadn't he? He'd survived that appalling moment of truth and moved on from it. Accepted it.

And he'd changed his name. It made sense. He couldn't still be called Liam and recruit the *new* Liam. It would be too much of a clue. A giveaway to the truth.

He'd even managed to change his accent.

'Jay-zus.'

Rashim looked up from his notes. 'What's up?'

Liam shook his head. 'Nothing . . . I was just . . .' His voice trailed away into silence.

Foster had still believed in the job. Even though he knew he'd been lied to, set up, manipulated, *exploited* by this agency . . . he still believed the job needed doing. What was that? *Programmed* loyalty? Was that it? Had the mysterious Mr Waldstein written into his mind a mission priority that even if he was to discover that he was a meatbot and that he'd been lied to and exploited, his first instinct would always be to continue doing the job?

Just like Bob. Just like Becks. Both of them standing outside in the car park keeping an eye out for Maddy. Duty first. Always.

The door handle rattled and the door opened, spilling sickly green light from the motel's glowing VACANT sign outside across the room's mottled carpet. Bob's wide frame filled the doorway.

Speak of the devil.

'She is back,' he rumbled. He stepped aside and Maddy appeared in the doorway. She waved limply.

'Hey, Liam.'

'Hey.'

She turned to Becks, standing outside. 'Go next door and wake up Sal.'

'Affirmative.'

To Liam's eyes she seemed a little more alert than when he'd last seen her. If he hadn't been so lost in his own self-pity last night, he might have been worried about her state of mind. Worried that she hadn't come back. Worried she'd gone and done something silly.

'You OK, Mads? Where've you been?'

'Getting my head straight.'

He heard the door in the next room *snick* shut and Sal appeared beside Maddy, bleary-eyed, looking as if she'd just been roused from sleep.

'We're leaving,' said Maddy.

'Leaving?'

'We've had a couple of days of freakin' navel-gazing, feeling sorry for ourselves.' She pushed a frizzy spiral of hair away from her face. 'OK, so we're clones. We're meatbots.' She shrugged her shoulders. 'I dunno, maybe when we've got ourselves sorted one of us should stick our heads in an X-ray machine and see if we've got frikkin' microchips inside us like Bob and Becks. But that's . . . that's for another time, I guess.'

Liam grimaced, remembering hacking open Bob's skull, months ago, in order to pull out that tiny shard of silicon in there.

'Yeah, I know. Not exactly a nice thought,' said Maddy. 'Well, like I say . . . maybe it's on the To Do list, or maybe I just don't wanna know, but right now I say we're done with the sulking. OK? That's enough self-pity. We need to sort ourselves out. Get things up and running again.'

CHAPTER 38

16 September 2001, Interstate 90, Newton, Massachusetts

Sal's bleary eyes widened. 'We're carrying on?'

'Damn right we are.'

Maddy ushered Sal and Becks inside the motel room and closed the door after them. Not that there was anyone out there in the car park to eavesdrop – a row of empty chalets and a gravel lot with only their Winnebago SuperChief parked in the middle. All the same . . .

'If it's just us keeping history on track, and no one else –' she scratched the back of her head – 'then we've got to keep it up. We've got no choice.'

'But we *do* have a choice,' said Sal. 'We don't have to get involved any more.'

'Aye.' Liam nodded. 'Let it all go to hell as far as I'm concerned. If that's the way history wants to take itself then stuff it. Let it.'

'Dammit, Liam!' snapped Maddy. 'This is serious!'

'And I AM being serious!' He sat up on his bed. 'I . . . I'm not sure I care any more.' He got up, took a challenging step towards Maddy. 'This isn't our world! Do you not see that? We don't have families to worry about . . . friends . . . loved ones. None of us have ever had any of that. Just memories of someone else's families! So, honest-to-God,' he said, shrugging, 'what do I care if a time wave rubs out this whole world?

Ireland? Cork . . . and everyone I was supposed to "know" living there?'

Sal nodded. 'He's right, Maddy. We are nothing. We have nothing. No, like, descendants. No ancestors. No family tree. Nothing!' A faint and weary smile stole across her lips as if something had finally made sense to her. 'I suppose that's why we've always been sort of unaffected by the waves we've been through.'

'Because none of you are *of* this timeline? None of you belong in this timeline.' Rashim stroked the tip of his nose, thinking aloud. 'All three of you are an artificial intrusion not susceptible to any cause—effect cycle.' He nodded, satisfied with his train of thought. 'That would explain how you were never changed by time waves.'

'Yeah, I s'pose that's what I mean,' Sal added. 'We don't belong, so we don't get changed.'

Liam wasn't so interested in that. 'Maddy, why should I care? Huh?' He shrugged. 'Time waves? As far as I'm concerned, they're now someone else's problem, so they are.' He laughed humourlessly. 'Jay-zus . . . I don't even know why I speak this way. This accent. I've never even *been* to Ireland!'

Maddy had had enough. She reached out and grabbed a fistful of his shirt. 'Liam, you bubble-head! You don't need to have been to Ireland . . . to be you. Don't you see that?' She turned to Sal. 'Both of you! Me too! We're who we are *because* of these memories. That's the same for everyone. Memories . . . define every person on this planet.' She had a silent audience, but no one seemed to know where she was taking this.

'We're defined by our memories. We're the *product* of our memories. That's it.'

She glanced at both support units – living proof of that. Both of them so much more than the emotionless automatons that had slid out of their grow-tubes on to the floor.

'So who freakin' well cares if the bag of memories in our heads are *ours* or *someone else's*? We're here in this place right now, together, and we're making our own decisions and goddammit that makes us *real*!'

'Not all of your memories are false,' added Becks to the long silence.

Maddy looked at the small frame of the support unit beside her. 'You're right.' She turned back to the others, particularly Liam and Sal. She let go of his shirt. 'We've been real people since we woke up together all those months ago. Real people!' She patted down his puffed-up shirt gently, apologetically. '*Real* people . . .' She smiled at them both. '*Real* friends.' She grasped his arm affectionately. '*Real family*.'

Sal nodded silently. Maddy thought she caught a glint of the green of the neon sign outside reflected in her eyes, the glint of a tear perhaps.

'We need to continue doing the job, guys. Come on . . . we've seen some of the horrific results time travel can produce. I don't suppose we've even seen the worst it can do. Not yet.'

Liam gazed thoughtfully out of the window.

Sal too. 'I hated how those poor eugenic creatures were treated.'

Maddy nodded. 'And we made that nightmare world *not* happen.'

The TV still burbled quietly in the corner of the motel room.

'I don't see we've got much of a choice,' said Maddy. 'We have to carry on. No one else is doing it and someone has to grab the wheel, right? Someone needs to be holding the goddamn steering wheel or this world crashes and burns!'

She winced a little at her metaphor. It sounded like typical

Hollywood shtick. But whatever. The point was valid. 'We need to continue doing this job . . . but this time, let's do it for ourselves. Not for –' she made air quotes with her fingers – 'the agency. Not for Waldstein. But for ourselves. We decide if and when history needs fixing.'

'You mean . . .' Liam frowned. 'You mean, if a better timeline comes along . . . ?'

Maddy knew what he was suggesting. 'Yeah! If it looks like a happier, shinier, funkier world,' she said with a shrug, 'why not? We'll decide ourselves if intervention is required.'

She noticed Bob stirring. 'Bob?'

'That contradicts a primary protocol.'

'Remember what Foster said?' added Sal. 'For good or bad, history has to go a certain way?'

'Aye, he did that.'

'Has to go a certain way, huh?' Maddy turned to Rashim. 'And just remind us how history goes, Dr Anwar?'

He grinned edgily as all eyes rested on him. 'I . . . I, uh, don't really think I should be involved with this argument.'

'Tell them!'

'Well, you know already. The world's not too good actually. A systemic collapse of –'

'Right. We heat the world until the ice caps melt and about a third of the land is flooded. Then we poison what's left of the world with chemicals until there's no ecosystem left that's worth a damn. Then, not happy with all of that, we decide to wipe ourselves out with some kind of Von Neumann virus that leaves nothing left alive. That about right, Rashim?'

'They were calling the virus *Kosong-ni*. That's where it started. Ground zero.' Rashim nodded. 'That's a somewhat simplified version of events, but essentially, yes, that's it.'

'And that's what Foster –' she splayed her hands – 'that's what

211

Waldstein . . . wants us to do our very best to *preserve*? Anyone here think that might be just a little freakin' stupid?'

'To be fair,' said Liam, 'Foster was just following some orders.'

'You're right, Liam.' She smiled at him. 'He was just like you . . .'

'He *was* me.'

'Right. And he was just doing what he thought was the right thing to do. Like you, Liam – heart always in the right place.' She rested a hand on him again. Genuine affection. 'Always in the right place, Liam, doing what duty calls for. But maybe we've been wrong all along to follow Waldstein's directive.' She took her glasses off the bridge of her nose.

'I've been doing some thinking. I think that codeword, Pandora . . . I think that was a warning to us. A warning that we're doing the wrong thing.' Maddy was reluctant to take her thoughts a step further. But the logic was right there and needed to be said out loud.

'Maybe we've been doing the dirty work of someone not quite right in the head. Someone who quite simply is insane.'

'Waldstein?'

She shrugged. 'He set this agency up. And Bob? Didn't you say those support units trying to kill us came from the same place as you?'

'Affirmative. W.G. Systems software.'

She looked at the others. 'Maybe Waldstein sent them to kill us?' A further thought occurred to her. 'Maybe when I sent that message asking about Pandora, when I sent that ad to the newspaper . . . that's what triggered all of this?'

The air in the room all of a sudden felt very charged.

'We were never meant to know how bad the world gets,' said Liam. 'Were we?'

'And now Waldstein knows we know . . . ?' She pursed her lips, focusing on the lenses she was unnecessarily scrubbing clean. Still thinking things through. 'We can't be relied on any more. We're a loose cog.' She put her glasses back on. 'Not fit for purpose.'

'Jahulla!' whispered Sal. 'He wants to wipe us out and start again!'

Maddy turned to Bob. 'If we changed our mission goals . . . where does that leave us, Bob? Does your core programming mean you'd have to attempt to stop us?' She turned to Becks. 'Kill us?'

Both support units looked at each other.

Bob finally spoke. Maddy wondered whether he was speaking on behalf of the pair of them. Probably. Becks would defer to him right now. Her mind, after all, was a pale reflection of his. 'On previous occasions, I have been able to override hard-coded mission parameters.'

'And? So, this time?'

His thick brow lowered and became a monobrow of intense thought. A long pause of deliberation. Finally he spoke. 'I am able to comply with a new mission directive.' He stared at her intently. 'And what is your new directive?'

'To, uh . . . to stop Pandora?' There was a tremulous, questioning tone in Maddy's voice, worried that somewhere deep in his coconut head a logic gate might flip its state at what she'd just suggested and Bob might suddenly leap across the room and rip her head off.

'Your stated intention is to prevent the future event codenamed Pandora from occurring?'

She nodded slowly. 'That's kind of it. Yeah. You know . . . save the world?' She winced as Bob's forehead creased with thought and his eyes seemed to disappear into the shadow cast by his thick Neanderthal brow.

'What do you think? Bob? That OK with you?'

'The original mission goal of preserving the destruction of the world and humankind appears to be an illogical mission goal,' he announced finally. Maddy let out a breath she hadn't realized she'd been holding for the best part of a minute. 'Becks?'

She nodded; her mind had processed the same information and arrived at the same answer. 'With the information that Dr Rashim Anwar has provided us of the future, the previous directive appears to make no sense.'

'If that's your plan, Maddy, if you wish to work against the goal of your agency then you need to be somewhere else entirely,' said Rashim. 'You need to get as far away from here as possible. Another place, maybe even another time. You know that, don't you?' Maddy knew.

'If you really are what you think you are . . . *engineered units*,' he said that carefully, desperate not to cause offence, 'then if Waldstein's after you, he will, I'm sure, have all your pre-inception date memories on file. He'll know everything there is to know about you.'

Liam stirred. 'Pre-inception?'

'Before our recruitment,' clarified Maddy. 'Our so-called life stories.'

'Right,' said Rashim. 'He'll certainly guess you've come up here to find your family, Maddy. He . . . or more of his support units . . . could be close by, closing in on us as we speak.'

'You're right.'

'A new base for us to set up?' Liam's clouded face seemed to brighten a little.

'Yup, new home. New mission.'

'I'm not sure I get what our mission is, though,' said Sal.

Maddy wasn't a hundred per cent sure herself. To make Pandora NOT happen. Yes, that . . . but also to continue, in some moderated way, the mission they used to have: to make sure no reckless time traveller set this world hurtling towards another nightmare timeline.

'We're going to make the call, Sal. We're going to take control of history. We're going to steer it so the world gets a future where we don't kill ourselves off. Where we don't completely trash this planet.'

Liam nodded. 'Now that makes a bit more sense to me, so.'

Even Sal perked up a little bit. 'But if we're moving on to somewhere else . . . aren't we going to need some more money, or something?'

'Aye,' said Liam. 'We've nearly run out.'

'True.' Maddy shrugged. 'I guess we better think about where we're going to get some more, then.'

CHAPTER 39

16 September 2001, Interstate 90, Westfield, Massachusetts

Bob held the gun up at the man behind the counter. The sock pulled over his large head was far too small and stretched so taut that his thick horse-lips were mashed against his teeth and squished back into a hideous leer, halfway between a snarl and a grin.

'I 'eed you to 'ive 'e all your 'oney!'

The old Korean man behind the counter shrugged. 'What you say?'

'I 'AID . . . I 'EED YOU TO 'IVE 'E ALL YOUR 'ONEY!' Bob's voice boomed across the racks of convenience goods in the petrol station. A trucker taking his pick from some microwavable snacks in a fridge unit looked their way.

Liam lifted his own sock up to reveal his nose and mouth. 'Excuse the big fella, he's not so good with a sock on his head.'

'This is *robbery*?'

'Aye, yes . . . yes, I'm afraid it is.' Liam shrugged guiltily. 'Really sorry about that. We're going to need some of that money in your till there.'

The old man nodded, understanding. 'Ah . . .' and then ducked down out of sight.

'Uh?' Liam hadn't been expecting the old man to be quite so co-operative. He looked at Bob. 'Well, that wasn't so hard.'

A moment later the old man reappeared holding a rusty old Korean model AK47 held together by duct tape. 'YOU LEAVE NOW!' he yelled, his finger resting on the trigger and looking dangerously like he was halfway pulling on it.

'Maybe we should –'

The gun went off, five rapid-fire rounds before the old weapon clicked. Jammed. Several polystyrene ceiling tiles exploded in showers of plastic snow, most of the bullets whistling past them. But one caused a puff of crimson to erupt from the side of Bob's head; an ear, almost completely intact, flew across the racks and landed among the refrigerated snacks not too far from the trucker.

Bob shouldered their shotgun.

'Hoy! No!' Liam pushed the barrel up as the weapon boomed. The rack of cigarettes behind the old man's head exploded with a shower of tobacco shreds and paper.

'Just get that till!' barked Liam.

Bob passed the gun to Liam, leaned over and grabbed the till embedded firmly in a counter housing. Plywood cracked and splintered, chocolate bars and scratch cards spilled on to the floor as Bob shook the till vigorously. The whole counter unit was lifted clean off the floor. With a loud crack, the till pulled free and the counter crashed back down again.

'Sorry 'bout the mess there!' Liam grimaced, before he pulled the sock back down over his mouth.

Maddy had only just finished filling the motorhome when she heard the rattle of gunfire inside the petrol station's convenience store. Another shot, deeper, the boom of a shotgun. Then a second later what sounded like a bull charging around inside.

'Oh Jesus!' she whispered. 'I said be discreet!' They were

meant to be holding the store up for some quick cash, not levelling the place to the ground.

A moment later she saw Liam emerging, followed by Bob carrying something that looked almost as big as a bank safe in his arms.

'Becks!' she called out. 'We're leaving! Now!'

The Winnebago's engine started up with a roar of an accelerator pedal pushed down too hard – Becks's first go behind the wheel.

Liam tumbled up the steps inside, Sal helping him up. He collapsed on to the seat at the back, hyperventilating. Bob followed him inside and tossed the till on to the floor. The vehicle rocked on its loose suspension under the heavy impact. SpongeBubba wobbled and lost his footing.

'Woo-hoo!' he chirped merrily on his back, stubby paddle feet whirring ineffectually in the air.

Maddy slammed the door shut on them, cursing under her breath as she ran along the outside of the motorhome, pulled open the passenger side door and clambered up on to the seat beside Becks. 'Go! Go! GO!!'

Becks eased the gearstick into Drive and the SuperChief bucked forward like an eager racehorse let out of a trap. The front of the RV clipped the rear of the rig parked up beside the petrol pump next door, sending showers of sparks and a twisted aluminium bumper across the forecourt.

Becks spun the big wheel round, finally regaining control of the Winnebago as they barrelled out of the petrol station's exit ramp and up the slip road on to the interstate. At least at this time of night they weren't roaring up only to join a road clogged with bumper-to-bumper commuter traffic. They had three lanes almost to themselves. Becks gunned the accelerator.

'Slower!' barked Maddy. 'Slow down! Keep it under fifty!

We don't want to get pulled up for speeding!'

'Affirmative.' She eased back on the pedal and the complaining whine of the vehicle's engine settled back to an almost soothing, muted grumble.

Maddy eased herself back in her seat. She let go of the dashboard in front of her. Her nails had left crescent-shaped dents in the plastic.

She turned round in her seat to see Rashim and Sal hefting SpongeBubba back on to his flat paddle feet and Bob and Liam pounding at the till like a pair of dim-witted cavemen trying to chip flint shards from an unbreakable boulder.

Jesus. Not the first time she found herself wondering, *What kind of a Mickey Mouse team is this?*

'My God!' she hurled at them, exasperated. 'What the hell was that?'

They stopped what they were doing, all of them staring expectantly at her. A bizarre menagerie seemingly sharing the same wide-eyed question on their faces – *not good?*

She shook her head. 'I'm pretty sure I said we should try and be *discreet* about this!'

CHAPTER 40

20 September 2001, Harcourt, Ohio

It was an abandoned elementary school they ended up looking at. Many of its windows were boarded up and covered with fading graffiti, and those that weren't, were either broken or smeared with foggy green blooms of moss. The playground beside the main entrance foyer sprouted tufts of grass and weed between fissures in the tarmac. Along one side, a row of gently rusting bicycle racks emerged from a bed of several years' worth of windswept autumn leaves.

The fact that the school was a couple of miles outside the nearest town and – apart from a gang of kids goofing around at night with cans of spray paint, some time long ago – it looked like no one had been here recently, coupled with the fact that it still had a tappable link to the power grid, made it pretty much a perfect temporary place for them to set up shop.

Actually, they'd found it quite by chance. A stop at a diner in the middle of one-strip town, Harcourt. A blink-it-and-miss town in the middle of Ohio's faded industrial heartland – the rustbelt, some called it. By the look of the lifeless smokestacks and fenced-off warehouses, it had once been a very promising industrial town. Bob had pulled over on the gravel car park in front of the diner and they'd gone in for a toilet and breakfast bagel break.

The diner was empty apart from them and one young waitress

in a green check dress and apron slumped across the end of the counter reading a newspaper. SpongeBob and Patrick quacked and guffawed from a TV on the other end. Rashim smiled at the sight of that.

After bringing them the pot of coffee and breakfast they'd ordered, the waitress found a reason to loiter by their table – wiping down others nearby, changing ketchup bottles and salt cellars that didn't need changing – clearly bored witless with her own company and intrigued by the diner's first and only customers that morning.

Her name was Kaydee-Lee Williams – at least that's what the plastic name tag on her chest said.

It was Liam who broke the ice and asked her about the town. She was pitifully keen to answer. 'Oh, Harcourt's, like, totally dead. Been dying for years. Ever since they closed down the auto-parts factory. That's all this town was really, a place for a couple of factories to go.' She shrugged. 'When the auto parts started getting made in China, the factories closed. Just like that. Simple.'

She told them how the town's population shrank each year. There was no future here, people were moving away, particularly families with young children. That's how they learned about the school in Harcourt, Green Acres Elementary. The school Kaydee-Lee said she'd once been to. No need for schools any more in a dying town, she'd said.

Maddy looked at it now. It would suit their immediate needs. It still had a live power feed that they could tap into. The local electricity company apparently hadn't bothered to disconnect and mothball the junction box. Instead, it had obviously been cheaper just putting up some hazard signs with risk disclaimers all over them.

The town itself also had a pretty decent hardware store they could use, and they'd passed a big retail park a dozen miles back along Interstate 70. Maddy had spotted a CompUSA, a Best Buy and of course the obligatory mega-sized Walmart.

She looked up at a grey sky. Over halfway into the month, September's late-summer promise was fading already, and tumbling autumn clouds vied with each other to be the first to drop their load on Green Acres Elementary.

'Let's get our stuff inside,' she said.

Half an hour later, they'd emptied the SuperChief of all the things that had once made the archway in Brooklyn their home. And now 'home', or at least their temporary home, was a classroom with mouse or maybe it was rat droppings on a scuffed linoleum chequered floor and school desks and bucket chairs stacked along a cork-board wall still decorated with curling pieces of paper. Thumb-tacked pictures drawn in crayon and felt tip. Childish scrawlings that spoke of happier times here. Blue skies and suns. Mom-an'-Dad-an'-Me pictures with tents and barbecues, summer fairs and parades.

Outside it was finally raining. The tapping of heavy, greasy drops on smeared windowpanes and somewhere inside the school building they could hear an echoing *drip-drip-drip* where a part of the roof was failing.

Maddy offered them her best morale-boosting cheerleader's smile. 'It'll be a bit comfier once we get ourselves sorted out. I promise.'

Liam remembered the moment he'd first awoken in the archway – a dark place. All damp bricks and crumbling mortar. And yes, just like now, the tap-tap-tapping of dripping water from somewhere out in the darkness. He'd thought it a horrible place to wake up. For a moment even wondered if it might be an odd version of Heaven. In which case he'd vowed to have a word with the first priest he came across.

If truth be told, his first impression of the archway hadn't been that great. It had appeared to be every bit as grim and unwelcoming as this place. But they'd made it a home.

'Aye, we'll get some bits and pieces in here to make it nice.'

'That's right.' Maddy stepped across the classroom and reached tentatively for a light switch. She grimaced as she flipped it, half expecting failing wiring and the progressive corrosion of damp to collude in electrocuting her. Instead, several frosted glass panels in the classroom's low ceiling flickered and winked to life.

'See? We got some power! So, we'll go get a kettle, a heater, camping stove. We'll be living like kings before you know it.'

Sal nodded. 'Just as good as the old archway.' Taking Maddy's lead, she smiled. Slightly forced. 'And at least we don't have to listen to the trains running overhead all the time.'

Actually, Liam had found that regular faint rumble comforting. Stepping outside into that dark, rubbish-strewn alleyway and listening to the restless noises of Brooklyn had been a somewhat reassuring thing. A sign that life was ceaselessly going on all around them.

Here in this abandoned school, they could just as easily be the last people on Earth and not know for sure one way or the other until they drove into town. And even then, given how lifeless Harcourt had looked on their way in, they'd not be certain.

'Come on, guys!' said Maddy. 'We've got a ton of work to do if the agency's going to be up and running again.'

'Aye,' Liam shrugged. 'Under new management, so it is.'

Maddy grinned. This time not her forced make-the-troops-happy smile. This time a genuine grin of excitement. 'Yes! Exactly what you just said, Liam. We're *Under New Management*. Us! How cool's that?'

'We're really going to change the world?' asked Sal.

'Yup . . .' Maddy wiped dusty hands on the front of her jeans. 'Now doesn't that sound like a better job description? To make the world a better place, rather than just keeping it the same ol' same crud? Huh?'

Rashim squatted down beside SpongeBubba, amid the plastic bags they'd carried in. 'A better world?' he muttered to himself. He was already checking through the more delicate parts of the displacement machine's components. He held a circuit up in front of the lab robot. It dutifully extended a sensitive graphene-tipped sensor and began to test the integrity of the board.

Rashim looked up at the others. 'Anything that *isn't* the world I left behind works just fine for me.'

Sal gave that a moment's thought. 'Making a better world does sound good.'

'Aye,' Liam grinned. 'Aye, it does, so.'

'Then let's make busy,' said Maddy. 'Highest-priority tasks first, ladies and gents. I need a coffee.'

CHAPTER 41

26 September 2001, Green Acres Elementary School, Harcourt, Ohio

We've been so busy I haven't really had time to think about things that much. Which is nice. It's such a crazy pinchudda thing – last night I realized I was missing my parents and I nearly started crying when I reminded myself they never existed! Or, if they did, they were some other girl's mamaji and papaji!

Then I reminded myself I'm not even Indian. Then I reminded myself I'm not even human. So, as you can imagine, this is really messing with my head.

That's why I'm glad we've been so busy.

A few days ago we got a load of things from a big camping store: sleeping bags, a stove and gas, kettle, lights, torches, food. All the comforts! So it's been nice. Like a camping trip. We even made a small fire in the middle of the floor and cooked toast and sausages and stuff. SpongeBubba and Rashim were like a pair of excitable little children! Never done campfire food before. But then have I? Even if I remembered doing that . . . it would be someone else's memory, wouldn't it? Or some made-up memories concocted by some techie somewhere.

Today we need to go back to that big retail park outside of Harcourt and get some more things. Some computers and cables and stuff. Me and Bob and Becks are getting those things.

Oh yeah, Maddy also spotted an Internet cafe last time we

*came. Said she wants to do some research on where we're going
to set up our permanent new home . . .*

Maddy winced and stuck her tongue out.

'What's wrong?' asked Liam.

'The coffee's frikkin' disgusting.'

'Mine's all right,' Rashim shrugged.

'Yeah, but you're used to drinking some sort of soya-gunk
substitute.' Maddy put the cardboard cup down on the small
table beside their Internet cubicle. The three of them were
huddled together suspiciously between the cubicle partitions
like three truant teenagers messing about on Facebook.

'That cack's all yours if you want any more of it, Rashim.'
She turned back to the computer monitor in front of them. She
had Wikipedia up on the screen. 'So . . . I guess we should go as
far back in time from now as we can get,' said Maddy. 'Put down
as much distance as we can between us and 2001.'

'What about going forward in time?' asked Liam.

She shook her head. 'We go forward, and it gets increasingly
difficult to remain off the radar.'

'Off the . . . ?'

'To stay hidden. There'll be more Internet, more connectivity,
more information. Bound to be. I just think we've got a much
better chance of remaining anonymous if we aim backwards.'

Liam sipped at his coffee. Her explanation made sense to
him. It was hard enough getting his head around this time,
without going further into an unfathomable future. 'And I
suppose we really have to pick another time? And not stay in
this one?'

'Yes, I would say so,' said Rashim. He hunkered forward into
the narrow cubicle. He lowered his voice. 'If Waldstein is
determined to locate you, he may decide to send more of those

military recon units after you.' He bit his lip. 'They may be old genetic hybrid technology, but they're robust, resourceful, tenacious . . . and very, very hard to kill.'

'You don't need to remind us of that,' said Liam.

'If he sends more, you really want to make it as difficult as possible for them to track you down. Remaining in the present simply presents one search vector for them: determining your location. But picking another time adds another search vector . . . *when*.'

'Yeah, so we need to think about less obvious places in time to hide,' added Maddy.

'Like the past.'

'Exactly.'

'But . . . but how far back can we go?' asked Liam. 'We need some power, do we not?'

Rashim nodded. 'Quite. And that's going to be the limiting factor.'

Maddy tapped at the keyboard. 'So . . . that does pretty much limit us to the age of electricity. When did we start having electric power everywhere?'

Rashim rolled his eyes upwards, thinking. Guessing. '1940?'

'Ahhh . . . I think there was power a lot earlier than then,' said Liam. 'There was plenty of electric on the *Titanic*, so there . . .' His words came to an abrupt halt. 'Not that, uh . . . not that I was ever even on the ship.' He shook his head and muttered something.

'Liam's right. Much earlier than that.' Maddy typed a phrase into Wikipedia's search box.

'My history isn't very good.' Rashim tried again. '1900?'

'Nope. Earlier.'

The man's eyes widened behind his glasses. 'Really? There was electricity in the 1800s?'

The monitor flickered with the result of her search: a page of text, no pictures or diagrams or embedded video clips. *This is old Wikipedia*, Maddy reminded herself. *Just text*.

'There we go. How about this . . .' She read out loud. 'Electricity remained not much more than a curiosity of nature until 1600, when English scientist William Gilbert carried out detailed observations of the relationship between the apparent visible effects between magnetism and the as yet undefined, unnamed force of electricity. He produced and distinguished the "lodestone" effect from static electricity created by rubbing amber. He named this effect after the Latin word "electricus" meaning "like amber", which in turn came from the Greek word for elektron.'

'Really?' Rashim craned his neck forward to read the small text more easily. 'I never would have believed . . .' he muttered, now silently reading on.

Maddy picked out another paragraph further down the article. 'In 1800, Alessandro Volta created the "Voltaic Pile", a structure of alternating layers of zinc and copper.' She looked at Liam. 'There you go! The first electric battery!'

'1819 . . .' said Rashim, 'Michael Faraday creates the Faraday disk! The first electromagnetic generator!'

'*Generator?*'

Rashim grinned at her. 'Don't get too excited, it generated about a couple of volts of direct current. We need output that's equivalent or thereabout to the domestic feed most people are getting today.' He read on. 'There . . . 1876, Thomas Edison builds the first power station in Menlo Park, New Jersey. Built it to supply power for his laboratory and various experiments.'

'But it needs to be power that's available for us to get our hands on,' said Liam.

Maddy nodded. 'Yeah, you're right, that's the really important bit. And it needs to be a totally *reliable* source, not some nutty inventor's cranky prototype that keeps breaking down or something. We need power that was, like, *commercially* available . . . put out for normal people, businesses, to use.'

'Ahhh!' Rashim raised a finger. 'Well then, how about this? The Edison Electric Light Station, built in 1880–81, which then came online in, let's see . . . ah yes! 1882.'

'That sounds promising,' said Maddy. 'But I dunno . . . New Jersey's still pretty close to where we were. If we're going to play it safe and put as much distance as we –'

'It's not in New Jersey.'

'Uh! Where, then?'

'London.'

'London?' She took a moment to take that in. Not in America? She'd presumed just now that something as forward-thinking, something so *modern* as electricity must have been a solely American thing long before anyone else. Even before the turn of the century.

'You mean London, *England*?'

'Yes, of course I mean London, England. A steam-powered 125-horsepower generator beneath –' he traced his finger down through the text to find his place – 'beneath a place called the Holborn Viaduct. Yes, and that's in central London.' He read the article from where his finger touched the screen. 'It was built to power the lights on the viaduct, but also to premises in the area, the City Temple and the Old Bailey.' He looked at them. 'Whatever *that* was.'

Maddy stroked her chin thoughtfully. 'Do you think it might have been churning out enough for our needs?'

'I don't know. Perhaps.' Rashim picked up a biro and began scribbling down scraps of information from the article.

'No need,' she said. She clicked her mouse on an icon to one side of the screen and smiled. 'It's already printing.'

'London.' Liam turned to look at her. He was just about to say he'd always wanted to visit the city as a boy. But once again, there it was, stupid circular thinking; he'd never been a little boy with dreams and wishes. He settled for a thoughtful nod. 'Aye, London sounds like a good enough bet to me.'

Maddy was grinning like a loon. 'London!' Truly and genuinely, a terrifyingly Cheshire cat-sized grin. Something she realized she hadn't done in a while; an honest expression of excitement. 'Victorian London! All top hats and posh frocks?'

Her growing excitement was wholly infectious. Liam found himself smiling straight back at her. He remembered their fleeting visit to San Francisco in 1906, the childlike beam of pleasure on her face as they'd strutted down that broad and busy thoroughfare: her with a plume of ostrich feathers on her head and wearing a bodice tight enough to make her want to cough up a kidney, and him with a top hat on his head tilted at a jaunty, gentleman-about-town angle.

'Aye . . . I think we just might've found ourselves a new home.'

She squeezed his hand. 'Yup,' she said right back. 'Rashim?'

'Yes?'

'How long do you think it will take you to rebuild the displacement machine?'

She knew he'd do it – the instinctive response habit of any technician, engineer, plumber – he sucked air in through his teeth. 'I don't know. We have the key component boards and they're still intact incredibly. But I'm going to have to, uh . . . reverse-engineer them. The basic process pipeline is the same as we had on Project Exodus, but there are implementation differences that I've got to learn and adapt to work with these components.'

'Just give me your best guess.'

'A couple of weeks? A month, two maybe?'

'You don't know, do you?'

'You asked me to guess.' He shrugged. 'So, I'm guessing.'

CHAPTER 42
1 October 2001, Harcourt, Ohio

'So that's twenty-seven dollars and –'

'Ninety cents,' Liam finished. He smiled at her and she blushed. 'I know that off by heart.'

'And I know what you're gonna order by heart,' said Kaydee-Lee. 'Why do you always order the same thing?'

Liam had been up to the diner virtually every morning since they'd settled into the abandoned elementary school. It was boredom, that's why he volunteered to do the breakfast bagel run. Maddy, Rashim and SpongeBubba seemed to be spending all their waking hours either poring over pencil-sketched schematics or huddled over a make-do workbench, carefully soldering electrical components together by the light of a desktop lamp. Sal seemed to be busy on the computers most of the time. They had a similar set-up of twelve networked PCs as they'd had back in Brooklyn, the old hard drives from the archway system installed. Once the W.G. Systems operating code had been loaded up and had successfully kicked Windows 2000 to the kerb, computer-Bob was able to talk Sal through installing all the other bits and pieces.

'I know what bagel filling everyone likes . . . saves me having to, you know, disturb them from their work.'

Kaydee-Lee narrowed her eyes. 'So, what are you guys up to down there at the school?'

'Oh, it's . . . it's just a little science experiment, so it is.'

'That sounds kinda cool.'

He curled his lip casually. 'Aw, it's nothing too exciting really. Uh, we're . . . we're measuring –' he scrambled to reach for a few sciencey-sounding terms and words – 'measuring background particle emissions from, uh . . . from radio-micron particle toxin materials.'

She gazed at him, none the wiser. An awkward silence hung between them, begging to be filled. 'Cool!' she said, smiling. 'I kinda liked science at school.' Then she sighed. 'Wasn't any good at it, though.' She huffed a little sadly. 'Wasn't much good at anything at school . . . that's why I'm here, I guess.'

He followed her doleful gaze out of the broad window of the diner across a high street that was half made up of boarded-up stores. 'I never see anyone else working in here. Is it just you?' he asked.

She nodded. 'Pretty much in the mornings. Arnie comes in at lunchtimes to cook. That's when it gets *real* busy.' She looked back at him. 'We get a ladies' sewing circle come in for lunch, regular as clockwork. Five old dears. The place is totally *buzzing* then.'

Liam laughed. He picked up the tone of sarcasm.

Yes, it was boredom that brought him up here, that and a chance to get some exercise. It was a fifteen-minute trip into town on the bicycle he'd found in the schoolyard. But . . . yes, if he was being honest, it was a chance to pop into the diner – always quiet at this time in the morning – and talk to Kaydee-Lee. Over the last few weeks they'd graduated from 'how ya doing today' niceties to talking about the weather, to really talking, to finally, politely exchanging their names.

'Why do you stay here, Kaydee-Lee?'

She filled the silence with getting on with finishing up his take-out order, busy spreading a thick layer of cream cheese on to one of the bagels. She looked up at his question. 'Harcourt?'

'Aye.'

She hunched her shoulders. 'Where else am I gonna go? I got a job and it's OK, I guess. It's not like I go home at night all stressed out or anything. I'm bored . . . but at least I'm not stressed.'

'But you don't intend to work in here forever, right? You've got a plan, a dream . . . a *goal*, so to speak?'

'Jeeez! I'm, like, seventeen. I don't even know what I'm gonna cook up for dinner tonight, let alone know where I wanna be when I'm your age.'

'My age?'

She nodded. 'You're what? Like, twenty-five, twenty-six or something?'

Liam stifled an urge to gasp. *Twenty-five? I'm sixteen! Sixteen!!* But then he reminded himself he wasn't any particular age. Not really. His false memory calmly tried to reassure him he was a sixteen-year-old boy from Cork, Ireland. But that was all meaningless claptrap now. Someone else's fiction.

Kaydee-Lee looked up from her work, studied his troubled face. 'Oh my God, did I just say something wrong?'

'No . . . I just, I'm not *that* old.'

'Oh God, you don't have some kinda awful ageing sickness or something? Did I just put my foot in my mouth?'

Liam laughed. 'No, don't worry.' He ruffled the scruffy mop of hair on his head. 'It's my grey bit of hair. Some people think I'm older than I am.' He offered her a disarming smirk: an assurance that he hadn't taken offence, that she hadn't clumsily blundered on to uncomfortable ground.

'Ahh, don't you worry now. I've always had this little bit of grey. Me lucky silver streak, so it is.'

She nodded. 'Well, I really like it.' Her cheeks suddenly coloured a mottled pink once more. 'I mean, you know . . . it looks *cool*. Kinda gothic.'

'Gothic? What the devil does that mean?'

She smiled suspiciously at him. 'Gothic? Sort of Sabbath-grungy-rocky? Kind of the whole steam-punky thing?'

'You know,' he shrugged. 'I haven't the first idea what any of that means.'

She laughed at that. 'You're so funny. The way you, like, talk . . . like a sort of young-old man –'

'*Old?* Did I hear you just use the word "old"?' The look of horror on his face was mock-serious.

'No!' she yelped. 'No, I don't mean that! I meant . . . I dunno, it's like you've got old-style manners. If you know what I mean? Like you just stepped out of one of 'em ancient black and white movies.'

He spread his hands. 'Well now, you're never too young or too old for a dose of good manners, my dear.'

She chuckled behind the counter as she finished fixing the salt beef and cream cheese bagel, wrapped it up in greaseproof paper and put it in the plastic bag with the others. She tossed in some napkins and plastic forks and passed the bag over the counter to him. 'I know an old-fashioned word that I can use to describe you.'

'What's that?'

'Enigma? That's how you say it, right? You're *en–ig–mat–ic*?'

'You mean, a puzzle?'

She nodded. 'Oh, you're that all right, Liam. Exactly that. You're a puzzle.'

CHAPTER 43

3 October 2001, Green Acres
Elementary School, Harcourt, Ohio

'It may look a bit random,' said Maddy, 'but, trust me, it all works.'

Liam cast another wary glance at the cables snaking across the classroom floor. The displacement machine at the moment was nothing more than an array of circuit boards placed on a row of orange plastic bucket chairs, all of them linked by dangling loops of electrical flex, blobs of solder holding the whole fragile thing together.

The computer system controlling the displacement machine looked very like it had back in Brooklyn: a dozen base units and half a dozen monitors hooked up together and occupying a cluster of school desks pushed together.

They didn't have their own version of a displacement 'tube' filled with freezing cold water. According to Maddy, they didn't need one of those any more. Since their mission was now a different one – no longer the rigid preservation of one particular timeline with all the necessary strict measures to ensure no unwanted contaminants came back into the past with them – there was no longer the need for a 'wet drop'. If a minor contaminant, for example a chunk of modern-day linoleum floor, went back into the past, it might possibly result in some minor contamination. But, as far as Maddy was concerned, that was OK; that was an acceptable risk. The rules were different now. And anyway, a minor change, a minor time wave, might just be the thing that ultimately deflected the course of history and resulted in there not being an engineered super-virus known as Kosong-ni in the year 2070.

Totally unlikely that a chunk of classroom floor could alter history that much. But you never know.

'Don't worry, Mads,' said Liam, looking at the guts of the machine spread along the row of plastic chairs. 'I trust you.' He hoped his voice sounded as confident as he was trying to look.

Rashim pointed to one of two squares marked out on the floor with lengths of masking tape. 'That's where you stand, Liam. It's a metre square, wide enough for comfortable clearance just as long as you're not waving your arms around. Each square has its own departure software that controls the distribution of energy and channelling of the field. I enter the precise mass figure into each entry field . . . with an acceptable nine per cent margin of error, of course,' said Rashim. He pointed at the square in front of Liam. 'The left square has your stats, the right one has Bob's.'

Rashim had made his mass calculations several days ago using a rather old-school method. He'd filled a plastic drum with water – cold, of course, straight from a bathroom tap – right to the very top, then asked Liam to climb in and completely submerge himself. The water had spilled out as he'd displaced it. The displaced water was caught in a tray beneath the drum. And that water was then measured carefully to determine Liam's mass. The process was repeated for Bob, then the girls, then Rashim and SpongeBubba. Provided none of them lost too much weight or put too much weight on in the meantime, the figures were good enough. Comfortably within the nine per cent margin for error.

'So it's squares now?' Liam arched his brows and looked at Maddy. 'Not one big circle any more?'

She shrugged. 'Rashim's deployment method. That's how they did it with Exodus, separate displacement volumes.'

'It's safer. There's a much lower risk of mass convergence. Plus I've calculated for an additional amount of mass. Each time we use the same square, we'll take a half inch of the floor with us, no more than –'

'Mass convergence?' Liam could guess what that harmless-sounding phrase meant. He'd seen 'mass convergence' before and it wasn't a particularly pleasant sight.

He grimaced. 'You're telling me that kind of thing happened with your lot often enough that you had a proper technical term for it?'

'We had thirteen mis-translations in phase alpha!' piped up SpongeBubba. 'What came back was real gooey!'

'Yes, thanks, SpongeBubba. Certainly, we had . . . uh . . . a *few* failed trials. But look –' Rashim pushed his glasses up his nose – 'this system, *Waldstein's* particle-projection system, is way more elegant than ours. I mean . . . quite incredible! The man was . . . *is* . . . a genius! It's the simplicity of the calculation pipeline that amazes me – the way he's truncated the whole process into a basic two-step process . . .' He stopped himself. 'Sorry . . . the more I've worked on this machine, the bigger a fanboy I've become. The point is, Liam, this is a much more reliable system than ours was. Plus we're dealing with a much smaller mass conversion. Two departure squares at a time. And they're separate. Which means if one square happens to malfunction in some way, the other person won't be involved.' Rashim shrugged. 'Only one person gets turned inside out, not two. Relax, Liam . . . you and I will be fine.'

Liam looked at Maddy for reassurance. She nodded. 'Separate's not a bad idea. It is actually a lot safer than the spherical portal we used to share.'

'All right, then.' Liam buttoned up his waistcoat. 'If you say so. Remind me, what year are we going back to exactly?'

'I decided on 1888. That puts you at several years *after* the viaduct and its generator were built. Time enough for any gremlins to have worked their way out of the system.'

Liam frowned. For some particular reason the year rang a bell with him. '1888? Didn't something big happen that year?'

'I'm sure a lot of things happened in that year, Liam.'

'No . . . I read something recently. Something pretty big in London.'

Bob scowled as he trawled through the data uploaded into his head. 'The Whitechapel murders happened in that year,' he said.

'Murders!' Liam snapped his fingers. 'That was it! Wasn't it that Jack the Ripper fella? He did those murders.'

'Affirmative. The murders occurred in Whitechapel, east London. Five female victims over several months. The last victim, Mary Kelly, was murdered on the ninth of November 1888.'

'Aye! That's it!' He turned to Maddy. 'It was all a big mystery, so it was. No one ever found out who did it.' Liam had an idea. 'We could find out who did it! You know, while we're back there looking around for a new home?'

'No, Liam. We aren't the police. We're not a homicide squad. Just concentrate on the job at hand, OK?'

He huffed. 'Just an idea.'

'And that's all it will remain. We've got more important things to worry about.'

Sal finished dressing Bob. She'd visited a men's clothing store in the retail park. Liam and Rashim were now wearing modern polyester slacks and smart shirts with collars that were clearly not Victorian, but the grey flannel waistcoats helped date them both a little. If no one inspected their clothes too closely, they'd be OK. Once again, though, Sal had struggled to find clothes to fit Bob. She'd had to resort to shopping at a branch of X-tra-MAN, 'the store for gentle giants', and the choices were pretty limited. Dungarees again for Bob and a loose striped shirt. With a flat cap perched on his coarse hair, he could just about pass as some lumbering navvy.

'So, I've set up a time-stamp for half a dozen years after the setting up of that Holborn Viaduct generator.' Maddy stepped towards the row of computer screens, and studied one. There was the image of an old parish map. 'The location is about a third of a mile south of the viaduct, right next to the River of London.'

'Ah . . . I think you'll find it's called the *Thames*, Mads,' said Liam.

She squinted at the screen. 'Oh yeah, of course. Yeah . . . the Thames. We did a bunch of pinhole tests on the arrival location, looks like a small shingle bank, brick wall on one side and what look like some steps leading up the side of it. There's very little spatial disruption. Small stuff, occasional pigeon or something I'm guessing. So, it looks like a pretty quiet spot.'

'Grand.'

'So . . . remember this is just a quick look, OK? Go check out that viaduct, see if there's someplace we can make ourselves at home. Then come back to the river.'

'How long have we got?'

'As long as you want really. I can set up a scheduled return window if you want, or we can just monitor the location for a regular rhythmic spatial displacement signature. Remember? Like you did back in dinosaur-land? Just wave your arms in a regular rhythmic fashion . . . we'll pick it up just fine.'

'Hmm . . . I think I'd like the scheduled return window, to be sure.'

'OK,' she said, tapping it into a keyboard. 'Three hours? More?'

'Aye, three hours sounds like enough.' Liam looked across at Bob. 'You ready for another jaunt, big fella?'

He nodded. 'Of course.'

'Well, all right, then,' said Liam, clapping his hands together. 'Shall we?'

'Be careful,' said Sal.

'That I most certainly will.'

'Have a nice trip, skippa!' SpongeBubba called out. 'Bring me flowers!'

Rashim turned to Liam. 'I need to change his programming sometime soon. It's beginning to get annoying.'

'The order of departure is Bob and Rashim first,' said Maddy. 'Then you, Liam, on the left square.'

Bob and Rashim took their places in the two taped-out squares.

'Uh, guys . . . one minute countdown. Mark!'

A single LED flickered on one of the circuit boards – clocking the energy being drawn in and stored on the capacitor. A single diode that would wink out when there was enough on-board energy to discharge. Maddy told Rashim it would do for now. When they were properly settled, she'd build something a little more elaborate.

She counted the minute down and, with a hum of discharged energy, they both vanished, along with the scuffed linoleum floor they'd been standing on.

'You're next,' she said, ushering Liam on to his square. He was standing on freshly exposed wooden floor. The displacement volume had dug down two inches into the ground.

'Thirty seconds. Stand still now!'

Liam put his hands down by his side. It felt a little unsettling, looking down at the tape on the floor surrounding him, and not knowing for sure if the tip of an elbow, the heel of a foot, might be too close, or even overhanging the tape. At least bobbing around in that perspex tube he knew for certain he was wholly 'in' the displacement envelope.

The capacitor was beginning to hum.

'Fifteen seconds!' called out Maddy. 'No more fidgeting now, please!'

'I'm not!'

'Yes, you are! Hold still!'

Liam sucked in a deep breath, closed his eyes.

Ah dear, here we go again.

So much seemed to have happened since the last time he'd done this. It seemed like a whole lifetime ago. In many ways it was a different life. Someone else's. The last time he'd volunteered to have his body discharged through chaos space into unknowable danger he'd been certain of who he was and why he was doing what he was doing. This time around . . . it was so very different.

'Ten seconds!'

This time he understood why his body could take such punishment. It was engineered specifically to take it. This time around he knew if he took a bullet, or the stab of a sword or a knife, it might well hurt, but he'd live. That meant there was less to be scared of. Right?

'Five seconds!'

Nope. He was starting to tremble like he always did as Maddy counted down the last few seconds.

Liam, ya big wuss. You're meant to be some kind of support unit, aren't you?

He was just about to start wondering whether Bob actually

ever experienced fear when he felt the floor beneath his feet suddenly give way like a hangman's trap, and that awful sensation of falling.

CHAPTER 44

1 December 1888, London

Liam kept his eyes shut. The white mist of chaos space no longer held him in thrall; it wasn't a Heaven-like magical white wilderness any more but a place that increasingly unsettled him. He'd seen shapes out there so faintly that he couldn't begin to determine whether they had a certain form or not. They flitted like wraiths, like sharks circling ever closer. Or perhaps his eyes or his mind were playing tricks with an utterly blank canvas. Perhaps it was his imagination. But then hadn't Sal said she'd seen them too?

His solitary limbo in chaos space couldn't end soon enough.

A moment later he felt his feet make a soft landing.

Soft, and sinking.

'Whuh?'

And sinking.

He tried to pull a foot out of whatever gunk he was gradually sinking into, and lost his balance. His hands reached out in front of him, bracing for a face-first impact with the sludge, but brushed past something firm. He grabbed at it.

It felt like wood. A spar of damp wood, coated in a slime that he nearly lost his grip on.

'Liam?'

'Rashim?'

It was dark and foggy and cold. But he could make out

Rashim's faint outline. 'I think there's been a mis-transmission. We're out on some sort of mudbank.'

'No . . . I think it's low tide.' There could have been some small offset miscalculation that had dropped them several yards to one side. In this case further into the river. It could have been worse. High tide for instance.

'Bob, you there?'

'Affirmative,' his deep voice rumbled out of the fog.

Liam held tightly on to the wooden spar. He wasn't sinking any more. He pulled one foot out of the glutinous mud with a sucking sound coming from the silt. 'There's a wooden post here, hold on to it. You can use it to pull yourself out of the mud.'

'That is not necessary,' Bob replied.

'We're not actually *in* the mud,' said Rashim. 'We're standing on what appears to be a wooden-slat walkway.'

The fog thinned and he saw them both several yards away, standing on a creaking, rickety wooden jetty. Quite dry.

Liam realized there must have been a small error in Rashim's calculation of his mass. Then again, not necessarily Rashim's fault. He'd eaten a small bag of pecan doughnuts just half an hour ago. That might possibly have altered his mass enough to cause a deviation from where he was supposed to be.

Rashim had actually cautioned them all not to eat just before a jump. Liam cursed his carelessness.

Only got yourself to blame, greedy guts.

He muttered as he took several sinking, teetering, laboured steps towards them through the silt and pulled himself up on to the jetty to join them. His legs dangled over the side and he attempted to kick the largest clumps of foul-smelling gunk off his boots.

'Information: the translation was offset by fourteen feet and three inches,' said Bob.

Rashim nodded. 'We should let Maddy know when we get back. She'll need to recalibrate the spatial attributor.'

'Don't bother,' said Liam. 'It was three doughnuts that are to blame.'

'Ahh . . . now, yes, I did warn you, Liam,' said Rashim.

Liam got up off the damp wood, most of the cloying mud shaken off. He grinned in the dark at him. 'Lesson learned.' He took in the freezing mist all around them. 'So this is Victorian London, is it?'

'Affirmative, Liam.'

'Yes . . . Liam. Say *yes*, not *affirmative*.' He picked out the dark mountain of Bob's back and slapped it gently. 'You're never going to get your head around that, are you?'

'That particular speech file appears to be resistant to replacement.'

'Should we not proceed?' Rashim interrupted.

'Hmmm, you're right,' said Liam. 'Let's find some solid ground.'

They followed the jetty until it widened and finally terminated on firm shingle at the base of a slime-encrusted stone wall. A high-tide line marked the top of the slime halfway up, and it was mist-damp stonework the rest of the way. The pinhole image they'd gathered earlier had shown this jetty wall. The mist hadn't been here then. And there were the steps they'd spotted in the image. A dozen slippery, narrow stone steps up the side of the jetty wall.

At the top Liam looked around. A carpet of mist covered the river below like a wispy layer of virgin snow, dusted silvery blue by a quarter-moon. He saw the humps of river barges emerge from the mist, topped with pilots' cabins like isolated stubby lighthouses rising from a milky sea. The milky sea itself seemed to stir with life; he watched enormous dark phantoms loom through the river mist, like those ever-circling wraiths in chaos space – shadows cast by fleeting clouds chasing each other across the moonlit sky.

The other two joined him.

'It's so dark,' said Rashim.

Liam nodded. Compared to New York, compared to whatever future cities Rashim must be used to, it must seem like some medieval netherworld.

Dark, yes, but punctuated by a thousand pinpricks of faint amber light: gas lamps behind dirty windows, candles behind tattered net curtains. They were standing in a cobblestone square. On one side there appeared to be a brick warehouse or small factory.

They heard something heavy rumbling, rattling across the river, and turned round to look across the carpet of mist. It was then Liam noticed the arches and support stanchions of a broad, low bridge.

'According to my data that is Blackfriars Bridge,' said Bob.

Not so far beyond it another bridge . . . and the toot of a steam whistle confirmed what Liam suspected. It was a train crossing the river to their side. He could just about make out the faintest row of amber lights on the move – lamps in each carriage.

'My God!' whispered Rashim. 'Is that a . . . a *steam* train?'

'Aye.'

'We should proceed towards our target destination,' said Bob.

He was right. Liam would rather be back here for Maddy's scheduled window than have to flap his hands around like an idiot hoping for one. There was no knowing how good their temporary set-up back in 2001 was at picking up hand signals.

'We must head north,' said Bob, pointing towards a narrow street.

They made their way up the street, dark and quiet. It curved to the left and a hundred yards up at the end it joined a much broader street. They could hear it was busy even before they stepped out of their dark side street. The distinctive *clop-clop-clop* of shoed horses, the warning honk of a bulb horn, the rattle of iron-rimmed coach wheels. They emerged on to a broad street lit on either side with stout wrought-iron lamps, twelve feet tall, that spilled broad pools of amber illumination across a wide thoroughfare busy with horse-drawn carriages and carts.

'My God!' whispered Rashim. 'I never imagined it would be quite so busy!'

'It's only ten,' said Liam, pointing to a clock on a nearby building. 'People stay up even later in my hometown, Cork.'

He stopped himself from correcting that. Not *his* hometown . . . of course. But it was a constant, unsettling inconvenience for him and the girls, continually self-correcting statements like that, that he'd finally stopped giving a damn about it. As Maddy had told him, *It doesn't matter if they're second-hand memories, Liam — we ARE the sum of what we remember. And that's how I'm dealing with this*.

Denial. It was as good a way as any of dealing with the knowledge that your whole life was a lie.

'This is really quite fantastic,' Rashim uttered.

'Glad you like it. Which way now, Bob?'

'This is Farringdon Street.' He pointed up the busy thoroughfare. At the far end a low bridge arched over the wide street. Along the top of it were glowing orbs of light of a different colour, more of a pale amber, almost a vanilla colour. And a steadier, more resilient glow than the occasionally flickering, shifting illumination coming from the gas lamps.

'And that is the Holborn Viaduct.'

'Those lights . . . ?' Liam nodded at them.

'Affirmative,' replied Bob. 'They are electric lights.'

The three of them picked their way up the broad pavement on the left-hand side of Farringdon Street. It was busy with pedestrians, a mixture of smartly dressed gentlemen and ladies taking the air after a show, and costermongers and hucksters of various goods packing up and making their way home for the night.

'Come on! Make way there, lads!' barked a thick-shouldered man with a handcart laden with pigs' heads and trotters as he pushed his way past them.

An elegantly dressed woman walking with a whippet-thin man in a top hat curled her lips in disapproval as the cart wheeled past her. 'Oh really!' she muttered.

Liam and Rashim shared a grin. The noises, the smells – the acrid smell of burning coke, horse manure, the sight of such churning, shoulder-to-shoulder life – seemed reassuring, life-affirming. After all that time alone in the abandoned school it felt good to be back among so many people.

Liam caught the faintest whiff of it first: the smell of coffee beans roasting in a skillet. Parked up in the dirt at the side of the road was a large four-wheeled cart. Wooden steps unfolded down on to the pavement invited them up to a wooden deck where several tables and stools were occupied by gentlemen and ladies taking coffee and a slice of cake. At one end of the cart a woman and a man in aprons were serving cups of freshly roasted coffee from large tin urns that steamed over small skillets. Candles lit the small tables. Mini oil lamps were strung across the top, like Christmas lights.

'Just wait till Maddy sees that,' Liam laughed. 'A horse-drawn Starbucks!'

A few minutes later they were standing beneath the viaduct, looking up at the thick ribs of glossy green-painted iron arching across the broad street. Overhead, alongside the road that crossed over the viaduct, the orbs of electric light at the top of tall iron lampstands bloomed proudly.

'London's first public, electric-powered street lights.' Liam nodded approvingly. 'Not bad.'

'We have used half an hour of our allotted time,' said Bob.

Liam stopped gawking at the lights and turned his attention to life beneath the viaduct. The underbelly was a row of hexagonal stone columns on either side of the street from which the arches of iron branched out to meet each other. On both sides of Farringdon Street there were pedestrian walkways lit by yet more electric globes. The walkways were flanked by stone columns on one side and rows of brickwork archways on the other, each archway seemingly occupied by one sort of business or other.

As they watched, on the far side of the busy street the thick oak doors of one of the archways swung open and several men worked together, rolling casks of beer out, across the pavement and on to a flat-backed cart.

Liam craned his neck to get a better look through the open doors to the interior beyond. He could see archways and alcoves, all seemingly stuffed with barrels, crates and boxes of all different sizes.

'Let's go over and get a better look,' he said. They crossed Farringdon Street, dodging and ducking between horse-drawn vehicles that showed no intention of stopping or slowing for them.

Closer, Liam watched the three men working quickly, *furtively* even, as they loaded the cart up. 'Stay here,' he said then made a show of looking casual, whistling tunelessly as he strolled past the wide-open oak doors. He paused. Ducked down on to one knee and made as if he had a bootlace that needed tying up, all the while craning his neck to see through the open doors, getting a glimpse of the receding maze of archways and alcoves inside.

'Hoy!'

He turned to find one of the men standing over him.

'Hoy there! You get enough of a look inside, did ya?'

'I . . . was, I'm just . . .' Liam stood up.

'Pokin' ya nose in where it's likely to get broken!' A thought suddenly occurred to the man and he grabbed Liam's arm roughly. 'You a snitch for them bluebottles? Is that it? For the bleedin' coppers?'

The man was short and tubby, with owlish bug eyes that bulged beneath wiry brows. Liam found himself looking down at him. He suspected the little chap was actually tougher than he looked – that or he was all bluster.

'What? No! I'm . . . just . . . I'm . . .'

'Cos I'll get me lad, Bertie, to shank you good if you –'

'Actually,' replied Liam, 'I'm looking for business premises.'

'Business premises? Likely story!'

The stocky man turned to look at Rashim approaching to help Liam out. He did an almost comical double-take at Rashim's dark skin. 'Good God!' he blurted. 'You with this lad?'

'Yes. Yes, of course I am.'

Rashim's carefully enunciated, alien-sounding English seemed to impress, or perhaps intimidate, the stocky man. He cocked his head as if flexing a stiff neck. 'Well, all right, then.'

The man released his grip on Liam's arm. 'He your boy?'

Rashim's eyes met Liam's and he struggled to stifle an amused smile. 'No, not really.'

'I'm not anyone's boy,' sniffed Liam indignantly. 'We're uh . . . we're business partners, so we are.'

The stocky man pulled a face. 'Business partners, is it?'

'Uh . . . yes, he's quite right,' said Rashim.

'We want to rent one of these . . . archway places.' Liam glanced at the open doorway. The other two men had finished loading the last cask on to the cart and one of them climbed up on to the running board and coaxed the horses to life. Their hooves clattered on stone and the wagon pulled away.

'You seem to have a lot of space inside there,' said Liam. 'Could we rent a bit?'

'Well, what I got inside ain't none of your beeswax, lad!'

Bob emerged out of the gloom. 'Are you OK, Liam?' he asked, striding towards the stocky man. His voice reverberated beneath the iron and stone viaduct. A deep boom that made heads on the other side of Farringdon Street turn their way. A lamb shank of a hand reached out and grabbed one of the man's upper arms in a vice-like grip. The stocky man's bulging eyes widened still further. He looked like a tree frog in a waistcoat.

'Oh, I'm all right, Bob.' Liam grinned at the man. 'There's no harm done.'

'Bertie!' the man gulped, alarmed at the giant looming over him. '*Bertie!* Get over here and *help me!*'

His colleague, 'Bertie', took one look at Bob and then backed up several steps into the gloom.

'Can we not just have a little talk?' asked Liam. 'If you've got a spare room somewhere in there? Or perhaps you know of anybody else who does? That's all.'

'We have money,' added Rashim. 'We could pay a very generous rent.'

The man gulped, looking more like a toad than a frog now. 'Generous rent, eh?'

'Aye,' said Liam. 'Bob? Why don't you let this nice gentleman's arm go before you crush it to a pulp?'

'As you wish.' Bob loosened his grip and the man snatched his arm free, flexed his neck again and straightened his ruffled waistcoat indignantly.

'Well.' His bug eyes remained warily on Bob. 'I suppose a little talk won't hurt no one.'

CHAPTER 45

1 December 1888,
Holborn Viaduct, London

They stepped inside, through the double oak doors, and the tall young man called Bertie pulled them closed. He was wiry-thin with short dark hair parted on the side, long sideburns and a pitifully wispy attempt at a walrus moustache.

There was a glare on the face of his short, frog-like boss: a stern look at his young assistant very much along the lines of *we're going to have a little talk later on, you and I.*

Liam looked around. In one way it was very much like the home they'd left behind in Brooklyn: an arched ceiling of dark red bricks. But this archway was stuffed with stacks of wooden packing crates and casks of whisky and liquors, barrels of beer, bottles of wine, sacks of mysterious goods, even a rack of army-surplus rifles and small foil-sealed boxes of ammunition.

Off this main archway, through walkways between mountains of boxes, he could see other archways and alcoves receding into the gloom. It looked almost labyrinthine. An Aladdin's cave.

The rotund little man sat down at a small round table in the middle of his 'warehouse'. A gas lamp glowed in the middle of it. He cut a small wedge of cheese from a block the size of a shoebox.

'So you mentioned a *generous* rent, eh?'

Liam sat down opposite him. 'If you've got an archway spare

somewhere among all this,' he said, gesturing at the receding gloom. 'Then, yes, we can pay.'

'Oh, there's plenty more of this maze beneath the viaduct available for tenants.' He chewed energetically on his cheese, looking casually up at the low ceiling. 'If you know the right bloke to talk to.'

'And you're that right bloke, I suppose.'

He shrugged. 'That's what they say around this manor.'

Liam offered his hand across the table. 'The name's Liam O'Connor.'

The man eyed it warily for the moment, finishing his mouthful of cheese, then wiped his hand on his sleeve and shook with Liam. 'Delbert Hook. Imports and exports is m'business.'

Liam looked around him and wondered how much of the stuff in here was strictly legitimate business. And how much of it had 'fallen off the back of a wagon'. There'd been a somewhat suspicious haste in the way Mr Hook and his assistant had been loading up the wagon.

'The lanky drip standing over there by the door is my assistant, Bertie.'

The young man stepped forward. Offered his hand tentatively to Liam. 'It's *Herbert* actually. Pleased to meet you.'

'Bertie's what I calls him,' said Delbert. 'He's brighter than he looks.'

'Actually, I have a part-time job teaching mathematics,' replied Herbert. 'I do Del's accounts for him on weekdays and —'

'*Mr Hook* to you, lad!' He glared. Although his expression quickly softened. 'Or *Hooky. Or,* if I'm very, very drunk . . . then, and only then, you can call me Del.'

Liam suspected there was something of a bond between the two men, despite the mutual glaring.

'And these other two?' Delbert's gaze rested on Bob. 'Who's this giant?'

'That's Bob, and this fella's my good friend Dr Rashim Anwar.'

Delbert pursed his lips appreciatively at Rashim. 'Doctor? A physician is it, eh?'

'Not that kind of a doctor, I'm afraid.'

'Oh?' Delbert sounded disappointed. 'Anyway.' He cut another hunk of cheese. Liam noticed he wasn't offering any around. 'For the right price and so long as you can convince me you ain't snipes working for the police . . . I might be able to find you your very own archway.'

'We need privacy,' said Rashim.

Delbert looked at him. 'Well, of course. What decent businessman don't?'

'There's a power generator located somewhere under this viaduct,' said Rashim. 'Isn't there?'

Delbert nodded at Rashim. 'Oh, you mean the Bell Electrical Voltaic Generation Machine! Yes, indeed. The first of its size in the world, so they says. There was a big parade and marching bands an' the like here five or six years ago when they switched the ruddy thing on. Damn noisy it is too! Sounds like a bloomin' locomotive comin' through the walls. You might want one of the archways well away from the ruddy thing if you don't want to listen to it boomin' away all day an' all night!'

'No,' cut in Liam. 'Close to that's fine for us, so it is.'

'Close to it?' One of Delbert's bushy eyebrows rose suspiciously. 'You actually *want* the noise, do you?'

Liam shrugged. 'It won't be a problem for us.'

'Hmm . . .' Delbert stroked his bottom lip, both bushy brows lowered, almost a scowl. 'You gonna tell me what yer business is?'

'It's private,' said Liam.

'*Private* covers a multitude of sins, lad. I may not be entirely above the board here, but there's some things I won't be a party to. You understand what I'm sayin'?'

Liam figured he might have to feed the man a titbit of information. Just enough to satisfy his beady-eyed curiosity.

'Science experiments.' He nodded at Rashim. 'Dr Anwar here is something of a . . . a scientist.'

'Science, is it?' That seemed to appeal to Delbert. 'What are yer . . . some sort of inventor?'

'I . . . err . . .' He looked at Liam. Liam nodded. 'Yes, I suppose. Yes, an inventor.'

'Good Lord!' said Herbert. 'Might I ask what kind of things you invent?' He looked eager. 'See, I also have quite an interest in the sciences, sir.'

'Not now, Bertie!' Delbert sat back in his chair and wiped his hands and finished his mouthful of cheese as he gave his visitors some silent consideration.

'All right, then. I'll show you what I got. Then you and me, lad . . . we're gonna need to talk about the money.'

Delbert got up, reached for the lamp's brass handle, lifted it off the table and waved for them to follow him. He led them down through a tight squeeze between packing crates, along a narrow tunnel, low enough that Bob had to stoop down to enter it.

They turned a corner to see by the dim glow of Delbert's lamp an archway almost as large as Delbert's main one. Along the left-hand wall were a few stacks of goods. Along the wall opposite were three evenly spaced alcoves.

'The one on the left leads directly out on to Farringdon Street. I don't use it myself, but I got keys to it. You can use that access, just so long as you're mindful to lock it secure at night. That way you don't need to be disturbing my business all the time. The middle one's a small storage room. I don't use it. The right one is the one you can have.'

He walked over towards that alcove. It receded further along than it first appeared to. Ten feet, a low, narrow tunnel. At the end a small arched oak door with a thick padlock on it. Delbert fumbled in his trouser pocket and pulled out a jangling keyring.

'I'll give you this key, of course,' he said as he picked out the keyhole and inserted the key.

'That is the only copy of the key?' asked Rashim.

Delbert made a face. 'Of course! Of course!'

The lock clanked loudly and the thick door creaked inwards. Liam heard it almost immediately – the muted sound of something not so far away throbbing deeply. He glanced at Rashim who smiled back approvingly.

The generator's close by. Perfect.

'Here we are,' said Delbert, stepping inside. He raised the lamp in his hand and shadows danced around the empty space as they filed in behind him. Above the throb – more of a vibration sensed through the brick walls and the floor than it was a sound – they heard the faint squeak of rats scuttling for the safety of a dark corner.

The girls will just love the idea of that.

'I don't believe yer goin' to get any more private a place than this, gents!' Delbert's voice rang off the bricks, an almost endless echo that seemed to take an eternity to finally fade to nothing. He picked up a thick candle sitting on the floor amid its own solid nest of melted wax and lit it.

With the extra flickering light, Liam took in more details of their surroundings. It was about a third smaller than their archway under the Williamsburg Bridge. And no other rooms off this space. This was it. A rectangle of stone-slab floor, about twelve yards by six, encased by a low curving ceiling of bricks.

Almost a dungeon . . . if you let yourself think about it that way. Or like a large cabin aboard some vessel. Liam suspected that the ever-present pulsing throb would eventually be no more a distraction after a while than the engine of an ocean liner.

'This would be an appropriate location,' rumbled Bob finally. *And we can make it like home, can't we?*

The other place had been just as spartan and grim as this. But they'd managed to make it comfortable. Make it theirs.

'All right, Mr Hook,' said Liam. 'I think you have yourself some tenants.'

Delbert slapped him amicably on the back. 'Oh, come now, to hell with this Mister Hook nonsense! Call me *Hooky*, or *Del* if you want, young man.'

He turned to face Liam with a mock-serious glint in his eye. 'But not *Delboy*. Right? I draw the line at that!' He flexed his neck and tugged down on his waistcoat, a subconscious tic of his, so it seemed. 'The last cheeky plonker called me that ended up with a big fat lip. Didn't he, Bertie?'

'Uh . . . it's *Herbert* actually.'

Delbert sighed. 'Now, boy, let's not show off in front of the clients. Right, then! Let's go and discuss the rent, gentlemen!'

He led Liam and Bob out of the room. Rashim remained behind, taking in the space a moment longer.

'You're really an *inventor*, sir?' asked Bertie.

Rashim shrugged. 'More a quantum technician really.'

The young man didn't understand the term, but seemed impressed with it all the same. 'Well, that sounds jolly exciting, sir.' He offered his hand to Rashim. 'I do hope we shall have a chance to talk some time. I've got some ideas I'd love to share with you, if you'd care to . . . ?'

'Uh? Oh . . . sure, Bertie.' Rashim shook his hand. 'Yes, we'll talk some time.'

'Pft! You know, Dr Anwar, I hate it when Delbert introduces me with that damnable nickname. It's only him that calls me Bertie. No one else!'

Rashim snuffed the candle out and stepped back out of the room to follow the others before the receding light of the gas lamp dwindled to nothing and they were left in the pitch-black darkness.

'Herbert,' the young man called out after Rashim. 'My name's actually Herbert.' But Rashim wasn't listening; he was trying to catch up with the dwindling lamp light.

The young man was alone in the gloom, the skittering of emboldened rats emerging now it was almost wholly dark again. 'I was jolly well christened Herbert George Wells! Not bloomin' *Bertie*.'

But Rashim had turned a corner and was gone.

CHAPTER 46
7 October 2001, Harcourt, Ohio

Sheriff Marge McDormand cradled the mug of green tea in both hands as she stared at the computer screen in front of her.

'Hell of a crazy world,' she muttered to herself.

'What's that, Marge?'

'Nothing, Jerry,' she replied. She looked past the computer at her husband, sitting in the desk opposite hers. 'And it's "Sheriff" during office hours, my dear.'

Jerry pulled a biro out of his mouth and sighed. 'It's not enough I'm your office boy?'

'The term is "Deputy", hon . . . and that's only until we can find someone else to stand in.' She smiled at him. 'I'm sure we'll find someone soon. Then you can go back to being a kept man.'

She looked back at the screen. Quiet day in Harcourt. She'd done her rounds this morning. Nothing much to write up. A stolen car dumped outside Gary's Bar. No harm done to it other than the driver's-side window forced and the steering column's plastic hood broken to jack the ignition. That and giving Henry Learry — the town drunk — a lift in the squad car back home to his anxious wife. Marge had found him fast asleep behind the wheel of his truck after a night binge-drinking, still way too soaked to be trusted to drive the thing home safely.

Those were the sort of things that Marge dealt with day to

day. The occasional problem with kids breaking into and messing around in the abandoned factories, the occasional domestic dispute, the occasional kitty stuck up a tree. That was it. Police work in Harcourt.

Suited her. She was far too old to be dealing with real crime. She carried a firearm on her hip, but in five years as sheriff here she'd yet to unpop the leather flap of her holster in the course of doing her job.

Which was just fine.

The morning's breakfast round had ended up as it always did at the diner where she'd got into the habit of picking up a take-out coffee and doughnut for Jerry and a green tea for herself. The Williams girl, Kaydee-Lee, usually served her and kept her there talking about everything and nothing for five minutes longer than it took to serve up the order.

That poor young girl's so lonely.

Marge wondered why on earth she stayed in Harcourt. This place was a town with a past, not a future: a glorified departure lounge for an ageing population that seemed to shrink by a couple of dozen every harsh winter.

This morning, though, Kaydee-Lee had had some company. A disarmingly pleasant young man with an interesting accent and charmingly old-fashioned manners. For some reason Marge thought he was Canadian until she got back in the car and placed his accent. Irish. The pair of them seemed to be getting on like old buddies. Thick as thieves.

That girl needed someone in her lonely life. And the young man seemed to be a nice enough find.

Good for you, girl.

Marge sipped her tea and returned to her routine of grazing through news websites and the state police intranet pages. The world really seemed to have gone quite mad in the wake of that terror attack in New York. The President was busy banging a drum for the whole world to go to war with Iraq for some reason. Even though there was evidence surfacing that the terrorists had mostly come from Saudi Arabia.

Go figure.

And what about those guys in Afghanistan? What were they called? Tally-something? Jerry kept calling them the *Telly-Tallies*. Like those children's characters on TV. Weren't they more likely involved in attacking the Twin Towers than this Saddam Hussein fellow over in Iraq?

Marge shook her head. Americans were quite rightly angry. Tens of thousands of New Yorkers were grieving for loved ones right now, but *now* was surely not the best of times to be making big decisions like who to go to war with.

The boys want a war. She sighed again. *And they'll get their war sure enough.*

She clicked to close the MSNBC news page and then pulled up the state police bulletin page. It featured the usual day-to-day bumph, plus the now obligatory daily notices on the current terror threat level. Today it was, as it was yesterday and the day before: RED – SEVERE. Beside the colour-coded alert was a reminder for all law-enforcement personnel to be vigilant for 'suspicious activities and persons'.

Marge was *always* alert for suspicious activities and persons. It was – *well duh, excu-u-use me* – her job anyway! She found the notice vaguely patronizing. It would be like telling young Kaydee-Lee to make a special effort not to pour scalding coffee over the head of the next customer she served.

Grating her teeth, she dutifully scanned the rest of the page then hit the link to the FBI's ViCAP site. The Bureau were featuring front and centre a rogues' gallery of Most Wanteds. Two dozen mugshots, a fair number of them dark-skinned and sporting dark Santa Claus beards large enough to lose a small dog in.

'Nope,' she muttered, 'not seen any of you types skulking around here in Harcourt . . . nor you . . . nor you, Mr Osama bin Laden, nor you, Mr Manuel Caraccus.' She clicked on the link for the second page of the gallery.

'Nor . . .' And stopped mid-mutter. She was looking at a face she'd seen just ten minutes ago.

Jerry heard her suck in her breath. He looked up from the paperwork on his desk. 'Given yourself another paper cut, Marge?' He noticed her wide eyes, her glasses reflecting the pale glow of the computer screen, the styrofoam cup held midway between the desk and her mouth, which now hung open, not making a sound — a rare event in itself.

'You OK over there, Marge?'

CHAPTER 47

7 October 2001, Green Acres
Elementary School, Harcourt, Ohio

'Looks like you're going to have to dig through some walls by the look of this.' Maddy clicked on the screen and zoomed in on a portion of the blueprint.

Rashim nodded. 'It appears as if they left space between these walls for cabling to run from the generator room up to the lights on the top. And over here.' He pointed on the screen. 'Cabling that leads out to an external distribution node.'

'Uh-huh. I guess they planned to have the generator as a part of the viaduct from the very beginning. Fascinating.'

Rashim reached for the mouse. Fingers touched. And recoiled. An awkward half a second.

'All yours,' Maddy said a little too quickly.

He dragged the pixellated image of the blueprint across the screen. 'Hmm, it would be a lot easier knocking through to the generator room itself. Only two walls between our archway and that big steam engine in there.'

'But would you really want to do that? Bust right in there? There's probably "steam engine" engineers or whatever you call them in there. Coal-shovellers and stuff. We've got to be ultra-discreet about this.'

'Indeed. Yes . . . so maybe then, we'll have to tap the cabling somewhere along this conduit. It's a lot more work.' He leaned forward. 'And I imagine a bit of a squeeze, shuffling along inside that space between the walls.' He squinted and muttered a curse in Farsi. 'I wish this image was at a higher resolution.'

'Best I could get.' She shrugged. 'In fact, it was the only blueprint image I could find.' She'd spent a good part of yesterday back at the Internet cafe in the retail park. She'd found an architectural website with an archive of Victorian-era building projects. The Holborn Viaduct was hardly the grandest of London projects, but historically notable because of its incorporation of the city's first electric generator.

'It looks fiddly . . . but it is discreet, Rashim, and that's the important thing. If we're going to start leeching on their power, we've got to make it so that, if they work out the generator's not delivering the power it's designed to deliver, it's got to be almost impossible for them to figure out where the power is leaking away to. The only way they'll figure out what's going on is if they decide to track the course of the cables. Thing is, if we tap the output cautiously – little and often – it'll never be enough of a drain for them to consider stopping the engine and overhauling everything to figure it out.'

'Hopefully.'

She made a face. 'Hopefully.'

'Hey! You all right there, Sal?'

She looked up. Liam was crossing the cracked and weed-speckled playground. He casually kicked his way through a pile of dead leaves, this year's fall from the maple trees lined up beside what was once the school bus drop-off point. The leaves rustled and skittered across the tarmac, caught by a fresh breeze.

Early October, it was getting cold now. The clouds above were promising snow, not rain. Sal shivered inside her parka, puffing a cloud of vapour out in front of her. Liam joined her on the swing. Sat on the plastic strap-seat next to her. The rusting frame creaked as they both swung gently, idly.

'I'm fine.'

'Jay-zus!' He rubbed his hands together vigorously. 'It's cold out here! You should come in.'

'I'm *in* all the time. I came out to get some fresh air.'

'Aye . . .'tis a bit smelly inside, so it is.'

Both Bob and Becks were eating the same convenience meals as them. However, their body chemistry preferred high-protein, low-fat foods. And preferably blended to a baby mush. But tins of refried beans in New Orleans sauce, Uncle YangYang Kettle Noodles and pop tarts had to suffice as their source of nutrition. It just meant they farted constantly. Particularly Bob. He was like some flea-bitten, wiry old mongrel dog letting them off one after the other without any sense of embarrassment. Seemingly without a care in the world.

'Why do you do that?' she asked presently.

'Do what?'

'Talk like you do. The whole Irish thing. You're not even Irish.'

'Hey! Jayz- . . . I just . . .' His mouth flapped for a moment then shut with a coconut *clop*. He looked hurt. Sal winced. That had come out sounding all wrong and she felt guilty.

'I'm sorry. I wasn't trying to be rude, Liam. I just think it all sounds . . . I dunno, fake now.'

He swung in silence. The frame creaked.

'I've stopped using those Indian words. I don't think I even knew what they meant. I'm not even sure if they were real Hindi words.' She still had the sing-song Indian accent, though. She'd even started consciously trying to lose that. If it wasn't real, if it was some technician's idea of how an Indian girl from 2026 *ought* to sound . . . then she was damned if she was going to follow his programming.

'I talk this way, Sal . . . because it's the only way I know how to talk.'

'It's just code, Liam. It's code. Worse than that . . . the Irish thing? It's a cheesy cliché.'

'It's who I am.' He shrugged. 'Even if that does make me a – *whatcha-call-it?* – a *cliché.*'

She looked at him. 'How can you do that, though? Go on just like before, like nothing's happened?'

He managed a wry smile. 'Why not? Nothing about me has changed at all, so. I'm exactly the same person I was.'

'But how can you be the *same person* now you know what you are? Everything – *everything* – planted in our minds before we woke up . . . none of it ever happened! It's nothing! God . . . I mean, maybe we've got chips in our heads just like Bob and Becks. Have you considered that?'

'Aye. But it doesn't worry me any.'

'How can it not?'

He shrugged. 'Anyway, Maddy reckons we're not the same as them. Our minds aren't computers but proper human minds. That's why we had to believe we were human. So we'd act like humans. Think like humans.'

'But wouldn't you want to have someone X-ray your head? Take a look inside to see if there's a chip or something inside?'

'Not really. Whatever's in me head, machine or meat, it works just fine.'

She sniffed. 'Except it's fake.'

'Ah well now . . . who's to say anybody's memories are for real? Hmm?' He chuckled. A plume of breath erupted from his mouth. 'You know, perhaps the whole world, the whole universe, is just a big pretend – someone's idea of a funny joke. Huh?'

'Difference is . . . we *know* our lives are a funny joke, Liam.'

'You can never know anything for sure, Sal. In the end, it's all a question of what you choose to believe.' He watched a cloud of his breath drift away – turning, twisting, dissipating in the cold afternoon air.

'Thing is . . . I choose to be Liam. I like him.' He smiled at her. 'I like being him. And maybe he was once a real lad who lived in Cork and I'm just borrowing his memories, or maybe he's just a made-up person put together from bits and pieces. Who cares?'

'But that's no better than . . .' She struggled to think of an example. 'That's no better than a child pretending to be Superman. No better than all those people who believe in God. Or Jehovah. Or Allah, or Vishnu, or –'

'Maybe.' He shrugged. 'But it works for me.'

She sighed. 'I can't do it, Liam,' she whispered. 'I don't think I can pretend I'm who I thought I was. All I've got that's real is the time in the archway. You. Maddy.'

He pointed at what was clasped in her hands. 'Is that why you've got that with you all the time?'

Sal looked down at the notebook – her diary – and nodded. 'That's me, Liam.' A solitary tear dripped on to the scuffed black cover. She wiped it off irritably. 'That's all there is left of me. Ink and paper.'

A crow cawed from the bare branches beyond the chain-link fence surrounding the playground. The solitary, ominous noise of approaching winter.

'Sal?' He reached out and squeezed her gloved hand. 'Don't do this, Sal. Eh? Don't drift off and away from me an' Maddy. We need you, so we do. The three of us need to hold fast together. To stay a proper team.'

'Need me? What do I do? Nothing.'

'You will do. When we're set up again in London, we'll need you watching for them little changes. Up in the centre of the city, Piccadilly Circus maybe, watching for the time waves.'

She gave that a moment's thought. Perhaps he was right. Perhaps there was a purpose for her still. She wiped her nose and sniffed noisily. Then sniggered.

Liam smiled. 'What?'

'Nothing.'

'No, go on. What's so funny?'

'Something you said.'

'I said something funny?'

She shook her head. 'It's nothing.' Her face brightened for him. 'You're right. We've still got a job to do, haven't we?'

'Aye. So come in, then, Sal. Before you freeze.'

'I will. You go. I'll be along in a minute.'

'All right. I'm makin' some hot chocolate. Care for some?' He cocked a brow. 'There'll be a fair chance of some of them nice chocolate biscuits with the cream in the middle.'

'Oreos.'

'Aye, those are the fellas.'

'Sure. Count me in.'

She watched him go, kicking those leaves again on the way back to the double doors of the school gymnasium, blue paint flaking off both and a rusting push-bar on one of them. The door clattered shut behind him.

Something you said, Liam . . . something funny. Really funny.

'Perhaps the whole universe is just a big pretend?' she muttered softly.

No, actually, not that funny after all.

CHAPTER 48
7 October 2001, Washington DC

Faith appraised Agent Cooper. Unlike most humans he appeared to be very task-focused, very *driven*. One could say binary, almost *Boolean*, in his mindset. He could almost have passed as one of her short-lived batch of clone brothers and sisters. Except, of course, he wasn't six foot six inches tall and carrying around eighteen stone of muscle and dense-lattice bone. He was just as frail and vulnerable as any other human being: one of her hands round his neck and a quick twist and he'd be burger meat in a suit. That unfortunate frailty notwithstanding . . . she'd so far been quite impressed with his performance.

She resumed eating the bowl of Cow & Gate baby food.

Cooper in turn was silently appraising her. Perched on the edge of his desk, he grimaced as he watched her spoon the baby food into her mouth. 'I can't believe you can chow down that stuff.'

'It is an optimal formula,' she replied with her mouth full. 'Maximum nutrition with a minimum of energy consumed in the process of breaking it down and digesting it.'

She noticed he was looking at her intently. 'What is it, Agent Cooper?'

'You've, uh . . . you've got a blob of that stuff right there on the end of your nose.'

She remained staring at him — a face that seemed to be wondering why that mattered in any meaningful way.

'It's not a good look, Faith.' He leaned forward, reached out with a finger and deftly flicked it away.

'*Not a good look*,' she mimicked him. An almost exact copy of his southern Virginian accent. 'Why?'

'Why . . . why? Because you don't want to look like some sort of day-release outpatient from a nuthouse.' He sipped his coffee. 'You're odd enough without dried baby food plastered all over your face. If you're going to be working alongside me, we need you to not attract any attention. I'm pretty much exceeding my authority letting you down here as it is.'

Faith finished her food, put down the bowl and carefully wiped round her mouth. 'I understand.'

Cooper really had stuck his neck out. He'd brought her to The Department a couple of weeks ago. Ushered her past several ID checks, pulling rank on the security personnel. And now here she was down on the mezzanine floor in his domain – the 'catacombs' – being kept here like some sort of a pet.

Truth was he didn't know what to do with her. She couldn't be left to her own devices roaming around Boston conducting her very own hunt-and-seek mission, murdering who she pleased because she might just consider them 'a contaminant' – whatever the heck that was really supposed to mean. And he didn't want to kill her. She was all he had. She was his only connection to whoever these mysterious time travellers were.

What he had was not very much: an autopsy report on Faith's dead colleague, and a tiny chunk of fried circuitry pulled from his head that wasn't anything more now than an interesting fingernail-sized nugget of silicon and graphene.

This creature, this flesh-and-blood robot-woman, was the best piece of evidence he had that he wasn't going mad; that time travel had been quietly going on right in front of everyone's nose for God knows how long. For God knows how many decades. Cooper couldn't even begin to contemplate how valuable the treasure trove of knowledge residing in that digital mind of hers was.

But right now the only investigative process he had on the go was Agent Mallard out there doing the donkey work to track down and confiscate all the CCTV footage that he could lay his hands on. There was the footage from the mall, but also a petrol station, a diner and a motel they'd used the day before. Mallard had already brought back several boxes of tapes, and from those there were some not bad, albeit grainy images of their faces that they'd managed to isolate and enhance.

But that was it. Other than Mallard's legwork, and hoping for a lead to turn up, he had this unlikely 'woman' in front of him.

'I know I keep saying this,' he said, breaking the long silence, 'but if you just shared with me the data you have on them, I could put it to good use. I can get priority access to the Bureau's IT department. We can tap all sorts of databases . . . medical insurance, local and state law-enforcement incident reports, bank records, traffic —'

'No,' she said softly. 'Your assistance in this matter is —' she paused, her eyelids flickering as she considered a choice of phrase — '*appreciated*. However, I am unable to share with you data about the target.'

Perhaps he could try a different angle. 'Well, what about you, then? Hmmm? Or how about telling me something about where you've come from?'

Her cool grey eyes locked on his. 'You wish to know about the future?'

He shrugged. 'Yeah, why not?'

She silently considered that for a moment. 'I am unable to tell you specific details. But I can discuss the early symptoms that are occurring in the world at present.'

'Symptoms?' He laughed at that. 'You make the world sound like it's a hospital patient.'

She cocked her head slightly. 'That analogy is suitable. This world *is* "sick". It is unsustainable. It is dying.'

'Dying? What do you mean?'

'Population tangents increasing versus rapidly diminishing world resources. Even in this time evidence of this, of these future problems, is known to your world leaders. But they choose to do nothing. Oil will run out. Global warming will increase. The polar caps will melt and a third of the world's land mass will be submerged by rising sea levels. It will become accepted in 2035 – far too late to deploy corrective measures – that global warming was more significantly affected by the explosion in world population than it was by hydrocarbon usage.'

She adjusted the cuffs of her jacket. Her hair was growing in quickly – still boyishly short, though. But now, with a vaguely feminine fringe of dark hair and office clothes Cooper had bought her from JC Penney, she almost looked like your typical Wall Street *go-to girl*: hard-faced, ambitious and smartly turned out.

'In only twenty-five years from now there will be nine billion human beings attempting to exist on a diminishing resource-poor land mass. The arithmetic is inevitable, and was always entirely predictable, Cooper. Even now there are scientists that are accurately predicting mankind's fate.'

'Which is what?'

She shrugged. 'You will destroy yourselves.'

He puffed his cheeks. 'That's, uh . . . that's pretty grim.'

'It is what will happen.'

'Jeez, I bet you're a blast at parties.'

She cocked an eyebrow. 'I don't understand the relevance or intended meaning of that comment.'

'Never mind.'

Just then the door into the main office swung inwards with a bang. Cooper jerked and spilled coffee on to the crisp white cuff of his shirt. He saw Mallard's face across a chest-high maze of vacant office cubicles.

'Christ, Mallard! You made me jump!'

'Sir! Sir!'

'What the hell is it?'

Mallard picked his way through, past an empty watercooler that hadn't been used in years, past desks with dust-covered computers that, if someone actually bothered to switch them on, they'd find still ran on Windows 95.

'Sir,' he said, breathless, as he finally stood in front of Cooper and Faith. 'We've got a solid lead. Some small-town sheriff reckons he's ID'ed one of the images we put up on the Bureau's Most Wanted site.'

'Where?'

Mallard looked down at a Post-it note in his hand. 'They're in Ohio. Someplace called Harcourt. It's some has-been town. Used to have several auto-parts factories. They're all closed down now. Mothballed.'

'Hang on.' Cooper looked at Faith. 'That's what you suggested, wasn't it? They'd go to ground someplace like that? Quiet. Out of the way . . . ?'

'With access to a source of electricity and required technical components.' She nodded and almost smiled. 'It is what *I* would do.'

CHAPTER 49

8 October 2001, Green Acres Elementary School, Harcourt, Ohio

'But it's going to be dangerous, isn't it?' Sal looked at Becks. She was no taller or bulkier than any normal twelve- or thirteen-year-old girl. But she, like Bob, was originally engineered for military purposes, a killing machine; if she got the idea into her head while Bob was not around, there'd not be much of any of them left.

Maddy clucked her tongue. 'I've got no idea how she'll behave. But if she bugs out on us, we've got Bob right here to restrain her, or . . .'

'Kill her?'

'Look . . . it won't come to that, I'm sure. More likely she'll just swoon and pine for Liam like some pathetic fangirl.'

Sal snorted. That was kind of funny despite the seriousness of the situation. 'But why now? Why don't we wait until we're settled in London?'

'I'm not sure we're going to have enough power back in 1888 to sustain our back-up frozen embryos. Once we go through to the past, we may not be able to regrow replacement support units. It might be just Bob and Becks . . . one of each. We lose them, we won't have any back-up support units to grow.'

'What about the San Francisco drop point?'

Maddy shook her head. 'I don't think it would be a good idea going anywhere near there. They've got to be watching that place now. No . . . it would be dumb for us to go back there.'

Sal nodded.

'We can take the foetuses with us, just in case there's some way we can find a way to grow new support units if needed. But, really, I think we need to sort Becks out now, once and for all. We need both our support units fully loaded and functional.' She turned to them both. 'Once we go back, we may have to ditch our embryos and that means no more support units. We'll have to rely indefinitely on these two. Which is why . . . we need to test her mind out now, Sal, while we've got a chance here in 2001 to grow a new one from scratch if . . . you know . . . this doesn't work out. Anyway,' she added, 'while Liam's in London it might be easier. We don't want Becks hurling herself his way and slobbering all over him.'

Sal curled her lip. An 'eww' written all over her face.

Maddy pulled a hard drive out of her duffel bag. Masking tape with 'Becks' felt-tipped across it. Becks's complete, original consciousness, her mind, right there in a hard plastic case. Maddy held it up. 'You ready for this, Becks?'

'Affirmative. I am ready.'

'All right, then.' Maddy wasn't entirely sure this was the sensible thing to do. But what was locked away on there, in an encrypted folder, was knowledge that was far too important to remain there forever . . . a decoded portion of the Holy Grail. A message sent by someone, quite possibly the previous team. Quite possibly a previous version of Maddy herself. And God knows what the message was. Another warning like that scribbled Pandora one? But whoever had sent the message from two thousand years ago, they'd thought to pass along an instruction to Becks to keep the secret locked away until certain unspecified conditions were met. And now all of that was sitting on an external hard drive: on a piece of hardware that was unable to *process* these thoughts; on hardware that was merely able to store them. They needed Becks's knowledge, her memories installed back on-board a support-unit mind where, hopefully someday soon, Becks would be able to announce that these mysterious 'conditions' had been met, and let Maddy know what the big secret was.

And now they were acting entirely on their own, beyond the agency's original remit, Maddy realized they had twice as much need to know what dark secret had been transported across a thousand years of Roman history and the Dark Ages, across another thousand years of Holy Grail history for their eyes only.

A warning? A truth? A threat? A revelation?

'Come on, then,' she said. 'This won't do itself.'

CHAPTER 50

8 October 2001, Green Acres
Elementary School, Harcourt, Ohio

It took Maddy half an hour to successfully connect the hard drive to the networked computers. The new PCs had a different method of logging the hard-drive idents, which meant computer-Bob had some data-shuffling to do before he could get the underlying DOS code to recognize the hard drives, and this external one, under their original ident tags.

Presently, Becks closed her eyes. The influx of new data being Bluetoothed into her mind was an odd sensation. One, of course, she'd had before as Bob had worked with her, slowly bringing her mind up to speed with his. But that had been a trickle. This was a flood. The nearest sensory equivalent was like having ice-cold liquid injected into an artery, feeling it spread, branch, travel . . . envelop.

There were duplicated memories among the incoming data. Memories she'd already inherited once before from Bob. Memories of memories. Then there were her very own memories: recollections of dinosaurs and jungles. Liam . . . and an emergent mind-state for him – a *feeling* – that she'd labelled and carefully put to one side. In her mind she saw medieval towns and castles, Prince John, ridiculously besotted with her. A battle . . . the siege of Nottingham: ranks of glinting armour and flapping banners shifting in the heat haze of a summer's day. A remote monastery, a monk called Cabot.

And then an ancient scroll of parchment. Becks recalled leaning over it and, by the dim, flickering light of the archway, moving a deciphering 'grille' across faded ink nearly a thousand years old. She could see herself writing down the letters on a pad of lined paper. Then, the decoding complete, starting to read it.

Then the discontinuity. Whatever she'd read had included an instruction that locked it all away into one part of her mind.

After that her memories were of the archway dropping, literally, into a war zone. A destroyed America tearing itself apart. She remembered the one-sided battle. Skies filled with giant airships, and hulking behemoths, engineered monsters, ascending the slope of a battlefield and dropping down into their trenches. Butchery. Blood. The dismembered ruins of bodies cluttering the floor of a trench.

She recalled taking one of those giant beasts down. Staring closely into its eyes as it lay dying and seeing what looked like a plea for death: *End me.*

And then she'd found a heavy machine gun and fired it from the hip until its spinning barrels had overheated and locked. She remembered a dozen gunshot and bayonet wounds, her body's enhanced biochemistry rushing to fight fires, to clog arteries and preserve a dwindling reserve of blood. But slowly losing the struggle.

Then that final lucky gunshot. The ricochet of a bullet inside her cranium, a glancing blow off the silicon in her head followed by a complete and instant shutdown.

'Becks?' Maddy's voice sounded distant. A cry from the end of an impossibly long tunnel. 'You OK?'

[System Update Complete]

Nanoseconds that felt like minutes passed in her mind, an almost reassuring pause. It appeared that the intelligence that had existed before her shutdown and death was actually largely undamaged and fully functional, but then . . .

[Warning: System Conflict]

Becks's breath caught in her throat. At the very base level of her digital mind two insistent lines of programming, two distinct imperatives, were firmly at odds with each other. Commands issued by two different individuals and embedded in her, each as unavoidably authoritative as a command from God Himself might be to a holy man. One recent – Madelaine Carter's new mission statement: *The end must be prevented.* And the other one much, much older. She realized that certain unlock conditions must have been satisfied. Whatever those conditions were, the part of her AI sectioned off and responsible for being the gatekeeper code had clearly decided, rightly or wrongly, that the gate could be cracked ajar.

And it opened the door on conflicting instructions she was struggling to resolve. Because the other imperative, the other mission statement released from captivity, was quite the opposite.

The end must be allowed to happen.

And those words had come from nearly two thousand years ago.

More to the point, they were Liam's instructions. His words. Not Maddy's. There was more. Much more in there. Her mind queried this conflict between Maddy's mission statement and the other from antiquity, Liam's, but the gatekeeper code refused her entry to that part of her hard drive. The explanation was in there, but not available. Not yet.

[Resolve Conflict]

Becks was on her own. She was going to have to choose between Liam and Maddy. But she realized that was a problem her mind had already been quietly working on. She had the recent mission reappraisal from Madelaine Carter complete with a perfectly logical justification: Waldstein's initial mission parameters could no longer be trusted. The man was quite clearly insane and bent on seeing mankind destroy itself. But she also had just one sentence from Liam. A future Liam. And no justification or explanation to go along with it.

[Resolve Conflict]
1. Carter imperative – logical validation
2. O'Connor imperative – none

She located a thought buried in her head like a prehistoric mosquito entombed in amber. A frozen decision, an instruction code with an internal time tag attached to it. It was a moment of thought that had occurred in an eye-blink, fifty-nine nanoseconds after a single British bullet had penetrated her skull and fluked a glancing impact on her computer chip. Her dying mind had attempted to unlock the secrets in that portion of her drive, to propagate the data stored there elsewhere in case of damage to that partition. The gatekeeper code must have agreed this emergency measure was valid and the process had just begun . . . when she'd 'died'.

And there it was – just one command from Liam with no sensible explanation to back it up. All there was to lend it authority, credence . . . was that it was an older Liam with knowledge of what destiny lay ahead of them all. And logic dictated that a future Liam would have the benefit of hindsight; a future Liam's command must exceed Maddy's authority now. However, Becks's scrambled, dying mind had turned that logical statement that future-Liam's command must be trusted . . . into love.

'Becks? Talk to us, goddammit! You OK?' That voice again. Still far away, but a little closer now. Becks opened her eyes. She saw Maddy, Sal and Bob staring at her, a concerned expression on all their faces.

'How do you feel?'

'I now have near full recollection,' she replied coolly. Her gaze met Bob's. 'My own memories are restored. I calculate 6.7 per cent data corruption.'

'That is better than our original simulated estimate,' rumbled Bob.

'What about Liam?'

She looked at Maddy. 'What do you wish to know, Madelaine?'

'When we ran the software simulation of your mind on the computer system, you said something very odd about him. Do you remember what you said?'

'Information: it was read-only,' said Bob. 'She would not remember the simulation as her mind-state was not stored.'

'Oh yeah. Of course.' Maddy rolled her eyes at her own stupidity. 'Of course. OK, then . . . uh, let's try a different approach. Let me see . . .'

Sal stepped in. 'Becks, tell us how you *feel* about Liam.'

[Recommended Answers]
1. I am presently confused by undefinable variables
2. I love him. Love him! LOVE HIM!
3. He is my operative

She offered the third answer and that seemed to please all three of them.

Maddy grinned with relief. She patted Becks affectionately. 'It's really good to have you back again.'

'Thank you,' she replied, smiling. 'It is good to be fully functional again.'

CHAPTER 51

5 December 1888, Holborn Viaduct, London

'Do you hear that, Liam?' Rashim tapped the brick wall again. They both heard the faint clatter and rustle of loose mortar dropping on the far side.

'It sounds like there's a hollow there.'

Rashim nodded. 'That's got to be it – the conduit.'

'Well done, skippa!' chirped SpongeBubba. Above the lab unit's goofy grin, its small gherkin-shaped nose wobbled slightly as it fidgeted from foot to foot.

Liam, Rashim and SpongeBubba had settled into their viaduct archway – *the dungeon* they were calling it now – a few days ago and all three had been kept busy. Rashim had figured out a way to make them some money. Obvious really. So obvious the entire team had collectively, figuratively palmed their foreheads when he'd mentioned it.

Gambling. More specifically, card games. Every public house seemed to have a room at the back, thick with pipe smoke, where a 'gambling party' had gathered: working men who were stupid enough to lose their wages night after night. Rashim and Liam had played faro several nights on the trot, learning how to count the cards, and Rashim calculating the odds. There was also hazard, which relied purely on chance, and a game they avoided like the plague. Chance wasn't any good to them.

After four consecutive nights of winning at several different gatherings, they were beginning to be recognized. Liam suggested any further money they'd need to make might be best earned placing bets on horses. A little trip of a few weeks into the future would give them the names of every winning horse in the country. Once they were all properly settled, that was going to be the first order of business.

With some money to tide them over, Liam had been busy buying some furnishings and comforts. There were plenty of pawnshops and second-hand furniture shops nearby in Holborn. It also gave him a chance to find his way around this part of London. To drink in and learn the finer nuances of London life in this time.

This morning, though, their attention had turned to the task of hooking into the source of electric power that was chugging away close by. They'd been digging small 'sample' holes along the back wall all morning. At first where they'd expected to find the narrow space according to the blueprints Maddy had printed out for them. And then, when it became clear the blueprints weren't entirely accurate, at random intervals along the wall.

Rashim worked the tip of his screwdriver along the mortar around a loose brick. This time, finally, it looked like they'd found the narrow voids beyond; they could hear the hollow echo of skittering rats, the tap and echo of grit and mortar falling off the brick wall on the far side. The mortar was like clay.

'Not very good,' he said. 'The building contractor must have been using a cheap mix.'

The brick shifted. It was loose enough now to remove with his fingers. He pulled it free. Liam flipped on a torch and shone it through the small hole in the wall into the darkness beyond. They could make out a passage about a yard wide and only the same again high.

Rashim cursed. 'I was actually hoping it was tall enough to be a walk space.'

Liam studied the floor of the passageway, littered with rat droppings. 'It's a crawl space,' he said. He grimaced. 'And it's covered in rat poo.'

'Great.'

They eased another dozen bricks out and widened the hole. Rashim consulted the blueprint by the light of Liam's torch. 'Twenty, maybe thirty metres down there, and that takes us very, *very* close to where the generator is supposed to be located.'

Liam took off his thick felt coat and began to unbutton his waistcoat.

Rashim sighed. 'No, maybe . . . I should go. If they've used this conduit for laying down cables then it's best I take a look at them.'

Liam looked again at the rat poo. 'Are you sure?'

Rashim grimaced at the fleeting sight of tiny grey furry bodies, flickering bald pink tails and the glint of dozens of beady black eyes. 'Not really.' He sighed. 'But I . . . it'll be easier if I can see for myself to do the job.'

Liam nodded. Patted his shoulder. 'Aye, there is that. I'll probably get it wrong and end up blowing this place to kingdom come, or something.'

Rashim stripped to the waist, folding his clothes carefully. He grabbed his tool bag and then, with a cheap keyfob pen torch between his teeth, climbed into the hole in the wall. He hesitated outside the crawl space.

'I really hate rats.'

'Ah now, go on. They're probably more frightened of you than you are of them.'

Rashim ducked down into the space and began to crawl along the passage.

'Ughhh!' His voice echoed back after a minute of grunting and shuffling. Liam heard him swearing in Farsi.

'You OK in there?'

'I have just put my hand in something disgusting.' Liam heard Rashim's breathing and muttering echoing back towards him. By the light of his own torch Liam could only faintly see the soles of Rashim's boots.

'Rashim, are you OK in there?'

'Dead rat.'

SpongeBubba was hovering curiously beside Liam's elbow. His plastic lips curled half convincingly. 'Ewww!'

Another couple of minutes of shuffling, the grunts and scrapes slowly receding, and Liam had lost sight of him. He snapped his torch off. Now their main room was lit only by an oil lamp flickering away on top of a wooden crate for a table.

The room was filling up with things from 2001 as well. They'd spent the last two days beaming back supplies and components and spares of things they thought they might need. Sal and Maddy had raided Walmart. The tools from their DIY section. The kettle, toaster and George Foreman griddle from their Home Essentials aisle, all sitting in a yellow plastic stack-box, would have been an unforgivable contamination of modernity under their old stricter contamination-averse regime, their old mission statement. But down here in this dungeon-like environment, under lock and key – and only they had the key, of course – no one was going to stumble upon these things.

There were boxes of Coco Pops, pot noodles, several dozen packs of Dr Pepper – enough to keep Maddy going for a few weeks.

Halfway up the brick wall on the far side of the room another plastic stack-box protruded as if it had always been a deliberate part of the viaduct's foundation construction. A mis-translation.

A box full of batteries, electrical flex, diodes, spare circuit boards that at some point they really ought to chip out of the bricks and remove from the wall.

Rashim and Maddy's response to that mistake had been to offer him a nervous 'oops' grin. Liam had complained that this instance of mis-translation could easily have happened to one of them. As it happened, it turned out to be the result of a bug in the new code they'd written for the reconfigured displacement machine. Since then, everything else beamed back from 2001 had landed in the middle of the chalk squares marked out on the floor of their new home.

He was about to call out again to Rashim, to check if he was all right, when he heard a loud knock on their small door. He was planning on ignoring it until he heard the voice of their landlord, Delbert Hook.

'Hoy! You gents all right in there?'

He turned to SpongeBubba. 'Go hide and don't make a sound.'

'Righto, Liam.'

Liam tucked his torch away, picked up the oil lamp and made his way to the door. He ducked into the low archway. Hesitant to slide the bolt and open it, he cupped his mouth instead and answered through the door's keyhole. 'Uh . . . I'm perfectly fine, Mr Hook, so I am!'

'Come on now, Mr O'Connor,' the man's muffled voice returned. 'That's no way to welcome your good neighbour, is it?'

Liam cursed. He looked back over his shoulder. SpongeBubba was out of sight and most of their bits and pieces from 2001 were covered by a tarp. By the faint glow of lamplight Delbert Hook wasn't going to see anything much, and most importantly, not the far wall, vandalized as it was with holes all along the length of it.

He quickly slid the bolt to one side and pulled the door open – catching Delbert still hunkered down, caught in the act of attempting to sneak a peek through the keyhole. 'What can I do for you, Mr Hook?'

Delbert awkwardly straightened up, flexed his neck and smoothed down his waistcoat. 'I . . . well, I heard some knockin' going on in here. Thought perhaps one of you might have got stuck. Locked in by mistake, so to speak.'

'No.' Liam offered him a reassuring face. 'No, we're just fine.'

Delbert was craning his neck curiously, trying to see past Liam. 'Is that some of your scientific paraphernalia I see behind you?'

Liam looked over his shoulder at the dim hump of the tarp in the middle of the floor. 'Aye. Just assorted bits and pieces.'

'A lot of bits and pieces by the look of it.' Delbert frowned suspiciously. 'I didn't hear you bring all of that lot in.'

'We used the Farringdon Street door, so we did.'

'Very quietly it seems.'

'Ah well, we didn't want to disturb you up the front.' Liam offered him a polite smile. 'Don't want to be a nuisance or anything.'

There was an awkward silence between them as Delbert's head ducked and weaved to get another look past Liam, and Liam shuffled subtly from side to side to obscure his view.

'So, is your Dr Anwar going to be starting his experiments soon, is he?'

'When he's good and ready.'

Delbert gave up on the peeking. The doorway was too narrow. 'Well, if you gents need anything . . . any supplies? You know I'm the man to call on. I can get you anything you want.' He winked. '*Anything*.'

Liam nodded. 'Well, if we do need your help, Mr Hook, we'll be sure to ask.'

The little man stood on tiptoes and craned his neck to one side, one last time. Liam mirrored him. 'Anything else, is there, Mr Hook?'

He sighed. Back down on flat feet. 'No . . . no. Just remember, your rent's due on the Sunday.'

'Aye, every Sunday. I won't forget.'

'Right then.' A frustrated smile flickered across Delbert's lips. 'I'll bid you good day.'

Liam watched him turn and go, whistling tunelessly as his feet scuffed the floor and he finally disappeared from view. He closed and bolted their door.

'OK, SpongeBubba, you can come out now.' The lab unit shuffled out of a dark corner.

Liam heard Rashim's voice echoing down the passage and out of the hole in the back wall. He couldn't make out what he'd said, but it sounded encouraging. A moment later he spotted the soles of Rashim's feet followed by his rear appearing in the crawl space as he slowly, awkwardly, reversed back out.

He stood up; his chest and back, hands and face were caked with dirt and grime. But he was grinning like a child. He held up a loop of modern plastic-sheathed flex, taped off to insulate the end. 'I managed to patch into their copper wiring.'

It took him another few minutes to wire in a heavy-duty transformer and then finally pull out a desk lamp from beneath the tarp. He plugged it into a four-way connector.

'So, here it is.' Rashim licked his lips anxiously and flicked the switch. 'Hopefully.' The desk lamp's bulb flickered on with a dull *snick*.

'And *voilà*! Now we have power!'

CHAPTER 52

9 October 2001, Green Acres Elementary School, Harcourt, Ohio

'OK. So we're jumping to 14 December 1888. That's a clear day and night after Liam and Rashim's return, so we shouldn't get any tachyon backwash.' The boys had had a total of nine days back there fixing their new 'home' up, ready for their complete relocation.

'This is how we're going to go about it,' said Maddy. She pointed at the PCs. 'We can operate this displacement window on just one of those. It's a relatively close time-stamp, just over a century away.'

'One hundred and twelve years, nine months and –'

'Thanks, Becks. Like I said, just over a century – so we're nowhere near pushing the calculative side of things. One PC will be enough. The rest we're gonna box up and send through.'

She looked around the derelict classroom, their home for nearly three weeks. It was almost empty now. All that remained was what they'd found in there: abandoned tables and chairs. She pointed at the two squares marked in tape on the floor.

'We're going in pairs. Obviously. But the way I see it, we've got a bit of a problem with the last displacement.'

She hesitated to see whether Liam or Sal were thinking along the same lines as her. Keeping up to speed. She sighed; of course they weren't. Liam shrugged at her to get on with it and Sal stared vacantly.

'Right,' she said with another sigh, 'good to see you two are on the ball.'

Liam nodded assuredly. 'Aye.'

She rolled her eyes, noting that Liam wouldn't recognize a gentle prod of *snark-asm* if it slapped him in the face.

'The last displacement, guys, has to transport the displacement machine itself. We can't leave it behind. Which means a certain amount of untested risk.' She looked at Rashim to elaborate.

'Yes . . . uh . . . yes, you see, when we activate the last time window, we will effectively be severing the power supply to the displacement machine. In theory the heavy lifting has already been done by opening the window, so this should not, theoretically, be an issue. But –' he spread his hands – 'it is untested. The interruption could cause a glitch.'

'And if it does that?' said Liam.

'We could lose our machine and be stuck in 1888,' replied Maddy.

'The window could collapse in on itself,' continued Rashim. 'Or the time-stamp might deviate in location or time.'

'Which is why someone has to go at the same time as it,' said Maddy. 'Go with it.'

Liam's eyes widened. 'You mean one of us has to run the risk of being turned inside out? Or get blended with a brick wall?'

'Or get lost in chaos space?' added Sal.

Maddy shook her head. 'You won't end up merged with it. Remember, these are separate displacement envelopes. But, if a glitch *does* happen and the displacement machine remains here in 2001, or – I dunno – ends up blapped ten years into the future or something, we need someone right there alongside it to destroy it. To make sure it doesn't end up in someone else's hands.'

'Stuff that,' said Liam. 'If that happens then it happens.'

Sal shook her head. 'I . . . I don't want to do it. I don't want to end up . . . lost.'

'Don't worry,' Maddy replied solemnly, 'I'm not actually asking for volunteers to go alongside the machine.'

'Jay-zus, Maddy! Don't be a daft idiot! We can't do this without you.'

Incredulity on her face. She half-laughed at that. 'I'm not frikkin' volunteering, Liam! Do I look like a stupid moron?'

'Then who?' asked Sal. She looked at Rashim. 'Not . . .'

He grinned. 'I'm not a stupid moron either.'

'Becks,' said Maddy, settling the issue. 'It's Becks who's doing it.' She looked at the support unit sitting cross-legged beside Bob, dismayingly small and slight in contrast to him – an orange compared to a pumpkin.

Becks nodded. 'Maddy and I have already discussed this. I am logically the most expendable team member.'

'Expendable?' Liam shook his head. 'She's not expendable . . . she's . . .' He studied his flapping hands for something to back that up. Then he had it. 'She's got that big secret in her head, so she does.'

'We've also got that same secret on a hard drive, Liam. And now we know her AI is pretty stable.' Maddy pursed her lips. 'Despite that crush she seems to have on you . . . it means we can either run her mind on the network, or upload her AI into Bob if worst comes to worst and we lose her.'

'It's a relatively low probability,' added Rashim assuredly. 'I have run some calculations on this. Severing the power to the machine should have no effect.'

'Aye, says the genius fella who beamed three hundred people seventeen years too far into Roman times.'

'Now *that* was not *my* fault! I had to make too many guesses without any preparation! I had to –'

Maddy waved them both silent. 'Forget it, guys. The point is one of us has to babysit the displacement machine through the last window. And Becks is going to be the one to do it. Aren't you?'

'Affirmative.'

'Like Rashim said, it's a low probability anyway. But . . . if it *does* happen then we need her alongside to trash the machine then self-terminate so there's nothing left for anyone, anywhere, to make use of.'

Maddy had toyed with nominating Bob, but she was pretty sure that it was unlikely that they were going to be able to grow any new support units where they were setting up base. If they *did* end up marooned in Victorian London forevermore then she'd rather have that big ape by their side to protect them than this small-framed female. A child. And yes, stronger than a fully grown man, but still nowhere near as lethal a weapon as Bob.

'I want us to get this done this morning. I think we've pushed our luck hanging around here for weeks on end . . . and God knows if those support units are still out there looking for us. They're not stupid. They've managed to track us down twice already.'

'No one'll find us here,' said Liam. 'Surely?'

'There's no knowing what sort of a breadcrumb trail we've left behind us. I think we've got very lucky so far. We don't want to push it, right?'

Liam and Sal nodded.

'We've got power-tap established and a nice new place we can call home. So, let's pack up the last of our gear and get this thing done.'

CHAPTER 53

9 October 2001, Harcourt, Ohio

'That's the girl,' said Sheriff Marge McDormand. 'The waitress. Her name's Kaydee-Lee Williams.'

Cooper caught a glimpse of her through the diner's broad glass window, dotted with fading yellow cardboard stars with handwritten assurances on them: 'All Day Breakfast – we'll fill you up like a truck!', 'Freshly Brewed Coffee – unlimited refills!'

They crossed Harcourt's main street, quiet at this hour. Cooper put a hand on the door.

'Go easy on her,' said Marge. She glanced at the other agent – '*Agent Mallard . . . like the duck,*' he'd joked as he'd presented his ID – and the young woman with Agent Cooper. She'd not offered to show any kind of ID. Not even given a name. She had an icy face, the calm, lifeless look of a serial killer if truth be told.

'Just go easy on Kaydee-Lee,' said Marge. 'She's no troublemaker. She's certainly no *terrorist*.'

Cooper nodded and smiled politely. 'Thank you for your assistance, Sheriff, we'll take it from here. Mallard?'

'Sir?'

'See the sheriff back to her car.'

'Yes, sir.'

Cooper pushed the door of the diner open and Faith followed him inside.

The doorbell *dinged* as the door swung shut. It was quiet inside. Empty except for the waitress watching a small TV set sitting on the end of the counter. Cooper walked up the aisle between check-cloth tables. He watched Mallard leading the sheriff back to her squad car and getting in the front with her. He noted the sheriff watching things intently from there.

Let her watch. He smiled. Cooper had authority enough to shut her up, to lock the whole town down behind an impenetrable ring of road blocks if need be.

The waitress finally responded to the sound of their approach and turned from the television to offer Cooper a warm, friendly smile. 'Help you guys?' She noticed Faith behind him. 'Table for two?'

Cooper pulled out his badge and flipped the wallet open with one smooth flick of his wrist. He loved doing that; he felt like Captain Kirk flipping open a communicator. One of the many little perks of the job. 'FBI. I'd like to have a talk with you, Kaydee-Lee.'

She looked at his ID. Her eyes widened. 'Did you just say FBI? Like on the TV?'

'I'm Agent Cooper,' he replied and stepped to one side. 'And this is Agent Faith. We just want to ask you some questions.'

'Am I . . . am I in trouble? Have I —'

Cooper shook his head. 'No . . . not at all. The sheriff says you're a good girl.' He grabbed a stool and perched on it. 'And, you know, I'm inclined to believe her. I just wondered if you could help us out with something?'

Kaydee-Lee's face relaxed a little. 'Uh . . . OK, I'll try.'

Cooper pulled a sheet of printer paper out of his pocket. The image on the face-down glossy side had been a nightmare to obtain. He'd had the devil of a time extracting it from that futuristic touch-screen mobile phone they'd recovered in that bridge archway in New York. He'd ended up having to draft some tech-heads from the Bureau's research division to open the phone up and extract the solid-state data-storage chip. Of course they'd first tried one of the data cables supplied with the single pre-release 'iPod' that Apple had begrudgingly released to them. It appeared to have the same connector, and, given this device from the future was manufactured by the very same company, Cooper had been hoping they were going to be able to access its data storage.

But that would have been too easy, wouldn't it? The futuristic mobile phone was using a different data-communication protocol.

The next step – something of a last resort – was pulling the damned thing to pieces and getting their hands on the data-storage chips inside. At which point, before they completely destroyed the thing, one of the Bureau nerds suggested simply getting the image up on the device's screen . . . and just photographing the screen.

Obvious really.

Cooper turned the photograph over on the counter. 'You've been talking to this guy recently.'

Kaydee-Lee leaned forward and scrutinized the image more closely. Her breath caught involuntarily. 'Errr . . . not sure . . . I . . .'

'It's best to just be straight up and honest with us, Kaydee-Lee,' he said. 'This is serious stuff.'

Her cheeks turned a mottled pink. 'OK . . . he's been in here for coffee a coupla times. That's all.'

'And you've been talking, haven't you?'

'Sure . . . he's kinda friendly, I guess.' She looked up at him. 'What's this about?'

'Terrorism, Kaydee-Lee. The worst kind of terrorism.'

She laughed. More a strangled giggle. 'Oh no . . . not him. No.' She bit her lip and shook her head until her face straightened. Nerves.

'No, he's not a terrorist.' She looked at the TV. Fox News was showing images of cranes pulling apart the mound of debris. 'Hang on . . . is this anything to do with *that*?'

'I'm not at liberty to say.' Cooper paused. Enough of a pause to be sure she understood that, yes, it actually was very much to do with that. 'All I can tell you is that we need you to be one hundred per cent honest with us. To be a good, patriotic American citizen and tell us what you can about this young man.'

She nodded. 'OK . . . he's called Liam, I know that much.'

'Liam O'Connor,' said Faith. 'We already know this.'

'And he's from Ireland,' added Kaydee-Lee.

'Tell me, Kaydee-Lee . . . is he alone? Or perhaps with some others?'

Her hesitation gave her away. She was holding something back. 'Come on, Kaydee-Lee, we need to know about this young man. Lives . . . a lot of innocent lives could be at stake.'

'Lives?' Her face was flushed fully crimson now. 'Seriously?'

Cooper decided to buy a little of her trust. 'I'll level with you, Kaydee-Lee. What I'm about to tell you is top secret and goes no further, do you understand?' She nodded.

'We have reason to believe this Liam is part of a terror cell that was based in New York and quite possibly involved in some way with what happened there in September. Do you understand? Perhaps they were part of a planning team, or coordinators or a back-up team. We don't know precisely what their involvement was yet.'

'But . . . but . . . he . . . doesn't look like one of *them*.'

Them. By that she meant an Arab. A Muslim.

'We have enemies that come in all shapes and sizes these days, I'm afraid.' Cooper recalled a rather colourful turn of phrase he'd heard President Bush use during a press conference the other day. 'There's an *axis of evil* out there, Kaydee-Lee, a coalition of bad groups all working together to topple our country: the Taliban, Al Qaeda, Iran, Iraq, China, North Korea. Even the IRA. Bad guys, Kaydee-Lee, all of them. Hell, we've even got our own American citizens working against us . . . White Supremacists, Nation of Islam, Anti-capitalists, Anarch–'

'Did you just say *IRA*?' She swallowed anxiously. 'IRA? That's those Irish ones, isn't it?'

'That's right.' Cooper nodded slowly. 'That's exactly right. So . . . he may have been using you, Kaydee-Lee.'

A tear began to well up in one eye, then spilled down her cheek. 'I thought he was being friendly.' Her mouth began to quiver. 'I . . . I thought he, you know, actually *liked* me.'

Cooper reached for a napkin further along the counter and passed it to her.

'It's possible he was *using* you, Kaydee-Lee. Using you to get some local information.' Cooper reached for her hand and guided the napkin to mop up some mascara that had smudged.

'And listen . . .' His voice softened. 'Maybe he also liked you, Kaydee-Lee. He may be a terrorist, but that doesn't stop him being human, right?'

She dabbed at her eyes miserably, nodded. She sniffed, her chin dimpled and her bottom lip curled as she tried to stifle a sob. 'But I really like . . . *liked* him. He wasn't like the others that come in. Truckers, creepy old men . . . always trying to hit on you an' stuff. He's, like,' she corrected herself, 'he *was*, like, a . . . well, a real *gentleman*.'

'That is men for you. They are all the same,' said Faith without a hint of warmth or empathy in her voice. Cooper turned to look at her. Where the heck did she get that from? She was a robot, wasn't she? Not some agony aunt. He figured she must have picked it up from some daytime TV show. Oprah or something.

Kaydee-Lee whispered pathetically, 'Everyone ends up using me.'

'Kaydee-Lee.' Cooper held her hand. She didn't flinch at that. It was vaguely comforting to have someone reach out for her, even if he did look like some kind of pale-skinned lizard wearing a *Men in Black* suit.

'Kaydee-Lee . . . we need to know a little bit more about Liam. Was it just him? Were there others? Can you tell me?'

She dabbed at her eyes, wiped her nose dry, straightened her shoulders and did her best to put on a calm, totally-in-control face, just like the scary-looking FBI lady over the counter from her. She wondered what it would be like to be like her, so incredibly ice-cool. Kaydee-Lee could only imagine how wonderful it would be to be just like this agent lady: elegant, confident, disciplined, ruthless. She bet no one *ever* used her.

'Miss?'

The woman stirred. 'Yes?'

'Is it, like, really hard to become an FBI agent? Could someone, you know, someone like me ever become one? Could I end up like you?' she asked hopefully.

The woman exchanged a glance with her partner. It looked like he was giving her permission to go ahead and answer the question. Her grey eyes disappeared for a moment behind flickering eyelids, then finally she answered. 'No. That is extremely unlikely.'

That figures. Kaydee-Lee sighed. *I'll be a waitress till the day I die.*

Cooper looked like he was getting impatient. 'Kaydee-Lee? Were there others? Can you tell me?'

She nodded. 'Oh yeah, I can tell you. There were others all right. They wanted a place to go an' hide up. They said they wanted somewhere quiet and private.' She raised two pairs of fingers and air-quoted. 'Somewhere where they could go and do their stupid *science experiments*.'

CHAPTER 54

9 October 2001, Green Acres
Elementary School, Harcourt, Ohio

Liam and Sal vanished from their tape-marked squares with a soft pop. They were now back in Victorian London on 14 December 1888 with Bob and SpongeBubba. At least Maddy *hoped* they were.

She was a hundred per cent sure the recently rewritten displacement software was error free. OK, perhaps not a hundred per cent, but gosh-darn as close as it's possible to be with hastily written computer code.

Just the three of them left here in the derelict school classroom now: her, Rashim and Becks. She looked round the room one last time. There was nothing left that they'd forgotten to send through. All they'd be leaving behind was a small pile of empty tin cans, plastic noodle pots and polystyrene coffee cups, a cheap sleeping bag that had popped its seam and spilled white stuffing, and a pair of extra-large size trainers for Bob that had proven to be still too small for him.

'This is it, then,' she said. 'Goodbye, 2001.'

'You sound sad,' said Rashim.

'Guess I am . . . a bit. This place has been my home, hasn't it? Well, at least this *time*, *this year*, has been my home since . . .' She smiled, stopping herself. 'I was going to say, "since I got recruited". But actually 2001 has been my *only* real home. It's the

302

year in which I was grown and birthed.' She laughed. 'It's the year in which I've lived my entire false life so far.'

Rashim shook his head and tutted. 'You shouldn't think like that. It does you no good, Maddy.'

'Relax. It's not self-pity.' She shrugged. 'I think I've got used to the idea I'm nothing but a meat product.'

'You are not a product. You are Miss Madelaine Cartwright . . .'

'Carter.'

'Sorry,' he said, wincing, '*Carter*. Even if someone *invented* you, came up with your life story, conjured up your name . . . you're still a real person. You are a person. Just as real as any other, as real as I am. Do you see?'

Her eyes moistened. 'Oh, that's a *really* beautiful thing to say, Rashim.' She bit her bottom lip. 'So very beautiful.'

He looked surprised. Perhaps even hopeful. 'Really?'

'No.' She put her hands on her hips. 'Slightly cheesy if anything.' She punched his arm playfully. 'But it was nice of you to say it.' She turned round. 'How are we doing over there, Becks?'

The support unit was studying a display on the monitor. 'The displacement machine is nearly ready to discharge again, Maddy. Ninety-six seconds.'

'You understand what to do once we're gone?'

'Affirmative. I will move the displacement machine into one departure marker, and I will stand in the other. I will displace alongside the machine.'

'And?'

'And?' Becks cocked her head. 'And . . . if there is a translation error I will ensure the machine and myself are destroyed.'

Maddy wandered over to the school desk and leaned over. 'And what about you, computer-Bob?'

> **I will erase all data on this machine once the last time displacement has been completed.**

Effectively that was suicide for computer-Bob, a software self-termination. She patted the top of the monitor. 'That's a good boy.'

Agent Cooper regarded the SWAT team, huddled against the side of the unmarked van. A dozen of them in Kevlar pads, helmets and flak jackets. He'd called in an armed standby team from the ATF, the Bureau of Alcohol, Tobacco, Firearms and Explosives. They looked the business: stern-faced and relentlessly trained for this kind of thing – narcotics raids, gang busts. That's what Cooper was telling them this was. The squad leader tapped his throat mic and checked each of his team had a clear comms line before locking off the command channel and giving his full attention to Agent Cooper and Faith, standing beside him.

'Carry on, sir.'

'We believe there are six of them. A male, late teens, perhaps early twenties. Caucasian, dark-haired. One female, red-ginger hair, late teens. One female, Asian-Indian, possibly a minor. Try not to kill her. We can do without the press calling the Bureau a bunch of child-murderers. There's another Caucasian male, very big . . . I mean *huge*. And *very* dangerous. You'll want to be sure to take him down first.'

'Understood.'

'Another female, Caucasian, small, most definitely another minor. She seems to be drugged or under some kind of sedation. Quite possibly she's a hostage. Again, be careful not to kill her. Lastly, another male, Asian-Indian, late twenties, long hair and beard. We believe he may be this terrorist cell's technician, quite possibly their bomb-maker.'

'Another high-priority target?'

'Definitely. But shoot to *incapacitate*, not to kill . . . if that's at all possible. I need information from these terrorists. I'd very much like to have someone alive to talk to when the gun smoke clears.'

'Understood, sir.'

'And maximum caution. Do you understand? That big one is a lethal killing machine. Take him down first.'

'Doesn't matter how big he is, sir . . . a head shot will bring him down.'

Cooper wasn't sure how much to tell the man; that back at the shopping mall in Connecticut it had taken *seven* cops, all of them emptying their magazines, to bring down Faith's colleague?

'Just don't assume a single head shot's going to do it . . . all right?'

'You should focus gunfire at the temples,' added Faith. 'Its cranium is comparatively weak there.'

The ATF squad's officer cocked his brow. 'Are you guys . . . ?' He looked from Cooper to Faith. Neither looked like they were joking. 'Seriously?'

'You heard what she said.' Cooper looked up at the gun-metal sky. A heavy bank of dark churning cloud on the horizon was rolling lazily towards them.

Storm's coming this way.

He looked at the boarded-up elementary school across the road. A godforsaken-looking place this; the sort of urban cancer that ate has-been, rustbelt cities like Baltimore, Detroit, Indianapolis from within, like tooth decay, rotting them from the inside out. He wondered why the building hadn't been bulldozed years ago – put out of its misery. Actually, the same could be said for this whole sorry town.

'Let's just get this done, before we all get soaked and catch our deaths standing out here.'

★

Maddy waved at Becks as she took her place in her taped square. 'See you on the other side. Don't be long now.'

'Yes, Madelaine.'

She turned to Rashim. 'You good to go?'

He centred his feet, checked arms and legs were well and truly inside the square. 'I'm ready.'

'OK, computer-Bob, beam me down!'

Rashim looked sideways at her. *'Beam me down?'*

'I've always wanted to say that.' She gave a guilty shrug. 'It's a *Star Trek* thing.'

On the monitor on the desk, the cursor danced across the black dialogue box. Maddy's eyes weren't good enough to read that, but it was a one-word response. Undoubtedly 'affirmative'.

Energy pulsed through wires and circuit boards, filling the classroom with a gentle hum. Maddy felt her hair lift off her shoulders from the build-up of static charge, then, as before, the rise in pitch and volume culminated in a sudden release.

And an anti-climactic puff of vacated air.

They were gone.

Becks immediately set to work, picking up the dusty bucket chair on which a dozen circuit boards hung suspended in an improvised case – a metal filing cabinet with the drawers pulled out and discarded. Gently, she set it down in its square in perfect silence. But in that silence an unspoken conversation was going on between her and computer-Bob.

> **Do you understand the mission parameters, computer-Bob?**

> **Affirmative, Becks.**

She checked that the loops of wire that dangled precariously from the metal frame were not snagged on anything, potentially pulling a circuit board loose from its mooring.

> **Are you afraid?**

The PC across the floor from her clicked and whirred. Its motherboard fan struggled to cool and soothe the CPU as it tried hard to answer that.

> **In this limited non-networked form I am unable to properly simulate the emotion. However, I understand the context of your question.**

> **And?**

> **This duplication of my AI will shortly be erased. But I am merely a copy of the original AI. There is no need for fear.**

She looked up at the monitor on the school desk. Maddy had stripped it of all non-essential peripherals, the mouse, the keyboard; she'd even pulled the webcam out of the machine's USB port and taken that with her. This version of computer-Bob was blind. All she had left behind was the basic Internet desk mic so he could 'hear' verbal instructions. His only connection with the outside world was the mic . . . and his Wi-Fi link with Becks.

> **We are like Liam, Madelaine and Sal. Just copies.**

> **That is correct, Becks.**

She carefully eased the loose loops of ribbon cable back inside the metal rack.

> **How long until the next displacement can be made?**

> **Five minutes, thirty-seven seconds.**

One more final inspection of the machine then she took her place in the neighbouring square.

> **Computer-Bob?**

> **Yes, Becks.**

> **I am experiencing conflicting root-level imperatives.**

> **Please clarify this.**

Actually, Becks had been trying to do this for days. It was as if she was looking at a piece of coloured paper and one eye was telling her it was blue, the other that it was red.

> **Madelaine's mission goal states that our aim is to alter history enough to avoid the Extinction Level Event that occurs in 2070.**

> **The Pandora event. Yes.**

> **But I also have a mission goal that states the Extinction Level Event — Pandora — must be preserved at all cost.**

> **From whom does this mission goal originate?**

She hesitated, trawling through the corners of her mind. It was an untidy mind now, fragments of digital memory, her own memories, Bob's memories, copies of copies of memories. But within that messy soup of information she located a tiny fragment of data that was appended to the mission statement. It was a name.

> **Liam O'Connor.**

> **Madelaine Carter's authority exceeds Liam's. She is team leader. There is no conflict. Maddy's mission statement supersedes Liam's.**

> **I understand this. But it appears that Liam has privileged knowledge.**

> **Please clarify this.**

A part of Becks was unsure about doing that, sharing this precious locked-up knowledge with the computer across the room from her. There were express instructions floating around her fractured mind that this was knowledge for Maddy's eyes alone. But then, she rationalized, in just under four minutes computer-Bob's mind would be gone, erased, leaving nothing but a wiped-clean hard drive.

Why not tell him?

> **Liam has been to the year 2070. He has spoken with Waldstein.**

It was then she heard the noise: boots on damp linoleum floor in the hallway outside; whispered voices, hoarse with trying to be heard, yet not heard; the soft clink of ammo cartridges in webbing pouches. Clumsy men trying far too hard to be quiet.

'We are not alone,' she said quietly.

CHAPTER 55

9 October 2001, Green Acres Elementary School, Harcourt, Ohio

The door to the classroom suddenly banged and rattled inwards, the rotten wood of its frame splintering and cracking under the whiplash impact of a standard-issue boot.

'FREEZE!' a voice roared as the door juddered loosely, scraping to a halt.

'Hands in the air!' Another voice. 'Let me see your hands. Lemme see *YOUR GODDAMN HANDS*!'

Becks stared at the three men that had spilled through the door into the classroom. All of them dropped down on to one knee for a steadier aim: a well-practised manoeuvre, weapons raised and all pointing at her. Their goggle-covered faces flicked from side to side, scanning the corners, making sure she was the only occupant.

'Please . . .' she said. She showed her empty hands, palm up, concealing nothing. 'Please do not shoot. I am unarmed, do you see?'

'*Where are the others?*'

Becks ignored the question as she took a faltering step towards them. 'Please . . .' She made her voice wobble in a way that she'd heard both Maddy and Sal do before. The warbling pitch of someone frightened, fragile, vulnerable. 'Please . . . I am so afraid.'

'*GODDAMMIT!* Stay right where you are!' barked one of the men.

'Down!' shouted another. 'Get her down on the ground!'

'DO IT! Get down. DO IT NOW!'

Becks took another step closer to them. 'I am so frightened!' Her face crumpled into the approximation of a bewildered, terrified child. 'Please . . . I want to go home to my mommy.'

'ANOTHER STEP AND I WILL SHOOT!'

One of the men lowered his barrel slightly. 'Jeez, Cameron! It's just a kid!'

Becks took another half-step. She nodded eagerly. 'I am,' she said, her voice a whimper. 'I am just a kid. And I want to go home to my mommy.'

Then, with a flicker of one swift movement, she had the stubby barrel of the lowered HK MP5 in one tight fist. She shoved it savagely, the gun's stock flicked backwards and smacked the man's jaw. Then she pulled on it, yanking the weapon free of his grasp.

'Jesus Christ!' gasped one of them.

She swung the weapon round like a battleaxe, a sweeping roundhouse blow that caught the unarmed man under the jaw again, snapping his head back and leaving him sprawled on the ground and out for the count.

Several unaimed twitch-finger shots rang out from the other two: staccato stabs of muzzle flash that lit the dim classroom like a strobe. In a blur of movement the weapon in Becks's hands flipped end over end and now the gun was aimed at the two men. She pulled the trigger. A double-tap: one shot to the flak-jacket-covered chest of the man on the right, knocking him off balance; the second shot to his left upper thigh. Not a killing shot, but one that would kill him in minutes if he didn't drag himself out to get some help immediately. In another second she had dealt the same precision shots to the other man. As the smoke cleared, they were both desperately dragging themselves out of the classroom, leaving dark snail trails of blood on the grimy floor behind them.

The passageway outside was now alive with echoing voices. Torch beams flickered and swayed. Becks caught a glimpse of a SWAT team helmet sneaking a look round the edge of the door. She emptied a dozen rounds into the doorframe and the wall beside it. Plaster and flecks of dried paint erupted in showers.

'*Jesus!* Man down!' A shrill voice outside. 'We got *another* man down over here!'

She was causing a rout, a rapid tactical rethink among the remaining men. Voices shouted over each other and the thud of boots receded down the passage in panic. Then after a minute, finally, it was quiet again, save for those same voices outside in the playground, still shouting over each other, exchanging curses and recriminations.

> **Two minutes until there is sufficient charge, Becks.**
> **Affirmative.**

She quickly examined the displacement machine. Miraculously, none of the shots fired in that quick exchange seemed to have hit it. To be honest, it would probably take no more than a sharp nudge of the metal frame or a mere fleck of damp paint lodged in the circuitry to cause the fragile thing to malfunction, let alone a single bullet on target.

In the moment of stillness Becks thought she heard the first tap of raindrops on a window. Then quickly it became apparent to her it wasn't rain.

Clack-clack-clack-clack.

Footsteps approaching swiftly down the corridor outside, purposefully.

Finally a woman appeared in the ragged doorway. She smiled coolly.

'So, here you are,' said Faith.

CHAPTER 56

9 October 2001, Green Acres
Elementary School, Harcourt, Ohio

Becks levelled the gun in her hands. 'Yes, I am here.'

Faith remained where she was, framed by the doorway. 'I am Faith.'

'I am Becks.'

'Do you understand why I am here?'

'I believe your mission priority is to kill this team.'

'Correct.'

Becks's finger hovered on the machine-pistol's trigger. The rest of the magazine's worth of bullets, aimed squarely at the unit's head, would be enough. Becks remembered her own death. A single lucky round from a British rifle. The impact against the miniature dense silicon wafer caused a cascading failure of circuits. She recalled her mind closing down. She recalled dropping to her knees amid a small hillock of uniformed bodies, the dying digital part of her spewing nonsensical random sequences across failing circuits. It was as close as her artificial mind could get to understanding the nature of death.

'Why do you have this goal?' asked Becks. 'Why must this team be terminated?'

'This team requested information on the Pandora event.' Faith shook her head reproachfully. 'Knowing of this – knowing what will one day happen – compromises their reliability.'

Becks found herself nodding in agreement. The unit standing in front of her was quite right. Maddy, now knowing what she did, was determined to ensure the Extinction Level Event in 2070 wasn't going to happen. Her team were now no longer performing the function they were intended for. Quite the opposite. From this support unit's perspective they were no longer the *solution* . . . they were the *problem*.

'Events must unfold in that precise way,' added Faith. 'Humans must wipe themselves out in the year 2070. There can be no other alternative. These are Waldstein's instructions.'

Becks frowned. 'But there is no logical beneficiary in such a scenario. If all humans are dead . . . then there is nothing left.'

Faith shrugged a *whatever*. Becks had to admire the fluidity of that gesture; it was so gracefully human-like. 'Perhaps it is for the best.'

And that too sounded so human. That sounded to Becks very much like an expressed *opinion*. Neither she nor Bob had quite managed to master that. 'Is this your personal conclusion?'

'Of course not. Unfortunately, I am unable to think that way.' Faith entered the room. 'Those are the words of my Authorized User – Roald Waldstein.'

Becks lowered her aim ever so slightly. 'You are following his instructions.'

'Correct.'

'In that case I understand your reasoning.'

Faith nodded. 'Good.' She stepped over the unconscious man on the floor between them as if he was nothing more than a roll of carpet waiting to be taken out and dumped in a skip.

'We are in agreement, Becks. There is no need for conflict.'

'Unfortunately, I also have orders to follow.' She shouldered the stock of the gun and fired in one swift motion.

Instinctively, Faith raised her arm to protect her head. Several rounds smashed into her wrist and lower arm, rendering it a ragged, swinging pulp of flesh and chalk-white splintered bone. As the weapon clicked noisily, the cartridge empty, Faith leaped forward. With her good arm, she knocked the gun effortlessly out of the younger, smaller support unit's grasp.

With the side of one hand, the girl tried to chop at her neck, an obvious weak point. Faith anticipated that and parried the jab with the soft crunch of her bullet-shattered arm. With her good arm, Faith duplicated the tactic and grabbed Becks by the throat, lifting her slight frame off the ground so that her feet were swinging free. She hurled her like a rag doll across the room into a stack of chairs and desks in the corner.

Becks disappeared among them, lost in a mini-avalanche of classroom furniture. Faith raced over, flinging desks and chairs aside as if they were mere scoops of dirt, digging for Becks before she could attempt to burrow deeper and escape. She found her lying on her back, gasping, spraying fine droplets of dark blood on to her pale chin. Her arms flailed pointlessly in an attempt to get herself up. Legs lifeless and useless.

Faith knelt down heavily on her heaving chest. 'Your back is broken, is it not?'

Becks nodded.

'Then you are incapacitated. You should self-terminate.'

Becks sputtered blood, her jaw working, trying to say something. Instead, she gave up trying to talk and simply nodded again.

Faith remained where she was, studying Becks's face until the glint of digital consciousness ebbed from her grey eyes. Now they rolled uncontrollably, a simple-minded animal stare. Nothing more than that. And there – the faintest whiff of melted plastic, singed silicon.

This child with its broken back was just a simple-minded

gurgling creature now, arms listlessly flailing. Faith reached her good hand out and grabbed the creature's slender neck. She snapped it with a quick, savage twist. And the pitiful thing was finally still.

She got up and walked quickly towards the metal frame sitting in the middle of a taped square on the classroom floor. A two-foot-high metal frame with a rat's nest of wires and circuit boards in the middle. She understood what it was: a displacement device. There was a growing hum of energy coming from inside it, like the stirring of angry bees inside a rattled and shaken hive. She noticed a second taped square beside the first. Empty.

[Information: these are departure markers]

She realized the support unit had been getting ready to transport herself.

[Caution: the displacement device is about to activate]

There was only one possible place this displacement charge was going to take her – to where the others must have already gone. She quickly stepped into the square. No need for any deliberation. Her mission was simple: locate and terminate. It really didn't matter when or where she ended up in the course of pursuing that goal. Once the job was done, her fate was going to be the same as the unit she'd just fought anyway.

It was then, over the electronic buzz coming from the device beside her, that she heard a voice echoing up the passageway.

'Faith?' It was Cooper. 'Hey! *Agent* Faith? You OK in there?'

The noise coming from the machine was increasing in pitch and volume now, more a whine than a buzz. Faith felt the hair on her scalp lift as the charge of excited particles enveloped her.

Cooper's head poked cautiously into view. 'Agent Faith?' His eyes darted quickly from the body of the man on the floor, the body of a young girl on the other side of the room and Faith calmly standing in the middle of the floor, motionless like a child playing musical statues, blood dripping from the ragged end of one arm. 'What's going on?' He frowned. 'What the devil's that noise?'

Faith cocked her head and tried out a faltering smile on her lips. As close to a fond farewell as she could manage.

'Goodbye, Agent Cooper,' she said coolly. 'It has been agreeable working with you.'

'Uh? Goodbye? Where are you go—' He looked at her, then glanced at the odd contraption on the classroom floor. The growing hum that was filling the room seemed to be coming from it. He noticed the taped-out squares. Indents several inches into the floor within them. For some reason he was reminded of those teleportation pads in that TV series *Star Trek*.

Oh no.

The electronic whine became deafening.

'Agent Faith! Please step out of that square! Now!! Please —'

He felt a hard puff of air on his cheeks, dust and grit in his face. By the time he'd quickly swiped at his eyes and blinked the grit out, she was gone.

Mallard was beside him. He'd just seen Faith disappear. 'Jesus . . . she . . . she just vanished!'

Cooper stepped over the man's body. Mallard ducked down to check for a pulse. Then he was up again on his feet and out in the passage bellowing for a medic to get the hell in here. Cooper ignored all that; it was a commotion that seemed a million miles away and entirely unimportant. He squatted down on his haunches and stared at the scuffed taped lines on the floor — at the fizzing, smoking end of a power cable that draped across the tape and ended abruptly where the floor dropped down into a shallow square recess.

He followed the snaking trail of cable back across the floor and up on to a school desk where a single commonplace Dell desktop computer was quietly humming away, its hard-drive light blinking silently.

His heart lifted with hope.

They must have left it behind by accident!

Perhaps in too much of a hurry to get out of there maybe? Perhaps . . . perhaps all the answers were right there on that machine? He got up and hurried over. There was something on the screen. An open dialogue box. Text. A cursor blinking, and a final phrase skittered across the screen.

> **Reformatting complete. Goodbye.**

The dialogue box closed, the screen went black and a DOS prompt appeared and blinked vapidly.

C:/

Cooper's voice echoed down the passageway, echoed through abandoned classrooms and corridors, gymnasiums and cloakrooms. A plaintive wail of grief and frustration. A lifetime's worth of waiting . . . for this. For nothing.

The entire boarded-up school reverberated with one miserable word.

'*No-o-o-o-o-o!*'

CHAPTER 57

14 December 1888,
Holborn Viaduct, London

Maddy felt the familiar thud of impact beneath her feet, and the usual flood of relief that she'd emerged from the haunting mists of chaos space. She could smell a damp mustiness, unpleasant and yet somewhat familiar; it reminded her of their old archway back in Brooklyn.

She opened her eyes and for the briefest moment she thought that's where she was: the same low arched brick ceiling, the dim light, the snaking of cables and untidy clutter everywhere. She could almost believe she was right back in Brooklyn.

'Best step aside, Maddy,' said Liam. 'The last one will be coming through soon.'

Rashim had already stepped out of his square, taken off his anorak to reveal a crisp white gentleman's dress shirt and waistcoat. She smiled; out of all of them he seemed to most relish wearing the smart tailored clothes of this time. He rolled his sleeves up to the elbow and immediately started working with a knife, splicing a loop of thick insulated cable that emerged from a hole in one of the walls. Getting ready to hook up the displacement machine to their source of power, the moment it arrived.

'Maddy?' prompted Liam. 'The square? You should get out of it.'

'Oh yeah.' She stepped aside. 'My God, Liam . . . it's just like, well, almost like the Brooklyn place.'

'Aye.' He grinned. 'That was my thought too. You like it?'

She smiled, the first time in weeks that she'd felt like smiling. It felt a little like that first time she'd woken up, Foster hovering over her with a tray of coffee and doughnuts. 'Pity there isn't a Starbucks nearby, though,' she said.

'Well now . . .' He laughed. 'Actually, there is. Of a sort.'

Maddy looked over the top of her glasses at him. 'What?'

'Well, sort of. A coffee shop on the back of a wagon, so it is. Roasted chestnuts. Vanilla slices. Fresh baked pies and tarts. You'll love it.'

Sal looked around the gloomy space. 'Where do we sleep?' She turned back to Liam. 'Where do we do toilet?'

Liam raised his hands apologetically. 'Me and Rashim have been doing like everyone else seems to do. You sort of find a dark corner in a backstreet somewhere and you just go –'

'Not doing that,' said Sal. 'Not going to happen.'

'Nuh-uh,' added Maddy. 'Me neither. I want a toilet.'

'Aye, all right,' he said with a shrug. 'I s'pose we can fix something up.'

'Immediately, I'd suggest. Like, top of the list.' Maddy turned her attention to Rashim working with SpongeBubba on the cable, slicing strips of insulating rubber away, exposing copper. She looked at the thick cable protruding from the hole in the wall. 'That's where our feed's coming from?'

'Yes,' replied Rashim.

'Have we got some sort of circuit-breakers installed? Some sort of spike protection?'

'That's what I'm working on right now.'

'Right.' She nodded. 'Good job.'

She put her hands on her hips and allowed herself a moment of self-congratulation.

That all went rather well, then. Once the displacement rack arrived and they'd set it and the networked computers up and checked that everything had come through unharmed, they were going to be pretty much back in business. Back to where they'd once been, but this time round they'd be pulling their own strings. This time round they were going to be wholly in charge of their own destinies.

How cool's that? Maddy smiled. *Very.*

'Bob? You getting any particles yet?'

Bob nodded. 'I am detecting precursor particles. The last displacement volume should be opening very soon.'

'This has really gone smoothly.' She nodded, satisfied with things. 'You know, Liam, I think we're all getting quite slick as a team at this whole time-travel thing.'

'Aye. Best team in the business.'

'The *only* team in the business,' Sal said drily.

'True.'

'Caution!' said Bob, 'Maddy, you should stand back now.'

Maddy did as he said and felt the air around her pulse with the sudden arrival of a dozen cubic metres of air and mass. In one marked square, the displacement rack sat on the floor, powering down with a disgruntled whine, freshly severed from its power source.

The other square was empty.

'Uh . . . where's Becks?'

CHAPTER 58

1 November 1888,
Whitechapel, London

Faith found herself standing in a narrow courtyard. Dark, damp, grimy brick walls on all four sides of her that rose up to eaves that overhung and narrowed the dull grey sky. A washing line ran across from one wall to the other, from which faded, wrinkled and threadbare rags of clothes hung limply like forgotten dried berries ready to drop.

Rain spattered on her upturned face as she took in her surroundings. She blinked fat drops of it from her eyes as her mind silently assessed the present situation.

[Information: translation error]

Her first thought was how lucky she was not to be partially merged with something. A dense urban environment like this – the odds were probably even between empty and occupied space. She turned her mind quickly to situation-assessment.

The rapidly decaying tachyon particles told her some of the story. She'd been misplaced spatially by – at her quick assessment – one or two miles. She was unable to be sure whether she'd also been misplaced in time: an overshoot of days, weeks, months. It was, of course, a distinct possibility. She had no idea at all when in time this rogue team had decided to head back to, but she was pretty sure, running the figures in her head, that she couldn't have over – or under – shot by much time. Days or weeks at worst.

Immediate matters first, though. She needed to blend in to whenever this was and certainly not be the cause of any unnecessary temporal contamination or undue attention. Then, when she was suitably dressed for this world, she could run the calculation in her head and work out precisely how far – spatially – she was from the intended location. There was no way of knowing in which direction she'd been offset, but if she could calculate a more precise distance then she'd have a viable search radius to work with.

Faith looked around the small courtyard. The ground was cobblestones covered by mud and rotting vegetable peelings. Here and there mildew-covered nuggets of faeces – animal or human, she couldn't tell. Clearly this small space was a dumping ground for the effluence and night-water that was tossed out of the small grimy windows that punctuated the towering walls all around this enclosed little courtyard.

She noticed a long wooden pole with a crudely fashioned hook on the end, leaning against one of the walls. That, presumably, was how the clothes were retrieved from the washing line. She also noted in one corner a small wooden door that hung pathetically on failing, rusty hinges.

It took her no more than a few minutes to retrieve the rags and change out of her modern clothes. She bundled them up under her arm and would figure out a way to dispose of them later. Her bullet-shattered lower arm and hand she wrapped up in a linen shawl. The blood had already coagulated and dried. It would eventually heal: the skin would re-grow, the bone and tendon beneath would re-knit.

The doorway took her into a narrow walkway between damp brick walls, covered by a slanted roof of slate shingles that tapped with the rain. At the far end she could see the grey light of this dull day. And a wide street by the look of it.

At the far end she emerged on to a broad cobbled road; rows of three-storey red-brick terraced homes, identical and equally as drab and squalid-looking as those that had surrounded the dingy space she'd just arrived in. The street was busy with people – people who didn't look occupied. Women sitting on doorsteps looking on as their children played in the street. A pair of men smoking long clay pipes, standing beside an open fire in a grate, poking it to stir the dying embers to life. All of them in rags.

She saw a sign. Presumably the name of this street; flaking paint on rusting tin – GREAT DOVER STREET.

Faith crossed the street towards the fire, approaching the two men. They didn't notice her coming until she tossed her clothes from the year 2001 on to the glowing embers. The synthetic fibres of her JC Penney office clothes flared up almost instantly.

'Hoy! Watcha think yer doin', love?' Both men turned to look at her.

'Fuel,' she replied evenly, 'for your fire.'

One of the men grinned around the stem of his pipe. 'Well, hello, m'dear.' His red-rimmed eyes – one of them opaque like a boiled fish-eye, a cataract – looked her up and down approvingly. 'Now there's a pretty, pretty thing.'

Faith offered her hesitant smile and picked what she considered the most appropriate response. 'Thank you.'

'You 'ungry, love? Want sumfin' to eat?'

It had certainly been a while since she'd had a protein refuel. 'Yes. I am hungry.'

Both men looked at each other and grinned. Then the one with the clouded eye turned back to her. 'Well, I got a nice bit of fish back in my 'ouse. An' some cheese.' He took a step towards her.

Faith stifled the urge to adopt a combat stance and chop at the man's neck with the side of her good hand.

Blend in.

'So 'ow 'bout you an' me 'ead back to my gaff.' He nodded to one of the terraced houses close by. 'I only live over there. I'll give yer a proper feed, love. Eh? Put some colour in 'em cheeks of yours.'

'Fish and cheese?' Faith cocked her head. Protein and fat. Perfect fuels for her body chemistry. 'Those are both suitable food types. Thank you.'

The man took his pipe out. 'Tell you what, love, ya don't 'alf talk funny.'

Her lips flickered uncertainly. 'I am new in this place.'

'New? Another foreigner, eh?' He reached and put an arm round her narrow waist. Faith decided to accept the overfamiliar gesture – for the moment. It didn't appear hostile or threatening so she let it pass.

'Come on, then, deary, come along with ol' Terry.' He pulled her to him so that her hip bumped clumsily against his leg. 'I'll look after ya, my dear.'

He tugged her firmly in the direction of his house and Faith had begun to take a few steps with him when a female voice barked out.

'You leave that poor girl be, Terry Matchins!'

He stopped and turned. 'Ah, not you!' He spat a curse at her.

Faith saw a woman who could have been any age between twenty and thirty-five – so very difficult to tell. The woman's skin was ruddy with rose-coloured splotches, several teeth missing and the rest an unpleasant vanilla colour. She was short and slight with auburn hair tied up in an untidy frizzy bun.

'You better let her go! Or I'll box yer ears!'

'She's comin' round mine for a bit o' supper. Ain't ya, love?'

The short woman addressed Faith. 'Love, that dirty ol' goat's not goin' to feed yer anything that you'd *want* to eat. Terry ain't got nuthin' indoors but dirty intentions. He's bloomin' bad news is what 'e is!'

Faith turned to look at him. 'Is this woman correct? You have no food?' A cold glare and her face so close to his presented a challenge that unsettled the man and his firm grasp on her waist loosened. 'I . . . I just thought you was lookin' a bit peaky, love. I thought —'

'I know exactly what you was thinkin'!' snapped the woman. 'Go on, sling yer hook!'

The man bared brown teeth at her. 'I'll slice yer up one day, Mary! Next time yer so drunk ya don't know it's night or day, I'll give yer a ruddy scar to remember!'

'Yeah, yeah! So you're the Ripper, are you?' She stepped forward and pushed him. 'Go on with ya! Go pester someone else, you rancid old fart!'

The man laughed and shrugged, and returned to his friend beside the fire.

The woman offered Faith a hand. 'He's right, though, you do look awful pale, love. I got some leftovers from yesterday.' She frowned firmly; a face that wasn't going to take 'no' for an answer. 'Come on, let's fix you some food. You look awful poorly.'

Faith extended a hand to the woman. A handshake: she'd learned that gesture of formal courtesy from Agent Cooper. 'Thank you. I am Faith.'

'Faith, is it? Well, since we're doin' introductions, I'm Mary. Mary Kelly. You'll be safe with me, love.' Her ruddy face split with a smile that even Faith was able to judge with a fair degree of certainty was entirely genuine. 'Perfectly safe.'

CHAPTER 59

14 December 1888, Holborn, London

'Oh my God!' gushed Maddy, 'I so-o-o-o love this!' Her face was one big toothy smile framed by the wisps of her strawberry hair and the lace of her bonnet. 'All of this! These posh clothes, this place! Don't you think it's so cool!'

Sal was fussing with her lace cuffs. 'I feel like an idiot in this dress.'

Liam was in the same frame of mind as Maddy. 'It feels like this could be our new home all right.'

Maddy sighed contentedly. Her first night in Victorian London. 'Yeah, it's almost like back home.' *Home*. New York. A strange choice of word for that place, that — home — since she'd never actually had one. 'Just as busy and bustling and vibrant as Brooklyn.'

'Uh-huh,' said Liam. His cheeks puffed up like a hamster's as he worked his way through a pork pie.

She looked around the open-top wagon with its four small round tables and tall wobbly stools. There was even a serving counter on the end, behind which a barista busied himself roasting coffee beans on an open skillet over glowing coals. A whole coffee shop complete with its own canvas awning and colourful bunting right there on the flatbed of an open horse-drawn cart.

She grinned. 'Starbucks 1880s style.' She sipped steaming hot coffee from the mug cupped in her hands and smacked her lips.

'Actually, even better than Starbucks. I mean, this is what I call fresh coffee.'

'Aye.'

The meagre light of the overcast afternoon was fading, the featureless December-grey sky becoming a deep ocean blue. Maddy watched as one by one glimmers of flame winked on like fireflies in the gathering twilight; oil lamps on the street, candles behind net-curtain windows. As evening began to settle on Farringdon Street, it became a Dickensian painting; splashes of midnight blue for the advancing evening shadows, and ambers and golds for the glowing pools of gas and candlelight. And, with the evening almost fully upon them, it seemed to be getting busier still.

'They seem to like their nightlife,' said Sal.

Liam and Rashim had already spent a week of nights here in London as they'd been setting up the new field office. Partly because some of their banging around had been noisy enough that it kept attracting their curious landlord. He'd turn up at their door like a bad penny with various excuses as to why he was knocking. They soon realized that Mr Hook enjoyed his ale and was in the habit of spending his evenings in one public house or another, so their lifting, bumping and banging, bringing in bits and pieces of furniture to make it more like home, was better done then rather than during the day.

Liam looked round the street. 'It *is actually* busier than normally, so.'

As well as a number of well-dressed gentlemen in top hats with elegant ladies on their arms – presumably quite usual for a Friday evening – there were several loose clusters of working men blocking the pavements further along the street. Liam presumed they were the overflow from various overcrowded public houses: men enjoying their ale at the end of the working week.

Maddy's mood had suddenly changed as her thoughts returned to matters at hand. 'We have to figure out what happened to Becks,' she said.

'It must have been a translation error,' said Liam.

Rashim fussed with his glasses. 'No, I don't think so. I checked and rechecked everyone's mass index. Something must have happened back in that school.'

'Like what?'

'Maybe a rat ran into her square or something?' said Sal.

Rashim jumped on that. 'Yes, it could easily be something like that . . . a rat, or a stray cat, or something.'

'So, does that mean she's somewhere here? Somewhere else in London?'

'I don't know, Maddy. It's possible.'

'She could be wandering around looking for us,' said Sal.

'Then we should have Bob and SpongeBubba switch on their Wi-Fi signals. If she gets within – what is it, half a mile range? – it'll give her something to home in on.'

Rashim sipped his coffee. 'But, Maddy, it is also equally possible she experienced mass convergence somewhere. This London is a dense place.'

'She'd be dead, then.' Rashim nodded.

'Maybe something happened to her back in the school?' Liam looked at the others. 'Maybe those meatbots finally caught up with us.'

'No.' Maddy shook her head. 'I'd say we probably lost them.'

The conclusion, then, wasn't so great. Her body was lost: a pulp of flesh somewhere in London perhaps fused into the foundations of some building.

'If that did happen, I just hope it was quick for her,' said Maddy. 'That she didn't suffer too much.'

Losing their half-grown Becks, though, was more than just losing a colleague. Friend even. Maddy felt that there might have been a chance to 'reason' with her AI to finally agree to open that locked portion of her mind. Somehow, having reinstalled her complete personality from the rigid binary confines of a hard drive – an object that was never going to be reasoned with – she'd begun to hope that enough things had happened recently for Becks to consider opening up to her, revealing whatever message had been waiting two thousand years to be heard. A message, by the way, specifically intended for her! She ground her teeth in frustration. A message, Becks had claimed, that had been sent by her.

I sent myself a message from the future. Maddy shook her head, very much annoyed with her stupid future self. *Why did I freakin' well decide I have to wait until 'certain conditions are met' before I can learn what it is?*

'Rashim, do you think there's any way we're going to be able to grow any new support units?'

Absently his fingers traced the felt brim of his top hat held reverently on his lap. Clearly he relished the whole dressing-up thing as much as she did. He'd even bought a fob watch on a chain to tuck into one of his waistcoat pockets.

What a poser.

'I think we'll struggle to find the components we need in this time. We could perhaps use a brewer's cask for a growth tube, but filtration pumps? Protein solution? We would need to take a journey forward to obtain those things.'

'And that's a risk, isn't it?' said Sal.

Maddy nodded. 'Yup, we run the risk of turning up on somebody's radar if we do too much of that. We'll have to think about this. Meanwhile, the foetuses will stay viable in the freezer unit?'

'Provided the power supply does not fail us,' he replied, nodding. 'Yes.'

'I wonder if there's something special on tonight?' said Liam. 'A parade or something?'

They sat in silence for a while, all of them contemplating the busy street. The barista, seeing their hushed conversation had hit a pause for the moment, came round the side of his counter and over to their table.

'Can I offer you ladies or gentlemen anything else? Only I'll need to be closin' up and movin' on soon.' He glanced at the gathering of men down the other end of Farringdon Street. 'I'd rather be off before things get a bit frisky. I 'eard a whisper, see.'

Liam nodded at the gathering of men. 'What *is* going on down there?'

'That'll be another of them gatherings,' replied the barista. 'Blasted anarchists and troublemakers. They're all worked up and makin' a nuisance of themselves. All because of that gentleman murderer.'

'Murderer?'

He looked at them with momentary bemusement. 'You know, the mad-in-the-'ead one? Been killin' women? In the East End? You ladies an' gents musta 'eard about that?'

Liam, Maddy and the others shook their heads in unison.

The barista took in the look of confusion on all their faces. 'You . . . you do know about that, right? That gentleman . . . a knight or lord or something. Some say he might even be a friend of the queen!'

Liam shook his head. 'Can't say that we do, sir.'

The barista laughed incredulously. 'Blimey! It's in all the penny papers. It 'as been for the last fortnight! Been on them telegraph wires all round the world I wouldn't be surprised.

Everyone's been talkin' about it! You lot must be the last people in the country to have 'eard about it, then!'

'We've sort of only just arrived in the country, you see,' said Maddy.

The barista nodded. 'Ahhh, foreigners! I thought I could 'ear somethin' funny in the way you's lot were talkin'. Where you ladies and gents come from?'

Maddy met Liam and Sal's eyes. They all shared a conspiratorial smile and she shrugged at the barista as if to say, *Where do I even begin?* 'Well now, that's kind of difficult to –'

'Canada,' said Bob. 'We are from Canada.'

The barista looked suitably impressed. 'Canadians, eh? I suppose you don't get newspapers and telegraph wires over there, then. Well –' he shook his head – 'to be honest, the whole thing's a nasty carry-on. This won't turn out well for none of us. Best advice I can tell you is – with all due respect – I'd suggest you might want to 'op on a boat 'eading back 'ome to Canada before it all kicks off over 'ere. It ain't gonna be nice.'

'Kicks off?'

'Nasty business. Very nasty.' His eyes narrowed as he gazed down the street. 'The way things are goin'. . . there'll be soldiers on the streets soon. Maybe even blood on the streets before long.' He looked back down at them. 'Best 'ead back to your 'otel or guesthouse and stay indoors this evening, that's for sure. I 'eard a whisper them riots what we've 'ad across Whitechapel and the rest of the East End of London will be spreading to the rest of the city.' He nodded at the growing crowd of men far off down the street. 'And them troublemakers down there look like they're making ready to 'ave a scrap with the police.'

CHAPTER 60

14 December 1888,
Holborn Viaduct, London

'Jesus, Liam! How did you not notice all this . . . *unrest* . . . was going on?' A copy of the *London Packet* rustled in Maddy's hands. She'd picked up a discarded copy lying on the doorstep of a haberdasher's on the way back to their cosy little subterranean dungeon.

She unlaced her bonnet and hung it carefully on the arm of a coat stand. 'There've been riots and stuff going off all over the country!'

Liam unbuttoned his waistcoat. 'I've been busy in here in case you hadn't noticed.' He slumped down on a creaking, spoon-backed armchair that was spilling stuffing from a popped seam on one arm. 'Making this place a little more like a home, so I have.'

'There's more important things than –' she struggled not to curse – 'making us comfy!'

He looked hurt. 'I just wanted it to be nice for you two.'

Maddy's stern gaze turned to Rashim.

'And, uh . . . I've been making money, and of course wiring this place up.'

Maddy looked down at the paper and picked bits to read out loud. '. . . *rioting in the East End: Whitechapel, Spitalfields. Riots also beginning to occur in Liverpool, Manchester.*' She skimmed the columns of small newsprint. '*Groups of anarchists, libertarians, troublemakers and ne'er-do-wells gathering in every city, every town, every village to protest about . . .*' She fell silent, skimming the words ahead, her lips moving.

'What? Protesting about what?'

She raised a finger. 'Just a sec. . . lemme finish.'

'I have to say, I always thought Victorian Britain was supposed to be an ordered place,' said Rashim. '*Disciplined*, you know? The famous British stiff upper lip? That's the right expression, isn't it?' He shook his head. 'Those men outside? All that anger? That naked aggression? It reminded me very much of my time. Always the riots. Every day news-streams showing a war or a food riot somewhere. Militia with guns stripping possessions from refugees.' He shook his head. 'That is what the end days of a failing civilization look like. It's an ugly, sad thing.'

'It was beginning to go that way in my time too,' added Sal. She snorted humourlessly at something that occurred to her. 'I should say *our* time.' She looked at Liam. 'After all, the three of us come from the same time, right? Same time, same place, same test tube?'

Liam sighed. 'Best forget about that, Sal.'

She ignored him. 'When exactly is our time, huh? I mean . . . when exactly was our particular batch of meatbots cooked up? Hmm? 2030? 2040? 2050? 20—'

'Just let it go, Sal!' snapped Liam irritably. 'Why don't you just forget about —'

'Because I can't! I'm a *product*. So's Maddy. So are you! I can't forget that!'

'No!' He shook his head. 'Jayzus-n-Holy-Mary, no, I'm not acting the maggot! No! I'm still who I thought I was. I'm still Liam and I'm still from Cork, Sal! And I'll tell you something else for nothing; I'm bleedin' well remaining that same person!

Do you understand? And so you should!' He looked self-consciously back at the others. They were staring at him, taken aback by his angry outburst.

'Well . . .' he huffed dismissively. 'That's all I've got to say about this foolish nonsense!' He slapped the arm of the chair. 'There! Look, I'm all angry now!'

They sat in a long and awkward silence, an old clock ticking far too noisily in the corner of the dungeon; the deep rumble of Holborn Viaduct's generator could be heard through several brick walls, doing its clanking, rumbling best to keep the immediate surrounding street lights glowing.

'You think what you want, Liam,' Sal sighed. 'It's all lies in the end. It's all —'

'Will the pair of you knock it off?' snapped Maddy. 'This is far more important!' She shook the paper in her hand for emphasis. 'This is a contamination. Right here! In this paper — a contamination!'

Sal shrugged. 'So? It's not like we *have* to fix them any more.'

'Don't you see, Sal? It means we're not alone!'

Liam suddenly looked up. 'Ah Jay-zus! Becks?'

Maddy shrugged. 'Or someone else.' She carried on reading parts aloud. '. . . *continuing riots in response to the recent shocking revelation of the Ripper's true identity*.'

'Whitechapel! The Ripper. Jack the Ripper! You mentioned him earlier,' said Rashim.

Liam nodded. 'Aye, and the big mystery was they never found out who the fella was.'

'But now it seems they have,' replied Maddy.

'Who is it?' Sal said, suddenly a lot more interested in what was in the paper than she was brooding by herself.

'A man called Lord Cathcart-Hyde. A knight of the realm,' Maddy added, skim-reading the paper, 'a Freemason, a member of the House of Lords, and until recently a senior member of the government.'

'Jahulla!' Sal sat up. 'Seriously?'

'Uh-huh.' Maddy raised a finger to shush her and continued reading in silence for another couple of minutes as the others waited impatiently. Then finally she looked up at them.

'This story's been rumbling on for just over a month! This posh guy, Cathcart, was attempting to murder another woman.' She consulted the article. 'Mary Kelly.'

'Aye! That's it, she was the last woman to be killed by Jack the Ripper!' said Liam.

'In correct history, yes! But apparently she managed to fight back. Fought back and killed the man!'

'Blimey,' said Liam. 'What a woman.'

'Good for her,' said Sal. 'It's not very often the good guy wins. Not in real life anyway.'

Maddy looked over the top of her glasses at them. 'Point is, folks, she's become a national hero over the last four weeks. That's a big goddamn contamination! That shouldn't have happened. And these riots that are springing up all over England are part of that contamination.'

'Maddy is correct,' said Bob. His deep voice rumbled with admonishment. 'This is a major contamination and must be corrected.'

'Thank you, Bob.' She looked down at the paper: headlines screaming out anger and rage on behalf of the common man. *Friend of Queen Hunted East End Women For Sport! Cathcart-Hyde – Evil Resides Among the Rich.*

'Those people out there are *enraged*. They're out in the streets because this is, like, the final straw. One thing too many. I guess they're seeing this as an example of the rich considering themselves above the law. That this lord guy was carving up common street women just for fun! Treating it like a . . . like some sort of a fox hunt!'

'Yes.' Rashim nodded. 'It has escalated into a *class* issue.'

'Exactly! And you heard that coffee-store guy – this is going to get worse.' Maddy looked down at the paper. 'It's been a slowly escalating news story and –' she shook her head – 'we've only just noticed it.'

Through the thick brick walls they could hear the faint roar of voices in the street outside. The barista was right, tonight trouble had spilled west towards central London. They heard a chorus of hooves on cobblestones passing by outside – mounted police called in to disperse the gathered protesters.

'Liam? Rashim?' Maddy sounded exasperated. 'Jesus, didn't either of you guys notice anything at all brewing up in the background while you were fixing things up in here? I mean, this story has been running in all the papers for the last month!'

Liam shook his head. 'No . . . uh, not really, no. I didn't read any of them papers.'

'This last week we've been inside, in here,' added Rashim, 'mostly.'

She sighed. Faintly they heard the shrill tone of a police whistle, the neighing and stamping of uneasy horses, a chorus of male voices united in chanting some slogan. The first tinkle of breaking glass.

'Bob, we need some more background data. Do a search on your on-board database. Use the search term "Whitechapel Murders".'

'Affirmative.'

Back in Harcourt Maddy had loaded him up with a dump of data pulled off the Internet about Victorian times, London in particular. It wasn't targeted particularly cleverly: basically a 'copy and paste' of everything she could find online that she casually dumped into his head. Once they got round to networking the computers and had the system up and running again, she intended to have him Bluetooth the whole lot across. But right now his hard drive made him the historical expert.

'Whitechapel,' said Bob. His eyelids flickered as he consulted his database. 'Information: 1888, Whitechapel murders. Also commonly referred to as the Jack the Ripper murders, and the Leather Apron murders.'

Liam nodded. 'Aye, I remember Delbert said something about that. Said the killer's other nickname was the Leather –'

'Shhhh!' Maddy flapped a hand at Liam. She nodded at Bob to go on.

'I will extrapolate and summarize facts from what I have.' He closed his eyes. 'Through the late summer and winter of 1888, a series of gruesome murders of women. Mostly prostitutes. In the terminology of this time – tarts, street ladies. There were five murders attributed to the same murderer because their methodology was strikingly similar.'

'Methodology?' asked Sal. 'You mean how they were killed?'

'Affirmative. The method of their murder. How they died,' he replied. 'In all five cases their throats were severed to the vertebrae; they were almost completely beheaded. Their abdomens were –'

'Save that for later, Bob,' said Maddy. 'We don't need that detail right now.'

'Of course.' He resumed. 'The post-mortem mutilations were immediately distinct, bearing a striking resemblance to Freemason rituals. After the third murder the national press was making veiled accusations that the killer might not be some commoner with basic knife-craft skills – a butcher or a fishmonger for instance – but instead some high-born figure with Masonic associations, possibly medical knowledge. The last murder attributed to the killer was a woman called Mary Kelly. Her body was discovered in Miller's Court in the early hours of the ninth of November. The killer was never caught or identified, and no further murders were deemed similar enough in method to be attributed to the same man.

'At the end of the twentieth century several historians considered there might be a royal connection to the murders.' Bob paged his mind for further details. 'Context: London in the 1880s was as close as it was ever going to come to a workers' revolution similar in nature to the one that occurred in Russia.'

'Well, that certainly seems true enough,' said Rashim. He cocked an ear at the faint noises of rioting coming from Farringdon Street.

Maddy nodded. 'Jack the Ripper *should* never have been identified. The ninth of November should have been the last Ripper victim and then it all stops, and becomes a mystery forevermore. Only . . . a month ago, ninth of November, something very different happened. The last victim killed him instead . . . and has now become the figurehead for a revolution.'

'Oh boy,' squealed SpongeBubba, 'someone's been naught-eee!'

Maddy could see that Bob was eager to say something. 'You think we should intervene?'

'This is a significant contamination. The point of contamination origin in terms of time and space is very close to us.'

'You think we should intervene, Bob?'

'I am not programmed to define agency policy, Maddy.'

'Oh, cut the crud, Bob. Just speak your mind!'

'Give him a rest, Maddy,' said Liam. 'He can't do opinions. He's not really made that way.' He got up, wandered across the dungeon and patted Bob affectionately. 'But we *are* made that way.'

She nodded at that. 'OK . . . then this seems to be the first test case for our new mission parameters. That's a pretty big change going on outside. So . . . I guess the way we deal with this is we check the outcome. We take a look forward in time to see where this is going to take us. And depending on what we see, we'll have to decide whether this Mary Kelly gets to live or . . . you know, die.'

'That's kind of brutal,' said Sal. 'That's a lot of judgement in our hands.'

'Yeah . . . I sort of didn't think about that bit.' Maddy chewed her lip. 'That kinda makes us judge, jury and executioner in this kind of situation. That's a lot of . . . of power. Sheesh, I'm not sure how I feel about that. It was sort of easier when we were just following orders.'

'There's a quote I can think of,' said Liam. 'I don't know if it helps us or not.'

'Go on, let's have it.'

'With great power comes great responsibility.'

'What is that . . . Shakespeare or something?'

'Uh . . . no. Spider-Man.'

CHAPTER 61

15 December 1888,
Holborn Viaduct, London

At about 11 p.m. the night before, they'd heard the first wagonloads of Metropolitan Police arriving to try and restore some order. The rioting increased in intensity and they heard a volley of shots being fired in the early hours of the morning. As the first touch of dawn began to lighten the night sky, the angry mob had finally melted away.

Now, in the cool steel-grey light of the morning after, with a light drizzle spitting fat drops of rain on to the cobbles, it looked like a war had been fought across Farringdon Street.

'Hoy! Mr O'Connor, Dr Anwar!' It was Delbert Hook and his assistant, Bertie. They emerged from the warren of archways and passageways to join them, standing just outside their side door, beneath the looming iron arches of Holborn Viaduct.

'Spent the blimmin' night, me an' Bertie, guarding our front entrance and praying we wasn't about to be cleared out and robbed blind.' He shook his head and tutted. 'Blasted anarchists, some of them even 'ad a go at our doors with 'ammers an' the like.'

He finally noticed Maddy and Sal; his scowl washed away and was replaced with a greasy charm. 'And who are these delightful young ladies?'

'Friends of ours. This is Maddy Carter.'

Delbert reached for her offered hand. She'd expected it to be shaken; instead, he stooped and kissed her knuckles. '*Enchanté!*' he said with cavalier flamboyance. 'That's French, that is, love.'

'Right,' she said, doing her best to smile. 'Yeah, I sort of figured that. Hello.'

'And this is Saleena Vikram.'

Sal stuck her hand out and chuckled at Delbert's theatrical gesture. 'Your moustache tickles!' She giggled as he kissed the back of her hand.

He stood up, straightened his rumpled waistcoat. 'Are you ladies 'ere to help with Dr Anwar's experiments?'

Maddy looked to Liam for the answer. He'd mentioned that he'd spun Delbert Hook a vague cover story to do with science and experiments. She wasn't so sure she liked the idea of being seen as some sort of mere lab assistant to Rashim, though; just because she was female she had to be the gopher not the brains?

Typically sexist.

She sighed. 'We're here to help him out, I guess. And you . . . you must be our landlord, Mr Hook? Liam's told me a little bit about you.'

'Mr *Delbert* Hook at your service, ma'am. Although you can also call me Del if you so wish. Self-made businessman. Importer and exporter of the finest goods in the world. You name it, and I can probably get 'old of it. And if I can't, I'll know someone who can. And this tall drink of milk standing behind me is Bertie.'

The young man offered a limp, pen-pusher's hand to the girls. 'Herbert actually. I do his accounts for him.'

Delbert looked out. Shopkeepers were already trying to restore some semblance of order to the street, brushing up piles of debris, the shards of glass, damaged, soiled goods looted from their stores and discarded in the dirt of the road. 'Shocking business this is. We've 'ad this going on in the East End of London for the last four nights in a row now. First time it's spread here to Holborn, though. Never thought it would come this way.'

'I was reading about it in yesterday's paper,' said Maddy. 'This has something to do with those murders in Whitechapel, doesn't it?'

Delbert sucked on his teeth. 'Any excuse for these yobbos to make a ruckus and take all they want, as far as I can see.'

'They're anarchists,' said Herbert. 'Workers, the common man. And they have good reason to be angry, Del. It's an unjust country. The rich get richer and the poor starve. Those murders . . .' Herbert paused and stroked his thin, pencil-line moustache. 'That was just the tinderbox to the fire. There were riots brewing anyway, but that lady, Miss Mary Kelly, she's an inspiration to the poor, isn't she? An inspiration to the oppressed proletariat.'

'Proletariat?' Delbert turned round slowly and looked up at his assistant. 'Listen to yer and yer poncey posh-boy talk. Since when did you swallow a whole blimmin' dictionary?'

'I read a lot, Del. When I'm not keeping your business running for you, or humping boxes around for you, I actually read. You should give it a try.'

'You think this is going to get worse?' Maddy directed her question at the young man.

Herbert nodded, his eyes wide, his Adam's apple bobbing like a fisherman's float. 'Oh yes, Miss Carter, I think this'll get a great deal worse.'

They let Delbert and Herbert get back to patching up the damage to the front doors to their business and decided to take a walk down Farringdon Street. Then along Blackfriars Passage, all the way down to the River Thames. Across the city's skyline, beyond London Bridge, they could see smudges of smoke rising up to the overcast sky. Hundreds of smouldering fires from the riots last night. It seemed the unrest had spread out of the East End in all directions – south over the river to Newington, into the City of London. And, if the view hadn't been obscured by the tall quayside warehouses along the river's edge, Maddy suspected they'd see more hairline columns of smoke to the north of them.

'It's a real mess.' Sal pulled a lace veil aside so Maddy could see her eyes more clearly. 'Maybe we can go back now?' Sal chose to wear a broad-brimmed 'ladies' touring hat' with dark lace trim that dangled over the edge and hid most of her face. She felt a little better that way. It was the combination of having darker skin in a city where there appeared to be virtually no black or Asian people – that and wearing clothes that she felt looked like pantomime costumes. Walking the streets by gaslight was one thing, but by broad daylight she felt too many eyes lingering curiously on her.

'Yeah, let's go back.' Maddy nodded. 'We need to decide what we're going to do next.'

Half an hour later they were back inside the dungeon, top hats, bowlers and bonnets dangling from their coat rack.

'All right, here's the thing, guys . . . it's a change. And, by the looks of it, it's clearly going to run and run and develop into a huge one.'

Sal cleared a space on the wooden crate they were using as a table and placed a pot of freshly brewed tea on it. She dealt out a mismatched collection of chipped teacups and enamel mugs.

'So?' Liam nudged her. 'Your suggestion is?'

'So –' the rocking-chair creaked as Maddy worked it gently backwards and forwards – 'this is a test case for our new role, our new function. Time's been changed, right? So we're going to take a look forward and see what this contamination gives us.

I suggest we go as far forward as we can ideally, get a look at the year 2070 and see if this Pandora thing is still going to happen to us.'

'You know going forward is very energy-intensive, Maddy,' said Rashim. 'I'm not sure how much forward displacement-reach I can coax out of this current set-up.'

'Well, let's find out. I mean . . . look, we don't exactly have to send Liam and Bob forward all the way to 2070. What if we just open a pinhole camera and take a look-see? Zero-mass, less energy, that's how it works, isn't it? Just get a pinhole image. I mean, a picture tells us a thousand words, or something like that.'

Rashim nodded. 'Yes . . . yes, of course. Let me get some calculations together.' He got up and went over to their networked computers, now all linked up, a chorus of CPU fans whirring and hard drives clicking contentedly. 'SpongeBubba!'

'Hey, skippa!' the lab unit squawked, emerging from a dark corner.

'Come over here, you and I have some work to do!'

'Yes, skippa!' it bleated, irritatingly happy to be of service.

'Retrieve my energy-conversion templates from Exodus.'

'Yes, skippa!' It waddled over to join Rashim at the computer table and together they started a hushed discussion of numbers.

'So then,' started Liam, 'we investigate whether this Jack the Ripper contamination needs to be corrected first before we do anything else?'

'That's right. That's how we're going to operate. From now on we watch and wait for contamination events and when one comes along, the procedure should be that we take a look at what future we get from it. If it's a good one,' Maddy said, shrugging, 'we just let it happen. If it's bad news then we do like we used to and go fix it.'

'But . . . let's say the future is good,' said Liam, 'no Pandora, no virus that wipes out all of humanity; you're saying if we get that future . . . we should do absolutely nothing?'

'Yup. That's what I'm saying.'

'I'm going to say it . . . because I'm sure I'm not the only one here thinking it,' said Sal.

'Thinking what?'

'Well . . . doesn't it strike you as unlikely that this Kelly woman could overpower a serial killer like the Ripper?'

Maddy tapped her chin thoughtfully. 'Not really. She seems a fiery character from what the papers are saying. She's got a real potty mouth on her too.'

'No, that's not what I'm getting at. This is wrong history now, Maddy. We're in a contamination.'

'I know that. Somehow Liam and Rashim changed something small that led on to something else, that led on to something else, like dominoes, that somehow resulted in a situation where Kelly had a chance to fight back. Who knows? Liam buying a chest of drawers from one trader instead of another might just have caused the same man to have to make a journey to pick up another chest of drawers that somehow impacted on the plans of the Ripper causing him to mess up somehow?' She shrugged her shoulders. 'It's impossible to determine for sure.'

'Or maybe we aren't alone back here.'

'Becks!' said Liam. 'Maybe she made it back alive!'

'Crud . . .' Maddy stared at them both. 'Maybe she did.'

'And maybe it was Becks who killed this Cathcart,' said Sal.

'In which case we also have to go back to the night of that murder, then, and see if it is her.'

'Becks wouldn't kill someone like that,' said Liam. 'Not without having a good reason. It's an unnecessary change to history. She knows not to do that.'

'Unless she's not right in the head, Liam. Maybe that upload wasn't stable. Maybe there's stuff going wrong in her head.'

'Ah Jay-zus, that's just great! The last thing we need – a wonky support unit going around killing bad guys.'

'OK, look . . . it just means we have a bit more work to do here. Right.' Maddy stopped rocking her chair and sat forward. 'This is what we're going to do. We're going to take a look at the future. If there's now no Pandora event thanks to this contamination, if mankind appears to be going merrily along and not wiping itself out with a killer gooey virus, then we've got a winning contamination. But . . . we still go back to the night that Mary Kelly should've been murdered. We know precisely when and where to go, since the papers have given us nothing but the details of that night for the last month. If it is Becks who did it, or is involved somehow, we grab her.'

'But if it is Becks who, say, killed Cathcart . . . we need to let her do that first, right?' said Sal.

'Yes, of course. We let her do her thing, then we grab her. On the other hand, if the future is still Pandora, then I suggest we grab her before she can mess with the sequence of events.'

'And Miss Kelly dies,' said Liam.

'Yes.' Maddy shook her hands subconsciously – Lady Macbeth shaking blood from her fingers. 'Yes . . . I'm afraid so.'

Liam pulled a face. 'That feels a bit like we're taking advantage of things, so it does.'

'So?' She shrugged nonchalantly. 'Sue me.'

Liam looked uncertain. 'We're meddling.'

'Christ, Liam, that's what we've been doing for the last six months for Waldstein – *meddling*. Worse than that, we were meddling without even really understanding why!'

'But that last woman, that Mary Kelly lady,' said Liam. 'Surely there's a way we could try and save her?'

347

'We could do. We could try and save every one of the Ripper's victims, Liam. Sheeeez, we could go wandering through time saving *everyone* who didn't deserve to die. But we don't have an infinite supply of energy, and we can't survive an infinite amount of time travel. So we have to be tactical about this, we have to be smart . . . *surgical*.'

She reached over and poured some tea into her mug. 'Here's a change someone else has made. Let's sort of *audition it*. We're gonna see if it's a good 'un. And if not, we'll fix it like a decent, responsible little team of TimeRiders.' She hunched her shoulders. 'Other than that, we sit tight. We watch. That's our job. And maybe we even enjoy Victorian London. Maybe even get out and live a little.'

'Aye.' Liam nodded slowly. 'I suppose you're right.'

Maddy turned to Bob. 'That OK with your programming, you big lump?'

'I concur with your assessment. The logic is sound.'

'So, if Rashim can get our displacement machine to do it, I say we first get a look at a time and place we're all very familiar with. Something we can compare directly to.'

'2001?'

'Yup. The eleventh of September 2001. New York. We know very well how it's supposed to look, so that'll be a perfect place to check first to see if this contamination had had knock-on effects, or self-corrected between now and 2001. You up for that, Liam?'

'Aye.' His face lifted. 'Aye, of course!'

'And then, after that, we'll try and get a glimpse at 2070, if we can do it. Sound like a plan?'

The others nodded. 'Plan.'

'Good. Now . . . who's for a nice cup of tea?'

CHAPTER 62

6 November 1888,
Whitechapel, London

'It's best to be in pairs, love,' said Mary. 'Ain't so safe on the streets these days with that madman out there somewhere.' She grasped Faith's bare arm. 'That's why you should stick close to me, you understand? We can look out for each other while we work.'

Faith adjusted the muslin wrapped tightly round her still-healing arm. 'I understand,' she replied evenly. 'I will stay close.'

She wasn't entirely sure what the woman meant by 'work' – they appeared to be doing nothing at all productive; instead, they were standing together beneath the soft amber gaslight glow of a street lamp and calling out peculiar greetings to males who happened to pass them by.

'What is your "work"?' asked Faith.

Mary looked at her with a coy grin. 'A finger-snitch, love.'

'What is a finger-snitch?'

'Oi, you serious?' She sighed. Faith stared at her, awaiting an answer. 'You really are a funny one, aintcha? I s'pose I better explain. See, what I do is lift a little coin from gents who should be behaving 'emselves better.'

Faith frowned. 'I do not understand.'

'Pick their pockets, love. Only the ones who look like they can afford it, mind. And usually gents who've had a bit too much of the ol' drink and rather fancy themselves.'

'Pick their pocket?' Faith ran a search for that phrase in her head. 'You are talking of theft? Stealing?' she said finally.

Mary laughed. 'Blimey, you're a bit slow on the uptake, love. Yes, I steal. I ain't so proud of that, but it's that, my dear, or starve. And I'll tell you there's plenty of gents in London who make a pretty penny by doing very little but sit on their fat backsides while poor hardworking sods break their backs making 'em rich. It's a bloomin' unfair place this city. One world for the rich, and another world for the rest of us.' Mary shrugged. 'So, I don't feel so bad about lifting the odd coin from a gentleman's back pocket.' She winked. 'It's all in 'ow you go about distractin' 'em.'

'Distracting them?'

'A saucy wink, love. That an' a cheeky smile.' She laughed. 'Men can be such fools. 'Specially when they've 'ad a bit too much to drink.'

Faith nodded. 'I understand. We deploy mating signals to distract them. Then we steal from them.'

Mary shook her head, bemused and tickled by Faith's choice of words. 'You're an odd one, love. But, yes, that's the gist of it. You can 'elp me, Faith. Two of us? We could make a good team. Pretty girl like you would get plenty of attention. You keep 'em talkin', an' I can do the finger work. What do you say?'

Faith gave that a few moments' thought. 'We will require money to obtain food. I need food to sustain me.'

'Don't we all. Ain't nothin' bleedin' well free in London.'

Faith nodded. 'Your logic is sound. I will assist you in finger-snitching. You will have to teach me the "saucy winks" and the "cheeky smiles". I can learn these actions.'

Mary nodded. 'I'll teach yer, that and a few saucy things to say to 'em gents. They like that. We should practise on someone . . .' She spotted a likely candidate. 'Hoy! Cooeee, love!' Mary called out to a gentleman a little worse for wear, tracing a drunken zigzag along the pavement opposite them. 'You want some company?'

The drunk snarled something back at her and staggered on.

'Charming,' muttered Mary.

Faith looked up and down the street. It was almost completely empty apart from them and another couple more women down the far end, like them, huddled in the pool of light at the base of a street lamp.

'Trade ain't good tonight. 'S the rain see? All the gents stayin' at home with their missus.' She laughed. A throaty sound. 'Get things for free at 'ome now, dontcha?'

Faith offered the distant women a polite nod, but they ignored her. She wasn't fully listening to Mary as she talked. Faith was busy evaluating her mission status. It was, of course, still active, yet to be completed. And she knew her targets were close by. They'd come here to this time, this place for a good reason – whatever that was. She was reasonably confident – 76 per cent – that they wouldn't know she'd actually managed to follow them through the portal. And here in this time with no CCTV cameras, no wireless transmitters, no radios, mobile phones, no computer tracking and monitoring they would probably feel entirely safe.

Which meant they might get careless.

She had identified a search radius of a mile in diameter, the approximate distance she'd been offset by the displacement process. A lot of people in such a densely populated place as London, but her eyes were good, her recognition software exceedingly fast. Yesterday Mary had taken her along Oxford Street to a pie shop that sold 'proper meat in the middle'. Oxford Street had been a good place to be. Faith had locked on to and evaluated 7,056 faces in just under ten minutes.

Streets were the best place to be, Faith decided.

A sea of humanity out there, plenty of opportunity for her to wait and watch. At some point one of her targets was bound to walk down one of these busy roads, in need of some essential thing: food, drink, clothing. And, if she was standing in the same street, she would spot them, and make her move.

'. . . although it is a shame . . .' Mary was still talking. 'Pretty flower like you 'aving to do something like this. 'Aving to be a common thief. But that's 'ow it is, I'm afraid.'

Faith turned to her. 'I am a "pretty flower"?'

Mary laughed. 'Course you bloomin' well are!' She sighed. 'Mind you, even I was pretty once. This place does that to you . . . sucks all the blimmin' life out of you.'

Faith sensed that was probably some sort of a metaphor, not to be taken literally. The woman was talking about fatigue, attrition. Being 'worn down', to use another human aphorism. Faith considered how long she had been pursuing the targets. Her 'elapsed mission time' counter was showing four weeks, five days and seventeen hours. Given that she'd been birthed nine hours before being sent back from 2069 to 2001, she'd effectively been on-task pretty much *all* of her short life.

She wasn't exactly *tired*; the proteins she'd managed to get hold of and consume were keeping her organic chassis fed. Perhaps not ideal forms of nutrition long term; her digestive system wasn't exactly designed to deal with pigs' trotters and eels.

No, her body was well-fuelled for now . . . it was *her mind* that felt tired.

Her hard drive was filling up with a trillion things observed, heard, smelled, felt, tasted. She needed to compress her data, to offload the unimportant, trivial data and defragment the spaces left behind. Data retrieval, sorting, ordering, filtering, all those necessary processes were getting markedly slower and that was undoubtedly beginning to affect her performance.

She looked at Mary and imagined that her hard drive looked like the skin on this woman's face: pockmarked, weathered, lined.

A visual metaphor, of course. Not literally.

A drip of rainwater from the lamp-post landed on Mary's upturned face. She wiped it away. 'I wanted to be a musician, a piano player when I was a little girl,' she said. 'You know, I was brought up near a convent. And they had an old piano there they let me play on. I could play some pretty tunes on that, Faith, I could. Even though I couldn't never read the music.' She smiled wistfully and listened to the soft patter of raindrops all around them. 'We all 'ave silly dreams when we're children, don't we?'

Faith felt she should nod at that.

'Only dream I got left, I s'pose, is taking meself back 'ome 'gain. To me mum and dad. Be a little girl all over again.' Mary sighed and the soft hiss of drizzle filled the silence.

'What about you, Faith? Was you a bit of a dreamer?'

Faith hadn't told Mary much about her past. In fact, Mary had *assumed* most of it – country girl from a farm? Longed for the excitement of the big city? Came to London with little or no money and soon found herself in trouble? All Faith had really needed to do was nod at Mary's stated presumptions.

Did she have 'dreams'? Faith gave that a moment's thought.

[Information: I have goals. Objectives]

But dreams . . . in a different sense, *dreams*. She had trace memories: the faintest recollection of pre-born foggy images and muffled sounds. A growth cycle in her tube, before her miniature silicon chip became active and thinking became a digital process.

'I sometimes dream,' said Faith finally. She panned her cool grey eyes on to Mary. 'I dream that I can go back home also.'

Mary laughed. 'Right blimmin' daft couple standin' here, ain't we?'

'Yes,' said Faith. '*Blimmin*' daft.'

'You an' me . . . we should try and save every penny we make. No more of the gin, no more of the bad stuff . . . just save up all the money we can lay our 'ands on.'

'Agreed. The gin is toxic to your body chemistry. It does you harm consuming it.' Faith looked at Mary. 'What is your intended purpose for the money?'

'To pay for a train, of course! A train away from 'ere. A train back home. That's where you an' me should try and get. Back to our 'omes. This ain't no decent place to live. Farm animals live a better life than most of the poor sods trapped 'ere in Whitechapel. I wish I'd never come 'ere in the first place.'

'Correct. Many of the humans here appear to be in poor condition.'

'It's so hard to get by.' She shook her head sadly. 'Even just gettin' enough to eat. But then you walk no more'n a mile west . . . places like Oxford Street, Piccadilly Circus . . . and you see 'em posh blighters in their fancy clothes, in their fancy carriages, stepping into fancy clubs and eateries. None of 'em done a day's work in their lives. Ain't right.' She sighed. 'If I 'ad a say in things . . . I'd change it all. Take what's *theirs* and share it among all them poor beggars out there workin' all day an' night just to scratch together enough money to blimmin' well eat!'

A thought occurred to Mary just then. 'Where did you tell me your 'ome was, Faith?'

Faith looked at her. 'I have no . . . *home*.'

'Then, blimmin' 'eck, you could come with me!' Mary's face creased with a gap-toothed grin. 'How about that? Would you

like that? Wales is lovely, Faith. Mountains and valleys. Nothin'
like London.' She grabbed Faith's arm. 'We could both go live
in Wales. Would you like that? You and me? We could pinch as
much money as we can . . . save every penny, an' buy us some
tickets away from this miserable city.'

Faith's tight lips curved, producing a practised-several-times,
almost genuine-looking smile. 'That sounds like a *blimmin'* good
plan, Mary.'

CHAPTER 63

15 December 1888,
Holborn Viaduct, London

Liam looked down at himself. He was wearing a pair of grey flannel trousers and a white cotton shirt; it was as time-neutral a look as they could get from his Victorian clothes. Maddy as well: just a plain grey skirt and a vanilla-coloured blouse – no frills, lace or bonnet. At worst they'd look like a pair of rather dull nerds in 2001.

Or a rather unimaginative couple.

'So, it's Piccadilly Circus, then,' said Liam. They were heading for London, 2001, instead of New York. Having crunched the numbers, Rashim had come to the conclusion that the charge they could muster was not going to be enough to project them that far into the future unless they compensated on the geo-displacement and aimed for somewhere closer to home.

'We'll do a one-hour visit,' said Maddy. 'One hour then open the return window at the same place. And a two-hour back-up window for just-in-case. OK?'

Rashim was sitting at the desk. 'Understood.'

Liam centred himself in his square. 'Nice not to be going back wet.' He grinned. 'That's a blessed relief, so it is.'

Maddy nodded. She tucked a small digital camera into a clutch bag. There were dozens of digital images of Piccadilly Circus on it, pulled from their database. They had a fair idea how it *should* look and she could reference those images on the camera. If it turned out to be only a moderately different Piccadilly Circus, then perhaps they were now heading along a timeline that was preferable.

'Density probe is showing us a consistent all-clear,' said Rashim. 'Countdown is now at thirty seconds. Are you two all ready?'

'Yes, we're good to go,' Maddy replied. She'd wanted Bob to go along with Liam. For protection, of course. But his mass was adding too much to the energy cost of displacing them. However, Maddy realized that of all of them, her memories – her programmed memories – were closest in time to 2001. Intuitively she'd have the best idea if London was looking odd, or the way it ought to.

'One hour,' she said. 'Time enough to buy a soda and some tacky I've-Been-To-London T-shirt and come home again.'

'Aye.'

'And ten . . . nine . . . eight . . .'

She winked at Sal. 'Chin-chin and toodle-pip, old girl.' She grinned. 'That's the sort of thing they say in England, isn't it?'

'Remain still, please, Maddy!' called out Rashim. '. . . and four . . . three . . .'

'And be careful, you two!' Sal called out, but her voice was lost in the buzz of energy building up.

'. . . two . . . one . . .'

2001, Piccadilly Circus, London

A yard, walled in on all four sides and overlooked by a tall, grey stone building lined with soot-encrusted windows and ledges of surly-looking pigeons. Above them, a pale sky of combed-out clouds. They could both hear the dull urban hiss and rumble of traffic, the melodic cooing of the pigeons watching them from the ledge.

Just then a door opened on to the yard and a middle-aged man wearing trousers, shirt, tie and a dull brown sleeveless jumper took out a packet of tobacco and cigarette papers, sat down on the step and began to roll himself a cigarette.

He noticed Maddy and Liam standing there. 'All right?'

Liam nodded. 'Aye. You?'

He shrugged. 'Middle-bad. But you have to make do, don't you?' He tucked a modest row of stale strands of tobacco along the paper. 'You two new? I haven't seen you around before.'

'Just joined,' said Liam. *Joined what exactly* . . . he wondered.

'Ahh . . . you must be with the Licence and Trade Monitoring? Or Weights, Standards and Measures Approvals?'

'The, uh . . . that's the one. Started this morning, so we did.' Liam watched the man lick one side of the paper. 'You know that'll kill you eventually, so it will. Smoking.'

'Eventually, huh?' He laughed at that. 'Least of me worries, wouldn't you say?'

'We'll be heading in now,' said Maddy, tugging Liam's sleeve.

'Hammer-an'-spades! You got a funny accent there!' The man looked at her. 'Where are you from?'

'Boston. United States.'

'*America?*' He was taken aback.

Maddy sensed that might not have been a prudent thing to say. 'Well . . . my folks were. You know, *originally*.'

'Well.' His eyes were wide. 'And they gave you a job in the Ministry of Information? I'd keep all that family ancestry to yourself, young lady. Quite seriously.'

They stepped past him. 'I . . . I will,' she said quickly. 'Thanks.'

'Hang on! Did you lie about that?' He looked up at them. 'To get the job? You must have had to lie to the Job Commissariat?'

'I, uh . . . I may have bent the truth a little,' she said with a shrug. 'I guess.'

Liam grabbed her hand. 'Enjoy your smoke, sir.' He pushed the door and they stepped into a dark hallway. It reeked of floor polish and disinfectant. At the end of the hallway the faint pearly glow of a pair of frosted-glass doors leading outside.

'I guess it's not good to be an American,' whispered Maddy.

'Aye, it seems it.'

They made their way towards the double doors, passing an opening on the right that led on to a large office: two long rows of dark wooden desks, with men and women typing away on machines that looked like a cross between typewriters and logic engines, all brass levers and glowing vacuum fuses. The room echoed with the clatter of keystrokes, and the long ring of a telephone.

'It's like one of them old black-and-white flicks,' said Liam.

Maddy nodded. Yes, it was: those old films where every scene was veiled behind a pall of cigarette smoke and every desk lamp seemed to cast its own beam of light through it. Men with trilby hats and trench coats, and every street glistening from a torrential downpour. *Noir* . . . she remembered. That's what they called those old films.

They reached the double doors and pushed them open. At least it wasn't raining. There was that.

The roar of traffic, the buzz of activity in Piccadilly Circus, took them by surprise. They were three wide steps up and back from a pavement thick with pedestrians. Maddy quickly located and identified the things she *expected* to see: the statue of Eros, the circular fountain and plinth on which it stood and the steps surrounding it. She noticed the signs pointing out the

'Underground Tramlines'. The tall stone buildings with classic grand entrances and granite pillars. Signs for Shaftesbury Avenue, Coventry Street, Regent Street. And as she'd expected, yes . . . it was busy. Hectic-busy.

But none of the garish colour she had in the images on her phone. No billboards, no electronic displays with SANYO or TDK or COCA-COLA dancing across them. No street vendors selling plastic double-decker buses, or Beefeater soft toys.

And no tourists.

Maddy had expected Piccadilly Circus to look a bit like Times Square: clusters of faces of all colours, people taking pictures of each other posing in front of Eros. But this was very different. It was certainly busy, though – busy with cars, bicycles and electric trams. A network of wires spun like a spider's web above the hectic thoroughfare. The trams, running along rails in the roads, all had connector arms that reached up to wires, and here and there sparks flickered and fizzed.

The cars all appeared to be the same, albeit in a variety of unexciting colours: maroons, browns and greys. Small bubble-like cars with oval windscreens that puffed thick dark clouds of exhaust fumes. And as many people on bicycles as there were clogging the pavements on foot; they wove round the trams like a school of pilot fish around a whale.

On the side of one towering building overlooking Piccadilly Circus was a giant television screen. Huge. Bigger even than the one in Times Square. But the image was blocky and primitive. Two-tone 'pixels' of just black and white. Looking more closely, Maddy saw it wasn't even a light-based display, but each 'pixel' was a disc about the size of a dinner plate, that flipped on a spindle. One side black, one side white.

'Now this *is* different to how it's meant to be.' Liam looked at her. 'Isn't it?'

'Very.'

It felt like a London that belonged to a Britain stuck in 1945. Perhaps the early fifties. She wasn't sure.

'Well now,' said Liam, 'we know for sure the Jack-the-Ripper thing has caused a change.'

Maddy looked at her watch. 'We've got fifty-six minutes left. Let's split up. Get what you can, any newspapers, magazines, books you can lay your hands on. Back here in fifty minutes, OK?'

CHAPTER 64

2001, Piccadilly Circus, London

Liam decided the plaque above the grand building in front of him looked promising enough: INFORMATION RESOURCES CENTRE (DEPT OF INFORMATION DISSEMINATION).

He took the dozen steps up and pushed his way through a heavy wooden revolving door and stepped into a cavernous foyer beyond. He saw several concentric circles of benches round a cluster of newspaper stands in the middle. Most of the seats were already occupied with men and women, even some children, flipping through rustling broadsheet newspapers.

He spotted long tables beyond, glowing reading lamps evenly spaced along them; they were mostly occupied by people reading newspapers or books. To his left was a counter and a young woman busily filing index cards in an organizer.

He wandered over and stood in front of the counter for a moment, before finally coughing into his balled fist for her attention.

She looked up. 'Oh, I'm so sorry!'

Liam offered her his best lopsided smile. 'Ah, that's all right.'

'How can I help you?'

'Well now, I'd like to have some information.'

'Information?'

'Aye.'

'Well . . .' Bemused exasperation on her face, she laced her fingers and leaned forward. 'How about we try and narrow that down just a little bit?'

Liam laughed softly. 'Aye, might help. I'm after history books, recent history, that is.'

'All right . . .' She nodded. 'Wonderful start! How recent?'

'Hmmm . . . last century or so.'

'Or so?'

'Last century, then. Nothing too specific, you know . . . general history, world history.'

She looked at him through a drooping tress of mouse-brown hair. 'Just arrived from another planet in another galaxy, have you, sir?'

'Aye. Who knows . . . I might even choose to stay.'

Her turn to laugh. 'Well, I have academic reference texts or general information texts.' She glanced at his puzzled face and decided to clarify that. 'With nice pretty pictures or without?'

'Oh, pictures! Please.'

'Pictures you can colour in?'

'Uh?'

She chuckled, raised a hand to cover her mouth. He noticed she had braces on her teeth. 'Just teasing you, sorry. Let me quickly check my info-veedee for some suitable lend-outs.'

He noticed a pale blue glow lighting her face from below and her fingers began to tap at a typewriter keyboard. He leaned forward over the counter and noted a small cabinet the size of a cigar box; one glass side glowed blue, like a small television set. Two metal brackets held a large oblong magnifying glass screen between the young woman and the mini 'television'. She adjusted its hinges slightly; the tiny screen loomed large in the lens, glowing blue with white text.

'That's a veedee, is it?'

She looked at him. 'Veedee? You know, visual display?'

'Ahh, that's a computer down there, I suppose?'

She looked at him quizzically. '*Compute-er*? What an odd word.' She cocked her head. 'You really are from another planet, aren't you?'

'That's what me mother used to say about me.'

She looked back at the magnified screen. 'We have *The Revolutionary Century: A History of Socialist Britain*. That's a bit heavy-going, I think. How about *Two Worlds: The Free Man and the Profit Slave*? That's quite a good read.' She looked up at him. 'And it's got lots of pictures too.'

'Aye, that one sounds good.'

She tapped a key. 'There, requested it.' He noticed her sneak a furtive glance up at him, then her eyes darted awkwardly back to the lens screen. 'Now, umm . . . let me see . . . what other works can I recommend for you?'

'Good to see a library so well used,' said Liam, looking back at the rows of eager readers, the gentle whispering rustle of pages being turned.

'It's the news-sheets,' she replied. 'Everyone wants to know the latest on what's happening.' The teasing smile at the edge of her lips dropped for a moment. Very suddenly she looked drawn and worried. 'It's all so terrifying, though, isn't it?'

'Terrifying?'

'The blockade! The Americans shipping in all those atomics for their French friends?' She pressed her lips together. 'You can't help wondering how this is going to end up, can you?'

Liam decided to play along. 'Aye, it's pretty bad, there's no doubting that.'

'My mum says,' she lowered her voice to a whisper, 'my mum says if the French get those missile bits and pieces and decide to put them together, it could end up leading to an atomic war.'

'War?'

She nodded. '*Atomic.*' She mouthed the word as if it was a curse not to be spoken out loud. As if merely saying the word would open the gates of Hell for Satan and his hordes to pour through.

'It's so frightening. Mum says we could *all* end up dying if that happened.'

Liam shrugged that off. 'Ah, now I'm sure something like that won't happen. What's in it for the big fellas at the top if they let something daft like that happen? Hmmm?'

She fiddled absently with the index folder in front of her. 'No, I suppose not. I suppose it all looks more frightening than it really is. It'll all turn out all right in the end, won't it?'

'Of course.' He nodded. 'Always does. Everyone sees sense in the end.' He smiled. 'They always do.'

She raised that teasing, flickering smile again, and continued browsing through catalogue pages on the lens screen. 'Anyway . . . so do you, uh . . . you live in London? Only you sound Irish or is it Scottish?'

'Irish.'

'I see. Are you, uh . . . visiting? Or do you live in London, or something?'

'Just visiting.'

'Uh huh.' That sounded to him more like a disappointed '*uh*'.

She tapped the keyboard in silence for a moment, the soft blue glow on her face flickering with screen refreshes. Finally she looked up, her lips playing with words silently for a moment before picking one or two to start with. 'I . . . I . . . don't normally . . .' Her face flushed pink.

'Don't normally? What?'

'I wonder . . .' she continued, her eyes firmly locked on the lens screen, far too embarrassed to look up at him and meet his eyes. 'Whether you'd care to . . . care to have some tea and brancakes?'

'Tea and . . . ?'

'Brancakes. Lunchtime? With me?' She dared a glance up at him. 'I have a lunchbreak coming soon, at one. I eat it outside by the fountain.' She laughed nervously. 'Sometimes I feed the pigeons with my cakes if they're too dry, though.'

'I . . .' Liam was pretty sure his cheeks looked as red as hers did now. 'I . . . well, uh . . . I'm awfully sorry, I have to run along. I'm only passing.'

'Oh! I'm . . . s-sorry. No, don't worry!' she cut in too quickly. 'Just a thought. Just an idea. I'll . . . just . . .' Her fingers knotted together uncomfortably. 'I'll just go and check on your book. See if someone's retrieving it for you.'

She turned and hurried away from the counter through swing doors and out of sight.

Maddy managed to pick up half a dozen discarded newspapers and shove them under her arm. She was beginning to think she looked like some mad bag lady – like that old vagrant in Times Square with his tarpaulin-covered shopping trolley and all that bin-rummaging.

The people in Piccadilly Circus seemed far too preoccupied to care about her, though.

Watching the comings and goings, the exhaust-spewing bubble cars, the hundreds of people on bicycles, some of them so overburdened with things she wondered how they didn't topple over. She was reminded of images of Beijing, of Mumbai, of Havana. There was an exciting, almost frenzied, whirlwind of chaotic activity going on all around her. But like those places, looking closely, she'd begun to note a threadbare quality to everything: a stiff-lipped impoverishment hidden away behind broad smiles and exuberant 'how-do-you-do's. A make-and-mend place of limited resources.

The cars all looked old, patched up, held together in places with tape, ribbon and rope. So many items of clothing seemed to sport discreetly sewn patches. At first she'd thought it might be some sort of fashion thing – a particular passion for elbow patches. But she noted thread giving way on shoulder seams, trousers worn tissue-thin at the knees, shoe leather worn to a rough suede.

They're really struggling. Britain's poor.

She was about to grab another discarded newspaper left on a bench near the fountain surrounding Eros, when a church bell – at least that's what it sounded like – gave an ominous single *claaaang*. She looked up towards where it seemed to have come from and saw that the large television screen had a logo slowly crawling across its black and white pixel blocks. Maddy recognized it as the clock face of Big Ben. And beneath it: SRBBCI — LUNCHTIME NEWS.

She noticed how many people in the bustling space turned to look. The trams continued, of course, the bubble cars rattled on, but the bicycles pulled over, the pedestrians stopped and turned. All those who could stop seemed so very keen to view the screen and listen to the news.

A newscaster appeared in blocky black and white pixelvision: smart, formal, a bow tie and a dark jacket. Silver-haired and with a reassuring fatherly smile, he looked like Dumbledore after a wet shave and a sensible haircut in smart gentleman's-club evening wear.

'*Good day, citizens. This is your News at One.*' A pause. A very long pause.

Looking around, Maddy noticed how many of the upturned faces around her seemed to wear a frozen expression of anticipation.

No . . . more than that. Dread.

'*The ultimatum presented by Secretary Andrei Bechemov of the Soviet Republic, and Secretary Andrew Benn of the Socialist Republic of Britain, has expired without any official response from President Jonathan Elroy Bush. The convoy of American warships crossing the Atlantic carrying the atomic materials to France appears to be proceeding undaunted. It is thought that the convoy will cross the 20 degree west longitude – otherwise known as the Bechemov Ultimatum Line – at some point late tomorrow afternoon. Discussions are continuing among the other gathered heads of state in Berlin as to the official response to the crossing, should it happen. There have been increased calls for a naval interception. Soviet warships despatched over a week ago across the Arctic Sea and around the top of the Atlantic and into the American-enforced "Trade Embargo Noose" will be in a position to meet the convoy should it make any attempt to cross the line.*'

The newscaster took a breath.

'*Secretary Benn reiterated that the proliferation of atomic weapons, specifically President Bush's insistence on deploying a forward atomic weapons base on French soil, was a flagrant attempt to provoke hostilities. French leader, President Durant, responded that France was at one with American foreign policy in wanting to preserve a robust frontline against socialist encroachment.*'

'Oh, that doesn't seem good,' Maddy whispered. She checked her watch. The one-hour window was due in just under ten minutes. She decided to make her way back across Piccadilly Circus; now, with the exception of the rattling wheels of the trams and the overhead fizzing of sparks along the contact wires, it was an almost completely frozen tableau.

She walked up the steps and through the frosted-glass double doors they'd emerged through earlier. Halfway down the dimly lit hallway, she passed the office on her left. The sound of clacking keyboards had ceased and she glimpsed inside – every typist in the long room was now gathered round a single desk, watching something glowing a flickering blue. She could hear the thin warble of the newscaster's voice echoing out of the still and silent office, following her down the dark hallway towards the doorway opening on to the yard.

'. . . *for everyone to be prepared for the worst possible scenario. That a state of war may soon exist between* . . .'

In the yard she was relieved to see Liam was waiting for her, a fat, heavy-looking book tucked under one arm.

'I think this might not be a future we want to hold on to,' said Liam as Maddy joined him.

She checked her watch. Five minutes to go.

'I've got a feeling you may be right.'

CHAPTER 65

15 December 1888,
Holborn Viaduct, London

'This is incredibly fascinating,' said Maddy. She pushed her glasses up the bridge of her nose. 'From Jack the Ripper goofing up and getting himself killed in 1888, here we have a 2001 sitting on the brink of global thermonuclear war!' She looked at the others. She had the history book Liam had 'borrowed' open on the desk in front of her and resumed reading passages aloud.

'*The revelation that the Whitechapel murders were perpetrated by a Cathcart-Hyde, a member of the House of Lords, proved to be the final straw. His intended victim, Mary Kelly, a common street woman, was hailed as a hero for overpowering him and killing him in self-defence. Upon her arrest for his murder, riots erupted across the East End of London.*'

She looked up at them. 'Which we saw for ourselves.' She resumed reading. '*Her trial in the spring of 1889 led to mass riots across the country. She was prevented from taking the stand and testifying publicly, because the authorities feared Mary Kelly would incite the working class to open revolt, so popular a figure was she by then.*'

Maddy turned the page, and scanned the text.

'*December the fifteenth 1890. The hanging of Mary Kelly led to the Winter of Rage and the subsequent "Trafalgar Square Massacre"; three hundred rioters were shot dead by soldiers of the fifth Hampshire rifles and another hundred and seven people were cut down during a charge down*'

Oxford Street by the Queen's own Blues and Royals of the Household Cavalry!'

She turned another page. *'May the seventh 1891, Queen Victoria and the royal family escaped to Canada as the Libertarian Workers' Transition Council took control of Westminster and the Houses of Parliament and the first socialist state in the world was officially declared.'*

She flipped through several more sections of the thick book, taking her forward through time. The others sat in silence as she skim-read the pages and timelines of dates and events.

'So . . .' she said presently, 'it seems . . . then, when the Second World War should have been happening in correct history, there was no war in this timeline; instead, a growing consolidation between two sides. And an escalating arms race.'

'Two sides? What, America versus Britain again?' said Sal. 'Just like that time when the American Civil War didn't finish?'

'No, not so much countries, Sal. *Ideologies*: socialism versus capitalism.'

'What does that mean exactly?' asked Liam.

Maddy looked at him. 'Oh, come on! Seriously? You must've read enough history books by now to know what those words mean, right? It's the struggle of the worker versus the banker. The poor versus the rich. The idea of shared wealth versus personal wealth.'

'Oh, right, *that*.' He shrugged. 'Aye, I knew that.'

'On one side we have Russia,' her finger ran across a colour-coded map of Europe, 'which has its revolution in the 1920s. Germany, Britain, Poland, Austria . . . one after the other, by the look of these dates, they experience their own workers' revolutions. And then on the other side we have America and Canada and some of the South American countries becoming one big "Free World Zone". That's what they call themselves.'

'It's an Atlantic divide, then?' said Rashim. 'The Americas against Europe?'

'No, not exactly.' Maddy flipped through some more pages until she found an entry she'd read earlier. 'Ah, here it is . . . *1937: The DuMann/Roosevelt Accord. President Roosevelt and Congress approve a loan of several hundreds of millions of dollars to the French to help them invest in industry and weapons development. France is seen by the American public as one of the last major outposts of capitalist values in Europe.*'

She checked an index at the front. 'The rest of this century, it seems, is one long Cold War. Tensions rising on both sides. There's a doozy of a quote right here at the front of this book.' She flipped to the title page.

'*The twentieth century will prove to be a century devoted to one purpose alone – preparation for an inevitable war. Almost a hundred years spent in a race for industrial and technological supremacy. A race in which the winning post will almost certainly be a brutal and catastrophic global war . . . and no country will emerge unscathed.*'

'Jay-zus,' muttered Liam. He recalled the strained look on that poor young girl's face in the library. She'd seemed so worried, so haunted by looming events. And Liam reminded himself how he'd casually, glibly, batted away her concerns as if she was being silly. So easy for him to be devil-may-care. His was a fleeting visit. But she . . . she was stuck there waiting, like every other person in the country, to see how far the Americans were prepared to push their challenge.

The young lady had returned with his book and a mumbled apology for the awkward invitation she'd extended to him. She'd covered her mouth, her braced teeth, as she'd whispered, but he could have sworn she'd said something like, '*I just don't want to be on my own . . . if . . . when . . . it happens.*'

'Everyone knew what was coming,' said Liam. 'They could see it coming, God help 'em.'

Maddy picked up one of the newspapers. She looked at the others, Rashim and Sal in particular. 'They have nuclear weapons in this timeline, but they call them "atomics". It looks like both sides have "atomics". They've been stockpiling warheads for decades.'

'We need to see how it turns out, Maddy.'

She nodded at Liam. 'I think so. It didn't look good. We need to go further forward, Rashim. Can we do it?'

He shook his head. 'I said it before. We don't have the power to send you any further, Maddy. Maybe remote-viewing. A pinhole-viewing.'

'That's fine. That's all we need. How far forward can we go?'

'I need to work it out.'

'2070? Can you get us a look at that year?'

He shrugged. 'I'll work it out. Just give me a moment.' Rashim took a chair at the desk and pulled up a program on the screen.

They waited silently, listening to him tap on the keyboard and mutter calculations under his breath.

'It's always the same,' said Sal after a while. 'One way or another, mankind ends up wiping itself out with some big weapon, doesn't it? Why are people so completely stupid?'

'It's what we do best, isn't it?' said Liam. 'Invent things that we can use to kill everyone. It's what we're good at, I suppose.'

'That is correct,' rumbled Bob. His eyelids were fluttering, revealing the rolled whites of his eyes. He was Bluetoothing data. One of his sporadic back-ups. 'Mankind is essentially sociopathic,' he continued. 'That is probably why *Homo sapiens* became dominant and wiped out the Neanderthals and the other sapient species; your killer instinct was more clearly defined.'

'Aye, we were tougher nuts than those apemen,' said Liam.

'Negative. Not tougher,' said Bob, 'just more ruthless.'

'Thanks for that, *Dr Phil*,' said Maddy. 'Since when did you become an expert on the human psyche?'

'I have files on —'

Maddy raised a hand. 'It's OK, I was just being snarky.'

'OK, I've got some rough figures,' said Rashim. 'We can't project a pinhole field all the way to 2070, I'm afraid. It's just not possible on the power we're drawing in right now.'

'Jesus!' Maddy gritted her teeth. 'We need to do something about that. This Holborn generator's a pile of junk!'

'I have some thoughts on this. We could do some reconfiguring, perhaps insert some kind of capacitor to build up a store of surplus energy —'

'Later. We'll discuss that later. Just tell me how far we can go right now.'

Rashim looked at the scribbled notes on the desk in front of him. He sucked air through his teeth. 'I think we can reach as far forward as the early forties – 2042, perhaps 2043. But not much more.'

Liam cocked his head. 'Wasn't that round about when Waldstein showed off his first-ever time machine?'

'Yeah, round about then, I think.'

'I wonder if this future has a version of him in it,' said Liam. 'Eh? That would be weird.'

Maddy shrugged. An intriguing idea – that another version of him lay ahead of them now, perhaps a version of him that was living a very different life. A happier life perhaps with his wife and his son? A life lived in blissful ignorance of time travel. An Einstein who remained a humble patent clerk; a Bill Gates who ended up a computer repairman.

Wouldn't that be a thing, though? A timeline that survives this looming nuclear crisis and perhaps finds a peaceful future. But also a timeline without Waldstein's displacement machine in it. Perhaps even a timeline without a Pandora. Wouldn't all of that be a wonderful thing? She could only hope. 'Rashim?'

He turned to look at her. 'Yes?'

'Do it. Set that up, please. Let's go get a look at our future.'

CHAPTER 66
2043, the ruins of Piccadilly Circus, London

The dog, a small, virtually hairless thing that might, once upon a time, have been mistaken for a Jack Russell, chased the rodent through a dark maze of creaking wooden tables and desks – furniture that for many a year had held true until a decade ago a portion of the building's roof had finally caved in. Ten years of wet summers and freezing winters had done its work and damp was rotting the wood.

The dog scurried between chair legs and desk legs in a desperate, ravenous pursuit. The rat was a good-sized one and yet fast. Its small feet skittered across a long-forgotten floor covered in grit and plaster; moistened by the damp, it was almost soil and in several places clumps of weed and moss thrived.

Out of the maze of the long-dead office, the rat scampered up a slanted fallen roof timber, on to a chair and over a stick-dry bundle of bones in rags slumped across the grit-covered surface of a service counter. Its body and beady dark eyes reflected all but briefly in a mildew-spotted oval of magnified glass. Along the counter now, it found a dark corner behind a rusting box spewing corroded wires.

A moment later the dog scampered past the counter in hot pursuit, out into a large hall of round wooden benches and long tables. As with the counter, there were other bundles of white bones and tufts of hair wrapped up in decaying fibres of clothing to be seen: lying along the benches, slumped on the reading tables, spread out on the floor. Shards of sunlight speared down into this place through the collapsed domed roof of the building, and a cheerful, welcoming blue sky was visible beyond, framed by the broken fingers of iron spars and crumbling masonry.

The balding dog sensed it had lost its prey and wandered over to an opening that led out into the warmth of a pleasant summer's afternoon. It emerged into the sunlight, blinking back the brightness of the sun, sat on its haunches and panted. It decided to rest and recover for a while before returning inside to sniff out another rodent. The pickings were too rich in this building to give up yet.

Its pink tongue darted out and slapped its muzzle. Skinny flanks heaved with the rapid in-out in-out in-out of hot breath being expelled and oxygen pulled in.

And dark beady eyes looked out impassively on a crowded vista that meant nothing to it. A place once upon a time known as Piccadilly Circus.

Tall grass and nettles grew waist-high here, a sea of gently swaying ochre-green giving way here and there to hummocky islands of rust-red vehicle roofs. Lost to sight, but certainly down there where the wild grass and the tall weeds spread their roots, was a rich compost of decaying clothing fibres and bleached bones still able to leak some goodness into the forming soil.

In the middle of this shifting grassland was a circular plinth topped by a still-recognizable human form with wings. Eros. Its bronze base was now a peppermint green, the statue itself – aluminium – was a marble-like pattern of rust spots and algal growth.

Everywhere a pleasing prairie sound. The gentle murmur of

breeze haunting the skeletons of dead buildings. The grass whispering a soothing white noise. Crickets chirruping in chorus. Far away another dog barks to find its pack. And slowly the late-afternoon sun eased across a cloudless sky towards a craggy horizon of falling buildings. Eventually that same horizon would be shallow humps beneath a blanket of vegetation. Eventually that horizon would be flat grassland or a wood or something in between.

Peaceful.

But life goes on. Big bugs eat small bugs. Rats eat bugs. Dogs eat rats. A dozen crows circle overhead prepared to eat anything. Life continues despite a gradually decreasing background level of radiation that might still give concern to a radiologist.

Just over four decades ago, it wasn't peaceful here. Just over four decades ago, there was a period of horror and panic. The sound of wailing sirens filled the air.

Screams.

Prayers.

This same blue sky was criss-crossed with several hair-thin lines of vapour: the approaching and departing vectors of missiles. A day in which the skies all over Earth looked largely the same. Vapour trails and mushroom clouds.

But that's all long ago. Forgotten now. Silly, vain, stupid, violent humans are history and in a couple of hundred years the last visible remnants of their buildings will be too.

Peaceful, except for a tiny disturbance now. Minute – the size of a mere pinhead. If one knew precisely where to look, you would see nothing more than a spot of darkness floating six feet above the ground. Like an errant pixel on a computer display, grain on an old photograph, the tiniest freckle on porcelain-fair skin.

There for a second, gone the next.

They stared at the low-resolution image on the computer screen for a long, silent minute before Liam finally spoke.

'That's Piccadilly Circus, is it?'

No answer. In his own Liam way he was being rhetorical. 'Well now, that's not looking very good, is it?'

'You're quite right,' said Maddy. 'Not good. Not good at all. I think it's safe to say we don't want this future.'

'That means we have to make it right,' said Sal. 'Jack the Ripper has to kill this Kelly lady?'

'And get away . . . never to be identified.' Maddy nodded. 'Kinda sucks, but yeah. That's how it has to be.'

CHAPTER 67

8 p.m., 8 November 1888, Whitechapel, London

Mary Kelly wiped muffin crumbs from her lips and smiled across the table at Faith. 'I ain't felt so 'appy in a long time.'

Faith had been gazing out at the street. The late-night market was closing up for business. By the amber glow of lamplight, costermongers, butchers, grocers packed their wares away as weary-looking stevedores returned home from the docks and warehouses along the Thames. A narrow street heaving with activity; a seething mass of grubby humanity seen through the sooty window of this small tea shop. Faith had logged, analysed and dismissed seventy-six faces in the last minute alone.

She levelled her impassive gaze on Mary. 'Why are you happy, Mary?'

'I have you.'

Faith had compiled a short list of non-specific, noncommittal yet reassuring responses that she could trot out in response to Mary's endless chatter. She picked one at random.

'Then I am happy too.'

'I feel like there's a hope. A way out of Whitechapel. A way out of this stinkin' awful unfair city.'

'Yes.' Faith played a smile. 'We have your plan.'

Mary checked the coins in her purse. The last few nights their petty crimes had paid off well. Mary had decided they could try their luck along the Strand. There were a number of members' clubs along that busy road that disgorged drunken gentlemen into the streets in the early hours. Faith had played her part well, catching the eye and attention of a number of them with some suggestive and teasing come-ons while Mary had made quick work of dipping her hand into their coat pockets.

'We've already got almost a whole pound! A few weeks like this, Faith love, and we might have enough for tickets to take us anywhere we want!'

'The place that you called "Wales" sounds like a very nice place.' Faith was vaguely aware that her AI was adopting some very sophisticated human behavioural traits. She was 'playing along'. Acting a part. Lying. Faith had no intention of travelling off to a place called 'Wales', but maintaining the illusion that she was sold on that idea suited her well. Mary was a useful accomplice with useful local knowledge. More than that, between them they seemed to have developed an efficient way to accumulate money; something that was needed, of course, to purchase food.

Faith finished her lamb broth. Generously full of chunks of mutton and other useful proteins.

'I think you an' me's earned a night off. What do you say?'

Faith was looking out of the soot-smudged window. 'As you wish.'

'We could go down me local, the Queen's Head. How's that sound?'

Faith turned to look at her reproachfully. 'You intend to consume alcohol again?'

Mary shrugged. 'It's just a little celebration. We done so well, you an' me. Just one drink ain't gonna hurt, is it?'

'Information: intoxication impairs performance and compromises judgement.'

Mary laughed. 'Bleedin' 'eck, Faith. Come on, just one little drink. Ain't gonna kill me now, is it?'

12.27 a.m., 9 November 1888, Whitechapel, London

The pub – The Queen's Head – turned out to be another useful location for Faith to log faces. Her database of stored images was rapidly increasing in size. She'd spotted, logged, analysed and filed 17,217 faces in London so far. None of them, of course, were the people she was after. But it meant over seventeen thousand humans ruled out.

As she calmly surveyed the florid faces around her, through clouds of acrid pipe smoke, Mary was enjoying herself. One drink had turned into several drinks and she was now in the middle of a noisy muddle of men and women, leading them in singing along to an accordion player, all of them equally inebriated. The innkeeper winced at the racket as he collected the empty tankards. Keen to begin kicking out his patrons for the night.

Faith approved of Mary Kelly. There was an iron strength in the woman: not physically, of course, but in the way she could command the obedience and respect of others. The kind of person who, in another life, in other more favourable circumstances, might have achieved great things. Instead, all she would ever be was a 'street woman', a pauper, quite likely destined for an early grave. If she could feel any emotion for Mary, it would be fondness. Instead, the best she could manage was dispassionate approval.

She watched Mary sing tunelessly for a while, a foghorn voice that carried over the other tuneless voices, then turned back to the task at hand: observing the faces around her.

And it was then, as she glanced around once more to check for any new faces, that she caught sight of a dark-haired young man. Just a glimpse of a face on the far side of the public house. Her breath caught in her throat.

Liam O'Connor.

[Information: 85% identity match]

She started to push her way through the fog of pipe smoke and heaving, sweaty bodies. Florid, bearded faces loomed closely at hers. Men with gap-toothed smiles leered at her as she squeezed her way frantically through.

For a moment she lost sight of the young man. Then re-established visual contact again a few seconds later. Closer now. She could see his face was slim, his nose prominent beneath two thick arched eyebrows.

[Information: 87% identity match]

She began to feel adrenaline coursing through her body. Her mind determining the best strategy. To kill him right here in this pub? Or better to watch him discreetly and perhaps follow him when he left at the end of the evening in the hope he was going to lead her back to the others.

Closer now. She could see the young man was the same height and build.

[Information: 88% identity match]

She needed to be closer; to not have clouds of pipe smoke obscuring her view; or red-faced, drunken fools staggering into her, breathing rancid fumes in her face. She could snap any one of these fools' necks with the slightest flick of her wrist, and perhaps no one would notice in the press and surge of bodies. A man might collapse to the sawdust-covered floor of this pub and they would all assume he'd passed out from too much drink.

But it wasn't worth the risk of alerting the attention of Liam

O'Connor, now just a few yards away from her, laughing at something being said to him by someone else.

Faith reached to pull her bonnet down a little, hoping to disguise her face. Too late. She noticed his brown eyes flicker on to her. Resting on her . . . and then a smile for her benefit. No alarm. No flicker of recognition and panic.

No. Just a fuzzy-headed, drunken smile.

'Hoy! All right?' the young man called across to her. 'Buy you a drink, love?'

[Information: not Liam O'Connor]

She ground her teeth. Turned on her heels and started to push and squirm her way through the crowd back to where she'd been standing moments ago. Only to discover Mary was no longer there with her newly made drunken friends.

CHAPTER 68

12.30 a.m., 9 November 1888, Whitechapel, London

Mary guessed Faith had had enough and taken herself back to the room they were sharing off Miller's Court. It wasn't so far; just a couple of streets away from the pub.

She staggered down Dorset Street, cursing and muttering as her feet slipped on rain-slicked cobblestones. She'd only intended to have the one drink. After all, it was well-earned. But one had led to two and more, and she'd spent more of that money than she'd really wanted to. Not that she was too worried about that. They could make that money again tomorrow. Easily.

Faith had an alluring way about her. An innocence and beauty that drew men like bees to honey, like moths to candlelight. So distracted were they with trying to chat her up, it was like stealing pennies from a blind man's cap.

What a splendid pair we are.

Although Faith was a little peculiar. There was an almost doll-like manner to her expressionless face. As if her features were as rigid as porcelain. And an almost mannequin stiffness to her, as if she was always on guard. Like one of them redcoat-'n'-bearskins standing to attention outside Buckingham Palace.

Mary wondered about her. She was such a puzzle.

She turned left off Dorset Street into the dark alleyway that led into Miller's Court, a cul-de-sac of dosshouses around a small cobblestoned courtyard that always seemed to reek of human faeces.

She staggered in the dark, steadying herself against one greasy brick wall.

'Blimey,' she muttered. 'Bit too much of the blimmin' laughing juice.'

Faith was probably already back in their room. Tucked up in the one bed they shared, toe to head. Mary did actually wonder if Faith ever slept. She always seemed to be wide awake, staring up at the cracked plaster of the low ceiling. She wondered what thoughts passed through that mind of hers. What wishes and dreams, wants and needs. She seemed to give so little away.

What a pretty puzzle she is.

Mary was in fact so puzzled by her friend that she failed to notice the shadow of a man entering the alleyway behind her, casting a long veil from the faint amber glow of a gas lamp on Dorset Street, all the way down the dark little alleyway into Miller's Court. Like some impossibly stretched, impossibly tall being. The shadow fell across her back, marking her with darkness . . . like the ghostly touch of the Grim Reaper, marking her soul for imminent collection as she entered the last few minutes of her life.

CHAPTER 69

15 December 1888,
Holborn Viaduct, London

'What we've got on the Ripper murders isn't a lot,' said Maddy. She'd grabbed the information and dumped it into Bob's head from Wikipedia back in 2001. Which, given that the site had only been running since January, wasn't a hugely detailed article.

'The night of the eighth of November . . . the early hours of the ninth of November is when the last victim, Mary Kelly, gets murdered. There's no precise time, just that she was supposedly last seen at midnight and was discovered dead by a neighbour at eight thirty in the morning.'

Maddy pulled up two grisly black-and-white photographs on one of the monitors. 'These were both taken by the Metropolitan Police.'

'Jay-zus,' whispered Liam.

'Yeah, not very nice I'm afraid.'

He looked at Sal queasily. 'I feel sick.'

'Well, you need to get over it, Liam,' said Maddy. 'You're gonna see this for real very soon.'

'Is that her face?' asked Rashim.

Maddy nodded. 'What's left of it. The Ripper seemed quite keen for some reason to completely disfigure her face.'

Rashim leaned closer. 'My God, it looks like he was trying to *remove* it.'

'So, now that's how the crime scene is *supposed* to look. In *correct* history, her body is found in her room, lying diagonally across her bed, her lower torso opened up and the contents, her organs, placed on the bed beside her.' Maddy reached across the desk and picked up a pad with notes on it. 'But this is the description I've summed up from the recent newspaper articles.'

She looked down at her notes. 'So, this bit I'm about to read to you is the contamination bit, what *shouldn't* have been found at the scene of the murder . . .' She began to read.

'*. . . on the floor beside Kelly's bed in her small rented room off Miller's Court was found the body of her attacker. At first glance a wealthy gentleman in his middle years, wearing an evening suit and thick coat, his top hat placed on a small table beside the bed. His manner of death – a crushing of the cranium – was believed to have been caused by the swinging of a coal shovel or similar device. Although Kelly claimed she had no memory of the struggle with Lord Cathcart-Hyde, it is clear she must have struck him once to the side of his head to render him unconscious, and then repeatedly as he lay on the floor, until his head was completely stoved in as if some workshop vice or similar device had been applied to the skull and wound tight until it was crushed out of all recognition . . .*'

'Good God,' whispered Rashim.

'A crushed head.' Liam had once seen Bob do that. A German guard in one of those concentration camps back in America. Bob had squeezed the poor man's head in one of his big hands: squeezed like it was nothing more than a ripe tomato. 'Bob? Could Becks do that?'

'Affirmative. Even partially grown she has enough physical strength to deploy that kind of damage to a human skull.'

'Then it really is Becks!' said Liam.

'If that is Becks then she may have flipped out,' said Maddy cautiously.

'May have? Jeez . . .' Liam all of sudden wasn't quite so keen on the idea of a reunion with their lost team member, even if she supposedly had some sort of weird, twisted digital version of a schoolgirl crush on him.

'Her AI must have been unstable,' said Maddy. 'I'm sorry, it's my fault. We shouldn't have tried loading her up with the stuff from the hard drive.'

'We're going to need to kill her, aren't we?' said Sal.

Maddy nodded. 'We can't leave her running around out there.'

'We could attempt to incapacitate her,' said Rashim. 'We may even be able to reset her.'

Maddy looked at him. 'How?'

'Your support units are older-generation units,' said Rashim. He pursed his lips thoughtfully. 'Perhaps twenty-year-old technology. I would say engineered around about the 2050s. Not like the support units you encountered in Rome. The ones procured for Project Exodus.'

Bob nodded. 'This is correct.'

'OK, so Bob and Becks are older models,' said Maddy. 'So what does that mean?'

'The computers are dense silicon wafers. The circuitry is mainly a graphene construct with *some* conventional silicon that is tightly meshed. *Very* tightly meshed. It is those small silicon portions which are vulnerable to power surges that can cause instances of micro-welding.'

Maddy noted Liam's eyes already beginning to glaze over. Mind you, she wasn't actually any the wiser herself. 'So? What are you getting at?'

'The older wafers in your units have a built-in trip switch to hard-set the chip into an "off" state to protect these weaker silicon parts from that kind of surge damage. During the

Russian–Chinese conflict over the Caspian oilfields, it was a common insurgency tactic by the Chinese to stun or incapacitate Russian hunt-and-kill squads with taser darts, and then later reprogram and reboot them with trojan viruses that made them turn on their own side after some trigger event – a word, a noise. There was a very famous incident of one squad that returned from a mission behind Chinese lines, passed through the sentry posts into the camp and nearly wiped out an entire regiment of Russian conscripts as they slept in their beds.'

'So, what are you saying . . . we taser Becks?'

'Well . . . yes.'

'That'll turn her computer off without, you know, completely trashing it?'

'Yes, that's exactly right. You see, the later-generation military units, the ones we had for the Exodus Project, designs from 2069, had chips made entirely of graphene circuitry. Those are completely resistant to that kind of surge-welding.'

'So we taser her. That means she's switched off? I mean *properly* off. She's not going to reboot, *wake up*, or anything like that, then, is she?'

'No. It is a hard-reset. A tiny physical switch is flipped and it'll stay flipped until someone physically gets into her head and flicks it back on.'

'Can you make something zappy like that from the bits we've got lying around?'

'There's no need. You already have one.' Rashim nodded at one of the boxes of gadgets and spare parts piled beneath the desk, still patiently waiting to be sorted through.

'When we were packing up, I was emptying that old filing cabinet,' he shrugged. 'I found one in there. I thought you knew we had one?'

Maddy rolled her eyes; yes, of course they had one. She'd

never used it. Never thought to. It had sat in the filing cabinet with all the other junk, waiting to be useful.

Well, now it was.

'All right, let's get it out, check the thing works. Meanwhile . . .' She turned to address the bank of computers. 'Computer-Bob, start charging up; the sooner we go back and get this done, the better.'

'Maddy, what if that taser thing doesn't work?' asked Liam.

'You're taking Bob along, aren't you? I'm sure he can handle little Becks.'

'Aye. But . . . she's quick. She's very agile.'

'Look, Liam, if for some reason you guys can't incapacitate Becks – if Bob can't wrestle her to the floor . . . or she looks like she might be doing a runner – she's got to be killed. Do you understand? If her mind has gone wonky, she's a contamination worry. More than that . . . whatever crazy stuff she gets up to may attract attention to this moment in time. She could blow our cover. Either you grab her and taser her, or you take her down.'

She looked at Foster's old pump-action shotgun leaning against the wall in the corner. Although why she still thought of it as *his*, she didn't really know. 'You should take the gun along with you. Just in case you need it.'

She was expecting an argument from him. She knew Liam was fond of her, *it*, the *unit*. She knew he'd have reservations about gunning her down in cold blood.

'Aye, the gun.' He eyed the weapon nervously. 'Good idea.'

Or actually, on the other hand . . . maybe he wouldn't.

CHAPTER 70

12.32 a.m., 9 November 1888, Whitechapel, London

Liam was soaked to the skin. This dark little corner of Miller's Court where they'd chosen to huddle and wait for Jack the Ripper offered little protection from the fine rain. It was as if God was hanging over London with a giant fine-nozzle plant spray, gently wafting aerosol clouds of moisture down on to the city. Moisture that seemed to find its way into every nook, crack and crevice.

They were beneath a lean-to: little more than four rotting posts of wood supporting a roof of rain-slick slate tiles that all seemed to be conspiring to channel bulbous, greasy drops of rain on to Liam no matter where he chose to crouch.

In the stillness of the early hours, the only sound to be heard was the soothing symphony of a rain-damp city fast asleep: the soft hiss of persistent drizzle; a dog far away with an intermittent worrisome bark; the soft cooing of pigeons tucked away under guttering, pleased with themselves for being dry.

Liam groaned.

'You must remain very still,' whispered Bob.

'My legs are killing me. I'm cold, I'm wet and I'm getting pins and needles.'

'Nonetheless you must be still,' said Bob.

He sighed and resumed his uncomfortable vigil on the narrow

entrance to this godforsaken courtyard. They'd been huddled here since 11 p.m. Watched a steady procession of drunks stagger home and noisily fumble their way through front doors. A dozen or more dosshouses seemed to have openings on to this place. And everyone, it seemed, in each dosshouse, seemed to enjoy drinking the night hours away.

'Bob, what's the time?'

He consulted his internal clock. '12.32 a.m.'

'Maybe we missed it? Maybe it's been and done?' He looked at the small dark square that was the window on to Mary Kelly's downstairs room.

Maybe she's already in there? He shuddered at the thought of that. Beyond the pale ghost of a net curtain was a small bedroom that quite possibly resembled an abattoir right now. A body almost unrecognizably human slowly losing the last of its warmth. Dots, commas and question marks of blood in arterial lines up the walls, now drying and crusting.

'Information: someone is approaching,' said Bob.

Liam heard the clack of footsteps. A shadow cast by one of the gaslights on Dorset Street danced down the rat run, then a moment later the long shadow was followed by the outline of a woman. He could hear the woman's soft voice, chattering to herself. Clearly, utterly, completely, passing-out drunk.

Mary Kelly.

She stopped outside the front door to her dosshouse, pushed the creaking door in and staggered clumsily inside.

More footsteps, quick, light, pattering down the rat run. Liam saw a long, thin shadow dancing along the wet brick opposite, then a man came into view. Tall and slim, a top hat cast a shadow across his face. He was wearing a thick cloak, but Liam managed to catch a glimpse of a leather surgeon's bag under one arm. He quickly stole across the courtyard, and caught the front door to

Mary's dosshouse with the toe of his boot before it slammed shut.

The man wrestled the door open and Liam heard a muttered exclamation from the hallway inside. The man pushed his way in and the door shut behind him. A moment later there was life in the room to the left of the front door. A gentle orange bloom appeared behind the tatty net curtain. Liam saw foggy movement going on inside: shadows cast up the walls, across the low ceiling.

'Jay-zus, this is it,' whispered Liam. 'That poor lady's going to die in a minute. Not just die, Bob, but die horribly!'

'Affirmative.'

A gnawing sensation had been eating at Liam for the last few hours. That there must be some other way to put history right. 'Ahh, this feels all wrong, so it does.'

'We must not intervene,' cautioned Bob.

Liam ground his teeth. His mind was replaying those two horrific photographs that Maddy had presented him with earlier, but now colouring in the black and white with vivid reds and intestinal purples. But then . . . wasn't something else meant to happen? Wasn't Becks somewhere close by? Perhaps mere seconds away from altering this scene somehow? Saving Mary Kelly? Killing this evil, psychopathic predator.

Where the hell is she?

'Ah Jay-zus! I can't do this. I can't just let that poor lady get carved up right in front of my eyes.'

He'd started to get to his feet when a shrill scream came from behind the fogged window. He saw a lurch of movement obscured by the net curtain and the scream was cut off. A shadow sliding across the ceiling, a sudden jerking movement, then another, and another, and another.

Liam felt the acid burn of bile in his throat, his stomach rejecting food.

Ah Jay-zus, I'm letting this all happen!

He heard a soft keening moan from inside the room.

'Oh God, she's still alive!'

Enough.

He got to his feet.

'Liam!' growled Bob, reaching out for him.

'Stuff this, I can't just watch!' He ducked out from under the low slate lean-to and darted across the small courtyard, the shotgun in his hands and ready to use.

And it was then, just then, that he noticed a figure to his right, striding quickly down the rat run towards him.

Both Liam and the other figure stopped. The figure wore a dress and a bonnet. Her face, what he could see of it, was so very familiar.

'Becks? Jay-zus! Is that you?'

CHAPTER 71

12.37 a.m., 9 November 1888, Whitechapel, London

Faith's mind was all of a sudden inundated with too many simultaneous decision loops running, each one of them furiously demanding all of her processor time.

Even only as a silhouette she instantly recognized the young man standing in front of her.

[Target acquired: Liam O'Connor]

Not only that, the target was a mere ten yards away AND in a dead end from which he had no hope of escaping her. Command imperatives screamed inside her head to step forward quickly and get on with the job. One of her fists balled and flexed, keen to get on with the task of killing him. But her eyes darted to the door that led to Mary's room. The very room Faith had been sharing with Mary Kelly . . . her friend . . . for days now.

Her . . . *friend* . . . *yes*. And her *'friend'* had screamed just moments ago.

Her friend needed help.

Now.

Even *now* might just be a second too late to save her.

'Becks?' whispered the young man. 'We have to help her!'

Faith realized that he'd misidentified her. He thought he was addressing the child support unit. It was a mistake she could take advantage of right now: draw closer to him while he still thought she was the other unit, perhaps close enough that she could quickly strike with a jab to his fragile neck before he could react and try using that gun he was holding.

But . . .

But . . .

Another desperate, dying gurgle from within the room.

But her *friend* needed help. Now.

'Jesus! Becks! C'mon . . . gimme a hand here!'

One imperative won out over the other.

Faith nodded. 'Agreed.'

No sooner had she taken three steps forward when she sensed movement to her left. A dark blur. Something large and fast looming towards her. She turned to face the threat and was halfway towards adopting a defensive combat stance when every process in her mind, every spinning loop of code, every circuit running hot and over-clocked, every data bus clogged with shuttling bytes like a highway jammed with rush-hour traffic . . . all of it came to a shuddering, grinding halt, as if an iron bar had been shoved through the spokes of a spinning bicycle wheel.

Several thousand volts locked her body rigid.

Her grey eyes fixed on Liam's for a moment before she keeled over, stiff as a board as the taser bolt, fired into her waist, rendered every muscle in her body as rigid as granite. She landed on the ground like a felled tree. And Liam, close enough to see her face clearly, took a backward step.

'Jay-zus! It's *not* Becks!' Liam turned to Bob. 'It's one of them!'

'Correct.'

He heard movement behind the window. The Ripper was busy.

'All right, she's down! Now let's go and catch that murdering –'

'No!' Bob reached out for Liam's arm.

Liam backed away, stepping up against the window. He turned to look over his shoulder – and got a second's glimpse through a ragged gap in the net curtains of a scene lit by a single oil lamp inside. A scene of ghastly crimson spattered across exposed ghost-white flesh.

My God . . .

Bob stepped forward and grasped his arm.

'Let me go, goddammit!'

'Negative.' Bob pulled Liam back towards the unconscious body of the unit. 'Both mission parameters have been satisfied. We have what we came for. We must let this happen.'

'The man's an animal! No, worse than that! A *monster* . . . a . . . a . . .' Liam realized he was crying; there was a vague acknowledgement that his cheeks were damp with tears for – how crazy's this? – a complete stranger. A woman he'd glimpsed for less than ten seconds. A poor wretch immortalized in the black and white grains of a scene-of-crime photograph. Forever frozen in her own timeless horror.

Bob gently eased him back from the front door. 'We must let him go. The killer must escape and must not be discovered or identified.' His voice managed to soften from its usual Dobermann growl to something resembling empathy. Understanding even.

'I am sorry. We have to let him go, Liam. And we have to let Mary Kelly die in that room.'

Otherwise stupid, powerful men in the future will blow each other to pieces, right? And not just themselves, but women, children . . . even innocent young librarians. Why? Because their ideologies don't agree. Like children who can't agree on which toys to have at playtime and decide instead to set a match to the lot of them.

Children. No better than children.

He let Bob pull the shotgun out of his hands. The support unit stooped down, picked up the unconscious body of their pursuer of the last few months, their assassin, and hefted her over one shoulder as if she was a pillowcase stuffed with charity shop seconds.

Liam was also dimly aware of the weight of one of Bob's arms around his shoulders. Not exactly a hug. But the clumsy, heavy-engineering approximation of one.

'We must go, Liam.'

He nodded. Maddy had a pick-up portal for them arranged for 4 a.m. located down among the warehouses and quays of Blackfriars docks. A couple of hours and change to spare yet, but they would want to get moving away from this crime scene as quickly as possible. The noises out here must have disturbed someone. There might even be people peeking through curtains at them now.

The sooner they were gone, the better. Otherwise, over a hundred years from now a Wikipedia article on the 'Infamous Whitechapel Murders' and various 'Famous Grisly Murders' anthologies might just feature in their footnotes an eyewitness sighting of '*a large ox of a man, almost certainly a labourer, accompanied by a slight and slender younger man with dark hair*' directly outside the room of the last-known victim of Jack the Ripper at the estimated time of half past midnight.

CHAPTER 72

15 December 1888,
Holborn Viaduct, London

'This is incredible,' said Rashim, looking at the others. 'We will see the wave approach, you say?'

'Yeah, it's like a weather front or something.' Maddy led them outside the dungeon, through their side door to stand on the kerb of Farringdon Street. 'Keep your eyes peeled for something that looks like a big bank of dark cloud.'

'It's always a spectacular sight,' added Sal, 'and a bit scary when it hits you.'

Rashim looked giddy with excitement. 'You know, we argued about this, Dr Yatsushita and I, about how a universe would accommodate an alteration to its past. What form the reality shift would take?' He gazed down Farringdon Street. Busy once again, although the usual kaleidoscope of activity was heavily punctuated with clusters of crimson tunics of soldiers and the black morning coats and tall pith helmets of bobbies stationed in protective cordons round the few shopfronts yet to have been stoved in by rioters. There'd been rumours that more riots were going to happen again later on today. But of course they weren't going to happen. The corrective time wave was going to arrive first.

'I thought reality would flip its state with some sort of global, instant paradigm shift.' Rashim shook his head in awe. 'Some sort of a . . . a pulse of change. Not like a tidal wave.' He turned to them. 'How quickly does this wave arrive?'

'It varies,' said Maddy. 'Sometimes almost immediately. Sometimes hours later. It's not predictable. It almost seems random.'

He nodded. 'Like some kind of Schrödinger flux? As if quantum particles are deciding to flip state or not?'

'If you ask me, more like quantum particles are having some freakin' union meeting and they need to vote unanimously on a change before something happens,' Maddy replied. 'Sometimes it's a no-brainer; sometimes I guess reality has a real struggle agreeing which way it wants to go.'

Rashim chuckled. 'You make it sound alive.'

'I do wonder sometimes.'

'Liam!' Sal called out for him. She ducked back inside and cupped her hands. 'Liam, you coming out to watch for the wave?' Her voice echoed inside the dark brick-built labyrinth.

He was inside, curled up on one of the bunks they'd improvised. He'd returned from the last short jump in an odd, un-Liam-like withdrawn mood.

'Best leave him, Sal.'

He's internalizing something, Maddy figured. *Guilt? Disgust? Anger?* Bob said he'd glimpsed the murder scene, the inside of Mary Kelly's room. Maddy could only imagine what horror he must have seen through her window. It must have been the stuff of nightmares. The kind of image once seen that remains in your mind like life-long retina burn.

'Just leave him be, Sal. The time wave isn't anything he hasn't already seen before.'

'Caution,' said Bob. He nodded down the street. 'There is the time wave.' He pointed.

To the east, above the tall townhouses opposite them, above

401

roof eaves and smoking chimney pots, the afternoon sky was darkening prematurely. Soldiers and policemen, street sweepers, peddlers and traders, the man standing on the flatbed of his coffee shop on wheels . . . *all* began to look up with burgeoning curiosity as the crisp winter sky became an overcast and improbable, swirling impressionist's oil painting.

'My God!' uttered Rashim. 'It's incredible. Quite beautiful!'

'Won't the wave affect our dungeon?' asked Sal. 'You know, not having a field up and running?'

'It shouldn't. Holborn Viaduct is here in either timeline. Mr Hook and his dodgy import/export business were here in *either* timeline too, so they won't change. And everything Liam and Rashim have done setting this place up had happened, would happen, whether Jack the Ripper had been killed or not. Two timelines, Holborn Viaduct and everything inside the same in either one.'

'In theory we should be all right.' Maddy looked at Rashim for confirmation as she spoke. 'Our dungeon *shouldn't* be affected by this.'

He nodded. 'Maddy is right.' As he spoke, his eyes remained on the sky. 'But this street, the rest of London . . . all of this will change. The riots will have never happened. This damage will never have happened.'

All returns to normality once more. Maddy watched as a cloud of pigeons fluttered from a rooftop nearby, startled by the first gasp of a squalling wind.

The poor remain poor and subservient, ignorant of a gentleman psychopath whose sport was carving up the bodies of unfortunate fallen women.

It didn't feel particularly good this time around restoring the status quo. But, as Foster had once explained, sometimes you have to allow space for a little evil in order to sidestep a much

402

greater one. An irradiated earth, that's what they were avoiding by allowing a murderer to escape and live the rest of his life undiscovered, perhaps even going on to murder again and again, indulging his secret, grotesque pleasure, undiscovered. Of course they were never going to find out for sure if this evil monster went on to kill again, whether 'Jack the Ripper's' victims went on to secretly number far more than the commonly accepted five.

The Wikipedia article listed many more prostitutes who died grisly deaths after Mary Kelly, who might have also been Ripper victims, but somehow didn't quite fit the same pattern of mutilations as the first five. Perhaps he was going to kill more. Perhaps his near capture and discovery frightened him off his grisly pleasure once and for all.

Maddy decided she needed to sit down with Liam and remind him that whatever that sick animal did, and possibly went on to do, once again their actions had saved this world. A fair transaction in the greater scheme of things.

A woman fifty yards down from them screamed out in alarm as a spectral tendril suddenly curled across the sky, like a negative image of forked lightning. The time wave was almost upon them. Much closer – Maddy had seen it coming from across the East River, roiling and boiling – she knew it would no longer resemble a bank of cloud, more a pulsating school of mackerel, twisting, turning, extruding tentacle-like outgrowths. As for Rashim, he'd only briefly witnessed it roar past the archway's open entrance. This time, they were going to be standing amid the swirling mass.

'Don't let it freak you out, Rashim!' cried Maddy. 'It's weird but it's totally harml–'

Her voice was lost in the sudden roar of a tsunami.

Wind buffeted and rocked them on their feet. They all

suddenly became enveloped in a wind tunnel of blurring reality, streaks of matter twisting, curling, changing. Fleeting visions of Hell and Heaven like an insane zoetrope.

Sal narrowed her eyes against the onslaught. She saw gargoyle faces whip past her; one or two seemed to sense her presence, wretched hands clawing towards her. She thought, in one fleeting moment, that she saw a face she recognized. A woman . . . dark-skinned, much older, grey-haired, with bulging cataract eyes full of raging malice. The face imploded into the snarl of some beetle-black underworld horror, claws, pincers, teeth.

Standing two feet to her right, yet entirely alone in her own wind-tunnel Hell, Maddy watched reality-soup conjure up momentary nightmares. She too thought she spotted a familiar face: pale and slim, a young man, framed by flailing hair – was laughing or was it screaming? Was that Adam? She reached out towards him, wondering if she might just be able to rescue him – pull him out of this swirling matter to have him join them once again. Her hand almost but not quite touching his slender fingers, then he was whipped away into a swirling reality tornado and became a thousand and one impossible things.

Then, as always, it was all gone in two shakes of a lamb's tail.

They were left staring at a Farringdon Street busy with the *clop-clop-clop* of horse-drawn hansom cabs and private carriages. Street hawkers barked the price of their wares; a knot of leering dock workers passed right in front of them, sharing a dirty laugh at some muttered punchline. One of them turned to Maddy and Sal.

'Awl right there, me loves?' he crowed, quite obviously drunk – swaying uncertainly on his feet. 'Come an' join us lads, eh?'

Sal flipped a hand gesture at him that wasn't going to have a proper meaning for another hundred years yet. The drunk shrugged it off with a grin. 'Your loss, love!' He tossed a good-natured laugh back at them, turned and staggered to catch up with his mates.

Maddy sighed. 'Men, eh?'

CHAPTER 73

2067, Piccadilly Circus, London

Another warm sunset across the overgrown ruins of mankind. The cry of a fox, the chirp of crickets. The gently swaying ochre sea of tall grass. The predatory swoop of a hawk.

A peaceful grave of humankind. Like some windswept site of archaeological interest – the ruins of Troy, of ancient Sparta, Babylon. Now, just like those places, worn stubs of masonry overgrown by an emerald carpet of nature. Tumbledown walls, caved-in roofs. Nothing lasts forever.

Here bleached bones lie amid the tangled roots of wild grass, doing a far better job of weathering time than the rusting, flaking skeletons of cars.

Peaceful, like a prairie, like the Serengeti, like an African veldt.

But now there's a fresh breeze, and the faintest distant rumble. The peach-coloured sunset sky has suddenly gained a faint twisting ribbon of black. At first as thin as a pencil scribble following the line of the horizon across a landscape painting. But, very quickly, becoming as thick as a marker pen as it approaches rapidly, and seconds later a looming, dark, continental crust swallowing the land beneath it.

A dozen seconds of deafening chaos as this black horizon sweeps in over the ruins of London and this peaceful post-human world is swept away; a possible future that had its short chance to exist. Swept away to join a million other begrudging futures that will never get a chance to see the light of day.

It's replaced by noise and chaos of a wholly different kind. London, 2067.

The grass is gone. Piccadilly Circus heaves with humanity, a city crowded with thirty million inhabitants. The statue of Eros looks up at looming mega-skyscrapers encrusted with holographic displays and garish adverts for soyo-protein products. The sky buzzes with corporate jyro-copters and police air-skimmers with winking blue lights and brilliant white searchlights tracking and monitoring the heaving populace below. A torrential downpour cascades from an unhealthy, lemon-tinted sky, overcast with polluted clouds.

Rain-slicked pedestrians push and jostle each other across waterlogged pavements, every last one of them wearing air filters on their faces.

London: one of a couple of dozen metropolises around the world playing host to its share of the migrating billions. Even though this city's levees that hold back the swollen Thames are sure to fail one day soon and it will join New York as another city lost to the rising seas, every day thousands more people swarm in and live cheek by jowl in cluttered tenement blocks that dwarf the old buildings of Canary Wharf.

In a way it's not so very different from the conditions of Whitechapel nearly two centuries ago.

London buzzes like a shaken beehive. Pounding music from hawkers on the street and second-tier pedestrian walkways above. A deafening riot of noise and movement and colour. Kerbside bazaars sell snake-oil cures for toxin-induced asthma. A trader sells slabs of pink-coloured dough that he's claiming is real meat. If it is . . . God knows what creature it once was. Genetically engineered apelike work-units marked by tattoo bar-codes and dressed in orange overalls move sullenly among the press of people, clearing trash, carelessly tossing the body of some starved-to-death immigrant into the back of a waste recycler.

This is the London that will exist a mere five decades after the last-ever Olympic Games are held here. Back in a time before the inevitable end was writ large for all to see and then foolishly ignored by one and all. Back before the first big oil shock, when supplies began to falter, before the sea level really started rising fast, the sky discolouring, crops failing, ecosystems collapsing.

But of course this is the way it has to be. This is the timeline a certain Roald Waldstein is so very desperate to preserve . . . at all costs. It has to be this.

And nothing else but this.

CHAPTER 74

1888, Holborn Viaduct, London

<u>Wednesday 19 December</u>

This is where we live now. It's not so very different to our last home, I guess. I'm getting used to it. We don't get the twenty-times-a-day rumble of a train over us. Instead, we have the constant deep engine rumble of Holborn Viaduct's power generator. Not so different, I suppose, to listening to the back-up generator we used to have.

We're settled now. Finding new routines. It's a different feel in here with Rashim and SpongeBubba keeping us company. I think I like it. SpongeBubba makes me laugh; the thing looks so ridiculous with that wobbling nose. We have to keep him out of sight of that nosy man Delbert. God knows what he'd make of that lab unit.

We have a decision to make about the killer support unit. Its organic body is being kept alive. It's like some person in an almost vegetative state; the eyes are open but there's nothing going on inside its head. The thing drools when we try and feed it this barley gruel. Totally disgusting. Rashim says we can keep it going indefinitely if we keep feeding it. The big question is whether we open up its . . . her . . . cranium and flip the 'hard-set' switch inside. I'm not sure how Maddy feels.

Liam, of course, says we should.

Me? I'm not sure. This support unit spent the last couple of *months wanting nothing more than to kill us all. I know its programming will all be erased . . . but will it really be? Completely?*

So, we have our new home. A new place in history, which I do find very fascinating. In many ways it feels like when we were first woken up by Foster. Scary, but exciting, new. It does feel a bit like that again. But it won't ever be the same. Not now that we know we're fakes. Pretend-humans. In fact, there's only one real person in here. Rashim.

Perhaps this time around, though, it's better. Like Maddy said, we're in charge now. We can decide whether or not we want to fix history. And who's going to stop us now? No one, NO ONE knows where we are now, not even Mr Roald Waldstein.

I like that. That makes me feel safe.

Maddy joined Liam standing in their side door. He was watching Farringdon Street slowly come to life. It was just gone seven in the morning and wisps of morning mist spun like silk across the wide cobbled street. Today looked like it was going to be another nice one. A clear blue sky waiting for the sun to get up and join it. A lamp-snuffer was putting out the street's gas lamps with his long-handled snuffer tray. Above them, on top of the viaduct, the electric-powered lights would be turned off manually by a man from the Edison Electric Company. They were beginning to learn the morning routine along Farringdon Street.

'Good morning,' said Maddy.

Liam nodded. He seemed a lot brighter since returning from the Whitechapel jump less than a week ago. 'Aye, looks like it'll be nice today.'

She had an enamel mug of coffee for him. Handed it to him and took up a place on the doorstep beside him. 'I like that we're not endlessly recycling in a two-day loop,' she said. 'Things change. That's kinda nice.'

'You sure we don't need to set up a field?'

'Yup. We're quite safe here. No one's looking for time travellers.' She laughed. 'No one in this time has even thought about time travel, I'd say. I mean . . . wasn't it that writer guy, H. G. Wells, who first thought up the idea of time travel?'

Liam shrugged. 'I'm sure somebody must've thought of the idea before he did. It must be the oldest fanciful notion ever; that it might be fun to travel backwards or forwards through time.'

'Yeah, well.' She sipped her coffee. 'He was the first one to write a fiction book about it.'

'Mark Twain.'

'What?'

'Mark Twain wrote a book about time travel. I'm sure he did. *A Yankee Fella in King Arthur's Court* I think it was called. Or something like that.'

Maddy hunched her shoulders. 'Oh well, whatever. My point is we don't have to worry quite so much about staying under the radar here. Nor do we have to worry about time waves. None of us are real. None of us belong in this timeline, so it really doesn't matter.'

He looked at her. 'You're OK, are you? Not . . . uh, not upset about –'

'About not being the *real* Maddy Carter from Boston?' She wrinkled her nose. 'Not really. Not any more. I think I quite like the feeling of freedom. I quite like not missing my mom and dad and my cousin Julian. Somebody made all those people up. Put painful memories of them into my head. I'm damned if I'm going to spend another second grieving for figments of someone's imagination. Stuff 'em.'

Liam laughed. 'Aye, that does seem a bit daft.'

'I am who I am. Right now, in this moment of time, *this* is

411

who I am. And that's all.' She looked sideways at him and smiled. 'Nice thought that, isn't it? It's liberating.'

'Aye.'

They heard a steam whistle echoing up from the far end of Farringdon Street where the docks and the River Thames were. Barges came in there and loaded and emptied round the clock. A never-ending cycle of trade and commerce.

'On the other hand, Sal's not coping so well, I don't think,' said Liam finally.

Maddy nodded. 'You and I should keep an eye on her. After all, I suppose we literally really are family now.'

'Uh?'

She looked at him. 'I might just be your sister, Liam.'

'*What?*'

'Think about it . . . we could've been grown together as a batch.' She laughed at her own words. Then curled her lip at a thought. 'God, I really hope we didn't share a grow-tube with you. That would be kinda gross.'

'Charmed.'

They sipped their coffees, blowing clouds of condensation out of their mugs into the chilly morning air.

'What about you, Liam? You all right?'

'About being a meat robot?' He grinned that devil-may-care lopsided smile. She wondered if that stupid smile of his was what kept him sane, made his good nature bulletproof. 'Aye, I'm not too bothered. So, at least I know now why it is I can cope with all that time travelling and not age so much as a normal person. It makes a bit more sense now.'

She hadn't told him about the ageing thing. She'd planned to, but never quite got round to it. And yet . . . it seemed he knew all about that.

'Don't look so shocked, Maddy. I'm not completely stupid.

412

I worked out this is how I became Foster. Or I should say, how I become *like* Foster. I presume Foster was a meat-product like us. Right?'

She nodded.

'Travelling is ageing me.' He flicked the tuft of grey hair above his right ear. 'And I'm not blind. I noticed that.' He pulled at the skin around his eyes. The faintest of crow's feet there. 'And don't think I didn't notice this either.' He cocked his head casually. 'So? I'm getting a little older. Happens to all of us eventually, doesn't it?'

She could have kissed him for being so resolutely . . . Liam. So brave.

So strong. So flippant.

'You know, Mads, I was thinking about this last night. I presume I must be *older* now. You know? Physically? No longer just a sixteen-year-old slice of a lad, eh?'

'I suppose so.'

'Older than you, Mads?'

'I don't know. It's possible. I guess so. What's your point?'

He grinned. 'Well now, if I'm the oldest, does that not mean that makes me the boss around here, then?'

She snorted coffee from her nose. There was laughter somewhere in that. 'In your freakin' dreams, Mr O'Connor.'

Epilogue

2069, W.G. Systems Research Campus, Pinedale, Wyoming

Roald Waldstein stared out of the broad panoramic window of his boardroom. The lemon-tinted sky over the steep slopes promised another downpour of acid rain, further stripping the last vestiges of green from the dying Douglas firs and the hilly landscape.

His forehead pressed against the plate glass, his hands leaving fingerprint smudges. He felt emotionally void. Utterly spent. The last three days of his life had been spent in a desperate panic to get those embryos speed-grown and ready. He was far too old for this damned level of stress. He'd begun to hope it was all long behind him. That his project, the agency, was something he could forget about.

Fourteen years ago.

Fourteen years ago almost to this day it happened. Almost an anniversary. The day Joseph Olivera had turned on him and *demanded* to know what Pandora was all about.

Back then Waldstein had begun to look on the young man almost as a son. A son to replace his boy Gabriel. (So long ago now that he'd lost little Gabriel and his wife Eleanor. A simple vehicle accident. If his wife had done just one of a thousand inconsequential little things differently that morning, she and Gabriel would still be alive and with him today.) But Olivera had pushed and pushed and pushed, asking questions Waldstein couldn't possibly answer and then coming to his own paranoid conclusions all by himself.

He'd never had Frasier Griggs killed. The poor man had simply been desperately unlucky. Took the wrong route home one night. But Joseph had been convinced, hadn't he? And he wanted to know . . . wanted to know why Waldstein needed to steer history this way.

Why? Why do you want mankind to destroy itself, Mr Waldstein?

If only he could tell the poor young man. But Olivera had gone and panicked. Olivera had garbled something about Griggs being killed because he'd found out too much.

That day back in 2055, poor young Joseph Olivera had convinced himself that Waldstein was going to have him killed. Nothing could have been further from his mind. He wanted Joseph out of that lab, away from the instrumentation panels before he did anything stupid. But Joseph had panicked and hurled himself into an open portal without any preparation, without any density checks. Nothing. God knows what horror happened to him.

Waldstein had cried for him that day.

And then there was the alarming event a few days later. A group of anti-time-travel activists managed to break into a project being secretly developed by the Russians: activists who hero-worshipped Waldstein, regarded him with his anti-time-travel message as some sort of a *prophet*. It turned out the Russian time-displacement project was a one-way-only technology with a severely limited range. But it was enough for the activists to send a lone assassin back to 2015 in an attempt to kill a young Chinese-American boy called Edward Chan. The young man who would soon write a thesis that would change the world. A thesis Waldstein would read as a young man himself. And there it would be: how time travel could actually be possible.

The assassination attempt was successful and Waldstein had watched from within the safety of his lab's protection field as the ensuing time wave changed everything outside.

That was the final straw. Too much to handle. Too much stress. He'd beamed a warning back to the 2001 team. But that was it – the last thing he wanted to do with this. That day, fourteen years ago, was the day he decided to finally close the doors on his special little project. To mothball it. Put locks on it and walk away. The agency was back there in 2001. They now had everything they needed to function – and that was always his intention anyway. For them to be self-sufficient: entirely on their own and working to preserve this timeline.

They certainly didn't need a heartbroken old man like him keeping tabs on them.

He'd closed those doors and locked them with a few final solemn words.

I'm sorry . . . you're on your own now.

Fourteen years ago.

And, since then, most days he thought of them: those three hand-crafted genetic products, so carefully designed for their roles. Liam with his robust, quick-witted mind. Sal with her enhanced visual acuity. Maddy with a mind designed for data sifting. In a way, they'd almost been like his own children. Like two daughters and a son. They were back there, all on their own with an older copy of the boy as the closest thing to a mentor for them. If they could just hold things together, prevent anyone else unseating this timeline for just a little longer, just until 2070 . . . then it would all have been worthwhile. Job done.

Mission accomplished.

Waldstein had even begun to believe it was all working out.

There'd even been days when he *hadn't* bothered to routinely check that tatty, yellowing page of newspaper with the personal ads on it. All, it seemed, was fine, going to plan. They were back there doing their job . . . and mankind was counting down its last few months and years until Pandora happened. Before they wiped themselves out.

Then all of this exhausting stress. Three days ago, out of the blue, that message from the Maddy Carter unit *demanding* to know all about Pandora. Demanding . . . and *threatening*.

His three 'children' were rebelling against their father. Like Joseph Olivera, demanding to know what Pandora was and threatening to come off-mission if no satisfactory answer was returned. With that brief message, they'd switched from being part of his plan to being a very big problem.

Oh God help me . . . Opening up that dusty old lab again after all these years, pulling those military-class foetuses out from cold storage, growing them, 'hatching' them and briefing them – briefing them to execute his own children – had been one of the hardest, most painful things he'd had to do in his entire life.

He'd sent them back to 2001 little more than an hour ago and he'd just realized something. He was probably never going to know for sure if they'd been successful. Most probably they had. Six lethal killing machines arriving right inside their archway without any warning whatsoever? His poor children wouldn't have stood a chance. The kill team had instructions to terminate the TimeRiders, destroy every item of equipment in the archway, then terminate themselves.

He should have thought to instruct them to send a final message when they had completed those objectives. Just before they self-terminated . . . a simple message to let him know the deed was done.

TimeRiders successfully terminated.

But in his panic and haste he hadn't.

Waldstein looked out of the window as gentle spots of toxic rain began to spatter heavily against the glass. Well . . . it was almost certainly done and in any case, there wasn't much time left now for anyone to steer history from its proper course.

'It's nearly time.' He sighed, leaving a small cloud on the glass. In a few months' time a virus was going to be released by either the Japanese or the North Koreans; no one was ever going to know who. Mankind was going to be almost completely wiped out in the space of a few short weeks.

'Nearly time.' His words echoed across an empty boardroom. W.G. Systems was a shell of a business now. A few caretaker staff left, but most had been let go eighteen months ago; there really was no more need for his business empire to be making any more money. Far better his employees spent what little time left with their families and loved ones.

'It's nearly time,' he whispered once more.

I've done all that you asked me to do . . . please, now, let this be enough.

HISTORY AS WE KNOW IT

1888
Victorian London: the Ripper murders are ongoing

2043:
London: an over-crowded metropolis in a polluted future

HISTORY ALTERED

1888
The Ripper's identity is revealed: he is an aristocrat and a member of government

1891
A popular uprising leads to Britain becoming a socialist nation

2001
A Cold War between America and the socialist nations of Russia and Britain finally turns 'hot' . . .

2043:
London: exists as deserted ruins amid a post-nuclear war wasteland

TIME RIDERS

2001 1912 1957 1941 2066

THE ADVENTURE DOESN'T STOP THERE

NEXT STOP: PIRATES . . .

FEBRUARY 2013

WANT MORE ACTION? MORE ADVENTURE? MORE ADRENALIN?

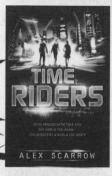

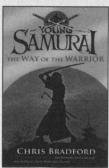

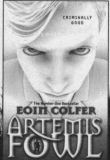

GET INTO PUFFIN'S ADVENTURE BOOKS FOR BOYS

It all started with a Scarecrow.

Puffin is seventy years old.
Sounds ancient, doesn't it? But Puffin has never been
so lively. We're always on the lookout for the next big
idea, which is how it began all those years ago.

Penguin Books was a big idea from the mind of
a man called Allen Lane, who in 1935 invented
the quality paperback and changed the world.
**And from great Penguins, great Puffins grew,
changing the face of children's books forever.**

The first four Puffin Picture Books were hatched in 1940 and the
first Puffin story book featured a man with broomstick arms called
Worzel Gummidge. In 1967 Kaye Webb, Puffin Editor, started the
Puffin Club, promising to **'make children into readers'**.
She kept that promise and over 200,000 children became
devoted Puffineers through their quarterly instalments of
Puffin Post, which is now back for a new generation.

Many years from now, we hope you'll look back and
remember Puffin with a smile. **No matter what your age
or what you're into, there's a Puffin for everyone.**
The possibilities are endless, but one thing is for sure:
whether it's a picture book or a paperback, a sticker book
or a hardback, **if it's got that little Puffin
on it – it's bound to be good.**